THE BEST AUSTRALIAN STORIES 2007

THE BEST AUSTRALIAN STORIES 2007

Edited by
ROBERT DREWE

Published by Black Inc.,
an imprint of Schwartz Publishing Pty Ltd

Level 5, 289 Flinders Lane
Melbourne Victoria 3000 Australia
email: enquiries@blackincbooks.com
http://www.blackincbooks.com

ISBN 9781863954181

Contents

Introduction

Robert Drewe

As I write this, I'm surrounded by short stories. Mounds of stories spill off the desk in my office and crowd the dining-room table and the coffee table and are heaped on the floor. Thousands of sheets of A4 paper-clipped together in hopeful bundles of maybe six or twelve, or sometimes twenty or thirty sheets – and thus transformed into *manuscripts* – threaten to overwhelm the house. Around my feet lie piles of magazines containing more short stories. There are so many new stories under the one roof – one thousand, seven hundred and thirty-two stories in all – that you can smell them when you enter the house.

The yeasty odour of raw paper and the sharp chemical whiff of computer printouts fills the rooms. I live in the sub-tropical north-coast hinterland of New South Wales and at present the weather is humid after ten days of solid rain. The stories all feel warm and slightly damp to the touch – as if strenuously exercised. Perhaps you can even smell the after-midnight creative sweat that went into them.

Don't let anyone tell you the Australian short story is dead. It's thriving. For six months last year, and for the same period this year, I was faced by this evidence every afternoon when I picked up that day's envelopes overflowing my post-office box and piled up on the counter of Connick's General Store, Post Office and Off-Licence ('For Honesty & Courtesy') in the tiny hamlet of Tintenbar. The stories came from everywhere, from all the capital cities of course, but just as many came from the countryside and regional towns. It seems there are many hundreds, maybe thousands, of people out there writing short fiction.

Are all these enthusiasts wasting their time? Not at all. Well, as with any art form, not the best of them anyway. Despite what the naysayers have been saying, there *are* plenty of magazines publishing short fiction. They're just not necessarily the mainstream, mostly American magazines traditionally associated with paying generously for short stories, like the *New Yorker* and *Harper's* and *Atlantic Monthly*. They are local, often new on the street, and staffed by young enthusiasts full of steam and vinegar. They are fresh, imaginatively designed, professionally polished and wide open to experiment.

Twenty different publications are represented in this anthology alone, and while we're singing the praises of the story here, it's appropriate to mention the *Sleepers Almanac, Griffith Review, Allnighter, Etchings, Voiceworks, Indigo, Bystander, Shotgun, Australian Literary Review,* the *UTS Writers' Anthology, Verandah, Coastlines, Overland, Meanjin, Westerly, Southerly, Island, Quadrant* and *HEAT*. And there are maybe three or four times as many others. Publications as varied and perhaps as unexpected as the *Alice Springs News,* the *Age,* the *Big Issue,* the *Bulletin* and the *Australian Women's Weekly* also publish seasonal short-story issues, often in conjunction with story competitions, and are represented in this anthology. I'll go out on a limb and say there have never been more story-friendly Australian publications than at the moment.

Where the crunch comes is not with the initial magazine publication of individual stories but with the next stage of the process: the publishing industry's reluctance to commit collections of short stories to book form. There are honourable exceptions – Black Inc., University of Queensland Press and my own publisher, Penguin, among them. But, generally speaking, unless the author is already established, or the collection in question comprises stories from many different (and celebrated) writers, the novel definitely rules.

What to do? How to right this terrible wrong? The writer Ann Patchett, current editor of *Best American Short Stories,* suggests that the short story needs a major literary scandal to bring it to public attention. It could do with some controversy. On past performance, the Australian media would certainly appreciate that. Perhaps we should call a press conference and confess that, sorry, our stories didn't actually occur. Even though they might seem convincing, they're not factual. Never happened. We made them up. The events described took place mainly in our heads. *Mea culpa.* Apologies all round. The stories are really *fiction.*

But well-told stories are fiction of a rare and precise power; a type of fiction that seems to speak to each of us personally, and in a sneaky manner that seems *real.* This is the point. Apart from its sharper focus, what the good short story has over the novel is that it sets up a need in us we weren't conscious of before we began to read – and then somehow fulfils it. As I said in this space last year, I've always appreciated that small miracle.

It's worth repeating my belief that what the gifted storyteller and the well-told story have accomplished ever since the ancient fireside tale is to strike a chord with the listener or reader whereby an essence of our own lives is extrapolated. You could call it the recognition or *wow!* factor. For a moment, or longer, we identify and we make some sense of the reckless human journey towards oblivion.

Obviously we're talking about an important and popular literary form, as well as one with an abiding Australian tradition. On the evidence of this anthology's past bestseller status, I think that readers of *Best Australian Stories 2007* will agree. Again, seeking diversity of form and content, I cast the widest possible net. As well as trawling for published stories through the nation's literary journals and all the various newspaper and magazine story competitions, I invited submissions of previously unpublished work from all over the country, open to everyone. Again, the proportion of published writing to new work ended up at about 2:1. About half my total selection came from well-known authors, but for me the most pleasing aspect of producing this anthology was discovering people I didn't know, especially young writers published here for the first time.

Rather than novellas or chapters of novels, what I was looking for in each case was a short (or shortish), complete-in-itself tale. The main test was whether it stuck in my mind after a couple of readings, even after reading hundreds of its fellows, and did

Edgar Allan Poe's simple definition of a short story ('a narrative that can be read at one sitting') genuinely apply.

I hope that readers will find intriguing and compelling stories here, some that resonate as particularly Australian – stories seriously concerned with contemporary life in both the cities and the bush – but also others telling of experiences outside our immediate physical and emotional boundaries. My selection guide was very subjective; another editor might have produced a quite different anthology from the material submitted. Again, many good stories missed out, not because they weren't admirable but because the book required a certain balance and, of course, necessarily reflects my own literary taste. I like to see an ebb and flow, with a humorous, lively or idiosyncratic story breaking up the more solemn narratives.

The stories that missed out on selection weigh heavily on me. (They loom over me now in three disappointed stacks.) In many of them I discerned heartbreak and hard times and immense life changes. I would have loved to produce another two or three anthologies. As a writer, I know from experience the physical effort, and often emotional anguish, that went into writing them. I know the pain of the literary knock-back. As I pointed out when calling for submissions, however, the sheer number of stories made it impossible for me to make individual responses or to offer personal editorial advice. (I have to get back to my own writing.) It might be some small compensation to know that the editor has been greatly impressed and moved by many of these stories, which will surely find a home elsewhere. I feel honoured to have read and absorbed these tales and to have guided *Best Australian Stories* for the past two issues.

Before departing the scene, I would like to acknowledge the selection assistance this year of Candida Baker, and the invaluable publishing assistance in 2006 and 2007 of Caitlin Yates, Chris Feik, Denise O'Dea and Nina Kenwood at Black Inc. Especially, I'd like to thank the publisher, Morry Schwartz, who generated *Best Australian Stories* in the first place and who should be held chiefly responsible for its continued success.

Robert Drewe

Tender

Cate Kennedy

Up in under her arm, that's where it aches. That's what worries her. They say the biopsy will be a minor invasive procedure, a couple of stitches at most, but she can't help thinking of that scalpel like an apple corer, going into her flesh, pushing in and twisting.

'You haven't written it on the calendar,' says Al when he comes in.

'It's at nine-fifteen.'

'So you'll – what – get the six-thirty-five train?'

'Yeah, I'll drive down and leave the car at the station for you to pick up. Then back in time after school.' She pauses, then mutters: 'Hopefully, I mean.'

'Why didn't you write it up?'

She stops grating cheese, stares at him. 'Why do you reckon?'

'Chris, the kids know. I told them last week you had to have a test at the hospital. They're fine about it. No point making it worse for them, keeping it all secret.'

'It's not going to be worse for them. They don't even need to think about it.' She looks down at the piece of roughened cheese in her hand, turns it to a new edge.

'What do they call it again?'

'A lumpectomy.'

She hates that word. Lump. The ugliest word in the English language. *Lumpen*. *Lumpy*. She thinks fleetingly of the story

Hannah developed an obsession for when she was three, which she'd demanded over and over, night after night. The princess with all the mattresses who still couldn't sleep because of that tiny lump disturbing her all night long; that hard, resilient pea rising cruelly and insistently through all those downy layers.

'Want a hand with something?'

'No,' she replies, taking a teatowel out of the drawer and pulling open the oven, 'I'm right.'

Hannah is off that story now. She's onto another one about a family who end up bringing two stray dogs home from the pound instead of one. Christine had fantasies when the kids were babies; of Jamie, three years older, reading to his little sister of a night in the big armchair. She'd imagined a golden halo of lamplight, polished floors, the strawbale walls finally rendered and whitewashed, everything as clean and wholesome as a cake of handmade soap.

Instead Jamie is forever setting up complicated wars of small action figures that bite painfully into your bare feet when you have to get up at night, battalions of tiny medieval knights with pointy plastic armour and shields. Hannah couldn't be less interested. Christine is having a few second thoughts, now, about the old nature versus nurture argument. What is it with boys and fighting? One hour of sanctioned TV a night and still Jamie sprawls on the floor, relishing battle-scenes, while Hannah flounces and squeals like some miniature Paris Hilton demanding to wear nail polish to kinder. Where have they absorbed all this from, this nasty flotsam leaking in like battery acid?

You couldn't have told her, seven years ago, she'd be worrying about this stuff, any more than she would have believed they'd even have a television or electric heaters.

She remembers Al and her, arguing over whether to render the walls with mud and cement or just mud – statistics about toxicity, about pure environments, about every bloody thing, things that buckled in the face of practicality and time. Now the solar panels are just a booster for an electric system like everyone else's, and to Christine that seems to sum up the whole experiment – it's a bonus, a gesture, a grand theory of sustainability modified to a more prosaic reality. The trees outside, which she'd imaged sprouting into a shady arbour, are taller and stalkier now but still unmistakably seedlings, painstakingly hand-watered from the dam and the bath. The piles of clay turned over by digging the house site still glint exposed through the thin groundcovers, and Jamie's BMX track has worn a looping circuit through the landscaping, turning her plans for terracing into an assortment of jumps and scrambles. Christine puts more wood in the firebox, and, with a familiar mix of guilt and resentment, dreams her nightly dream of an electric oven.

It's not that she doesn't love the house. She does – it's just still so makeshift and unfinished. The spare windows are still stacked under a tarp in the shed and they've spread rugs over the spots where the floor dips and cracks. You can't have a bath without bucketing out the water saved from the last one onto some dry patch of ground. She can hear Al giving the kids a bath now. That's Al's version of a fun activity with kids – stick them in the bath and try to foam up some bubbles with the biodegradable shampoo.

'Mum!' she hears Hannah bawling from the tub.

'What?'

'I need my SHOWER CAP!'

'Get Dad to find it.'

Now Al's voice, muffled and distracted. 'It's not in here.'

'Have you looked in the shower?'

She hears the shower-screen door open, then silence, a belated muttered thanks. Too late though.

'My hair's ALL WET ALREADY!' comes Hannah's wail, then that whiny crying that always sets Christine's teeth on edge. Does Hannah do it at kinder? Do the workers there tut and roll their eyes about lack of discipline at home?

'Shut UP!' comes Jamie's voice. Irritated splashing, then another high-pitched scream. Why doesn't Al do something to intervene?

She pulls open the big drawer with an irritated tug and gets out knives and forks.

Al had been the first one she'd told, of course, after she'd found it. She recalls his face as he raised himself on one elbow in bed, reaching for the bedside lamp, how he'd rubbed a hand over his eyes, pinching the bridge of his nose between thumb and forefinger. Then the radiographer, chatting with her as she'd got up on the table, joking about how cold the gel was, running the transducer across Christine's skin and then pausing, going quiet. Christine remembers the suddenly intent way she'd leaned her head closer to the image on the screen, her hand carefully clicking, moving the mouse, clicking again, the lighthearted talk abruptly over.

Then the doctor, finally, looking through the ultrasound films as he made a point of giving her the reassuring statistics of how many lumps turn out to be benign. She'd hated the way he'd stared off over her head as his fingers had coolly explored the lump, gazing into the distance like someone solving a mental equation.

'How does that feel?' he'd said.

'Pretty tender, actually.' Trying to breathe normally. Him writing something on her card, like his final answer in a quiz, before meeting her eyes again.

'Best to take that out and have a good look at it, I think,' he'd said.

Christine sits at the kitchen table now and listens to the wrangling in the bathroom, her husband's ineffectual protestations as the children fight over a certain squeaky bath toy they both lay claim to. From out of the corner of her eye, she sees the familiar tiny dark shape of a mouse run the length of the skirting. If she puts another trap out, she'd have to remember to tell Al to check them before the kids get up tomorrow. Finding a dead mouse is likely to set them both off, demanding a funeral and burial which would make them late for school.

She gets up and finds two traps in the pantry, in behind the jars and plastic containers and the box full of herbal cough and cold remedies, valerian tea and rescue remedy. Back when the kids were born, she and Al would never have dreamed of treating them with any commercial preparations from the chemist. And they'd been lucky – the kids never got sick, she hadn't been in a hospital since Hannah was born.

Rescue remedy, she thinks as she replaces the little bottle on the shelf. And can't stop her mouth twisting into a humourless, cynical curl as she dabs some peanut butter onto the mousetraps and sets them, pushing them carefully back into shadowy corners with the tip of her finger.

'Al!' she calls at last. 'Will you get the kids out of the bath, for God's sake? Dinner's been ready for half an hour!'

She finds herself watching him, sometimes, still a little incredulous at the dreamy way he handles things, how everything seems to flow around him. Once at a barbecue held at the community centre where he works she'd impulsively asked a colleague how he managed everything there at the office.

'Oh, fine,' the woman had said, surprised. 'Al just does his own thing, you know? It all comes together in the end.'

Here at home, she never sees it coming together. Everything, on the contrary, seems teetering on the verge of coming apart. That, or just sinking into neglect, like the wheelbarrow half full of compost and the shovel which has been buried in the weeds for over a fortnight, outside the kitchen window.

He never rises to the bait, either. Once, when he'd wandered in from the study and said 'What have you got planned for dinner?' she'd snapped: 'What have YOU got planned?' but he'd only looked surprised and answered mildly, 'Nothing. Is it my turn?'

He only makes one dinner though – tuna and pasta casserole. Christine supposes she should be grateful he's so laid-back – relaxed with the kids, always in the same amiable mood. But he's so vague, that's the trouble, so blind to how much *organising* she has to do around him to keep everything running. It's like she has three kids, not two. Now she watches him absently dump clean folded clothes out of the washing basket onto the rug, slowly picking through the pile looking for clean pyjamas for the kids.

'Hurry, Dad! Hurry!' whines Hannah, jiggling naked and impatient on the spot. Christine drinks in the sight of her strong little back, the sturdy muscles in her legs as she jumps from one foot to the other. Al looks up at Hannah and raises his eyebrows, tickles her with one teasing forefinger.

'Don't get your knickers in a twist,' he says, and Jamie guffaws with laughter at his sister, who complains even louder and kicks out at him. He aims his Jedi fighter-plane warningly at her. Al doesn't even notice. He glances down at the pyjama top he's holding and with one distracted but surprisingly adept movement reaches his hand inside to the label and shakes it rightway out.

If they do the tests in the afternoon, Christine wonders, would they keep her down there tomorrow night if the results are bad? She tries the word in her head, exploratively, trying to take the white-hot sting out of it. *Malignant. Malignant.* Would they be so prompt, or would some other specialist have to make the decision? Does she have tuna and pasta in the pantry, just in case?

'I need a cardboard box,' Jamie announces after dinner, 'for my school project.'

Christine finds him an old four-litre wine cask.

'What's this for?' she asks as he carefully cuts a hole in one end.

'We're making models. It's going to be a little world, kind of.' he says. 'Like, I'm going to put blue paper in here, for sky? And some little sticks like trees. And when people look through the hole it's going to look like a real place.'

'Wow, that sounds good. When does it have to be ready?'

'Tomorrow,' he replies calmly. God, sometimes he's so like Al it scares her.

'Shall we go and cut some sticks and twigs, then?' she suggests.

He glances out at the twilight and shrugs.

'O.K.'

'What are you going to stick them in, to make them stand up?'

She watches his serious seven-year-old face consider it, and wants to take his arm and plant a kiss on the faded temporary tattoo of Buzz Lightyear there on his skinny bicep.

'Playdough,' he says at last.

'Right.'

'Covered in grass so you can't see it.'

Christine feels the ardent rush of helpless, terrible love.

'Let's do it.'

She feels it catch, like a little stabbing stitch, when she reaches up to snip off some wattle sprigs. In the armpit again, like it's buried in her lymph nodes instead of the pale, pliant skin at the side of her breast. She'd been in the shower when she first felt it six weeks ago, soaping herself after a dusty day collecting bricks for paving. Her fingers had brushed over it and she'd felt her pulse leap and thud, racketing, to the roof of her mouth, and traced her fingers back to the tender place, tasting sudden adrenaline like solder. Yes, like a pea, buried but resilient, a small sly sphere nesting disguised between layers of flesh and tissue. Keeping you awake all night. Wondering how long it'd been there unnoticed, and what it might be collecting darkly into itself, like a little Death Star.

'What colour playdough?' she asks now, squeezing her arm next to her side, breathing deeply. 'Are you going to do stars, or clouds?'

As she makes tomorrow's lunches she watches Jamie at the kitchen table, assembling what he needs, pasting a pale sky inside the box with a glue-stick as his tongue jerks across his bottom lip in concentration.

'How long have you had this project?' grumbles Al when Jamie is nowhere near finished at bedtime. 'You should have started it earlier.'

Al, whose half-finished bookshelves they all step over on the way to the carport, who leaves the wet washing in the basket at the line while he drives into town for more pegs, who can't seem to shut a drawer once he's opened it.

'You really do have to get to bed soon,' Christine says to Jamie. His face goes blankly mutinous.

'There's these other kids,' he says as he pats chopped grass clippings down, 'who always have their things ready early? Always on the first day? Tomorrow they'll have theirs finished.'

He stares down disconsolately at the box and reaches in suddenly for the little plastic soldiers he's arranged in combat inside.

'Got to take these out,' he mutters. 'These aren't right.'

Christine feels an aching warmth bloom briefly in her chest, the tightness of tears.

'Ten more minutes,' orders Al, who wants the kids in bed so he can surf the net on the computer he'd once sworn he'd never own.

Everything's quiet by the time Christine finds a packet of icy-pole sticks in the kitchen drawer. Jamie has gone to bed resignedly and Al is in some chatroom, off in his study. On the table lies the box, some cottonwool balls for clouds waiting till morning. She can imagine him studiously gluing them on as he shovels cereal into his mouth, how closed and intent his face will be. She'll be on the train by then, the city a polluted Gotham on the distant horizon.

Well, maybe she can surprise him. She reaches inside the packet and breaks three icy-pole sticks in half and digs the pieces into the playdough to make a perfect little fence in the box. When you look through the eyehole it's like a diorama, one of those stagy, rustic sets from *The Wizard of Oz*. She arranges some grass around the bases, then glues some of the sticks together and sets them on an angle like a part-opened gate.

Look at me, she grins to herself, shaking her head, *I'm turning into one of those parents who takes over their kids' school projects.*

In the back of the wardrobe she finds an old handbag she remembers and removes a small mirror, which she arranges semi-buried in the grass, like a little reflective pond. Pokes the wattle sprigs around it, bending like she-oaks by the water.

It's ten-thirty now. There's another little galloping mouse-shadow she catches in her peripheral vision running across the kitchen floor into the pantry to disappear in behind the recycled paper and compost bucket, and she moves distractedly to set yet another mousetrap inside a cupboard. No wonder they sell the things in packs of six. She's back sitting at the kitchen table before she even realises, ducking her head to squint through the hole in the box. The trick is going to be letting enough light in the roof to simulate real sunshine. She hunts in a bag of Christmas wrapping in the hall cupboard and finds a square of yellow cellophane, cuts it to size and fits it between the layers of cardboard like a skylight. With the desk lamp she checks how the light will look. Golden afternoon sun pouring over an Enid Blyton countryside. Magic hour.

Al comes in yawning, sees her and chortles.

'Don't even start,' she says. 'I can't help myself.'

He puts the kettle on. 'Hey, remember that papier-mâché volcano on display at parent–teacher night, that we were all meant to believe had been made by a kid in grade two?' He laughs again at the memory, scratching his head as he gets two cups out and starts stacking the plates to wash up.

'I'm imagining the surprise when he comes down tomorrow,' she says. 'But if I ever go any further than this, tell me.'

Al dunks a glass in the sink. 'Don't worry about tomorrow, OK?' he says after a while. 'I'm sure everything will work out fine.'

She doesn't look up, but she senses him standing there with his back to her, washing the glass until it's way beyond clean.

Getting on for midnight. She sits back and stretches. Sand, that's what she needs. To glue carefully round the edges of the mirror, to simulate a shore. She steps outside and takes a few pinches from the dark pile next to the paving bricks. One thing about living in a house like this – raw materials are never far away. She glues a wavy, natural line around the mirror, and sticks on some dry stalks like reeds, holding them in place with tweezers as they dry.

She knows Hannah's got some black plasticine somewhere, for some swans. Maybe in her toybox, or in her little desk? Christine creeps into her daughter's room, and stands listening to the rhythmic steadiness of Hannah's breathing, gazes at her sprawled sideways on the bed like she's just landed from a great height. Hannah; healthy, respiring, her cells a blur of miraculously multiplying and flowering growth, life coursing through her flawless and perfect down to the last crescent moon fingernail. Christine, who once slept with a hand cupped around that tiny kicking foot praying for a safe delivery, now stands holding scissors and a page of silver stars, making impossible bargains at the speed of light. Her own heart knocking in her chest and something else, something dark and airless, trickling through her bloodstream, that black, dense shadow on the ultrasound searching for somewhere to colonise. Her feet take her into Jamie's room and she stands gazing at him too. Her children, perfect, made with her own once-trustworthy body.

She gets up again, silently, at five o'clock, nagged by an unfinished vision and the feel of the night draining away. Out in the garden she's calm again, feeling the dew drench her ankles and the bottom of her white cotton nightdress. She can sleep on the train, anyway. She walks slowly through the hillocks and raised beds, seeing her nightdress billow like a faintly luminous ghost, pausing to inhale deep spicy breaths of the lemon-scented gum. She sees Jamie in the morning, milky-breathed and drowsy, finding the box, looking through the eyehole with a shock of pleasure, being finished early for once in his life.

She glances up at the house. Yellow light in the square window, her family sleeping warm and secure. She clutches the sprig of Chinese elm she's found, which will look just like an apple tree, and crouches by the pile of paving stones. Her fingers search blindly and carefully into the damp crevices of the stack. Somewhere in here, she knows, is some moss; cool and velvety, perfect for the distant green hills behind the open gate in that little microcosmic landscape.

She'll leave it at his place at the table, ready. And their lunchboxes packed at the front of the fridge, where Al won't miss them. For some reason, she keeps recalling Al, suddenly surprising her by shaking those pyjamas right-way-out with that one deft easy motion. She can't think why, but the image comforts her.

Back inside, the dawn light reaching the kitchen, she checks the time again: thirty minutes till the train, just over three hours till she's in that doctor's room again. She looks out the unpainted window at their little patch of bush, and at what's becoming visible out there – the ridges of hard clay subsoil showing palely defiant through the grass, like a healing scar.

Then, cold but wide awake and ready, she locates each of the five mousetraps she's set and kneels down in front of each of them in turn. Carefully, with the flat of her hand, she releases the springs so that the small metal trays of bait slip from the jagged hook holding them in place. She's humming to herself as she grasps each straining metal bar and guides it back to let it settle, with a benign and harmless snap, against the small rectangle of wood.

Mrs Porter and the Rock

David Malouf

The Rock is Ayers Rock, Uluru. Mrs Porter's son, Donald, has brought her out to look at it. They are at breakfast, on the second day of a three-day tour, in the Desert Rose Room of the Yullara Sheraton. Mrs Porter, sucking voluptuously, is on her third cigarette, while Donald, a born letter-writer who will happily spend half an hour shaping and reshaping a description in his head, or putting a dazzling sheen on an ironical observation, is engaged in one of the airy rockets, all fizz and sparkle and recondite allusions, that he can barely wait, once he is out of town, to launch in the direction of his more discerning friends. In a large, loose, schoolboyish hand, on the Sheraton's notepaper, he writes:

To complete the scene, only the sacred river is missing, for this resort is surely inspired by the great tent city of Kubla Khan. Nestling among spinifex dunes, it rises, like a late version of the impossible East, out of the rust-red sands, a postmodern Bedouin encampment, all pink and apricot turrets and slender aluminium poles that hum and twang as they prick the skyline. Over the walkaways and public spaces hover huge, shadow-making sails that are meant to evoke, in those of us for whom deserts create a sense of spiritual unease, the ocean we left two thousand miles back.

So there you have it. The pitched tents of the modern nomads. That tribe of the internationally restless who have come on here from the Holy Land, or from Taos or Porto Cervo or Nepal, to stare for a bit on an imaginable wonder – when, that is, they can lift their eyes from the spa pool, or in pauses between the Tasmanian salmon and the crème brûlée ...

Mrs Porter is here on sufferance, accepting, with minimal grace, what Donald had intended as a treat. Frankly she'd rather be at Jupiter's playing the pokies. She takes a good drag on her cigarette, looks up from the plate – as yet untouched – of scrambled egg, baked beans and golden croquettes, and is astonished to find herself confronting, high up on the translucent canopy of the dining-room ceiling, a pair of colossal feet. The fat soles are sloshing about up there in ripples of light. Unnaturally magnified, and with the glare beyond them, diffuse, almost blinding, of the Central Australian sun. She gives a small cry and ducks. And Donald, who keeps a keen eye on her and is responsive to all her jerks and twitches, observing the movement but not for the moment its cause, demands, 'What? What's the matter? What is it?'

Mrs Porter shakes her head. He frowns, subjects her to worried scrutiny – one of his what's-she-up-to-now looks. She keeps her head down. After a moment, with another wary glance in her direction, he goes back to his letter.

Mrs Porter throws a swift glance upward.

Mmm, the feet are still there. Beyond them, distorted by fans of watery light, is the outline of a body, almost transparent – shoulders, a gigantic trunk. Black. This one is black. An enormous *black* man is up there wielding a length of hose, and the water is red. The big feet are bleeding. Well, that's a new one.

Mrs Porter nibbles at her toast. She needs to think about this. Between bites, she takes long, sweet drags on her cigarette. If she ignores this latest apparition, she thinks, maybe it will go away.

Lately – well, for quite a while now – she's been getting these visitations – apparitions is how she thinks of them, though they appear at such odd times, and in such unexpected guises, that she wonders if they aren't in fact *re*visitations that she herself has called up out of bits and pieces of her past, her now scattered and inconsiderate memory.

In the beginning she thought they might be messengers – well, to put it more plainly, angels. But their only message seemed to be one she already knew: that the world she found herself in these days was a stranger place than she'd bargained for, and getting stranger.

She had wondered as well – but this was only at the start – if they might be tormentors, visitors from places she'd never been, like Antarctica, bringing with them a breath of icebergs. But that, she'd decided pretty smartly, was foolish. Dulcie, she told herself, you're being a fool! She wasn't the sort of person that anyone out there would want to torment. All *her* apparitions did was make themselves visible, hang around for a bit, disturbing the afternoon or whatever with a sudden chill, and drift off.

Ghosts might have been a more common word for them – she believes in ghosts. But if that's what they are, they're the ghosts of people she's never met. And surely, if they were ghosts, her husband Leonard would be one of them.

Unless he has decided for some reason to give her a miss.

She finds this possibility distressing. She doesn't particularly want to see Leonard, but the thought that he could appear to her if he wanted and has chosen not to puts a clamp on her heart, makes her go damp and miserable.

All this is a puzzle and she would like to ask someone about it, get a few answers, but is afraid of what she might hear. In the meantime she turns her attention to Donald. Let the feet go their own way. Let them just go!

Donald looks sweet when he is writing. He sits with one shoulder dipped and his arm circling the page, forever worried, like a child, that someone might be looking over his shoulder and trying to copy. His tongue is at the corner of his mouth. Like a sweet-natured forty-three-year-old, very earnest and absorbed, practising pot-hooks.

Poor Donald, she thinks. He has spent his whole life waiting for her to become a mother of another sort. The sort who'll take an interest. Well, she *is* interested. She's interested, right now, in those feet! But what Donald means is interested in what interests him, and she can't for the life of her see what all this stuff *is* that he gets so excited about, and Donald, for all his cleverness, can't tell her. When she asks, he gets angry. The questions she comes up with are just the ones, it seems, that Donald cannot answer. They're too simple. He loses his cool – that's what people say these days – but all that does is make him feel bad, and the next moment he is coming after her with hugs, and little offerings out of the *Herald* that she could perfectly well read for herself, or out of books! Because she's made him feel guilty.

This capacity she appears to possess for making grown men feel guilty – she had the same effect on Donald's father – surprises her. Guilt is not one of the things she herself suffers from.

Duty. Responsibility. Guilt. Leonard was very strong on all three. So is Donald. He is very like his father in all sorts of ways, though not physically – Leonard was a very *thin* man.

Leonard too would have liked her to take an interest. Only Leonard was kinder, more understanding – she had almost said forgiving. It wasn't her fault that she'd left school at thirteen – loads of girls did in those days, and clever men married them just the same. Leonard was careful always not to let her see that in this way she had failed him; that in the part of his nature that looked out into the world and was baffled, or which brought him moments of almost boyish elation, she could not join him, he was alone.

She was sorry for that, but she didn't feel guilty. People are what they are. Leonard knew that as well as she did.

Donald's generation, she has decided, are less willing to make allowances. Less indulgent. Or maybe that is just Donald. Even as a tiny tot he was always imposing what he felt on others. His need to 'share,' as he calls it, does have its nice side, she knows that. But it is very consuming. 'Look at this, Mum,' he would shout, his whole tiny body in a fury. 'You're not *looking! Look!*'

In those days it would be a caterpillar, some nasty black thing. An armoured black dragon that she thought of as Japanese-looking and found particularly repulsive. Or a picture of an air battle, all dotted lines that were supposed to be machine-gun bullets, and jagged flame. Later it was books – Proust. She'd had a whole year of that one, that *Proust.* Now it was this Rock.

High maintenance, that's what they called it these days. She got that from her neighbour, Tess Hyland. Donald was high maintenance.

'What's up?' he asks now, seeing her dip her shoulder again and flinch. 'What's the matter?'

'Nothing's the matter,' she snaps back. 'What's the matter yourself?'

She has discovered that the best way of dealing with Donald's questions is to return them. Backhand. As a girl she was quite a decent tennis player.

She continues to crouch. There is plenty of space up there under the cantilevered ceiling, no shortage of space; but the fact that twenty feet over your head the splayed toes of some giant black acrobat are sloshing about in blood is not an easy thing to ignore, especially at breakfast. She is reminded of the roofs of some of the cathedrals they'd seen – with Leonard it was cathedrals. They visited seven of them once, seven in a row. But over there the angels existed mostly from the waist up. You were supposed to ignore what existed below. They hung out over the damp aisles blowing trumpets or shaking tambourines. Here, it seems, you did get the lower parts and they were armed with hosepipes. Well, that was logical enough. They were in the southern hemisphere.

Donald is eyeing her again, though he is pretending not to. They are all at it these days – Donald, Douglas, Shirley. She has become an object of interest. She knows why. They're on the lookout for some sign that she is losing her marbles.

'Why aren't you eating your breakfast?' Donald demands.

'I am,' she tells him.

As if in retaliation for all those years when she forced one thing or another into their reluctant mouths – gooey eggs, strips of limp bread and butter, mashed banana, cod-liver oil – they have begun, this last year, to torment her with her unwillingness to do more than pick about at her food. When Donald says, 'Come on now, just one more mouthful,' he is reproducing, whether he knows it or not, exactly the coax and whine of her own voice from forty years ago, and so accurately that, with a sickening rush, as if she had missed a step and fallen through four decades, she finds herself back in the dingy, cockroach-infested maisonette at West End that was all Leonard was able to find for them in the Shortage after the war. The linoleum! Except in the corners and under the immoveable sideboard, roses worn to a dishwater brown. A gas heater in the bathroom that when she shut her eyes and put a match to it went off like a bunger and threatened to blast her eyebrows off. Donald in his highchair chucking crusts all over the floor, and Douglas hauling himself up to the open piano, preparing to thump. To get away from that vision she's willing even to face the feet.

She glances upward – ah, they're gone! – then away to where an oversized ranger in a khaki uniform and wide-brimmed Akubra is examining the leaves of a rainforest shrub that goes all the way to the ceiling. For all the world as if he was out in the open somewhere and had just climbed out of a ute or off a horse.

'You shouldn't have taken all that,' Donald is saying – she knows this one too – 'if all you're going to do is let it sit on your plate.'

Dear me, she thinks, is he going to go through the whole routine? The poor little children in England? What a pain I must have been!

In fact, she doesn't intend to eat any of this stuff. Breakfast is just an excuse, so far as she is concerned, for a cigarette.

But the buffet table here is a feature. Donald leads her to it each morning as if it was an altar. Leonard too had a weakness for altars.

This one is garishly and unseasonably festive.

A big blue Japanese pumpkin is surrounded by several smaller ones, bright orange, with shells like fine bone china and pimpled.

There are wheatsheaves, loaves of rye and five-grain bread, spilled walnuts, almonds, a couple of hibiscus flowers. It's hard to know what is for decoration and what is to eat.

And the effect, whatever was intended, has been ruined because some joker has, without ceremony, *unceremoniously*, plonked his saddle down right in the middle of it. Its straps all discoloured with sweat, and with worn and frayed stitching, this saddle has simply been plonked down and left among the cereal jars, the plates of cheese, sliced ham and smoked salmon, the bowls of stewed prunes, tinned apricots, orange quarters, crystallised pears ...

But food is of no interest to her. She has helped herself so generously to the hot buffet not because she is hungry and intends to eat any of this stuff but so she'll have something to look at. Something other than *it*.

It is everywhere. The whole place has been designed so that whichever way you turn, it's there, displaying itself on the horizon. Sitting out there like a great slab of purple-brown liver going off in the sun. No, not liver, something else, she can't think quite what.

And then she can. Suddenly she can. That's why she has been so unwilling to look at it!

She is seven, maybe eight years old. Along with her friends of that time, Isobel and Betty Olds, she is squatting on her heels on the beach at Etty Bay in front of their discovery, a hump-backed sea creature bigger than any fish they have ever seen, which has been washed up on this familiar bit of beach and is lying stranded on the silvery wet sand. Its one visible eye, as yet unclouded, which is blue like a far-off moon, is open to the sky. It is alive and breathing. You can see the opening and closing of its gills.

The sea often tosses up flotsam of one kind or another. Big green-glass balls netted with rope. Toadfish that when you roll them with a big toe puff up and puff up till you think they'd burst. But nothing as big and sad-looking as this. You can imagine putting your arms around it like a person. Like a person that has maybe been *turned* into a fish by a witch's curse and is unable to tell you that once, not so long ago, it was a princess. It breathes and is silent. Cut off in a silence that makes you aware suddenly of your own breathing, while the gulls rise shrieking overhead.

They have the beach to themselves. They sit there watching while the tide goes out. No longer swirling and trying to catch your feet, it goes far out, leaving the sand polished like a mirror to a silvery gleam in which the light comes and goes in flashes and the colours of the late-afternoon sky are gaudily reflected.

And slowly, as they watch, the creature begins to change – the blue-black back, the golden belly. The big fish begins to throw off colours in electric flashes. Mauve, pink, a yellowish pale green, they have never seen anything like it. Slow fireworks. As if, out of its element, in a world where it had no other means of expression, the big fish was trying to reveal to them some vision of what it was and where it had come from, a lost secret they were meant to remember and pass on. Well, maybe the others had grasped it. All she had done was gape and feel the slow wonder spread through her.

So they had squatted there, all three, and watched the big fish slowly die.

It was a fish dolphin, a dorado, and it had been dying. That's what she knew now. The show had been its last. That's why she didn't want to look at this Rock. Just as she wouldn't want to look at the fish dolphin either if it was lying out there now. No matter what sort of performance it put on.

She finds herself fidgeting. She stubs out the last of her cigarette, takes up a fork.

'*My mother,*' Donald writes to his friend Sherman, offering yet another glimpse of a character who never fails to amuse, '*has for some reason taken against the scenery. Can you imagine? In fact it's what she's been doing all her life. If she can't accommodate a thing, it isn't there. Grand as it is, not even Ayers Rock stands a chance against her magnificent indifference. She simply chain-smokes and looks the other way. I begin to get an idea, after all these years, of how poor old Leonard must have felt.*

'The hotel, on the other hand, has her completely absorbed. She devotes whole mealtimes to the perusal of the menu.

'Not that she deigns to taste more than a bite or two. But she does like to know what is there for the choosing.'

He pauses and looks up, feeling a twinge at having yet again offered her up as a figure of fun, this woman who has never ceased to puzzle and thwart him but who still commands the largest part of his heart. He knows this is odd. He covers himself by making her appear to his friends as a burden he has taken on that cannot, in all honour, be thrown off; an endless source, in the meantime, of amusing stories and flat-footed comments and attitudes.

'What would Dulcie think of it?' his friends Sherman and Jack Anderson say, and try, amid shouts of laughter, to reproduce one of her dead ordinary ways of looking at things, without ever quite catching her tone.

She eludes them – 'One for you, Dulcie,' Donald tells himself – as she has for so long eluded him.

He watches her now, fork in hand, pushing baked beans about, piling them into modest heaps, then rearranging them in steep hills and ridges, then using the prongs of the fork to redistribute them in lines and circles, and finds himself thinking of the view from the plane window as they flew in from Alice: a panorama of scorched, reddish rock that must have been created, he thinks, in a spirit of wilfulness very like his mother's as she goes now at the beans.

He smiles. The idea amuses him. His mother as demiurge.

He continues to watch, allowing the image to undergo in his head the quiet miracle of transformation, then once again begins to write.

Mrs Porter sits in the tourist bus and smokes. Smoking isn't allowed of course, but there is nobody about. She has the bus to herself. She has no qualms about the breaking of rules.

The bus is parked in the shade but is not cool. Heated air pours in at the open window, bearing flies. She is using the smoke to keep them off. Outside, the earth bakes.

To her left, country that is flat. Orange-red with clumps of grey-green spiky bushes. *It*, the Rock, is a little way off to her right. She does not look.

People, among them Donald, are hauling themselves up it in relays; dark lines of them against the Rock's glowing red. Occasionally there is a flash as the sun bounces off a watch or a belt buckle, or a camera round someone's neck. Madness, she thinks. Why would anyone want to do it? But she knows the answer to that one. Because it's *there*.

Except that for most of the time, it hadn't been – not in her book. And what's more, she hadn't missed it, so there! When they drew maps at school they hadn't even bothered to put it in! She had got through life – dawdling her way past picket fences, barefoot, in a faded frock, pulling cosmos or daisies through the gaps to make bouquets, parsing sentences, getting her teeth drilled, going back and forth to the dairy on Saturday mornings for jugs of cream – with no awareness whatsoever that this great lump of a thing was sitting out here in the middle of nowhere and was considered sacred.

She resents the suggestion, transmitted to her via Donald, that she had been missing out on something, some other – dimension. How many dimensions are there? And how many could a body actually cope with and still get the washing on the line and tea on the table?

That's the trouble with young people. They think everything outside their own lives is lacking in something. Some dimension. How would they know, unless they were mind-readers or you told them (and then you'd have to find the words, and they'd have to *listen*), what it felt like – that little honey-sack at the end of a plumbago when it suddenly bursts on your tongue, or the roughness of Dezzy McGee's big toe when he rubbed it once on her belly when she was sunbaking at the Townsville Baths. 'Waddabout a root, Dulce?' That's what he had whispered.

She laughs, then looks about to see if anyone has heard, then laughs again. Eleven she was, and Dezzy must have been twelve. Blond and buck-toothed, the baker's boy.

All that seems closer now than this Rock ever was. Closer than last week.

Plus a butcher-bird her uncle Clary owned that was called Tom Leach after a mate he'd lost in France. Which was where – a good deal later of course – she lost Leonard. It could whistle like a champ. And a little stage set, no bigger than a cigar box, that belonged to Beverley Buss's mother, that consisted of a single room with walls that were all mirrors, and little gold tables and chairs, and a boy in silk breeches presenting to a girl in a hooped skirt a perfect silver rose. It played a tune, but the mechanism was broken so she never got to hear it. She had pushed her face so close once, to the tiny open door, that her hot breath fogged up all the mirrors, and Beverley Buss had said, 'Look, Dulce, you've made a different weather.'

Cancer. Beverley Buss, she'd heard, had died of cancer. Beverley McGowan by then.

She had loved that little theatre, and would, if she could, have willed herself small enough to squeeze right in through the narrow doorway and join that boy and girl in their charmed life that was so different from her own barefooted one – she bet *that* girl didn't have warts on her thumb or get ringworm or nits – but had managed it only once, in a dream, and was so shocked to be confronted with herself over and over again in the seven mirrors, which were only too clear on that occasion, that she burst into tears and had to pinch herself awake not to die of shame in front of such a perfect pair.

So what did this Rock have to do with any of that?

Nothing. How could it? It wasn't on the map. It wasn't even on the *list* – there was a list, and you had to find out where the names belonged and mark them in. Capes, bays, the river systems, even the ones that ran only for a month or two each year. You marked them in with a dotted line. But this Rock that everyone makes such a fuss of now wasn't on the list, let alone the map. So there!

It certainly wasn't on *her* map. Her map, in those days, was five or six cross-streets between their weatherboard, her school, the open-air pictures where coloured people sat on the other side of a latticed partition, and the Townsville Baths. Later, in Brisbane after the war, it was the streets around West End as she dragged Douglas and pushed Donald, up to the shops and then back again in the boiling sun, her route determined by the places where you could get a stroller over the kerb.

Big grasshoppers would be chugging past, and at nesting time you had to watch out for magpies. Nothing to see on the way. A stray dog sniffing then lifting its leg in the weeds round a lamppost. Roadmen at work round a fenced-off hole. A steamroller laying a carpet of hot tar, and that smell, burning pitch or hellfire, and the fellers in army boots and shorts at work beside it, most of them leaning on shovels or sitting on one heel with a fag hanging from their lip, waiting for the billy to boil over a pile of sticks. The tar smell thinning at last to the peppery scent that came through a paling fence. Dry stalks in a spare allotment.

Sometimes she stopped off to have morning tea with her only friend at that time, a Chinese lady called Mrs Wau Hing.

Mrs Wau Hing had a cabinet in her front room made of carved cherrywood, with shelves and brackets and appliquéd ivory flowers, chrysanthemums and little fine-winged hummingbirds. It was beautiful. Though you wouldn't really know what to do with it. Mrs Wau Hing called it decorative.

Mrs Wau Hing called *her* Blossom (which was silly really, but she liked it) and gave her chicken in garlicky black sauce to take home, which Leonard said was 'different.' Too different for her, but never mind, it was the thought.

What pleased her was the fine blue-whiteness of the bowl her friend sent it home in, with its design of pinpricks filled with transparent glaze.

When she went out barefoot in her nightie to get a glass of water at the kitchen sink, there it was, rinsed and shining in the wooden rack along with her own familiar crockery.

So what did the Rock have to do with any of that? Or with the stone she had in her kidneys in 1973?

These days, mind you, it's everywhere. Including on TV. Turns up dripping with tomato sauce as a hamburger, or as a long red-clay mould that starts to heave, then cracks open, and when all the bits fall away there's a flash-looking car inside, a Ford Fairlane – stuff like that. Its red shadow turned into a dingo one night and took that baby.

Suddenly it has plonked itself down in the middle of people's lives like something that has just landed from outer space, or pushed up out of the centre of the earth, and occupies the gap that was filled once by – by what? She can't think. Movie stars? Jesus? The Royal Family? It has opened people's minds – this is Donald again – in the direction of the *incommensurable.* What a mouthful! It is exerting an *influence.* Well, not on her it isn't! She gives it a quick dismissive glance and takes another deep drag on her Winfield.

Cathedrals. With Leonard it was cathedrals. As soon as the war was over and the big liners were on the go again he started planning their trip. They made it at last in 1976.

Cathedrals. Great sooty piles at the end of crooked little streets, more often than not with something missing, like the veterans they made a space for, *mutilés*, on every bus.

Or on islands. Or high up on cliffs. Leonard's eyes went all watery just at the sight of one of them and she felt him move quietly away.

He wasn't religious in a praying way. When Leonard got down on his knees each morning it was to polish his boots – Nugget boot polish was what he believed in. The smell of it hung about in the hallway long after he had taken his briefcase and hat and run off to the tram. But with cathedrals, she'd decided, it was the gloom that got him. Which had been brewing there for centuries, and connected with some part of his nature she recognised, and felt soft towards, but had never felt free to enter. She associated it with the bald patch on top of his head, which you only saw, or *she* did, when he got down on his knees in the hallway on a sheet of newspaper, and held one boot, then the other, very lovingly to his heart, and stroked it till it shone.

She felt such a surge of tenderness for him then. For his reliability, his decency. And for that bald spot, which was the only thing she could see in him that he couldn't, a hidden weakness. That's the sort of thing that got her. But cathedrals, no thanks!

When she did manage to feel something, other than a chill in her bones that was like creeping death, was if the organ happened to be playing, or the sun, which was rare enough, was dropping colours from a stained-glass window on to the stony floor, in a play of pink and gold.

As for the proportions, as Leonard called them, well, she didn't go in for height, she decided; all *that* gave you was a crick in the neck. What she liked was distance. A good long view towards the sunset, or at a certain soft hour at home, towards an empty intersection, and if you got a glimpse of something more it would be the way the hills blurred off into blueness beyond the last of the flashing roofs. You would feel small then, in a way she found comforting.

What really put her off was when Leonard, half lying in one of the pews, with the guide laid open in his lap and his arms extended along the wooden back, rolled his eyes up, like suffering Jesus or one of their Catholic saints. Where, she wondered, had he got *that* from? As far as she knew he was a Methodist.

As they moved on from Cologne to those others – the French ones – she'd taken against the cathedrals, started to really resent them. The way you resent a teacher (that Miss Bishop in third grade for instance) who has got a set against you and decided you're a dill, or some little miss at the bank.

She had never had to worry, as some do, about other women, but she'd felt then that Leonard was being stolen from her. The moment they pushed through the doors and the cold hit her heart, she felt the change in him. Lying awake at his side in poky rooms, she would stare up at the ceiling and have to prevent herself from reaching out to see if he was still there.

She began to feel a kind of dread. The sight of yet another of those Gothic monsters looming up out of a side street and opening its stone arms to him was more than she could face.

But when it happened it wasn't in a cathedral but in one of the hotels, and for two days afterwards she sat waiting in the room beside their ports, eating nothing, till at last Donald arrived to reclaim her and take his father home.

'It's something you should *see*,' Donald had told her, speaking of this Rock.

'Why?'

'Because you should, that's all.'

'You mean before I die,' she said, and gave a rough laugh.

It's what Leonard had said. 'I want to see Cologne cathedral before I die.' But after Cologne he had got in another six.

'Are there any more of these things?' she asked of the Rock. 'Or is there just the one?'

Donald gave her a hard look. He wondered sometimes if she wasn't sharper than she let on.

She had come out here to please him. He was easily pleased and she knew that if she didn't he would sulk. It was a break as well from the unit, and from having to show up at Tess Hyland's every afternoon at five-thirty – the Happy Hour – and listen to her complaints about the other owners and what the dogs were doing to her philodendrons.

Tess Hyland had been a convent mouse from Rockhampton when, in all the excitement after the war, she was recruited by UNRWA and went to work in the DP camps in Europe, then spent twenty-five years as a secretary at the UN in New York, where she had picked up a style that included daiquiris at five-thirty in the afternoon and little bits of this and that on 'crackers.'

Five-thirty, the Happy Hour. Personally it was a time she had always hated, when a good many people might think seriously of cutting their throat.

She would also miss out, just this once, on babysitting her three grandchildren, Les, Brett and Candy, on a Saturday night, and her drive in the back seat of Douglas's Toyota on Sunday afternoon.

They had given her a room out here with an en suite, and the menu, even at breakfast, was 'extensive.' It was only three nights.

*

The first thing she'd done when Donald left her alone in the room was to have a good go-through of the cupboards. She didn't know what she was looking for, but people, she knew, were inclined to leave things, and if there was a dirty sock somewhere, or a suspender belt or a used tissue, she wouldn't feel the place was her own.

The drawers for a start. There were two deep ones under the table where they had put her port, and two more at the end of the long cupboard. When you opened the cupboard a light came on. There was a good six feet of hanging space in there, with a dozen or so good hangers. Real ones, not fixed to the rail so you couldn't walk off with them like the ones in France.

But all that hanging space! All those shelves and drawers! Who had they been expecting? Madame Melba? How many frocks and matinee coats and smart little suits and jackets would you have to have, how many hankies and pairs of stockings and undies, to do justice to the facilities they had provided? She had brought too little. And even that, when she opened her port and looked at it, seemed more than she would need. And why were there two beds? Both *double*.

In the fridge, when she looked, and in the bar recess above, was all you would need to put on a good-sized party: cans of VB, bottles of Carlsberg, Cascade, champagne, wicker baskets packed like a Christmas hamper with Cheezels, crisps, Picnic and Snickers bars and tins of macadamia nuts and cashews.

So what am I in for? she wondered. Who should I be expecting? And what about those double beds?

Casting another panicky glance in the direction of so many tantalising but unwelcome possibilities, she fled to the en suite and snicked the lock on the door.

The whole place gleamed, you couldn't fault them on that. Every steel bar and granite surface gave off a blinding reflection. There was a band of satiny paper across the lid of the lav. You had to break it to use the thing. Like cutting the ribbon on a bridge.

You could crack your skull in there. That's what she thought. Easily. It was so shiny and full of edges. Or fall and break a hip.

She settled on the rim of the bath and considered her predicament. Just stepping into a place like this was a *big risk.*

Suddenly she saw something.

On the floor between the gleaming white lav and the wall was a cockroach, lying on its back with its curled-up legs in the air. It could hardly be the victim of a broken hip, so must have died of something the room had been sprayed with, that was safe for humans – well, it had better be! – but fatal to cockies and such. She got down on her knees and took a good look at it.

Cockroaches, she had heard, were the oldest living creatures on earth. Survivors. Unkillable. Well, obviously you could kill individuals like this one, but not the species. They would outlast anything. Even a nuclear explosion. She sat back on her heels and considered this.

The cockie statistics were impressive, but when it came to survival you couldn't beat people, that was her view. People were amazing. They just went on and on. No matter how poor they were, how pinched and cramped their lives, how much pain they had, or bad luck, or how unjust the world was, or how many times they had been struck down. Look at Mrs Ormond with her one breast and that husband of hers who was always after the little boys. Look at those fellers in Changi and on the railway – Dezzy McGee had been one of those. Look at that cripple you saw down at the Quay, in a wheelchair with his head lolling and the snot running down into his mouth. Living there – sleeping and all – in a wheelchair, with no other shelter, and young fellers running in off the ferries in relays to wheel him into the gents and put him on the lavvie and clean him up afterwards at one of the basins. Look at the derros with their yellow beards and bare, blackened feet, shifting about among the suits in Martin Place. They were all up and moving – well, not that one in the wheelchair – pushing on to the next day and the next and the one after, unkillable, in spite of the bombs and the gas chambers, needing only a mouthful of pap to live on, like those Africans on the TV, and the least bit of hope. Hanging on to it. To life and one another.

She took the cockroach very gingerly by one of its brittle legs, used the side of the bathtub to heave herself upright, went through to the bedroom, and tossed it out into a garden bed. Something out there, ants or that, would get a meal off it. Good luck to them!

But when she turned back to the room and saw the wide-open empty cupboard with its blaze of light she regretted it. She could have thrown the cockroach in there. A dead cockroach was all right. It wouldn't have disturbed her sleep. Not like a dirty sock.

She closed the cupboard door and squinnied through a crack to see that the light was off, then sat quietly on one of the beds. Then, after a moment, shifted to the other.

She was saved by a light knocking at the door. Donald. Afternoon tea. But when she came back the problem was still there. All that cupboard space, the second bed.

She did what she could by distributing her belongings in as many places as possible – one shoe in one drawer, one in another, the same with her undies, her four hankies and the things from her handbag: lipstick, a little hand mirror, an emery board, half a roll of Quick-Eze, a photograph of Donald and friends from the Arts Ball in Shanghai, another of Les, Brett and Candy in school uniform. But it looked so inadequate after a moment or two, so hopeless, that she gathered everything up again, put it back in her handbag, then repacked her port and left it to sit there, all locked and buckled, on the rack, as if only her unclaimed luggage had arrived in the room, and she as yet had acquired no responsibilities. Then she stretched out fully clothed on one of the beds and slept.

'What now?'

Donald had lowered the novel he was reading and was watching her, over the top of his glasses, slide down, just an inch at a time, between the arms of the yielding silk-covered lounge chair. They were in one of the hotel's grand reception rooms after dinner.

'What now what?' she demanded.

'What are you doing?'

'Nothing,' she told him. 'Getting comfortable.'

Dim lighting, the lampshades glowing gold. Outside the beginnings of night, blue-luminous. The long room suspended out there in reflection so that the lounge chairs and gold-legged glass-topped tables floated above a carpet of lawn, among shrubs that might simply have sprouted through the floorboards, and they too, she and Donald, and some people who were standing in a group behind them, also floating and transparent, in double exposure like ghosts.

Meanwhile, shoes off, stockinged feet extended, slumped sideways in the welcoming softness, she was getting her right hand down between the arm of the chair and the cushion, almost to the elbow now, right down in the crease there, feeling for coins, or a biro or lost earring. You could find all sorts of things in such places if you got deep enough, as she knew from cleaning at home. Not just dustballs.

Once, in a big hotel at Eaglehawk Neck in Tasmania, where she had gone to play in a bridge tournament, Tess Hyland had found a used condom. Really! They must have been doing it right there in the lounge, whoever it was, late at night, in the dark. She hoped her fingers, as they felt about now, didn't come across anything like that! But she was ready – you had to be. For *whatever.*

The tips of her fingers encountered metal. She slipped lower in the chair, settling in a lopsided position, very nearly horizontal, like a drunk, and closed her fist on one, two, three coins, more – and a pen, but only plastic.

'For heaven's sake,' Donald exploded.

Maybe she looked as if she was having an attack. She abandoned the pen. With some difficulty she wiggled her fist free and, pushing upright, smoothed her skirt and sat up, very straight now and defiant. Donald, with a puzzled look, went back to his novel but continued to throw her glances.

She snapped her handbag open, met his gaze and, very adroitly she thought, slipped the coins in. Two one-dollar pieces, a twenty cents and some fives. Not bad. She estimated there were about thirty such armchairs in the lounge, plus another half-dozen three-seaters. Up to a hundred dollars that would make, lurking about as buried treasure in the near vicinity. Quite a haul if you got in before the staff.

She wondered if she could risk moving to the third of the armchairs round their table, but decided she'd better not. Donald was already on the watch.

What pleased her, amid all these ghostly reflections, was that the coins down there in their hidden places, like the ones she had just slipped into her purse, maybe because they had slipped deep down and smuggled themselves out of sight, had retained their lovely solidity and weight. That was a good trick.

What she had to do was work out how *she* might manage it.

Mid-morning. They were out under the sails beside the pool. Donald was writing again. She wondered sometimes what on earth he found to say. She had been with him all the time they were here. Nothing had *happened.*

On the wide lawn bodies were sunbaking, laid out on folding chairs, white plastic, that could also become beds, their oiled limbs sleek in the sun.

Three Japanese boys who looked like twelve-year-olds, and not at all the sort who would rape nuns, were larking about at the deep end, throwing one another over and over again into the pool. They were doctors, down here, Donald had discovered, to celebrate their graduation.

Four women in bikinis that showed their belly buttons and yellow-tanned bellies – women as old as herself she thought – were at a table together, sipping coloured drinks. They wore sunglasses and a lot of heavy gold, though all one of them had to show was a stack of red, white and green plastic bangles up her arm. She recognised her as a person she had spoken to once before, maybe yesterday. She was from a place called Spokane. Or was she the one from Tucson, Arizona? Either way, she had found their encounter disturbing.

Spokane! She'd never heard of it. Never even knew it existed. A big place too, over four hundred thousand. All learning to talk and walk and read and getting the papers delivered and feeling one another up in the backs of cars. This woman had lived her whole life there.

What you don't know can't hurt you, her mother used to say. Well, lately she'd begun to have her doubts. There was so much. This Rock, for instance, those people in the *camps*. All the time she had been spooning Farax into Douglas, then Donald, these people in Spokane or Tucson, Arizona, had been going to bed and the others into gas ovens. You couldn't keep up.

'Where is it?' she had asked the woman from Tucson, Arizona, who was perched on the edge of one plastic chair with her foot up on another, painting her toenails an iridescent pink.

The woman paused in her painting. 'Well, do you know Phoenix?'

'What?'

'Phoenix,' the woman repeated. 'Tucson is a two-hour drive from Phoenix. South.'

'Oh,' she'd said.

So now there was this other place as well. She'd never heard of either one. But then, she thought, these people have probably never heard of Hurstville!'

Still, it disturbed her, all these unknown places. Like that second *bed*.

There were six old men in the spa, all in a circle as if they were playing ring-a-ring-a-rosie, their arms extended along the tiled edge, the bluish water hopping about under their chins.

They were baldies most of them, but one had a peak of snow-white hair like a cockatoo and surprisingly black eyebrows, in a face that was long and tanned.

Occasionally one of them would sink, and as he went down his toes would surface. So there was more to them than just the head and shoulders.

These old fellers had not lost their vim. You could see it in their eyes and in the champagne that bubbled up between their legs. The spa was *buzzing*. Most of it was these old guys' voices. It was like a ceremony, that's what she thought.

She shifted her chair to hear them better.

'Tallahassee,' she heard. That was a new one! 'Jerusalem.'

She pretended to be looking for something under her chair, and trying not to let Donald see, jerked it closer to the spa. These old fellers were up to something.

Gnomes, is what she thought of. The gnomes of Zurich. Shoulders, some of them with tufts of white hair, long faces above the boiling surface. Hiding the real source of things, the plumbing. Which was lower down.

She had never fathomed what men were really up to, what they wanted. What it was they were asking for, but never openly, and when they didn't get it, brooded and fretted over and clenched their jaws and inwardly went dark, or clenched their fists and beat one another senseless, or their wives and kiddies, or rolled their eyes up and yearned for it in a silence that filled their mouths like tongues.

The pool was whispering again.

'Odessa,' she heard. 'Schenectady.' Then, after a whole lot more she couldn't catch, very clearly, in a voice she recognised over the buzzing of the water, 'unceremonious,' a word she wouldn't have picked up if she hadn't heard it on a previous occasion.

Unceremonious.

Mrs Porter stood in the middle of her room and did not know which way to turn. Each time she came back to it, it was like a place she was stepping into for the first time. She recognised nothing.

When something like that happens over and over again it shakes you. As if you'd left no mark.

It wasn't simply that the moment she went out they slipped in and removed all trace of her. It was the room itself. It was so perfect it didn't need you. It certainly didn't need *her.*

She thought of breaking something. But what? A mirror would be bad luck.

She picked up a heavy glass ashtray, considered a moment, then flipped it out the window. Like that cockroach. It disappeared with a clunk into a flowerbed.

Well, that was a start. She looked for something else she could chuck out.

The one thing she couldn't get rid of was that Rock. It sat dead centre there in the window. Just dumped there throbbing in the late sunlight, and so red it hurt her eyes.

To save herself from having to look at it she shut herself in the bathroom. At least you could make an impression on that. You could use the lav or turn the shower on and make the place so steamy all the mirrors fogged up and the walls lost some of their terrible brightness.

The place had its dangers of course, but was safe enough if all you did was lower the toilet seat and sit. Only how long could a body just sit?

Unceremonious.

He had saved that up till the last moment, when he thought she was no longer listening, and had hissed it out, but so softly that if she hadn't had her head down trying to catch his last breath she mightn't have heard it at all.

What a thing to say. What a word to come up with!

She thought she might have got it wrong, but it wasn't a word *she* could have produced, she hardly knew what it meant. So what was it, an accusation? Even now, after so long, it made her furious.

To have *that* thrown at you! In a dingy little room in a place where the words were strange enough anyway, not to speak of the food, and the dim light bulbs, and the wobbly ironwork lift that shook the bones half out of you, and the smell of the bedding.

One of her bitterest memories of that dank little room was of Leonard kneeling on that last morning in front of the grate and putting what must have been the last of his strength into removing the dust of France from the cracks in his boots. His breath rasping with each pass of the cloth. His body leaning into the work as if his blessèd soul depended on the quality of the shine.

And then, just minutes later, that word between them. 'Unceremonious.'

For heaven's sake, what did they expect? How many meals did you have to dish up? How many sheets did you have to wash and peg out and fold and put away or smooth over and tuck under? How many times did you have to lick your thumb and test the iron? How many times did you have to go fishing with a safety pin in their pyjama bottoms to find a lost cord?

Angrily she ripped a page off the little notepad they provided on the table between the beds and scribbled the word. Let someone else deal with it, spelled out there in her round, state-school hand.

She opened a drawer and dropped it in. *Unceremonious.* Posted it to the dead.

Then quickly, one after another, scribbled more words, till she had a pile of ripped-out pages.

Dimension, she wrote.

Bon Ami.

Flat 2, 19 Hampstead Road, West End, she wrote.

Root, she wrote, and many more words, till she had emptied herself, like a woman who has done all her housework, swept the house, made the beds, got the washing on the line, and, with nothing to do now but wait for the kiddies to come home from school and her husband from work, can afford to have a bit of a lie-down. She posted each page in a different drawer until all the drawers were occupied, then stretched out on one of the beds, the one on the left, and slept. Badly.

Back home in her unit, dust would be gathering, settling grain by grain on all her things: on the top of the television, between the knots of her crocheted doilies, in the hearts of the blood-red artificial roses that filled the glass vase on her bedside table.

On one petal of each rose was a raindrop, as if a few sports of rain had fallen. But when you touched the drop it was hard, like one of those lumps of red-gold resin they used to chew when they were kids, that had bled out of the rough trunk of a gum.

If it was rain that had fallen, even a few spots, her things would be wet and the heart of the rose would have been washed clean. But what she found herself sitting in, in her dream, was a slow fall of dust. Everything, everything, was being covered and choked with it.

Well, it's what they'd always said: dust to dust – only she hadn't believed it. The last word. *Dust.*

It worried her now that when she'd made her list she had left it out, and now it had got into her head she'd never be rid of it. She'd just go on sitting there forever watching it gather around her. Watching it fall grain by grain over her things, over *her*, like a grainy twilight that was the start of another sort of night, but one that would go on and on and never pass.

The Hoover, she shouted in her sleep. Get the Hoover.

She woke then. On this double bed in a room from which every bit of dust, as far as she could see, had been expunged.

And now, at last, the others arrived.

One of them lay down beside her. She refused to turn and look, and the bed was wide enough for her to ignore him, though at one point he began to whisper. More *words.*

The others, a couple, lay down on the second bed and began to make love, and so as not to see who it was who had come to her own bed, and most of all not to have to listen to his words, she turned towards them and watched. They were shadowy. Maybe black.

She didn't mind them using the bed, they didn't disturb her. Probably had nowhere to go, poor things. And they weren't noisy.

She must have gone back to sleep then, because when she woke again the room seemed lighter, less thick with breath. She was alone.

There was a humming in the room. Low. It made the veins in her forehead throb.

She got up and went, in her stockinged feet, to the window.

It was as if something out there at the end of the night was sending out gonglike vibrations that made the whole room hum and glow. The Rock, darkly veined and shimmering, was sitting like a cloud a hundred feet above the earth. Had simply risen up, ignoring the millions of tons it must weigh, and was stalled there on the horizon like an immense spacecraft, and the light it gave off was a sound with a voice at the centre of it saying, *Look at this. So, what do you reckon now?*

Mrs Porter looked at it askance, but she did look. And what she felt was an immediate and unaccountable happiness, as if the Rock's new-found lightness was catching. And she remembered something: a time when Donald had just begun to stand unsteadily on his own plump little legs and had discovered the joy of running away from her towards a flower he had glimpsed in a garden bed, or a puppy dog or his brother's red tricycle. When she called he would give a quick glance over his shoulder and run further. Suddenly unburdened, she had had to hang on to things – the sink, Leonard's Stelzner upright – so as not to go floating clean off the linoleum, as if, after so many months of carrying them, inside her body or on her hip, first the one, then the other, she had forgotten the trick of letting gravity alone hold her down.

Now, looking at the Rock, she felt as if she had let go of something and was free to join it. To go floating. Like a balloon some small child – Donald perhaps – had let go of and which was free to go now wherever the world might take it. She glanced down. She was hovering a foot above the carpet.

So it had happened. She was off.

Immediately she began to worry about Donald. She needed to get word to him.

That did it. She came down with a bump. And with her heart beating fast in the fear that it might already be too late, she made for the door. She needed to reassure him, if he didn't already know, that she hadn't really minded all those times when he'd hung on to her skirt and dragged her off to look at this and that. So full of need and bullying insistence, she saw now, because if she didn't look, and confirm that yes it was amazing, it really was, he couldn't be sure that either he or it was there.

She had gone grudgingly, and looked and pretended. Because she had never given up the hard little knot of selfishness that her mother had warned would one day do her in. Well, her mother was wrong. It had saved her. Without it she would have been no more than a space for others to curl up in for a time then walk away from. All this, in her new-found lightness, she understood at last and wanted to explain to the one person who was left who might understand it and forgive. Still wearing the frock she had lain down in, she flung the door open and, barely hearing the click as it closed behind her, stepped out into the hotel corridor. Only then did she realise that she did not know the number of Donald's room.

'You fool, Dulcie,' she told herself. The voice was Leonard's. In these latter years, Leonard's had become the voice she used for speaking to herself. It made her see things more clearly. Though Leonard would never have said to her the sort of things she said to herself. 'Stupid *woman*. Bloody old fool.'

She walked up and down a little. All the doors looked the same.

She put her ear to one, then to another, to see if she could hear Donald's snoring, but behind their identical doors all the rooms preserved an identical breathless silence.

A little further along, beside the door to a linen closet where she had sometimes seen a trolley stacked with towels and the little coloured bottles and soap packs that went into the various bathrooms, there was a chair. In a state now of angry alarm, she seized occupation of it and sat, commanding the empty corridor. She'd been too quick off the mark. She needed to sit now and have a think.

But the corridor, with its rows of ceiling lights and doors all blindly closed on their separate dreams, gave her the creeps. She felt breathless.

She made for a small flight of stairs at the far end that went down to a door, and when she opened it, and it too clicked shut behind her, found herself outside the building altogether, standing in her stockinged feet on stone flags that were still warm. The warmth came right up through her, and all about were night-flowering shrubs, and bigger trees with boughs that drooped. She took a good breath. The air was heavy with scent – with different scents. Night insects were twittering. All was clear moonlight, as still as still.

She began to walk – how simple things could be! – enjoying her own lightness and wondering if she wasn't still asleep and dreaming. Only in dreams did your body dispose of itself so easily. She walked on springy lawn. But they must have been watering it, because almost immediately her stockings were soaked. She sat down on a low wall and peeled them off, and when she looked back gave a little laugh at the look of them there on the shadowy grass. Like two snakeskins, a couple. That'll make 'em guess!

Soon she was in a car park, empty but flooded with moonlight, then out again into soft sand. Red sand, still with the warmth of the sun in it, but cooler when you worked your naked toes in. Luxurious. She waded to the top of a dune and let herself go, half sliding, half rolling, till she came to a stop and was on level ground again. She righted herself and, seated in warm sand, checked for broken bones. All around her the bushes, which were spiky and had seemed dull by day, were giving off light like slow-burning fireworks. Big clouds rolled across the moon, thin as smoke, then darker. There was a twittering, though she could see no birds. Everywhere, things were happening – that's what she felt. Small things that for a long time now she had failed to notice. To see them you had to get down to where she was now, close to the ground. At kiddie level. Otherwise there were so many other things to demand your attention that you got distracted, you lost the habit of looking, of listening, unless some kiddie down there dragged at your skirt and demanded, 'Look, Mum, look.'

That twittering for instance. She knew what it was now. Not birds but the Station Master's office at Babinda. It was years, donkey's years, since that particular sound had come to her, yet here it was. Must have been going on all around her for ages, and she was too busy listening to other things to notice.

Babinda.

For a whole year after she was married, with Leonard away in New Guinea, she had been with the railways, an emergency worker while the boys were at the war. Those were the days! She was off the shelf, so that was settled, and she had no domestic responsibilities. She had never in her life felt so free. She loved the noise and bustle of the Station Master's office when things were on the go; the buzzing and tinkling when the First Division was held up by floods below the Burdekin or when, outside the regular timetable, a special came though, a troop-transport with all the boys hanging out the windows wolf-whistling and calling across the tracks to where she was walking up and down with a lantern, to ask her name. Then the long sleepy periods when nothing was happening at all and you could get your head into *Photoplay*.

The Station Master, Mr O'Leary, was a gardener, his platform a tame jungle of staghorns, elkhorns, hoyas, maidenhair ferns in hanging baskets, tree orchids cut straight from the trunk. He was out there in all weathers in his shirtsleeves whispering to his favourites. 'Hullo, ducky,' he'd be singing, 'here's a nice drop of water for you. That's a girl! You'll enjoy this.'

She'd pause at her knitting to listen to him. He used the same tone when he was talking to her. It made her feel quite tender towards him. But he was always respectful – she was, after all, a married woman.

Sometimes, in the late afternoon, when everything was at a low point and even the bush sounds had dropped to nothing, he would talk of his son Reggie, the footballer, who had been in her class at primary school and was now a POW in Malaya. Reggie had played the mouth organ, that's what she remembered. A chunk of honeycomb at his lips and his breath swarming in the golden cells, that's what she remembered. 'The Flight of the Bumble Bee.'

'It's a blessing his mother's already gone,' Mr O'Leary would tell her softly while the light slanted and turned pink. 'At least she's spared the waiting. Once you've got kiddies, Dulce, you're never free, not ever. I spend half my time asking myself what he's getting to eat, he's such a big feller. If he's got a mate an' that. I'm only half here sometimes.'

She listened and was sympathetic but did not understand, not really. Douglas and Donald were still way off in the future, waiting there in the shadows beyond the track; they had not yet found her. But she liked listening to Mr O'Leary. No one had ever thought her worth confiding in, not till this. She felt quite grown up. An independent woman. She was all of twenty-three.

Under the influence of the many unscheduled trains that were running up and down the line, all those lives the war had forced out of their expected course, she was led to wonder what direction she herself might be headed in. Odd, she thought now, that she had never considered her marriage a direction, let alone a terminus. But that was the times, the war. Everything normal was suspended for the duration. Afterwards, anything might be possible.

'You won't find me stickin' round once the war is over.'

This was Jim Haddy, the Station Master's Assistant. 'No fear! I'll be off like a shot. You watch my dust!'

At sixteen, Jim Haddy was the most amazing boy she'd ever come across. He was so full of things, so dedicated. He thought the Queensland Railways were God and got quite upset if you threw off at them or said things like, 'You know the theme song of the Queensland Railways, don't you? "I Walk Beside You."' He thought Mr O'Leary was 'slack' because when they went out with their flags and lamps and things to wave a train through, he left the tabs on his waistcoat unfastened. Jim was a stickler. He did not roll his sleeves up on even the muggiest days. Always wore his soft felt Railway hat. And his waistcoat, even if it was unbuttoned in front, was always properly buckled at the sides.

He was a soft-faced kid who got overexcited and had, as Mr O'Leary put it, to be watched. He knew all there was to know about the Royal Houses of Europe, and talked about the Teck Mecklenburgs and the Bourbon Parmas as if they owned cane farms down the road, and Queen Marie of Romania and King Zog as if they were his auntie and uncle. He spent a lot of the

Railway's time settling them like starlings in their family trees on sheets of austerity butcher's paper.

'What a funny boy you are,' she would tell him dreamily as she leaned over his shoulder to watch.

The summer sun would be sheeting down, a wall of impenetrable light, and when it stopped, the view would be back, so green it hurt your eyes, and the earth in Mr O'Leary's flowerbeds would steam and give off smells. The little room where they sat at the end of the platform would be all misty with heat. She'd be thinking: When I get home I'll have to take Leonard's shoes out of the lowboy and brush the mould off. 'Where *is* Montenegro?' she'd ask, and Jim was only too happy to tell, though she was none the wiser.

That boy needs watching.

But she had lost sight of him. Like so much else from that time. And from other times. She was surprised now that he had come back, and so clearly that as she leaned over his shoulder she caught the vinegary smell of his neck under the raw haircut.

'What happened to you, Jim Haddy?' she found herself asking in her own voice, her feet in the powdery red soil. 'Where are you, I wonder? And where are Queen Marie and King Zog?' She hadn't heard much of them lately either.

'I'm here,' she announced, in case Jim was somewhere in the vicinity and listening.

She looked about and saw that she was in the midst of a lot of small grey-green bushes, with daylight coming and no landmarks she could recognise.

'My God,' she said to herself, 'where? *Where* am I? This isn't my life.'

Off in the distance a train was rumbling in over the tracks: a great whooshing sound that grew and grew, and before she knew it passed so close to where she was standing that she was blown clear off her feet in a blaze of dust. It cleared, and she realised that high up in a window of one of the carriages as it went thundering past she had seen her own face, dreaming behind the glass and smiling. Going south. She picked herself up and got going again.

The Rock was there. Looming. Dark against the skyline. She made for that.

The sun was coming up, hot out of the oven, and almost immediately now the earth grew too hot to walk on. The bushes around her went suddenly dry; her mouth parched, she sat down dump. There was no shade. She must have dozed off.

When she looked up again a small boy was squatting in front of her. Not Donald. And not Douglas either. He was about five years old and black. He squatted on his heels. When her eyes clicked open he stared at her for a moment, then took off shouting.

When she opened her eyes again there were others, six or seven of them. Shy but curious, with big eyes. They squatted and stared. When she raised a hand they drew back. Dared one another to come closer. Poked. Then giggled and sprang away.

At last one little girl, older than the rest, trotted off and came back with some scraps of bread and a cup full of water. The others looked on while the little girl pushed dry crusts into the open mouth, as if feeding a sick bird, and tipped the cup. The cup was old and crumpled, the child's fingers rather dirty. Oh well, she thought, it's a bit late to be worrying over my peck of dirt.

She swallowed, and the children watched as her old throat dealt with the warmish water, got it down.

She saw that it was a test. To see what she was. Old woman or spirit.

No need to look so puzzled, she told them, though not in so many words. It's just me, Dulcie MacIntyre. It's no use expecting anything more. This is it.

But they continued to watch as if they were not convinced.

She lay like a package while they sat waiting. As if, when the package finally unwrapped itself, it might contain something interesting. Oh well, she thought, they'll find out. If they're disappointed, that's their lookout.

After a while she must have seemed permanent and familiar to them as any other lump of earth because they got bored, some of them – the littlies – and went back to whatever game they'd been playing when that first one interrupted them, shouting, 'Hey, look what I found! Over here!'

But two or three of them stayed. Watching the old lizard turn its head on the wrinkled, outstretched neck. Slowly lifting its gaze. Shifting it north. Then east. The dry mouth open.

They fed her dribbles of water. Went off in relays and brought back armfuls of dry scrub and built a screen to keep the sun off, which was fierce, and moved it as the sun moved so that she was always in shade. She had never in all her life felt so closely attended to, cared for. They continued to sit close beside her and watch. They were waiting for something else now. But what?

'I told you,' she said weakly, 'it's no good expecting anything more.' They had been watching so long, poor things. It was a shame they had to be disappointed.

They must have waited all day, because at last she felt the sun's heat fall from her shoulders, though its light was still full in the face of her watchers. Then a shadow moved over them. The shadow of the Rock. She knew this because they kept lifting their eyes towards it, from her to it then back again. The Rock was changing colour now as the sun sank behind it.

The shadow continued to move, like a giant red scarf that was being drawn over them. The Rock, which had been hoarding the sun's heat all day, was giving it off now in a kindlier form as it turned from orange-red to purple. If she could swing her body around now to face it, to look at it, she might understand something. Might. But then again she might not. Better to take what she could, this gentle heat, and leave the show to these others.

I'm sorry, she chuckled, I can't compete.

She was beginning to rise up now, feeling even what was lightest in her, her thoughts, drop gently away. And the children, poor things, had their eyes fixed in the wrong place. No, she wanted to shout to them. Here I am. Up here.

One of the little ones, sitting there with a look of such intense puzzlement on his face, and baffled expectation, was Donald. I'm sorry, Donald, she said softly. But he too was looking in the wrong place.

The big fish dolphin lay stranded. The smaller waves no longer reached it. There were sandgrits in its eyes, the mouth was open, a pulse throbbed under its gills. It was changing colour like a sunset: electric pink and mauve flashes, blushings of yellow-green.

'What is it?' Betty Olds asked. 'What's happening to it?'

'Shush,' Isobel told her.

So they sat, all three and watched. The waves continued to whisper at the edge of the beach. The colours continued to play over the humped back and belly, flushing, changing, until slowly they became less vivid. The pulsing under the gills fluttered, then ceased, and the flesh, slowly as they watched, grew silvery-grey, then leaden.

'What's happened?' Betty asked again. 'Is it dead now?'

'I think so,' Isobel told her. Then, seeing Betty's lip begin to quiver, put her arm around her sister's shoulder and drew her close. 'It's all right, Bets,' she whispered. 'It was old.'

Dulcie said nothing. She too was breathless. This was a moment, she knew, that she would never forget. Never. As long as she lived. She also knew, with certainty, that she would live forever.

Every Move You Make

Letter to A

Alice Pung

You ripped down the wallpaper one day when you were fourteen, ripped it right off the walls all four of them and then stuck up posters all over the room to hide the scabby paint. One day it will get painted over, you told yourself. One day the broken window will get fixed. One day the carpets will get changed. One day the ceiling will not fall down. One day the cracks will not be there, one day the smell will not be there, and when that day comes you will be out. Out of there. You will not be there to see it all. One day you will be out of there and one day you will live a freshly whitewashed life. Yes you will, and the ceiling will no longer peel and fall on top of you and these four walls will no longer close in on you, and you will have cauterised your wants.

There is a depression in the wall. These depressions come about when your knuckles itch and your upper deltoids ache to exert themselves and your mind is nothing but a blank black hole screaming to see red, that is when you strike and don't think of the consequences. This is when your inarticulate rage causes you to bunch up your fist and punch the wall so hard that the clock falls down on the other side, since there is no one to listen to your choked half-finished sentences about a cousin, a cousin who was once like a brother but is now nothing more than crap for all you care, a cousin so far gone that you don't think of the money he has borrowed from you or the money he owes you, the money to get out, you do not think about it at all because you do not want to think about him. To think about him is to stumble down the path of despair and once you are on that path, you have to keep running, keep running or else if you stop and pause to see what direction you are going, you will sink to your knees and realise how much you need water, water like the water bottles they carry down the streets of Richmond and you can always tell which ones are the ones on the habit because of these water bottles.

We were powerpoints, powerpoints with the three holes, two that slanted upwards and one that was a straight stroke down, straight and narrow and sad, like the prospect of some of us spending the rest of our lives doing Powerpoint presentations because our names are Andrew Chan and we wear glasses and sit in front of our PCs after school each evening because our parents want us to study hard and become successful, because this is a land of great opportunity and we must not waste it, it is a land of great fairness where even Ah Chan selling BanCao at the market in Saigon can raise a son who can decipher strange symbols in front of a screen merely by pressing many buttons in different combinations on a black pad, and it assures him to hear the clackity clack noise like an old abacus coming from his son's room, because then he knows that his son knows more than he does. Old Ah Chan doesn't have a clue about what the information superhighway is, all he knows is that there are no casualties, none at all, and that it can only go up from here. And so he buys his son the magic machine with the clopclop buttons and with a few clackity clacks and clicks he can transport himself to a nice office and a house in the suburbs and a shiny new blue Mazda.

Chink is an insult, but chink is also the sound that money makes as it rattles in your father's pockets, it is also the sound that those machines at the casino make when he hits the jackpot, so chink is not necessarily too bad a word. Chink is the only word that governs the life of your father, chink chink chink of the coins in the gaming machine, chink chink chink one at a time and not all at once, and so he sits there to wait for the sound of all-at-once chinks, meanwhile at home the boy and the mother and the kid brother sit together for a dinner of rice and vegetables and bits of beef before parting to play computer games or watch Chinese serials in separate rooms. You go off to your room and turn up the music, real loud music, and you look at the white wall which you had determined to paint a mural on, 'cause your art teacher says that you have real talent, but what the hell, what now? What is determination now, when the father won't come back and when the father won't stop spending the money and won't stop believing in the glorious sound of the chinkchinkchink of the machine.

A steady beat of chinks from the coins in his pocket, waiting for the rapid succession of chinkchinkchinks like the quickening of a heartbeat until the glorious rushing sound cannot be separated into its individual tinkles but all pours forth like a mad gold rush.

This is a different gold rush from the gold rush of the nineteenth century when we men had to carry heavy buckets and sift away to find the little pieces, and we needed strong stomachs to swallow the pieces and keen eyes to sift through the processes of our digestive tracts to find that little hard lump.

Meanwhile, swallow that lump in your throat you big sook, 'cause big boys aren't sooks goddam it, and look at your comic books and pictures of *Dragonball Z* and pick up the phone to call the number of that little pale-faced girl with the dark eyes and the black hair, even if she makes you write her letters instead of wanting to talk in person. Let the phone ring and ring and goddam is there anyone home? Keep your finger on the little soft grey 'off' button on the cordless phone in case her parents pick up and interrogate you worse than those Mao guards during the bloody cultural revolution that would not leave your family alone, that sent them to Vietnam, and then to this new land where little white-faced girls with black hair laugh at your stories of killing chickens in the Guangzhou countryside, and all your history becomes a funny after-dinner anecdote. Others would see your acts as barbaric, and squeeze their clean faces into squished looks of shudder-shake – 'eww, how gross' – even as they are seated opposite you eating a McChicken burger or severing the joints of the skinny bones of KFC chicken-wings with shiny fingers.

And so you lie on your bed in your room waiting for the father to come home, and you can hear the sound of your mother's footsteps padding to the kitchen to wash the dishes from dinner. You sit up and decide to write the girl a letter, a poem even, although you know all of this means nothing to you even though the girl means something to you, little ivory-faced girl in a tower. Grab a few sheets of Reflex paper, A4, nothing fancy. Goddam if the girl is expecting perfumed notepaper, well this was the best she was going to get and she had better be happy with it. Bloody hell how are you going to do this when you couldn't give a damn about this decomposed Keats your English teacher keeps mentioning?

Words are there to convey action, not an endless quagmire of feelings, and whatever you are feeling is transformed into action. And that is why for the life of you, you can't understand why the girl will not go out with you and all she wants to do is to write these bloody letters to you and wants you to write these bloody letters back to her. The surest way to get to know a person is to meet them, and take them out in your car with your recently attained Ps, God you are proud of these plates, and ask her questions but not too many, and do something fun like going to a movie or something.

But this girl, she's a strange girl. You wonder whether you should pursue her, whether this stupid poem will persuade her to actually go out with you. Grant you that date so you can be with someone for once and not have to say a word and just forget about things and have fun. But this girl, this girl looks like she can't have fun. Something about the look in her eyes, as if she is a little scared of what she sees in the world around her. Like she spends a lot of time thinking about why it is all so terrifying, and keeping quiet about her answers. You have no time for enigmas, you want to get out there and get some action, although not necessarily from this girl, because she is a good girl. You are sick to death of sitting still, of doing nothing.

You pick up the phone again and dial the number of the girl. 'Hello?' Ah, the familiar voice, you can imagine her now, sitting at her desk, which is where you imagine her to be, if you are not imagining her in other more pleasant places that suit your fancy but probably not her reality. You have called to chat to get your mind off things, but she does not want to chat, this girl. She wants to talk, goddam it why is it that the stereotype is true, why do women always want to talk about feelings and shit as if these feelings will change anything?

Dingdong. That's the bell. The father is home, the mother must be lying in bed, wide awake. You swear you can almost hear the bedsprings creak as she gets up. Creak creak. You can certainly hear the footsteps, the creak creak snap snap of the tendons of her feet and ankles as she shuffles to the door. You wonder whether the little brother is asleep, and whether he is going to wake up this evening. You wait to hear the inevitable question. 'Where have you been?' Even though your mother knows the answer she asks it anyway.

She can see the chinkchinkchink in his eyes, see the bags beneath. Dark bags beneath carrying phantasmagoric gold coins. He blinks once or twice, and the illusion is gone. He is tired. So tired. The bags hang down to his cheekbones, they become bags of bones, he *is* a bag of bones. 'How much did you use?' your mother demands. 'How much did you lose?' the terms are interchangeable, and it doesn't matter which one comes out.

'I'm hungry, woman, haven't had dinner yet,' the sad man in the old brown leather jacket with the elastic at the bottom grumbles.

'If you came home earlier, you wouldn't have to eat leftovers,' grumbles the mother, as she shuffles to the kitchen, but she brings out the beef from the stove, the beef she would not let you eat too much of because she was saving it for him.

The Concern

Roger McDonald

An elderly man, Kingsley Colts, tall, crow-faced, sag-bellied with wasted potency, stood on the corner of a narrow Kirribilli street clutching a cardboard box of rubbish as a garbage truck roared towards him.

His intention was to step into the road and throw the box in the truck, and the garbos, seeing this, moved fast.

'We'll handle it for you, mate' – taking an elbow, steering the old bloke away – but Kingsley broke off, sped on his big, flat feet to the rear of the truck and hurled the box in with an exhausted laugh; then staggered back, watching the teeth of the compactor crush down on bundles of papers and old photographs.

'You could have killed yourself,' they said, steadying him with dirty hands. Kingsley gazed after the truck – its hydraulic crusher bright yellow like the crest of a sulphur-crested cockatoo. 'I did kill myself, but it's all right, mate, I'm alive,' he wheezed, making as much sense as any other nutter on an average garbo run.

Kingsley Colts sat on a horse blanket in hot shade making friends with ants and beetles. His sister, Barbara, brought him drinks of red cordial and a paper bag of rainbow balls to suck until they turned white. Cockatoos screeched overhead.

Kingsley's eyes searched the horizon.

Earliest memory: a column of dust rising closer, with a darker shape inside it, a man named Adrian Fripp. Kingsley jumped to his feet, stood tall as he could, and watched Fripp emerging from the dust, driving a 'finger slapper' road grader drawn by two blinkered draught horses.

Next memory, the grader pulled by a steam tractor bearing a yellow painted sign: 'Colts and Fripp (ex-AIF), Tanksinkers and Road Contractors.' Fripp called it 'the concern,' what he did. The children were born into it, Fripp always said, through their father, the late Colonel Colts, being its founder. Fripp was the children's legal guardian, his idea of the role being to stamp them with his own inclinations. If they grew up belligerent towards the wrong sort, all would be well. 'Made by Adrian Fripp' was the brand they would carry into ripe old age.

Freed from work, the Clydesdales – Old George and Mrs Dinah – munched nosebags dusty with chaff. They were bleary and affectionate, wiry whiskers on rubbery lips, shaggy hairs matted over hooves as heavy as boulders. Their breath smelled sweet as flaked tobacco. Ambling closer they gave Kingsley the feeling they were about to stand on his toes, a delicious fear to be held until he screamed and jumped back.

'Those two are immortal,' said Fripp, and Kingsley believed him.

After their retirement, the horses were agisted in a paddock near the Darling River, destroying the bark of coolibah trees, eating thistles and rare green pick. They had the stars for company and occasional visits from a boundary rider or jackaroo to see they weren't bogged, foundered or caught in wire. Fripp, if he was lucky, saw them once a year, bringing Kingsley and sometimes Barbara with him.

Veronica Baxter's caravan stood nearby, shuttered tight against dust, birds and mice. It was one of the couple's legendary love nests. After marrying Fripp, Veronica, an artist, kept her own name and bank account. 'Call her Mum,' said Fripp. But they couldn't. 'Call me Veronica,' she said, but they couldn't manage that either: so they shyly called her 'Vee.' Back in Sydney they would give excited reports to her. A painted arch gave shade, with the paint cracked and faded – a wreath of dancers and gum leaves. When the bolts shot back it was always the same – tins of meat, baked beans and drums of powdered milk arranged on shelves, like a grocery shop, with bottles of vinegar and black sauce forming palace guards at attention and old grey army blankets stacked on a chair. Throughout her childhood, Barbara went through with a dustpan and brush playing house. Kingsley learned to read there, and outside learned to shoot, swam in the clay-smelling river, caught catfish and cod.

While the road plant shifted from depot to depot, the caravan mostly stayed put, with roly-poly grass piling underneath. When it was time to go, Kingsley watched until it sank into the trees, twisting his head around to keep it in sight. He thought it was Fripp but in the end, Veronica would brand him cleanest.

They found the plant wherever it was working – Fripp doing 'flash inspections' – somewhere in NSW or just over the border into Victoria, South Australia, or up into western Queensland, where mirages shimmered like lakes of opal.

Kingsley Colts finalises his affairs, not before time at eighty-six – that banana box of old Kodaks last on his list of chuck-outs. The dimpled, crazed surfaces of the photographs rouse a feeling of sour hunger for an era that is utterly gone: Kingsley had wanted to change it, had had a hand in the try, yes, had throttled some bloody life out of it as a union rep 1948–82.

That confounded road plant lined up for inspection – it still haunts him: graders, scoops, lorries, water tanks, the rickety, pneumatic-tyred cookhouse. Men standing around in early morning light smoking, drinking tea from enamel mugs, awaiting their orders – a ramshackle parade of the grateful, whose payment was in pride of the work done, and not much else.

As the childhood episodes ended they came to 'Limestone Hills,' east of Wellington, the low-roofed, deep-windowed house taken back from a share farmer and almost in ruin.

Kingsley sat on a stump with his knees jammed under his chin. A yellow road-grader loomed up, an original 'Leviathan,' blade glancing the earth, sending out sparks and the acrid smell of gunpowder rocks. Kingsley gazed at the metal apparition longing for a wave from Fripp and the chance to jump on. The grader worked away towards a dry ridge without him. It travelled under dusty fig trees heavy with fruit and past kurrajongs with leaves glossy in the heat. Down it came into the dry creekbed and up again. It scraped nothing more than a path for farm lorries on rugged limestone, but to Kingsley the grader defied gravity with its angular leaning wheels and shining blade diminishing in perspective. Only last night he had dreamed of its spectacular qualities, a recurring dream still pursuing him into his dotage: a machine driving through the sky, parting dust-clouds in a celestial parade. Something obvious about road graders was being told him every time: that they returned from the distance without turning around – that was their trick. Every time Kingsley woke, he was amazed by the wonder of it – 'That's how it's done, how it's really done' – until the thrill of knowledge faded to ordinary daylight and awareness of aches and pains.

Fripp banged the controls, flipped levers, spun handwheels. His hatchet face and military moustache came into view covered in dust and streaked with lines of sweat. Kingsley copied his expressions, twisted his lips, curled his mouth in distaste at opposing opinions.

Fripp wore his ex-army slouch hat with a leather chin-strap and a khaki shirt with the sleeves rolled down. Whenever he passed, Kingsley drank the rush of heat that came in a cloud of oily fumes. Then suddenly this memory: the 'Leviathan' standing before him idling in dust and clatter, huge as King Kong.

Before Kingsley could act, Barbara was on her feet: 'Last one up's a rotten egg!' She balanced on a strut while Fripp reached down for Kingsley. But just as Fripp was about to haul him up, Kingsley let go the monkey grip, jumped back, shook his head. Fripp shrugged, frowned sideways, looked around for another taker. So it was to be Barbara darling – and there she went, perched on the high seat with her floral skirt clutched between her knees and her golden hair flying. Fripp held her steady with a hand on the small of her back. The blade clipped gravel, throwing daytime sparks as Kingsley ran alongside.

On the lumpy homestead tennis courts using a racquet dangling broken strings, Kingsley smashed, volleyed, lobbed and cut with a ferocity that wiped away smiles. Fripp played to win but Kingsley toppled him. Barbara wasn't all that good, yet the way she ran for a shot, concentrated on preparing a serve, laughed when she lost a point or received service badly, the way she thumped to earth after collecting a high lob and stood there laughing – just for the fun of it, didn't matter. 'I'm done,' said Barbara. 'You've got us licked, you cow,' said Fripp.

Those two could go far away and Kingsley could bring them back. He wore himself out like a sheepdog in devotion.

One night Kingsley wakes sweating, trembling with awareness of a judgement day. 'It gets no easier,' is the motto of old age. On his way from the toilet he shuffles to the side window of his one-bedroomed flat where he gains a fragmented, steep-angled view of the Harbour Bridge, its metal arch lifting to the clouds. Now he remembers. There was a dream with a floating, released, joyous quality, a realisation of the meaning of life connected to metal. Upon waking, it is this.

At different times in the past, Kingsley has thrown out Fripp's shirt studs, his pigskin hairbrush, his bundles of worthless forestry shares. The photographs will be next. The Veronica Baxter portrait, where Fripp appears like a glossy-faced beetle rearing from dry leaf mould, he donated to the State Library some years ago. It has never been hung. And who remembers the two books Fripp wrote in the 1930s – *Blazeroo*, the Great War memoir; *Wake UP*, the novel? Kingsley Colts is the only one. At moments like this, to have been dedicated in youth to the ideal of Fripp feels like shame; to have led a life in opposition to Fripp feels like betrayal. He made the break, but the rusty machine of the man's inheritance won't go away.

'Coming in,' Fripp called it – enjoying the comforts of Sydney after roughing it in the bush. On starry nights after tea, Fripp joined Kingsley for a midnight scramble. They lived at Castlecrag in the Walter Burley Griffin house that Veronica bought, and Fripp, on first sighting it, made the judgement of the raised eyebrow.

'Righty-oh, Kings, show me that cliff. If I fall off and you don't, that's kismet.'

They carried a torch but rarely used it, enjoying the sensations of the night-time bush, whooshing owls, ghostly moths, haunting nocturnal bird-calls. Kingsley led a way down nimbly as a possum, foothold by handhold, almost hanging upside-down in places, using smooth, corkscrewed angophora branches like slippery slides, while Adrian Fripp, wheezing with effort, stuck close behind him.

Fripp involved himself in '30s politics, stirring strife. 'Not very savoury,' he said, 'but needed.' What it involved only slowly became clear to Kingsley as he reached his teenage years. Breaking up meetings. Confronting strikers with clubs and following them home in unmarked cars.

Kingsley remembers being taken to parades in lonely clearings, uneasy, now, over his guardian's aversions, a sinewy boy clenching his fist for slogans he did not believe. Battle lines were drawn, pinkos to the left, property defenders to the right. Fripp's mates were trusted from trench days and prepared for the worst – the red revolution, no less. Fripp introduced Kingsley around as the late colonel's son – getting him into the legend without the entry fee, as he liked to dig. When the bugle sounded, if it blew the retreat, they would survive in the outback on split peas and raw peanuts.

Kingsley saw Fripp asleep on the couch when he 'came in' but Barbara knew better, that he went to his wife's room later, and they argued. It was politics drove them apart. Barbara interpreted the drift of cigarette smoke and the urgent conversations, that often concluded with Fripp on the living-room couch again. Barbara talked to Kingsley about a love of ideas that changed worlds for the better; it was where Fripp appealed to him, too, only at a level low as the dirt, and he began to look higher.

When Kingsley peered into that room, he saw Fripp's eyeballs like shining marble. 'Take a single reed,' said Fripp. 'It bends. Bind it together with ten times ten of reeds you have a strong weapon.'

Kingsley stood in the dark, in the shadows. 'That's Mussolini,' he said.

'Musso is the man to watch. Good night to you, son,' he said in his basso profundo, after which Kingsley slept uneasily, as if a bottle-cap had been knocked from his fizz.

When Kingsley read Fripp's books as a boy he savoured the malcontent feel with a sensation of sick excitement. It was a world of double-dealing and underhand betrayal that Fripp represented, with a background of unblemished honour apportioned to the few. Soon it would all turn over. The world would take sides, Fripp would turn sullen, resentful – await the call to go back into uniform but find himself bypassed by army chiefs offering no more than command of neglected district depots.

Men smoking small acrid pipes dealt with agents of European powers in opium dens. Weak-spined women in white satin cocktail dresses spoke in beguiling accents from mouths like puckered strawberries. Orientals were beyond the pale. Old diggers lived on honour like blowflies. The books were on railway bookstall stands, but nobody read them much. King Harry walked the field of battle being mistaken for a gentleman, stating that cowards were unfit to die at his side, were excused the fight and could take their passports home. Kingsley had a strange conversation with Fripp, who warned him to look in the letterbox in case he found a white feather. Later in New Guinea, Kingsley took a bullet in the lung through a stupid mistake in cane grass and his war ended before it had really started.

After a breakfast of wheatgrains soaked eight hours and eaten with wildflower honey and cream, Fripp left early, making little sound in the house, just a sensation of exhaled breath as the screen door was let shut.

Kingsley heard the crank handle turn and the firing of the Bedford. He had the notion of Fripp driving from place to place wearing his dusty cotton motoring-coat and crumpled chamois driving-gloves, his grey felt hat tilted back from his forehead. He was off making contact with his men before he went back to the road camp, the old soldiers from the battalion who were all wonderful fellows. 'But they aren't, all of them,' Veronica said, 'they are the rabble left after he spouts his ideas.' He was off making demands of those who questioned him, 'all scabs and renegades.' – 'But they aren't,' said Veronica, 'they are the ones with thoughtfulness and correct information and hearts to be moved.' He was gone making trouble on behalf of, raising funds for, distributing blankets to, finding food and furniture for, returned men's families on the skids. 'Depending on if their papas side with baloney,' said Veronica.

*

One day Kingsley stood under the Harbour Bridge, that great arc of studded steel, a boy with his head tipped back, eyes narrowed, hands in pockets and knees throbbing from growing pains. He listened to the roar of trains passing overhead. Their vibration trembled his spine. The trains moved in a cage of fury suspended by lines of force. Thunder had nothing on them. Lightning came through the rails. Everything had the feeling of a KO punch.

Wake UP was published by Angus and Robertson in 1936. The book ended in battle scenes of hopeless heroism, depicting the true khakis, a few brave men of Great War vintage and their sons, nephews, and Legacy wards hurling themselves across the rail tracks of the Harbour Bridge against the enemy pinko hordes.

A bomb called the Bangalore Torpedo was used to clear barbed-wire entanglements on the bridge's railway lines. A nitropilpowered battering ram, it was carried forward in a team and hurled by boys ready to die for what they believed in. Even failure, even suicidal attacks, would immortalise their cause and multiply their followers.

The finale was a pitched battle at Bulli Pass, which the true khakis lost.

It was a wild stab at fiction. Fripp wrote it in six weeks to get Australians off their arses. Then he went back bulldozing, leaving Kingsley in boarding school until the Jap war.

Kingsley Colts watches the evening news with its tally of suicide bombings and intractable oppositions hammered home with virtuous certainty across broad swathes of the world map. He sees himself disappearing as a young man in a blaze of light – a blaze of heroic light under Fripp's inspiration and only a fictional hair's breadth from this sort of thing.

'I came out from under it,' Kingsley reminds himself, as he heads off to bed; 'I lived, it's something, I made a dent.'

The next morning he goes out into the street, dumps the photographs in the garbage compactor ... That night, and for many nights afterwards, he re-experiences a wonderful elation on waking. But it no longer leaves him, on properly waking, with a feeling of distaste.

Because now, and for what time he has left, Kingsley dreams not of road graders, but of garbage trucks with sulphur-yellow superstructure driving across the sky, shreds of mulched papers drifting away below them like cockatoo feathers floating in the blue. 'Ahhh, that's how it's done,' he tells himself. 'How it's really done.'

Bulletin

Endgame

Louise Swinn

The class was told that I'd found my mother burning and I had never corrected them. Nobody said it to my face anyway. We filed out to morning assembly and I stood leaning against the brick wall up the back listening to the principal call out winners of last week's basketball. I watched the cloud through the window as it darkened and exploded into massive drops of loud rain. Our teacher flicked the hall lights on. I expected her to tell me to stop leaning against the back wall but she didn't.

The night had been spent ironing shirts and making sandwiches for the freezer. We put videos on. *Diff'rent Strokes*, *Fame*, *Back to the Future*, *Good Morning Vietnam*. My instant coffees had got to six spoonfuls but Deborah was up to eight already which probably isn't good for a thirteen-year-old. I had almost burnt one of my white school-shirts without enough water in the iron, dragging the sticky metal across the thin fabric. Deborah picked up Danny and took him to bed. On her way back, she checked that the phone was on the hook. She looked out the window to the driveway and I watched her and pretended that I wasn't.

Claire had woken up as usual, not exactly crying, and I had made her some Milo in the microwave and told her how school gets better when you're in year nine. I switched off the iron and Deborah looked up from her book. When it's nearly one in the morning and you can't go to bed because you can't sleep from the instant coffee and because your dad's not home, there's no point trying so we stayed up till four and made popcorn.

My teacher looks across at me and I look straight ahead, listening to the announcement about this year's school play. It is *Godspell*. It should be *Endgame* if they want me to be in it. I know that's why she's looking at me, trying to see whether I want a part. I keep looking straight ahead. I wonder which sandwiches I put in my bag, can't remember if I did or not. The kid in front of me stands up and we all clap while he walks to the stage and receives a medal for public speaking. I can see Deborah turning round and looking at me. She turns back before I decide to smile. You wouldn't believe how long it takes for me to decide to smile.

My name is called out and in the back of my head I recall that this was going to happen but it's a dull recollection. I am supposed to walk to the front so I do and people are clapping. It's about the piece I wrote for the local paper. I get a medal. Forget to smile. Lucky Claire's not at our school yet or she'd be crying. No point looking at Deborah. I stand for a moment with the medal around my neck and look out at the faces of all the students. It hasn't changed me so much as it inhabits me. I'll tell Dad I got a medal and he'll be proud. I walk back to my spot at the back of the hall, and you wouldn't believe how much easier that walk is on the way back.

I had missed the first few weeks of *The Harp in the South* and I am only reading every second page because I can't decide if I want to commit to it yet so Deborah's read it for me and we talk about it at night. Deborah's convinced Ruth Park is a good name for a novelist but I don't really understand why your name matters. She is studying *Tirra Lirra by the River* and I've read that because it's shorter and because Deborah loved it so it gives us something to talk about. She won't read any of the Stephen Kings I leave in her room now because she did try one once – *The Stand* – and I think maybe I shouldn't have started her on that one and I want to take it back and get her to start with something else. Maybe *Carrie* or *It*. But she's not interested. Her favourite book at the moment is *Nausea*. Mine is either *Brave New World* or *My Name is Asher Lev*. For a while we both had the same favourite book: *Lord of the Flies*. Then I went through my Shakespeare stage and Deborah devoted herself to Australian authors. I think she's moving out of that phase now. She says *The Diary of Anne Frank* is her bible.

I've still got the medal round my neck while we go back to the classroom and one of the kids from the year above me puts his hand on my shoulder for a moment and says, well done on your award and on your article. I know he's the editor of the school yearbook so I don't want to get into a conversation with him because I think he will ask me to write something for it. I nod and walk faster.

The classroom is freezing so our teacher puts the heater on and I watch it overhead as the orange lines start to glow. The boy who sits next to me, Michael, says congratulations on the medal and I am glad he's reminded me it's still there. I take it off and put it in my bag. We're studying the Vietnam War in History.

There's an awkward moment when we turn to the page in our textbook with the photo of the naked girl running away from the war and there is fire in that photo and no one laughs even though she's naked and no one looks at me but I can sense them. This is what Deborah has to look forward to next year. I think about telling them what happened but I am afraid that they will have more questions than I know the answers to. Looking at the photo doesn't make me think of Mum because I didn't see her until after it was over and that was different. I think Dad saw her as she was burning before he could reach her but I am not sure. We're going to have to move house again because the rental place we're staying in isn't big enough for us all really – it was just temporary anyway, we all knew that – and my bedroom is too far away from everyone else's.

I daydream that Dad comes to school and picks us up and says we don't have to go to school anymore and that he's not going to work anymore and the first thing we're going to do is find a house that is just right for our family and settle down into it. We won't have to make so many sandwiches all at once because we can make them when we want them, or we can have noodles for lunch. I know that Dad won't really do that because we need a lot of money just to live. If you have four kids and one income then you can't afford to lose your job and that's why Dad needs to work so late. I don't think we'll have a timber house next time.

It will have fire extinguishers in every room. It will be brick, and one-level. If one of us goes, we all go.

I can't wait for this class to end. Michael offers me some chewing gum and I take it and nod. Unwrapping it proves noisy and our teacher looks up and sees it's me and then goes on and I feel powerful but it doesn't last. They are letting me off the hook and I wonder how long that will go on for.

After History we have English in the same classroom. I push myself away from the desk waiting for the English teacher to come. Michael tells me about the paintball that he played on the weekend and asks if I would like to do it with them sometime. I am not sure but I say yes. Our English teacher comes into the room. She's the only teacher who has asked us to call her by her first name, which is Tanya. I am worried that we respect her less because we use her first name. Everybody likes her class.

I write a few notes about *The Harp in the South* in my notebook and then I think about what I will do after school tonight. I am starting a chess tournament and we have to decide whether Danny's old enough to be in it. Deborah thinks he is but I am not sure. We have to rake the yard before it gets dark because we all forgot to do it yesterday. I need to find my family tree from last year so that Deborah can copy mine because we don't want to have to ask Dad. I try to remember how to make tandoori chicken the way Mum made it. I write something in my notebook: mix tandoori paste with yoghurt. Then I am thinking, what happens if we have no plain yoghurt? I think we could substitute sour cream if we have some. Otherwise, what? I draw a question mark. The class finishes. Tanya asks me to stay back and I am already standing up when she says it so I stay standing at my desk, looking at my neat pile of books. I push my chair in and wait till everyone's gone. The heater is still on.

Tanya sits down on a desk in front of me and says she wants to talk to me about the school play because I was the star of the show last year. I am embarrassed but I try to look at her anyway. There is no way I can act right now. She says that she hopes I am interested in doing this one and she is going to recommend me for the lead role. I comment that I would prefer if it was *Endgame*, then it would feel more appropriate. She says why is that, and I am not sure if I can answer her so I just shake my head. She says can you at least tell me that you will give some serious consideration to the part? I am looking right at her face which is very difficult and I keep on doing it and soon I realise I am crying. I keep looking at her and don't do anything about the tears.

Tanya says I know that you have had a very difficult time lately but things will get better over time. You have to give yourself time, she says. I know what's happening because I can picture my face from her perspective but I stand there anyway, with my mouth shut while my tears are falling down my face and each swallow is painful but I still stand there and I keep looking at her. She says, you are a very talented actor – can you tell me that you will consider taking a part in the play? And I fight with myself to control the tears and look at her through them and she watches me while I do that, and it's difficult because she can't touch me but if I wasn't a student she probably would, and it's difficult because I am at an awkward age and it's not a good time to lose your mother. But I know that I have to try to do the right thing so I start to nod and while I nod I smile, even though I am crying. Finally, I say again that I wish it was *Endgame* instead of *Godspell* and she says, stop saying that. Then she says she's got some instant coffee in the staffroom and I look like I could use a cup and she won't take no for an answer, and I think that was the right thing to say because otherwise I would have said no. So we walk out of the classroom and while we're walking to the staffroom we talk about being in the school play and by the time she has poured the hot water I realise I have already decided that I am going to try out for it, and I can't wait to get home to tell Deborah.

Humble Pie

Kate Grenville

In the damp room in Slack's Rents off Bermondsey High Street, Sal Thornhill had owned no such thing as a pie dish, let alone one with a scalloped edge and the mark of a good Staffordshire potter on the bottom. Brim's baker had done a good pie, but a person needed tuppence, and the Thornhill household had not often run to tuppences.

Now, on the other side of the world from Bermondsey, a pie could come to seem more than just a meal. Mrs Ogilvie's grandmother had been Lady Horsham of Locksley Hall, and Mrs Ogilvie herself was the nearest thing the Colony of New South Wales had to royalty. When she gave Sal a special kind of chicken pie in a special kind of dish, made to her grandmother's recipe, the gesture was as important to Thornhill's wife as his pardon was to him. He still carried it in his pocket wrapped in a bit of oilcloth. He could not read it, but he knew what it meant: that he was as good as the next man.

The convict girl Meg brought the pie to the table, set it in front of Sal and handed her the brand-new silver pie-slice. Sal managed the thing awkwardly, trying to be ladylike and not touch the food with her fingers. She scolded the children when they left their crusts.

'This is Mrs Ogilvie's mother's recipe,' she cried. 'From Locksley Hall!'

Thornhill ate through his piece and did not share his thought with Sal: that it was on the dry side. He would as soon have had a good warm stew, even if it did not come from Locksley Hall. He loved his wife, but was troubled by what had been done to her by the pardon in his pocket, their fine stone house, their mahogany table with the double-damask cloth. Miracles had taken place in this new land, but they were miracles solely to do with the power of money. He knew, as Sal did not, that Ogilvie himself, a duffer who had got into strife with a sandalwood venture gone wrong, owed Thornhill nigh on £500. A pie in a fancy dish was the least he could do to butter up the man who could ruin him.

It had been years since anyone had reminded Thornhill that he had once worn the stripes. Old Colonialist – that was what they called him. Everyone knew what it meant, but as long as they called him Mr Thornhill and did his bidding he did not care what went on in their heads. But unlike Sal, he had no illusions.

Next day, the pie finished and the dish washed, she came to him all in a fluster.

'Look at this here,' she said, 'a crack.'

He glanced: a line like a hair, running down from one of the scallops.

'What I got to know, Will, is this: was it there when she give us it?'

He wanted to laugh, but saw how it mattered to her.

'If I give it back to her cracked and it weren't cracked before, she will think real bad of us,' Sal said. 'Emancipists, you know.'

'I seen them at Howes',' he said. 'Just the very same make, two pounds. Get her a new one.'

'Yes, but Will,' Sal cried, her voice thin and high with the puzzle of it, 'but see, if it were cracked before, and she gets back one not cracked, well' – she laughed, a sudden high-strained laugh – 'she'll think I'm cracked!'

Her worn face was screwed up with the worry of it.

'See? Either way, I've got myself in a pickle.'

At the start, the Thornhills had lived in a slab hut that leaked, with a lean-to on the side where they served rum to the travellers up and down the river. Now they had three boats doing the cedar trade, it was as good as a licence to print money. The Sign of the

Rose had become a neat place with sawn boards and glass in the windows, and up the hill – out of earshot and out of range of the smell of rum – was the grand stone house where Mr and Mrs Thornhill took their ease.

Up there, from time to time, they could be persuaded to cater to an altogether better class of customer. It seemed that the great crags and plunging cliffs of the place they had come to were thought of by a certain type of gentry and their lady-folk as picturesque and interesting beyond anything. Thornhill had fitted out a suite of rooms for them, good enough even for the Governor himself, who had stayed once with his lady wife and pronounced the place splendid and the views of the cliffs very grand indeed.

To Thornhill's eye the place was simply barren and difficult. He knew, from having tamed it to bear grain and fruit, and run cattle and hogs, that it was a place that put every obstacle in the way of a man out to make good, but he did not share this knowledge with them. When some woman in an unnecessary fur muff exclaimed that it was the most romantic landscape she had ever seen, he glanced out at it – at the parched-looking leaves of the forest everywhere around, the lowering cliffs that cut off the sky – as if it was something he had produced himself, just for her satisfaction, and found his mouth curving into the unfamiliar shape of a smile.

The cliffs alone were worth another pound a day to gentry seeking a thrill on their honeymoon.

He was not comfortable in the company of these gentrified customers. Behind their smiles and their round-mouthed exclamations of delight waited always the stab of humiliation for the Emancipist who had brought it all into being. But Sal basked in the company and the flattery, wagged her head along with the songs Palmer pounded out on the new piano in the parlour.

'It is just like Home, Will,' she said once, her eyes shining, during a night of songs, and he agreed. He did not say what he thought, which was that Home had never been near as good as this.

The business of Major and Mrs Nicholson was a rude shock for Sal.

Both newly arrived in the colony, and newly wed at St James', they had arranged to spend their honeymoon at Thornhills'. Several of their friends had already enjoyed the frisson of being up close to the wilds while still lapped-about in linen sheets and chintz armchairs. After the peaceful garrison at Green Hills, where Major Nicholson was quartered, they were eager to experience the picturesque wilds of the lower Hawkesbury.

Sal had fussed around, and made Meg fuss, too. Had the upstairs apartment made ready for the party, flowers in the vases, bed-linen starched and blued to glassy perfection. He had heard her scolding Meg for not ironing the pillowcases to her liking – heard her voice growing shrill, as she held one up and pointed to a spot where the iron had ironed in the creases instead of ironing them out.

'This is the way we did it at Home,' he heard her telling Meg. When she remembered, she put on a new way of talking now, with her lips tightened up. She had the idea it sounded ladylike. Thornhill thought she sounded like someone talking through their bumhole.

'Yes, Mrs Thornhill,' he heard Meg say.

There was no joke in it for her.

You would never have thought that sheets of any kind were a new thing for Sal Thornhill, much less sheets of the finest Irish linen. Even if Sal had forgotten, he could still remember the heaps of musty rags where they had slept in Slack's Rents, the fleas that rose from them in clouds when you shifted them, the bugs that nipped you in the night. He frowned, listening outside the laundry door as she nagged on about the starch.

Meg was put to it then to get every puff of dust out of every corner, with Sal coming along after and poking under the chest of drawers, running her finger along the top of the doorframe, getting her to do it again.

'It seems a little dusty there, Meg,' she said. There was a pitch in her voice – high and reedy – that went with the bumhole mouth.

'Best do it again, and proper this time.'

So Meg trudged upstairs again with the mop and the bucket, and Sal sat in the armchair there, watching to make sure she went all the way under the chest of drawers, and into the dark corner past the bed again, and ran the rag around the skirtings, twice.

'To make sure certain, Meg, if you please.'

Meg said nothing, only 'Yes, Mrs Thornhill,' and bent to the wet rag again.

Major Nicholson was a weather-beaten old soldier with 500 acres on Hunter's River and the best herd of breeding cattle in the colony. He, or that fertile spread of his, had managed to snare for himself a Miss Fortescue, a silly, spoilt girl fresh from Surrey and a cousin of Mrs Ogilvie, who had learnt nothing of life except how to speak a little French, sit down without creasing her gown, and to put her feet down as prettily on Thornhill's best rug as if picking her way between cow pats.

The Nicholsons stayed two days and in all that time, they did not address a single word to Sal or to Thornhill: not even as you would treat a servant, much less your host and hostess. In particular Mrs Nicholson kept her distance from Thornhill. It was as if she thought he might smell. Coming down the stairs on one occasion, and seeing him about to come up, she had turned and gone back to their room until he was gone. If Thornhill should enter a room where the two were sitting – his own sitting-room, for example – the Major immediately stood up and placed himself between his wife and Thornhill, as if instructed to protect her.

Thornhill and Meg were by chance together in the sitting-room on the second morning of the Nicholsons' visit, Meg crouching by the fire, blacking the grate in the way Sal had discovered she could not live without. She was not a bad girl, Thornhill had found, and knew Slack's Rents, had an aunt there.

Mrs Nicholson was just beyond the parlour window, out on the verandah in the armchair Thornhill himself liked to sit in and watch the river. He wished to go out there, but did not want to have to see her draw her skirts away from him and turn away as he came out the door, and was waiting by the cold fireplace, out of sight behind the curtain, until she chose to leave.

It could feel like imprisonment all over again, but he would not allow it to. Mrs Nicholson was paying through the nose for the privilege of drawing her skirts away.

Now through the window, he and Meg could hear Sal come up from the garden.

'Good afternoon, Mrs Nicholson,' they heard her say in her

best mincing ladylike manner. 'You have brung the fine weather with you, looks like.'

They could hear her smiling.

Meg met Thornhill's eye for a moment and they shared the unspoken thought: *sucking up*. They listened for a reply, but the girl did not speak. They heard the creak of the chair as she got up, heard her little tripping steps crunch quickly across the gravel. There was the squeak of the gate as she opened it and went out towards the road. In the silence that followed, Thornhill and Meg glanced at each other again. Then Sal burst in: flushed, congested with fury.

'That rotten little hussy,' she hissed. 'Cut me dead on my own porch.'

Then she noticed Meg.

'Meg, leave them damn things,' she said. 'Get away out of it back to the kitchen.'

Meg left the blacking things where they were and went out.

'Steady on Sal,' Thornhill said, 'Meg done nothing to deserve that tone.'

But Sal was too angry to listen.

'Turned her face away like I was dirt,' she said, but soft, so as not to be heard outside the room.

He could see her thinking about it, smoothing the damask on the mahogany table that was not, after all, a passport to respectability. She began to cry, quietly, desperately.

'Sal,' he started, 'she is just a silly girl.'

But she rushed out of the room and he heard her go up the stairs to their bedroom.

After a moment Meg came back in quietly, meekly, and picked up the blacking rags.

'I best get this finished,' she said, almost apologising, not looking at him.

'She didn't ought to use that tone with you, Meg,' Thornhill said. 'High-handed and that.'

'Thank you, Mr Thornhill,' Meg said, and hesitated with the rag in her hand. 'But she were just passing it along to me, what that other woman done to her. I seen that.'

They were both surprised when Sal came in again, Mrs Ogilvie's fancy pie dish in her hand.

'Meg,' she said, in her own voice, not the pursed-up one. 'I spoke to you real sharp before. There weren't no call for it.'

She sat down in the other armchair.

'That Mrs Ogilvie and her blooming cracked dish,' she said. 'Thought she beat the band showing us how they did it in Locksley Hall.'

She laughed so that all the lines on her face relaxed, and Thornhill realised how long it was since he had seen her not trying to be dignified.

'Make us one of your plum duffs, Meg. Full up to the top, mind, hide the damned crack.'

She held out the pie dish.

'Plenty of lard now, pet, make it nice the way you know how. Our precious Lady Ogilvie can see how we do things in Slack's Rents.'

Bulletin

Mac Attack

Sally Breen

Back in the very early nineties McDonalds is still number one. Before Nandos and Subway and juice bars, and Sushi Trains, and fancy delis and ubiquitous alfresco dining. Before cardboard salads and *Super Size Me* and pistachio gelati, Maccas is still the big thing. The big 'M,' the golden arch glowing on every built-up horizon; the only thing open in Queensland apart from Seven Elevens and Night Owls and service stations on long quiet roads in the suburban night. One of the only places where a young kid can hang out, pick up or pick a fight.

I'm thirteen when I start work at McDonalds Aspley. You have to be fourteen to work legally in Queensland but with my parents' signature on a yellow form everything can be arranged. McDonalds Aspley is huge, part of the old-school manifestation of Ronald McDonald architecture; not express size or arranged boutique, it's mega-eighties and mega-American. The drive-through does not wind around the carpark inconspicuously; it's definitely hard on the clutch. You inch up to the Taj Mahal of cheese on a massive concrete ramp. Like something out of *Star Wars,* the cars bank up, headlights rearing, awaiting assignment or expedition to space or another land. People cue endlessly, on the ramp or twelve deep on the registers in the dining room – an unquestionable popularity.

McDonalds is the gastronomical monopolist and a certain amount of cred comes from working there. Every working-class kid in my generation is lining up for the big gigs – Hypermarkets, Westfield Shopping Centres, Pizza Huts, KFC or Sizzlers (though Sizzlers, it is widely known, is only for spastics). If you work at Maccas you're part of a scene; a code developed out of both its public and covert reputations. Maccas, every kid knows, is no walk in the park. In the mini-nations of suburban megaplexes Maccas is the warmonger. I know I'm up against the unquestionable standing and rhetoric of the great suburban coloniser, the international giant of late capitalism and I'm determined not to get beat. I'd do anything to salvage my spirit and subsist. I get a uniform, a badge, a half-successful brainwash and the ability to develop my own cloak-and-dagger survival strategies. Surviving with stripes. Failure is not an option.

Lots of cool kids work at Maccas in the eighties and early nineties. And there are many more who aren't cool because Maccas requires much young flesh to fill its coffers. There are hundreds of us. Kids working the vats and the grills and the double-decker drive-throughs like we're sending up coal from mines. Maccas likes us young; it takes nearly three hours to make ten bucks. The going rate for your average thirteen-year-old in the late eighties is $3.75 an hour.

The volume of what we move, cook and pack is incredible. Every few days the massive semi-trailers come, subtly branded, opening their back doors and unloading a torrent of perishables and merchandising. The sugar buns arrive in great yellow plastic-tray towers and stack up everywhere in the rush. There are thousands of boxes of pre-cut meat patties and French fries in plastic bags and countless varieties of lids, cups, wrappers and accompanying implements. Buckets of pickles and packed-down pre-shredded lettuce, and great cylinders of sauces await, ready to be loaded into guns and shot over toasted buns at high speed. The stock is all downstairs in colossal bays and freezers. No matter how well prepared we think we are, kids constantly run down the stairs to collect more, coming back loaded with so many boxes and trays they no longer have bodies, just fingers and legs. There are always hundreds of buzzers going off. The last thing you want to be is a gumby. The last thing you want to hear is someone yell out, 'bus load!'

*

The only people on staff older than sixteen are the managers and sometimes the day ladies who fill in when us slaves go to school. The day ladies are cool – plucky middle-aged women who find themselves, mid-term, wiping down plastic tables for some reason or another. They never seem to be able to move fast enough. It's as if the tiny spaces, work stations and production units of the Maccas assembly line have been built to factor in the agility and fearlessness of youth.

Maccas managers are another species. They wear blue uniforms just like cops. Steely and infallible. They aren't packing guns but something a whole lot worse – McDonalds boot-camp procedures; all laws, expectations and punishments non-negotiable. We all know that McDonalds managers have been to McDonalds-manager schools: they are no longer human.

The worst and the most feared of managers at McDonalds Aspley is Wendy: tall and thin as a steel pole with a manner and constitution just as hard. Her uniform, hair and shoes are always perfect. Wendy is never late and she never makes a mistake. Wendy is a machine. The skin on her face is smooth and taut with the thin drawn on eyebrows and impenetrability of an old-school movie star. Indeed, there is something very Joan Crawford about her; something nasty and impeccable. Wendy doesn't like anybody but if you're good at your job she gives you shifts. Playing ball with her is always tenuous. You have to be nice; you have to perform even though all you ever want to do is tell her to fuck off.

Wendy is store manager – and often on shift. When I arrive (usually flustered and late) rushing through those great glass doors, my heart sinks when I see her. The vibe is edgy; inevitably she's gonna strip shreds off somebody; it might as well be me. Wendy expects 180%. The type of manager who asks you to mop the entire three-storey dining room twenty minutes before the end of a shift; who makes you wait in the dingy crew-room downstairs for over an hour before the call is sent to start; who rags you out in front of customers for some minor trespass or other. Wendy reduces less-capable crew members to tears and bears down on them with her unfailing capability until gradually they are reduced to mush. It's painful to watch. Kids shake and choke and stumble on their words. Whatever fuck-up they've made gets worse as their cheeks burn and their tears slide unceremoniously into brown paper bags or hot vats. A strange kind of silence descends over the rest of us. We work harder to cover for them like we're giving penance to the fallen or as a mark of respect but in the end there's nothing we can do. We know what's coming. This is their last shift. If Wendy's really pissed she'll fire them on the spot.

There is nothing harder or more humiliating when you are thirteen than walking out of a McDonalds heart in your stomach, bag in your hand, trying not to look back. Some kids are confident enough to rage against her, yelling out something funny as they leave. Most go quietly. Wendy will ring their parents three days later to ask for their uniform back. Wendy only smiles at customers and even then the movement on her face seems mechanical like the button to her mouth is stuck and has to be held down hard to make it work. You can't fault her service but something about it leaves me cold. She's drawn too tight, she's too officious. No wonder the more adventurous of us want to be rock-stars. By the time we're seventeen we know working for the man sucks.

Wendy only tries to fire me once. She calls me into the party room downstairs – the room she does the rosters in, the room where (on her good days) she lets me sit with her. There's a hint of something between us but really I'm just trying to get good shifts for my mates. By this time I'm a bit of a Maccas favourite, a success story. I have mastered the transitions of Maccas stations from the pre-pubescent suffering of dressing, to chicken and fish, to fries, to front counter, to children's party hostess and drive-through Queen Bee.

It's amazing how important you can feel wearing a Maccas headset. When your voice is the one the boys can hear on grill when the cars come in relentless. Speakers pump the sound into the kitchen so the crew can be prepared for the unexpected call of twenty-five Big Macs which has the power to throw the whole delicate system of sending those burgers down the shoot way out of whack. The boys keep half an ear out while doing five million other things at once because that's just the way it is at Maccas – no more staff to take the load, just more multi-tasking. I learn pretty fast how to have three conversations at once – to the speaker, to the car next to me, to the chicks on the floor. How to punch in orders while taking the money for another one, run two registers – left hand punching, right hand taking. Brain and body split right down the middle but not even thinking about it. That's the thing about being hot crew. You learn how to act like you're not even doing it. Getting flustered is not cool. Only when you get home do the synapses start unravelling. When you've had five showers and just can't get that smell of white fat off your skin and the phone rings and you say, 'Welcome-to-McDonalds-Drive-Through-Can-I-Take-Your-Order-Please?' That's when you know this imitation machine shit is just no good for you.

Sometimes when I'm up in the solitary confinement of the first drive-through window, I miss the rush and heat of the floor, my common days – getting down and dirty with the rest of the crew. I stare out the plate-glass windows through the pixilated forms of Grimace and Hamburgler to the blue sky rising over the Hypermarket thinking that being here's like reaching any kind of pinnacle: you look around and there's just no one there with you.

I liked it out back with the guys – cutting my teeth on the vats, pining for a chance to be out on front counter with the other girls who weren't all greased, thinking it'd be better, but Wendy keeps me on chicken and fish 'cause I'm a legend at it. I can make thirty Filet'o'Fish, sixteen apple pies, answer calls for packs of nuggets, and still have time to help pack for the fry guy and cut tomatoes in the mega-slicer for the geek who's losing it on dressing. Really, I'm not like those slick counter-chicks with their perfect hair and big asses in their tight Maccas pants out the front who act superior and yell at us when there's not enough hot stock. I'm one of the guys. By the time the managers do eventually let me loose on the floor I've got enough gumption to remember where I've come from. I can cut it both sides.

But now it's all over. Wendy is giving me the sack. Leading me into the party room, which looks sinister unlit: warped plastic Ronald heads. What is it, I wonder, that I'm supposed to have done? I've done enough bad shit before and gotten away with it. I've filled those brown paper bags with free burgers for the cute friends of the cool crew. I've put 2000 sashays of salt in a bag when some asshole screamed into the speaker for extra. I've told my Dad to piss off when he pulled up to the speaker in drive-through – everyone thought that was a cack – especially when he leaned in and asked rather sheepishly: 'Is that you Sal?' I've passed out one early morning under the front counter and no one found me until the store opened; stole a kilo bag of caramel sundae sauce when fetching stock, changed the timers on the food from, 'should throw out at big-hand six' to 'OK to sit here and harden until big-hand hits ten'.

Like everyone else, I've also eaten and drunk anything I could; nuggets under the bain-marie, orange juice in the walk-in fridge, apple pies in drive-through and handfuls of French fries on the way to the wash-up bay.

But it's not for any of this that Wendy calls me into the party room. Wendy wants me out for giving a staff member a Summer-size chocolate shake when he only paid for a standard. That's approximately fifty mls extra of sugared milk and he looked like he needed a decent feed but McDonalds is not in the business of forgiving empathetic lapses in judgement.

I look at her and wonder. How can she do this? How can she fire me for fifty mls of shake after four years? Four years – nearly my whole high-school life. I wonder why she's brought me down here into our room, why she didn't just fire me on the day. It's been three days since the alleged crime and she's been stewing on it. Like the Terminator, like her programming's all fucked up, like she wants to be human but the procedure, always the procedure.

We're in here and the lights are dim as if she doesn't want anyone to see. I realise that I'm just not gonna let her do it. I need this job. How else am I supposed to get into town on all those nights I tell my Dad I'm closing and the boys pick me up from round the back, Maccas uniform and clothes suitable for a dark nightclub in the Valley in my bag. Maccas is where I meet the guys in the bands for godsake, the ones who have the cars, and the cool hair, who pick me up and drop me off, who watch me take my legs out of trackpants and into black stockings in the back seats of their cars. Maccas is my ticket – for sometimes what amounts to less than fifty bucks a week – out of Albany Creek. There's just no way Wendy is ever going to understand this.

I try a different tack. I incite her Maccas patriotism, I tell her this place is just like another family, that maybe someday I might be able to wear blue, just like her, that I'm very sorry, it was a mistake, and I'll never do it again, that I'll work harder and never even spill a bit of shake let alone black market it, that she can't do this because I've worked hard for her, that I've given my all to this place. I'm getting heated. She really can't do this. I look around the room for inspiration. My last line: 'And anyway, I'm the best damn party hostess you ever had.'

Then Wendy's crying. I can't believe it.

And it's not big crying with hints of sound and movement – it's as though her eyes are leaking. And they're softer, but her face is just the same. I know I've won. Won my freedom; my key to the city from the big suburban coloniser, from Wendy. I don't even really hear what she says next, some quietly spoken spiel about chances and departures from courses of action and exceptions because *I've* had a victory, *I've* kicked a goal. I look up at her and catch just the last sentence. 'We will never mention this again.'

'Of course. Of course,' I say. 'Never.'

And I know Wendy means the crying more than anything else. When we leave the room I almost salute her.

Griffith Review

Floating above the Village

Lee Kofman

My mother eats herring for breakfast. She uses her fingers to retrieve the bare bones out of her mouth and to put them back on her paper plate. She sucks in the moist flesh and stares blankly at me, as I clean my brushes.

'Mama, would you like anything else to eat?'

'Don't worry, I'll manage.'

Feeding her is never simple. She only eats kosher food and refuses to use any of my kitchenware because it is 'impure.' Since her arrival in Australia, a week ago, we shop for her food around Elsternwick and East St Kilda. We enter the dark shabby shops stuffed untidily with imported goods bearing Hebrew labels. The floors are sticky and the shop assistants wear bouffant wigs like my mother. She feels at home there, perhaps more than in our sunny flat, full of my paintings. We come back loaded with canned gefilte fish, egg salad and frozen *cholent*.

My mother watches me experiment, mixing cornflower blue with lemon chiffon, but as always, she doesn't ask me anything about my painting. She is bent over the food, her elbows solidly on the table. Her lips are oily with the fish.

'Are you OK?' I am as disgusted as I used to be in my childhood.

'Shhh…' says my mother, 'The kabbalah teaches that when we're eating, we feel God's presence.'

She finishes her meal, absentmindedly picks her teeth and whispers an aftermeal *brakha.*

'So what are you going to do today?' Daniel breaks the silence. It is Sunday, but he has to work. Here is the day I have been dreading since her visit began; the two of us alone. For the first time since I left Israel five years ago.

'Look! Look! Chagall!' inside the National Gallery my mother urges me past stony, industrial-looking floors and walls. What a setting for the luxury of past art – is it mere misunderstanding, or the deliberate contempt of pioneers used to asceticism? I always feel incurably foreign here, craving long marble stairways and chandeliers, soft silk and polished boots from my Russian childhood. My memories draw an invisible frontier between me and my new home.

We walk past the modern art section. The minimalist exhibits, bleak like anorexic party-girls, match the building's spirit and make me wonder whether my own paintings depicting lewd, masked beauties with gold and silver splashes of colour, have any future in this country. The critics write I am too European; as though it is a new measurement of failure; as though decadence is outdated in Australia, and equivalent to *decay*.

I feel more comfortable in the Modernists section.

'*Dochenka,* Chagall was Jewish!' my mother pants behind me. We stand before a large canvas depicting a village of black fences and cherry-red roofs. Its houses, trees and hedges – painted in rough, thick brushstrokes – are pushing, climbing on top of each other, invading. I step back from this density, and from my mother. From the distance, as I breathe more deeply, I see two lovers in the painting, dressed in dark clothes like mourners. They float in a spacious, yellowgreen sky, high above the village. The young man with curly hair gently cups the breast of his beloved. In their sad, dark eyes there is a reflection of their village. Perhaps they are eloping, but will they ever break free from this memory? I feel like crying. I want to be alone.

My mother grabs my arm: 'Chagall was born in Russia just like us. *Nyet,* actually it was Byelorussia. What a rotten place, I tell you, those Byelorussians, they hated Jews so much. There were always pogroms, always pogroms. After the revolution when

Chagall ran away to Paris, all he ever painted was his village. But how could he, after everything they'd done to us?'

She lets go of my arm only to put up a wavering finger: 'Look at these people, flying. He always painted dreams. What a big dreamer he was … to paint Russia like some fairytale. Huh! What a joke. He should have got on with his life, just like I did.'

Her voice has always been young and slender. I can picture her back in Israel, lecturing to her students: '… so I said to those Russians: "Either you let us out of this country, or I'll burn myself right in Red Square." They let us go. What could they do?'

I shut my eyes, pretending she is her voice.

My mother is truly excited. I've never observed her before in such public situations. In Israel we'd meet over nervous Sabbath dinners: *Dochenka, your dress is too short. Wash your hands. Be quiet now, papa is praying* … Even now in my home where she is my guest, it is the same on Friday nights: *Daniel, wear this yarmulke. Hurry, let's light the candles.* She will not calm down until the conditions are just right, the *Kiddush* wine gulped and the bread blessed, but even then she seems busy. I snap at her more often than I would like: 'You and your God … What would you do without him?' But she just ignores me. She sneaked a photo of the late Rabbi Lubavitch into my car 'for safe driving.' On long drives I stare crankily at the holy man's austere, bearded face, but feel oddly secure.

We have never just spent time together, so it has never occurred to me that we both might admire paintings. I try to draw out the moment and introduce her to one of my little passions.

'See this painting? It's Dorothea Tanning, one of the only women surrealists in Paris in the 1920s. These surrealists, they wrote a manifesto saying a woman's job was to inspire. Women weren't supposed to paint. She's been excluded from most art books, but here, look she's next to Magritte; he's probably turning in his grave.' I smile at my mother.

'Tanning …' she repeats slowly. 'Didn't she have a Jewish husband?'

*

I also have a Jewish husband, but, as my mother knows, we didn't have a traditional Jewish wedding. I didn't circle Daniel seven times and he didn't break a glass under the *huppa*, instead he took me to Kakadu for a honeymoon. Perhaps this is what my mother is here to do now, to remind us of our Jewish duties. Purposes make her happy. Chagall makes her happy, not Dorothea Tanning.

We decide to go see the Early Renaissance. Before the *Madonna and Child* my mother says, 'You should have babies. I told Daniel, all this painting-shmainting ... My silly girl.' She pats me with her oily-fishy fingers. I shake her off.

'Mama, stop it! Let's have fun. C'mon, I'll show you Melbourne.'

It is her first trip outside Israel, but all she wants to do is iron our clothes and vacuum the carpets. It is not housework she performs, but an elaborate dance, tiptoeing skilfully on her sore toes, as though if she stopped, she might cease to exist.

She says, 'I came to see *you*, not Melbourne, you silly girl. One day you'll have your own daughter ... All right, all right. Anyway, when you have your own, you'll understand.'

Melbourne grants us a beautiful day. The sun peeps green through the abundant foliage and the scant wind cools our sweating bodies. I navigate between the cars: 'Mama, look at the Yarra.'

Small boats glide across its glossy surface like swans.

'Very nice,' my mother nods. Her gaze is fixed on my profile. Intermittently she watches the road reading the signs out loud: *Left to City Road; slow down, children crossing; seventeen parking spots available.* Occasionally she advises, 'The truck behind is going too fast. Careful!'

I have no idea how others manage to go for a coffee or movies with their parents. My mother was always too busy for leisurely things, preferring productive activities, like studying kabbalah, marking her students' homework, arguing with my father or cooking large Sabbath dinners.

I keep driving, but rather than enjoying the view she grooms her new pet project, Daniel's family tree: 'His paternal grandfather was from Poland? And what did he do for a living?'

*

Since her arrival, I've started breaking things. The frame of my newly mounted painting. Daniel's glasses. I trod on my palette, flooding the carpet with sparkling gold. I can't work anymore. I just want her to go. Since her arrival I've counted not the days, but the hours. This is the secret I keep from Daniel. My secrets are mounting, not my paintings.

Last night I pushed Daniel away. 'Have I done something wrong?' he asked.

My tears flooded his chest.

'She's in the other room. She's alone ...'

'So what? What's the big drama? She seems pretty happy to me. Anyway, soon she'll be back with your father, babe.'

I hid my face in his chest. How could I explain? How could I explain my drifting father, daydreaming with the Russian radio as his lullaby? How could I explain my mother's constant erratic movement, as though she were escaping some memory? Or her bare legs, which she'd shown only to me? Their dark purple veins trap her like fishing net.

The night was metallic blue. Daniel's breathing had grown steady. I stood on the balcony, peering into the giant orange windows of the city's skyscrapers, bright like stars. I wished my paintings were bold like them, dazzling onlookers, filling them with emotion. How do you paint feelings if you're not Chagall?

I could paint the thick veins on my mother's legs and the reviewers could again praise the virtuosity of my brushstrokes, the intricacy of patterns. But it would be just another failure.

I couldn't sell you so cheaply, Mama. I want them to see my pain. That choking pain on seeing your ageing legs. But how?

Perhaps I'll paint you as you used to be, when we rented a wooden hut in a Siberian village and in the frosty mornings my father used to drown mice in the outside toilet. You wore that red dress there, the one with puffy princess-sleeves you'd got on the black market. You'd saved for five months and had then stood before my father, your hourglass body tight-wrapped. *A new haircut?* He'd asked. Then went back to his books.

I want to show my mother my iridescent, sparkling Melbourne – but instead we drive in circles.

'What else would you like to see?' I ask, casually turning the wrong direction into a one-way street. I know the answer. Something like: *All I want to see is you and Daniel. That's my greatest pleasure. Besides, of course, having grandchildren …*

'I have to see a kangaroo.'

I almost collide with a car heading towards us. Rabbi Lubavitch, with his white Santa Claus beard, promptly rescues us while giving my cleavage a nasty look.

'Your father told me not to come back until I'd seen a kangaroo!'

We leave the city behind. The houses recede, the horizon yawns its grand, pink mouth, and the energy of the city lets us go. Even Rabbi Lubavitch lets go of my cleavage. I open the window, breathing in the smell of warm grass. I long to transplant this smell and the endless Australian meadows onto my canvas. This will be my version of pioneering, a way to possess this tough land.

But perhaps, like my mother says, I'm just vain and self-absorbed.

My mother ignores the changing landscape, the low hills and small makeshift graveyards. Instead, she looks at me; I can smell her breath: 'At your age I already had two children. I wasn't so silly. I knew what was really important.'

'I'm not you. You wanted to make babies, I'm making paintings.'

'Do you think that I wanted to have children so early?' My mother diverts her hazel, perpetually intense gaze from me. 'Those were different times then. In Russia you had to bribe the Abortion Commission. We were students and didn't have the money. When we got married, they kicked us out of the university hostel.'

I stop the car. My hands are shaking: 'You never told me these things.'

She stares blankly ahead, her wig is askew.

'Why did they kick you out?'

'Because we were PhD candidates, because we were too good,' she says slowly. 'We had to focus on our studies, not babies. They gave us the privilege of sacrificing our youth for the mother country. It was either career or marriage; no grey areas. You'd never have understood.'

I look at my mother as though she is a stranger. For the first time I notice how smooth her skin is, how unusually smooth is her voice. She sits very still.

'The day they kicked us out, your papa sat on a bench at the bus station, not moving … it was winter, minus forty. I wandered around in a neighbouring village, knocking on doors, begging people to let us in, to rent us a room. I didn't even have time to think about an abortion.'

She sobs quietly; her fleshy cheeks shine crimson. She wipes her eyes with a determined gesture and adjusts her wig. I want to hold her, but I can't; that's not how things are between us. When I was younger, I craved to make her happy, but she always said happiness was God's business. And perhaps this memory is just another excuse.

'Russia was no good to its people,' says my mother. 'It ate them like that Australian spider that eats its children. What's its name?'

'I don't know.'

'You know, I'm really happy for you, *dochenka*. It's different today. Your papa and I didn't have our own place in our first years together. I'm so happy …' she sobs.

I'm weighed down with her sorrow, the sorrow that has always – since I was very young – driven me away to the strangest of places: kinky nightclubs, artistic communes, and now, Australia. She has infected me with incurable restlessness. But today, rather than running away I have an odd urgency to get to our destination.

'*Mamochka*, please don't cry. Another ten minutes and we'll see the kangaroos …'

I repeat these words like mantra, then turn on some music.

'Would you mind turning it down?' asks my mother.

'Mama, remember in Russia when we'd listen to opera records together? You told me the story of *Onegin*.'

'I can't believe you remember that.'

'I remember more: your red dress. I thought you were a princess.'

'Me? A princess? You mean your papa was a prince, always the prince – not from this world. He was so spoiled …'

'Mama! Listen …'

'Sorry, sorry. Go on.'

'*You* were like a princess. Remember? You weren't religious then. Your hair was long. You were beautiful, mama. We played piano together. Remember how I could never get it right? But you didn't care. You never cared about those things.'

My mother stares straight ahead into the snaky road, 'Who would think children could remember so well …' but, this time she doesn't cry.

At the Healesville Sanctuary my mother limps towards the fresh green spaces, her heavy buttocks moving quickly under her skirt.

'Hey, mama, I've got seeds for you to feed the animals.'

'Oy, oy,' says my mother.

'Here, have some.'

'Oy, oy,' my mother repeats, 'If only your father could see this … a real kangaroo … in Australia …' Her eyes are glued to the smooth-skinned kangaroos as they stroll around looking regal. She grabs both seed cones from me, gathers up her skirt and, panting heavily but determined, she pushes her way to the front of a group of school children. Her limp is severe, but the cones remain steady in her hands.

'Mama, will you give me one, please? I want to feed them too.'

There is no reply.

The sky is transparent, light blue. Two trembling naked figures float high above; their movements awkward and mismatched. The man is perhaps my young father with a head full of curly hair. He shyly covers his groin with one hand and puts the other on my mother's abundant milky breast. I can just hear her prayer: *Baruch Ata Adonai … Blessed are you, God. You who has saved us from our village …* She rises suddenly upwards, then sinks back, below my father, and again till eventually she disappears and only her voice remains.

Baruch Ata Adonai …

*

Back on earth – blackskirted, she is sprawled frivolously like an odalisque on the humid grass, fondling the muscular body of a grey kangaroo.

'What the hell are you doing?! It's dangerous!'

But she is busy calling to a fat, pale wallaby, spilling words like seeds: 'You lazy boy! Look how they've spoiled you here in Australia. You can't even be bothered coming to get your food … Come on, lazy. Come on, beautiful!' Her voice rises and rises, its music stripping her of her body, of our shared memories, of her age.

'Look how sweet he is.' The wallaby has eventually accepted her invitation and is swaying towards her. She stretches out an open palm laden with food for *lazy boy*.

I sit down close to her: 'Mama, you're spoiling him. In case you didn't know, he's not Jewish.'

My mother smiles at me and lifts her head, glaring intensely at the summer sky, as if she too can see the floating lovers.

Island

Repossession

Michael Meehan

Tom O'Reilly took two shotgun cartridge cases and rolled his note and secured it inside, forcing the lip of one case into the other till it was watertight. Then he pitched it to the darkness. A year or two later and well after his death and only by an extraordinary chance a dog out chasing kangaroos toppled into the abandoned well-shaft and stayed there barking, unable to climb the crumbling walls and save itself until they lowered the youngest of his sons into the well-shaft on a rope.

The red flash of the cartridge caught his eye, half buried in the dried mud and the sand.

A year later, the sons were called to rescue a child stuck up a hollow pine. The boy, down from the city, had gone up to steal a Major Mitchell's egg. He climbed too high and out along a branch, and was unable to get back. When they went up to fetch him, they found high up in the crevice a cigarette pack wrapped in plastic with a further note inside.

After that time they went on to discover other notes, Tom's nine children now starting to scour the wilderness for further messages, with now and then a cartridge case appearing, or a bottle or a matchbox or cigarette pack hidden within a hollow log or in a cockatoo's nest lodged high up in a blasted Murray pine and even, once, deep in a rabbit burrow. All knew by then that through those last months of his life, Tom O'Reilly, with tumour spreading through his brain and all around him the lands that were mingled with his sweat and labour now shrinking apace, roamed out across those tracts of recent dispossession to plant his mysteries and his presence, to seed his lost lands with fragments of some message, the whole of which was never to be found.

Tom discovered just months before the tumour took its hold that the leasehold on all the land that he and his forbears had cleared, settled and straightened for a hundred years was now to be resumed, the stock hunted out, the fences uprooted, the sheds demolished and the dams choked off, with Tom and his heirs left clinging to each other on a withered three-hundred-acre freehold fragment at the core. The word resumed did not mean in this instance a return to any state of being that ever was before, when the first inhabitants tracked across that wilderness. It did not mean a vacating of the land for other wandering pilgrims to return, or restoration to some pristine state where the land might learn to speak in its own voice. It was rather for the imprint of a bureaucratic story, of this way and not that way and nine to five and make sure the gate is closed. The new Decalogue was spelt out in signs and bins and chains and padlocks, the pathways and tracks closely charted and signposted with the strictest prohibitions, and camping here and not there and, of course, no open fires. The stringy box and buloke and stark stands of pine were now lost to regulation, the early nomad wanderings of Tom O'Reilly and his brothers and sisters below the vast white gums that lined the ancient lakebeds now boxed back to the padlocked gate, the official map, the jackboot grid of Management Vehicles Only.

Thus Tom O'Reilly with spreading tumour and with shrinking lands crossed the boundaries of that last and fragile island freehold and tracked out at night into the coarse tracts of scrub and seas of box and buloke and mallee and Murray pine, taking within him his lode of secret messages, now hiding his voice in hollow trees and wash-holes and soaks and under fallen logs and in rabbit burrows and in parrots' nests, seeding the landscape with his messages but always in secret and in hidden places, with just enough to be discovered for all to know there must be many others across that landscape. With his own life and holding now buckled to restriction Tom still raged against that dying and that shrinking, forging at last these new and lasting forms of possession, new ways of living with a landscape that would run far beyond *I own* towards *I know, I love, I understand,* bred from an intuition fed perhaps by the secret marks of those previous travellers who had moved across that landscape, their presence never quite eroded, their fragile but rich possession still marked for those with eyes skilled to see it in the middens, soaks and canoe trees, and in other hidden places.

What did the notes say? That if you walked two hundred metres directly to the east you would come across a mallee fowl's nest. That if you crossed the sand ridge three hundred metres to the left, you would find the last of a trapper's hut. That if you made for the tall pine that capped the huge drift to the east you would in less than one hundred metres find a hidden soak. No more than fragments. Not maps, but only parts of maps. Fragments not touching other fragments. As though Tom O'Reilly knew that it was in full order and design that his own destruction lay, that it was in incompleteness and broken tracks and hidden vignettes only that there was life and hope of continuing possession. The tumour in his brain telling him at last the deepest truths of our nomadic condition, against which no kind of fencing, no kind of signposting might give reassurance, he knew, though perhaps in deep unconsciousness, that this smallest shift from frame to frame, the living that one did within the short space that ran from abandoned well to mallee fowl nest, from hollow tree to trapper's hut, from hidden soak to canoe tree, was the best form of mapping that there could be. That the best way to tell the story was not to wrap up the story but to replace it with a lasting conversation. That the best way to possess was not in deed or map or charter but in the adding of one's voice to all the voices that had passed, to be part of the disorder and not the regulation, part of the fount and not the boundary, part of the mystery but not the explanation

How many further maps, how many further secrets? If you asked his widow, years afterwards, what Tom O'Reilly thought he was doing, the answer was quite clear and simple, that he liked to find old bottles in the bush and even once high in a hollow tree; that once or twice in all that time he had found things with old writing in them, and thought it would be good for those after him to find these things as well. The richness of his artistry perhaps being as well spelt-out in her few words as ever surly Tom would have attempted, he never telling anyone or trying to explain those silent night-time journeys, linking his messages with the flints of rock and the marks in the trees, the nests and new growths of mallee; innumerable, boundless and not subject to resumption. His family, as though knowing, even before that first note was discovered, decided at his death to build the box themselves and bury him on the last of the freehold. His casket was rough-hewn from that same strain of Murray pine in which he left his messages, the coarse adzed planks sawn and nailed and screwed together, the boards scarce meeting at the seams so that he might quickly meet the earth and be possessed in turn, his body running out to join his words. The nine children, each risking a splinter, carried him to his grave, set on a high ridge beyond the house and towards the sand drifts, to overlook the margins of the freehold fragment, the boundary fence, and beyond, out over the wild and ever renewed and now illimitable tracts of Tom O'Reilly's mysterious repossession.

Meanjin

Slowly Last Summer

Peter Goldsworthy

Universe, Milky Way, Solar System, Earth, Southern Hemisphere, Australia, South Australia, The South-East, Pinetown, Church Street, 32. I always scribbled my galactic address *backwards* on my things; it seemed to offer a more logical pathway home if something found itself lost, especially in another galaxy. I flipped my new 28-inch bike upside down and carved the same sequence into the rawhide underbelly of the saddle, although if that beautiful machine – a Christmas reward as Top Boy at the end of primary school – loved me as much as I loved it, it would surely come freewheeling home, riderless, whenever I whistled.

I suppose I was always happy, if mostly of a kind of even, steady happiness that largely escaped my notice then. Happiness was a default state; a given, like the town that I was born in, the family I was born into. Like the mind that I *grew* into, the brain I'd begun slowly to fill.

Summer was another given, a recurring given. Billy Currie was also a given; we had been best friends since he first moved to town, a lifetime – a child's boundless lifetime – before. It was arranged friendship, like most from childhood: a match made by geography and limited opportunity. We had shared the same desk throughout primary school. We went to the same church; Reverend Stevenson had helped sponsor the various Currie families when they made the move into town from the mission. We played in the same Caledonian band; me on pipes, Billy on kettle. We both had stick-thin bodies with big, difficult-to-balance heads, and even bigger mouths that were forever getting us into trouble.

We were both *expected* to get into trouble; me because I had a cop for a father, Billy because he was an Abo.

He inherited my 26-inch Malvern Star that Christmas, after a lengthy bargaining process. My Dad, who saw himself as some sort of local protector, or benefactor, of Aborigines, offered the old bike for free; Billy's Dad, a proud man who worked plenty of overtime at the sawmill, didn't want charity. Somehow a price was agreed on; money went one way and the bike went the other in a terse, wordless ceremony outside the front gate of the station. I overheard the liturgy later that night, a muffled whispering behind my parents' bedroom door. *Not as if they don't need the money. You'd think they'd be grateful. You've done so much for those people, Bob.*

In our boy-world, both bikes were common boy-property. Bare-chested and barefoot, but with thickly Brylcreemed hair, Billy and I rode everywhere that summer, rode to the ends of the known world, or at least to the ends of our endurance, whichever came first.

We spent long mornings excavating treasures at the dump south of town, and long afternoons losing ourselves in the cool, dense-packed pine forests to the east and west. On the hottest January days we cycled north to the flooded limestone quarries and sinkholes out beyond the vineyards. Our given corner of the universe, the south east of South Australia, Earth, Solar System, sat on a thousand-square-mile slab of porous limestone, a great artesian sponge so sodden with winter rain that even in summer the water was pressed upwards and outwards into swamps and springs and creeklets by the sheer, wet weight of itself.

We, however, were utterly weightless as we dived and swam in those vast limestone holes. Here was another kind of flying, in a different kind of sky. The sunlight fell unobstructed through the deep, clear water as if it were air, the rocky floors and walls were as lime-white and dazzling as a beach. Even twenty feet down the light still hurt our eyes, and the underwater world of yabbie-infested crevices and tiny freshwater fish was as vivid to the senses as a *National Geographic* pictorial. Legend had it that horses, cattle, tractors and even entire picnicking families had fallen through the thin limestone crust and vanished forever into this watery world (it had happened to friends of all my parents' friends) but we dived for horse bones and human skulls and other sunken treasure in vain. On the long haul back to town, waterlogged, bladders bursting, we stopped frequently to piss among the vines and eat the ripening grapes; later in life, I came to wonder if the fame of the great vintages of those years might owe something to our copious boy-piss foaming about the vine-roots.

Apart from the occasional ride-by mealtime, or comb-through of fresh Brylcreem after a weekly shower, we were seldom at home that summer. Once or twice we camped in the depths of the forest, if only to terrify ourselves, but there were no rabbits there, and rabbits were our subsistence crop, worth four bob a brace at Jeffrey's Butchery. Farmers everywhere welcomed us, directed us to the biggest warrens and best camp sites. Short, sweet nights these, at the end of long, exhausting days. After setting our traps we would light a fire, lay out our blanket-rolls and smoke pilfered tailor-mades or pungent rollies of newspaper and palm-crumbled stringy-bark. Probably the first freshly skinned rabbit would be roasting on a rough twig-spit between us, and with luck, there would be something to drink, perhaps a bottle of Autumn Brown sweet sherry that Billy had filched from his Uncle Doug, who lived on its pungent, brown mother's milk. More traps would be springing shut in the darkness about us, more rabbits crying to be released, if only from pain, but very soon we would have eaten too much meat and drunk too much sherry to move, or even to stay awake.

'Tell another science-fiction story,' Billy might mumble across this sleepy twilight zone.

'Tell me the one about the planet where the people grow wheels instead of legs. Four wheels...'

'The people have *two* wheels,' I remind him. 'Like bikes. They're a kind of centaur. It's a really flat planet. All the *other* animals have four wheels.'

'Same diff. Tell it again.'

I was always happy to tell it again, I was happy to tell all my stories again, although usually one of us would be asleep before I finished.

'What if we're not in the same class at high school?' He shook me awake on another night towards the end of summer, perhaps even the same night.

Giddy, and barely sensible, I couldn't move. What on Earth was the time – at least on *this* corner of Earth? Halfway to morning, and then some. The fire was dead, the moon and stars all shifted and strange.

'Hughie said they done this test on the first day. Last year. Next day they put everyone in a different class.'

'Go back to sleep, Billy.'

'*Can't* sleep. What we gonna do if we're in a different class?'

'We won't be in a different class.'

He rolled across onto my swag and jammed a headlock on me. 'You'll be in the *brainy* class for sure.'

'Let go, bugger you! *You're* brainy enough. You know more than me about *lots* of stuff.'

His grip was a vice. 'I'm *dumb*. Everyone knows I'm dumb. I'll be in the dumb class. What stuff?'

He had been in this half-tearful, half-violent state before; sweet sherry especially could get him started on everything that might go wrong with his life, or *had* gone wrong since leaving the mission and an idyllic childhood of swan-egging and fishing and messing about in boats.

'That tiger snake we killed at the Dump,' I remembered. '*You* knew how to skin it.'

Open sesame; he released the headlock. '*Course* I knew. We used to eat 'em back on the mission.'

I didn't fully believe him. That is, I believed that a Currie uncle or cousin had probably eaten a snake, somewhere, some time back – but not Billy. He hadn't wanted to eat our tiger snake.

'What'd they taste like?'

'Like fish. Mullet. A bit muddy.'

'I grabbed a king brown by the tail once,' I told him.

He didn't really believe that either, but we didn't have to believe each other, especially this late at night. The story was the thing, whether set in the the future or the even more astounding past, and now he needed to hear the rest.

Soon enough he was asleep, but I couldn't follow. My neck hurt a little – Billy's affectionate violence often left me sore. And although the giddiness of the sherry had faded, nausea remained. I slipped out of my blanket-roll, took a long purifying piss out into the darkness, then grabbed my torch and knife and wandered off to check the traps. Rabbits might be a plague, but they shouldn't be left to suffer according to my old man. Or left (*his* old man was a Scot, after all) to work their two-bob carcass free, or drag a ten-bob trap down a burrow from where it would have to be dug out. Less hunter than gatherer tonight, I twisted two rabbit necks, slit open their bellies by torchlight, and flung the guts between my legs far out into the darkness. A four-bob night already; I didn't bother re-setting the traps. I emptied the last of the Autumn Brown into my big, chipped enamel mug, and stoked up the fire. High school was suddenly no more than a few days away. *Would* we end up in the same class, or even – the root cause of Billy's panic, I see now – in the same friendship? Time would tell; far more interesting to me that night was the promise of high school itself, growing closer with each less-small hour. I liked school, I was good at it; I played up from time to time, played the smart-aleck, but unlike every other boy my age I couldn't make myself pretend to hate it.

Billy slept on; I stirred the embers and picked over the rabbit bones and sipped at my mug, alone in my default happiness, in my default corner of the big, default universe. That summer night is forty years past, now – but the sting of eucalyptus smoke in my eyes and the ruffle of the night breeze in my hair feels as fresh and new and vivid as ever. Pinewood, South Australia, might have been the width of a paddock or the width of a galaxy away; no matter. In the morning our two bikes would find their way home easily enough, bed-rolls and skinned carcasses and rattling traps strapped to their wheel racks, the two of us half asleep in our saddles, our long morning shadows pacing us, neck and neck, flat shadow-centaurs of boy-flesh and steel tubing and spinning wheels, made one.

From the Wreck

Robert Williams

My bike was a tart. It was gleaming purple with a little chrome wheel at the front and a big one at the rear and a big chopper seat with huge Marlon bars and three gears on its twin columns. It didn't have streamers but it might as well have. It was truly a poofter and I rode it with pride in a part of town where you could get your head kicked for it.

I'm aboard the chopper and have just flicked my second Stuyvesant Gold of the morning as I approach the cyclone and barbed-wire gates of the school. I'm cruising in with Margle. He has the standard bike, all shame and mismatched components. It was standard by contrivance, like everybody else's, crafted to be inconspicuous.

Our school is on the northern fringe of the city of Melbourne. A city that blows hot dust in from the north and blizzards in from the south. Dust that warms you then blinds you and Antarctic ice that cuts you in half and then freezes your arse off.

Sometimes all in the same day.

The school is stratified. There are 120 boys doing form four at our school – streamed into Gold, who do Latin 'cause they're smart, and Red and Blue who do Tech Drag because they are dumb. Margle is so smart that he's brilliantly contrived to hide it. That way he can avoid Latin and bludge in Tech Drag while most of the smart kids are getting bored shitless by ancient Rome and getting the cuts for being stupid or 'running their own race.'

We're in the long driveway now. Bernie Biedel will be here soon. Looking to give me some shit to see if I fight back. And I won't. Margle assures me he'll be too good for me. That he can really fight. That he's a bona fide skin 'ead with bona fide skin mates. But it's not Margle's fault that I won't fight. In my last fight I was well pitted against a kid I hate. But his bigger brothers kept punching me or holding me down every time I started to get on top. I was over that two-hour ordeal. It just made me a bit more careful.

Bernie had a witch's head and face right down to the missing teeth. Gums like a graveyard. Teeth like tombstones. I wouldn't fight him because there was nothing I could take away from him. He had nothing to lose. And I was afraid of that.

As I wheel my purple chopper past the first of the low grey buildings made of concrete blocks with flat angled roofs, concrete blocks that steady me, like Latin, I begin to get over that little panic.

The headmaster, Brother Lyon, takes Latin. I am a certified Latin genius. Nobody can stop me. The harder it gets, the better I get. In the earlier forms, there used to be two of us that ruled Latin, like consuls. The other kid usually shaded me then but these days I've taken over. I am the self-proclaimed Emperor of Latin. I can put the laurels on my own head and even Brother Lyon is in awe of me. I could just make up new Latin words and they would go back in time and put themselves in the dictionary. My head appears in marble form in history books – with real laurels.

No sign of Bernie yet.

I haven't done my Latin homework today. There is a standard practice in Latin class. Every boy who hasn't done it has to stand. If I am sitting they all get the cuts. If I stand Lyon spares the rod. Sometimes I don't think even Lyon has noticed this. Looks like it's a lucky day for Latin backsliders.

The grounds fall away to my left as I wheel past the concrete blocks of the rear building towards the bike racks. Fall away under acres of rough weeds, dust and volcanic rocks that are half way through a grand entrance from the underworld.

Right next to the tuckshop there's a cesspit. The sewage from all the neighbouring buildings (our school, the new co-ed senior school and the almost empty babies' home) drains out of an open pipe into a huge trough with a hinge at its base. It flips from side to side as it fills with effluent. Like a Japanese water-feature for shit. It creaks like tortured metal and then goes clang as Margle and I pass it.

Then I see Bernie. His head's at a tilt and he's sneering at me. But today he doesn't say anything much to me except 'Wow, that's a fucken grouse bike. Did you lose the streamers off it? Ya cocksucker.' And I let it slide and Margle ignores it and we rack our bikes and head into class. Him to Red with Bernie, and me alone to Gold.

Lino's waiting by our door. He's the toughest motherfucker in Gold. We love 'motherfucker.' It's in all the books we're reading. All the best songs. He stands me for some dead-arm. Him first. He lets rip with a fourteen-stone-backed right to the base of the bump on my arm where the shoulder muscle finishes but he misses the spot so it just bruises. My turn. I can hit almost as hard as him but he knows my accuracy and he winces in anticipation. Bullseye. And his arm's fucked. Motherfucked. So I just swagger into class.

It's religion. Lyon takes religion. I'm still of an age where I think about God. Where I try to make sense of what hits me in terms of God. But Lyon can't help me.

I like to ask hypothetical questions. 'What if you had to kill an innocent man in order to save a guilty woman but the woman was your mother, what should you do?' 'What if your father is a really good father but he doesn't get baptised so he goes to Limbo but you've been baptised and you are good and you go to Heaven but your dad can't go so you're in Heaven but really unhappy because you miss your dad? So what if you're unhappy in Heaven?' And on and on until he goes insane with it.

There's this cool new chaplain who's supposed to take form-four religion from time to time. A stranger to us. We've seen him around the streets – Margle's sister says he's over at their school all the time. He's got a Ned Kelly beard and long hair and a hot red ute with mags but even though he's been chaplain for a year, we haven't seen him over here yet. Not for religion. Not for nuthen. But he'll come one day. I know he will.

The morning is pretty much a cruise with us just making smart-arse comments after Lyon transmogrifies into a sheila trying to teach geography then she morphs into a bullfrog lecturing in accounting. The joint's an asylum. What can ya do? We just stuff up by asking stupid questions and making fart noises and coughing ingenious obscenities.

It's lunchtime. Me and Margle don't hang around together at school. We run our own race, him sticking with Red and me with Gold. I'm mucking around with Lino while we eat lunch, sitting on a fixed pew outside our class for the compulsory fifteen minutes. He wants to string some gorbies. That's compulsory too. Some poofter whinges that he's trying to eat lunch but we just give him 'Bums against the wall. Poofter on the loose' and go about our impressive work.

Our year's achievements are strung up from the rafters outside our class. We can't believe that nobody from the staff has noticed them. It's like they're charmed, these foot-long strings of snot that we've slagged up to the rafters. They've congealed in place over months. They're our trophies. Everybody wants one but only me and Lino can spit that high and we have the gift of viscosity. Mine is the jewel.

Today Lino drinks a full carton of Big M and then he lets rip with a history-making gorbie. One that just keeps dripping lower and lower all through lunch-eating and clinging triumphantly to the rafter of champions. Even after we are set loose for our handball games it keeps finding new length. It went on all day. It would go on all year. Lino's historic gorbie. My masterpiece had been exceeded. My trophy surpassed.

And to close a loser's lunch, the kid who belted me up with his older brothers last year flogs me at handball.

Now it's English with Horne. Sometimes we play a game where we all crack our dictionaries and we ask him the meaning of the hardest words we can find. Real long ones and if he doesn't know the answer straight up he works it out in front of us from the Greek or Latin roots. I want this power. Years later I study Greek (Attic) for a year at university to complete my skills but I never match him. Horne's dead now but he will always have bettered me.

But no games today. It's *The Power and the Glory* by Graham

Greene. It's about a whisky priest in a desert. He's at me wanting to know if I have finished it. And I tell him that I can't, that it's too depressing. He knows it's killing me and then he starts with this really camp suppressed guffaw, choking a belly laugh and he says to himself out loud 'Oh my God, he gets it.'

But I don't know what I get. I just know it's fucken killing me like a poem. Like a poem about a filly that becomes a beautiful shipwreck. Or like a poem about 'Batter my heart, three-personed God.' Then I notice him giving me an odd look.

And I know that look. I've got looks just like it. I use 'em mainly in church. Sly looks. One of the looks is about how I'd do that girl in the green outfit a thousand times. But that's not the look. It's the other one. It's for the girl in the pale yellow.

It's 'Yeah, I'd give her one.' That's the way he's looking at me right now. But he can't hide the pity.

And then it's time for the beautiful boredom of Latin. Time for me to express my total mastery of the realm. The opening of the class is customary.

'Stand up all those who haven't done their homework.' It's the other kids' lucky day as I stand. And then something that has never happened in four years, happens. The unthinkable.

'Stand in line to receive six cuts.' Four was standard, two on a good day but six? Has he noticed that I'm standing? What the hell can he be thinking? For Christ's sake – six. I'm just caught off guard. I'm flummoxed. That's what I am. Fucken flummoxed.

'So, you people want to run your own race, eh? So what are you, idiots? Line up straight.'

He'll be exhausted by the time he gets through the first dozen or so of us but I don't settle at the rear of the line. I push through to the front. But Lino gets there first and he won't surrender. So I'm second. Second to face the cuts from the ferocious Lyon.

For everybody else it's just another miserable August day but for me it's beginning to feel like the fifteenth of March. The ides. And Lino's getting his good, three across each hand and his dumb grinning face is reddening and getting dumber above the pain. And now he's shaking his hands and walking away and he mouths 'poofter' to me and I mouth 'motherfucker' back. And Lyon sees me and he's genuinely shocked and he goes cold with it and then he bends me over the desk.

From there I could see through the window in the door and out into the quadrangle and beyond to the toilets and the tuckshop and the cesspit. A red ute pulls up and parks anarchically next to the bike racks. And I can hear the class go still, hear the birds through the quiet as the strap reaches the top of its arc and pauses for an instant. And whack.

It caught me off guard with its ferocity. Like it taught you why they call a blow on the arse with a pickled, hand-stitched, multi-layered leather weapon, a 'cut.' I was sure he'd go easy on me. That's why I pushed to the front. So I could test my faith. But I don't reckon he could have put any more into that cut.

And I can feel that Lyon's arm is pointing to twelve o'clock again. Feel its stillness before the air runs away from it and it strikes six o'clock on my arse and then the cesspit groans and clangs like the doors of a city giving way to a siege. And the strap clock and the Japanese water torture feature are out of sync and the pain of the blow is swelling my buttocks and my face.

I focus on the picture through the window of the chaplain and his two visitors from the girls' school in his hoon-mobile. And as I watch the happy trio get out of the car I hear the silence of the strap striking twelve and feel the air run away and then the blow drives the blood away from my buttocks and into the last empty pockets of my face.

Through the window of the freshly painted ply door the chaplain locks his red ute and checks it, trying each of the doorhandles. Why, when he never visits us does the chaplain choose class-time to finally front? Why does his red ute spend its time parked neatly in a dedicated bay at the girls' school up the road in genteel Glenroy and never slink down the highway to our gloomy desert fringe? Broadie's the home of the red ute. And why, when he finally stumbles into our concentration camp does he bring girls with him?

And the air runs away as twelve o'clock turns to six in a split second arc and time stops with the contact and my purple face begins to swell beyond its dam walls. And the cesspit trough groans and snaps and spills shit and piss over the rocky pit.

The whip reached twelve again, ages ago as I watch the visitors walk across the quadrangle towards a window framing a fourteen-year-old boy bent over a desk beneath a black-soutaned man wielding a twelve-inch whip with cold ferocity against quivering buttocks.

And as the whip strikes six again I swear he's getting stronger. And I swear one of those girls was holding the hand of the pussy priest as they walked straight past my door and disappeared out of view. I can hear the clip-clopping of the two fillies he's got in tow, fading. But the air stops again and the cesspit groans and Lyon's leather heels skip over the concrete floor as he steps into the strike and I'm praying for it to stop now. Praying to a bearded man with two disciples who's just walked straight past us and left me to the whim of my captor.

And the air runs away and the whip finds its puffy target and my neck has given way so my head falls 'cause I'm not going to make it through the next onslaught of a single blow. Twelve o'clock, six o'clock, it doesn't matter. Eight-thirty to three-thirty is a bigger problem. I don't think I can last another blow. I don't think I can last another day at this motherfucken school.

A whip reaches its zenith and too slowly for the speed of it, its nadir. The blow is at least one too many and for the first time I notice the wetness on my face. It has burst spilling its load of piss and shit. It's over.

Nobody gives me crap as I hobble back to my desk. They're looking at me. They know what's brought me low. That it's worse than pain, that it's betrayal. I've got my head held high, looking up at the ceiling as I choke out my grief trying to get the tears to run down the holes in the corner of my eyes instead of on my scalded face.

And it was their lucky day. They got the lightest six cuts of all time. Lyon had to rest half way through the run and knocked off before he'd finished. They said later they thought he was going to have a heart attack. I didn't say nuthen for the rest of the class. Just stared out of the windows over at the babies' home where they used to torture orphan babies in the name of charity. And what do ya s'pose happened to the mothers?

When the bell went I walked towards the bike racks and there's Bernie waiting to give it to me. So I spent the next fifteen minutes belting the shit out of him, the last five minutes of it with my knees on his supine shoulders and my fists trying to knock the tombstones out of his mouth. He'd passed out by the time they got me off him.

The Age

The Bodyguard

Tom Cho

Someone is stalking Whitney Houston and I have been hired to be her bodyguard. However, I soon discover that guarding Whitney Houston is not as easy a job as I might have thought. It turns out that she and I do not get along very well. She complains that my protection of her is too strict and that she cannot do what she wants to anymore. As a result, even as she becomes more and more frightened of the stalker, she begins acting up. I do not take very well to her acting up so I begin acting more aloof. This behaviour soon becomes a pattern for us. Interestingly, even in times when strong emotions are present, I have a tendency to – perhaps mechanistically – call on my sense of logic. Thus, I eventually express to Whitney Houston the following either/or statement: either she will continue to refuse my protection and end up being gruesomely killed by the stalker who I will eventually track down and apprehend and then and only then will I write a bittersweet yet poignant song about my love for her such that her sister will become very jealous of my talent, or she will allow me to protect her and we will fall in love and one night we will end up having sex at my place and then and only then will I modify my body such that I will be able to defeat her stalker. Presented with these options, Whitney Houston decides that the latter scenario is best. Thus, we end up sleeping together the following night. Later that night, as we lie together on my bed, I hold her and she tells me that she has never felt this safe before. This makes me feel proud. But then, as a child, I always did have romantic ideas about being the protector of all the girls. On the other hand, I cannot help feeling that, by sleeping with my client, I have somehow breached the limits of acceptable bodyguard–client relations. Thus, the next morning I tell her that we should not have slept together and that we must revert to a proper bodyguard–client relationship. Whitney Houston is very upset about this and we begin to argue and Whitney Houston soon begins acting up and so I begin acting more aloof. Eventually, Whitney Houston falls silent for a moment and then she simply tells me that she is in love with me and that she still wants me. I do not know how to respond to this, so I say nothing.

Over the next few weeks, the tension between Whitney Houston and I worsens. She is hurt and angry with me, and she becomes more and more unco-operative about receiving my protection. One night, she holds a party after one of her performances. At the party, I stand in a corner drinking a protein shake as I watch her mingling with her guests. She looks truly beautiful, as always. It is then that I notice that Greg Portman is at the party. Portman is a bodyguard I have worked with. I walk over to Portman and greet him. He says hello to me in return, and he tells me that he is guarding another one of the guests at the party. We begin chatting. As always, Portman starts talking about some of the more recent technological innovations that have been changing the face of bodyguarding. He tells me that, thanks to major advances in the development of force-fields, bionic limbs, and cybernetic exoskeletons, his job as a bodyguard has become so much easier. I give Portman my usual response that I am not interested in adopting any of these technological advances into my bodyguarding work. He laughs at me and tells me that I am still the same old-fashioned guy with his bodyguard fantasies of being chivalrous and protecting women. Sometimes I regret having told Portman about my fantasies of chivalry. At any rate, just as Portman begins telling me that going bionic is the best thing that ever happened to him, Whitney Houston comes up to us. I smile at her but she ignores me and smiles at Portman instead. She places her hand on his arm and asks him to tell her all about bionics. As Portman begins to tell her about his very first experience with a neurostimulation implant, I walk away from them and head out to the balcony. On the balcony, I look out at the cityscape. I think about the conflict that is occurring between me and Whitney Houston and the effect it is having upon me. As always, I find myself wishing that I was a stronger and tougher man – someone a little more indestructible. After a while, I come to a decision: it is time for me to seek expert advice about my situation.

So, a few days later, I meet up with someone who has a special place in my life. I have always thought of him as a strong and tough man. He is also someone who has had many sexual adventures with women over the years. This person is my Uncle Shen. Uncle Shen has always projected a very physical and confident kind of masculinity. It is a type of masculinity that attracts many women to him and, as a result, I suspect that he is an expert on matters relating to women and desire. So, over beers at a pub, I tell Uncle Shen about what has been happening between Whitney Houston and me. I then mention to him that I have always admired his masculinity and the way it attracts women. Upon hearing this, Uncle Shen confesses to me that he has modelled aspects of his masculinity on Marlon Brando's animalistic, swaggering portrayal of Stanley Kowalski in the film *A Streetcar Named Desire*. He tells me that he saw the film as a teenager and was struck by the sexual power of Brando's Kowalski. He adds that he loves the power of having women want him. He then begins talking about his experiences of having flings with girls he meets in bars. Smiling, he tells me that his favourite line from *A Streetcar Named Desire* is 'I have always depended on the vaginas of strangers.' He says that he has adopted this line as his life philosophy. I do not have the heart to tell Uncle Shen that he has based his life philosophy upon misquoting Tennessee Williams, so I simply nod and tell him that I understand. Uncle Shen then winks and tells me that he has had many pleasurable journeys on 'the streetcar named desire.' Me, I can only think about how some of my deepest desires are unattainable, so I say nothing. Uncle Shen notices that I have gone quiet. He tells me that there are too many good things about desire for one to get too sad about it. He adds that the opposite situation – a life without desire – would be far worse. In spite of my mood, I can't help seeing some truth in what he is saying. So, as Uncle Shen begins talking about some of the things he finds attractive in women, I smile and join in. As a result, we spend the rest of the evening discussing our interest in 'a streetcar named lingerie.'

After saying goodbye to Uncle Shen, I head back to Whitney Houston's mansion. She is waiting up for me and wants to talk. She says that she wants to apologise for her behaviour towards me. She confesses that she is very scared of the stalker and that she wants my protection now more than ever. She also tells me that she has been nominated for an Oscar and that, even though it may be dangerous, she would still like to go to the awards ceremony. I congratulate her on her nomination. She blushes and thanks me. I look at her and I realise that I want to remain her bodyguard for now so I tell her that she can go to the awards ceremony. She smiles at me and thanks me once again. As she walks away from me in her baby-pink satin slip with its lace detail, side split, and embroidered contrast trim, I also make a silent vow to myself that I will do whatever is necessary to ensure that she is safe.

On Oscars night, Whitney Houston is understandably nervous about her safety. Crowds of people are everywhere and she looks almost ill with worry. I look at her and I realise that perhaps it was a mistake for me to tell her my theory that the stalker is going to strike tonight. At any rate, the night gets much better for her when, four-and-a-half hours later, it is announced that she has won her award. When the announcement is made, she raises her hands to her face in shock. The orchestra begins playing and everyone applauds as she makes her way to the stage. As she walks up to the podium to accept her award, I turn around and am surprised to discover that Portman is standing near me. I say hello to him but he looks a little awkward as he greets me in response. It is then that I realise the truth: Portman is the stalker and he is at the Oscars to launch his ultimate attack on Whitney Houston. Sure enough, just as she is about to make her acceptance speech, I notice that Portman's left bionic eye has begun to glow red. I immediately run out onto the stage and make a flying leap in front of Whitney Houston and push her out of the way. A laser beam from Portman's eye hits me in the shoulder. Everyone in the auditorium screams. I stand up and face

Portman, my shoulder wound closing in a matter of seconds. He is shocked to see my wound heal so quickly. I inform him that I have changed since we last met at the party and that I too have embraced the more recent technological innovations that have been changing the face of bodyguarding. I explain that I have always wanted to be unbreakable and thus I have now acquired super-fast healing powers and had my entire skeleton laced with an indestructible alloy called adamantium. Portman suddenly activates his personal force-field and tells me that, as long as I can never land a hit on him, he will be undefeatable. In response, I unsheathe three-foot-long super-sharp metal claws from each hand. Everyone in the auditorium screams once again as Portman and I begin to fight. However, it is not long before I have Portman on the defensive. Once he realises how powerful I have become, his confidence begins to fade. Thus, I am eventually able to corner him and slash through his force-field with my claws. Yet, just as I deliver the final blow to defeat Portman, he fires one last blast from his bionic eye into my chest. This blast is delivered from virtually point-blank range. As Portman sinks to the ground, I fall backwards, blood pouring out of my chest. Whitney Houston screams and rushes over to cradle me in her arms. She cries and begs me not to die on her. But, once again, my wound heals in a matter of seconds, and so Whitney Houston and I look at each other and we smile.

A week later, Whitney Houston and I are saying goodbye to each other on an airport tarmac. She is doing her best to not cry. We hug each other and we say our farewells. She walks away from me and enters her private plane. As I watch the plane slowly turn away from me and begin taxiing down the runway, I find myself feeling very sad. It seems that I am not so indestructible after all. Yet, in the midst of my sadness, I am able once again to call on my sense of logic. Thus, I formulate the following either/or statement: either I will stoically watch the plane depart and Whitney Houston will get the pilot to stop the plane so that she can run out to kiss me and then and only then will I resume my life as a bodyguard without her such that she will end up singing a song about our relationship, or I will decide that there is no logical reason why I cannot be her bodyguard as well as her lover so I will make a flying leap onto one of the plane's wings and unsheathe my claws and use them to rip a hole in the side of the plane so that I can climb in and grab Whitney Houston and we can kiss and then and only then will I tell her that I have come to realise that being both her bodyguard and her lover is a perfect combination of fantasies for me such that she will offer me an ongoing contract to work as both her bodyguard and her lover. Presented with these options, I decide that the latter scenario is best. Thus, Whitney Houston ends up in my arms, smiling at me, and offering to discuss the terms of my contract.

Her Voice Was Full of Money – and They Were Careless People

Carmel Bird

The Lisieux Convent. This was not situated as you might expect in rural France, but in Leafland, a 'comfortable, affluent' suburb of Melbourne, Australia. Such suburbs are often described as 'leafy,' and this one certainly was lined with lovely European trees as well as rows of flowering gums all of which mysteriously did not suffer badly from the drought that gripped the country in 2007. Yes, the country was *in the grip* of drought. Rainbow lorikeets chattered, flittered and darted from the blossoms of the gums that bloomed forever in a kind of long long hot forever and ever. Summer, autumn, winter – the drought-affected gum trees sent out honeyed fluffy pink and creamy white puffs all across the leafy lanes. The aroma of the honey! Never had there been so many lorikeets living for so long among the flowers and insects of Leafland. They were luminously bright birds, all the colours of the rainbow in splashes and splats and stripes, if you looked at them up close. Some of the sisters at Lisieux were French, and the school was renowned for its success in teaching languages and music.

Olga Bongiorno was five when she went to school at Lisieux. She was educated there for the following twelve years – a dozen years from 1952 to 1964. She was from the beginning one of those girls whose broad linen collar was always starched white, perfect as a seagull. In 1965 Olga went to the university, and then she went to the teachers' college, and then she returned to Lisieux where she taught French and English until she retired at the age of sixty. She herself would say if you asked her that she walked in the valley of the shadow and that she feared no evil. This grandiose biblical conversation-stopper concealed the death of a fiancé in a motorcycle accident when Olga was twenty-five. It wasn't as if Olga was a nun exactly, but it wasn't as if she wasn't one either, if you can follow that. She did one world trip with her sister and they went to London and Paris and Rome – and also Loreto where Olga was keen to visit the Holy House. She was interested in miracles. But Olga truly was happiest in her role as senior mistress of French and English at Lisieux, and she was mildly famous and widely celebrated among the families whose lives she touched through her years of teaching. As for what Olga did after retirement – those matters are not relevant to this story. For our purposes she is the Beloved Miss Bongiorno, sometimes known as Old Olga da Polga, named for the character of a guinea pig in a children's picture book. The guinea pig was a teller of tall tales, very tall tales, wild exaggerations. Nothing could be further from the character of Olga Bongiorno who resembled rather the aunt in a poem by Hilaire Belloc, an aunt 'who from her earliest youth had kept a strict regard for truth.' Olga was a woman of high moral principles and a virtuous Catholic morality. What she saw and what she heard in and around her classroom were frequently matters of severe distress to her. She worried so about her girls, and was known to be, as a result of her anxieties, a devoted lighter of votive candles in the Chapel of the Little Flower.

Some of these things I tell you for the purposes only of clarification and ornamentation, since my focus is in fact on the year of the drought, the year 2007, and on Olga and her class of final year students of English. I should add at this point that Loyola, the brother school, was situated just three leafy lanes away as the tram runs. Now that Loyola has entered the picture, things are becoming more promising, and you can begin to sense where they are moving.

In Olga's English class in the year of the drought Marina Delaney was known to be sleeping with Caroline Herbert's boyfriend. The other girls in the group rallied behind and around Caro, and they turned on Marina in a pack. To the Loyola boy in the case (one Teddy Buchan) there attached, it appeared, no blame whatsoever for Marina's misdemeanours. Sometimes in the classroom it seemed to Olga that all nineteen cells vibrated and lit up in unison, as the news of the progress of the Marina–Teddy Affair travelled in thrilling bee-lines across the desks, down the leafy lanes, over tennis courts and football ovals, round and round the garden like a teddy bear.

Caroline wept. Marina wept. Juliette, Tiffany, Marie-Claire, Ching Ye and Veronica sighed and frowned and gurgled. Trinity and Pieta squirmed. Wanda the Giggler giggled.

So it was not always possible, as you might appreciate, to teach the girls very much. Not that Olga had ever really understood, in all her years of teaching English and French, quite how the process of teaching really worked. Somehow her students ended up as literate, fluent, engaged, informed young women, but the chemistry or the physics or the metaphysics of the thing remained a mystery. All Olga knew at this point was that the Buchan boy was a terrible nuisance to her, that he was getting in the way of everything. He was the son of Buchan the leather-furnishing millionaire, and Olga knew his grandmother, Violet Fish, who had had her front teeth knocked out at the Lisieuz–Good Counsel hockey final in 1961. But that's really just another irrelevant little factoid. No, Olga couldn't get very much into the heads of her girls who were a flurry and sizzle of pink and grey dresses with the same huge white detachable collars as Olga used to wear. Some of theirs resembled hers in seagull snowy starch, but most did not. Olga must proceed, and so the day arrived when the curriculum, like a tram on a track, brought them all to chapter one of *The Great Gatsby* by F. Scott Fitzgerald.

And still the bee-lines hummed in the zipped or unzipped side pockets of the pink and grey dresses. If you half closed your eyes those dresses resembled a shimmering, spreading splat of young and healthy brain tissue. Would Teddy ever go back to poor darling Caro? Would that slut Marina ever give him up? You can of course guess what happens here – on the tram Teddy Buchan meets the cute blonde mega-slut from New Hudson High, a tart in a short black skirt and tiny satin thong, and before you can say honey pot he's dropped Marina (serves her right), forgotten all about Caroline (brave but inconsolable) and has 'moved on.'

'Now, girls, the plot turns on a hit-run accident.' The sleepy sun slants across the honey-coloured desks, stopping to glitter on the tiny diamond in the ear of Ginny King. Some cells glow and hum as the bee-lines are kept open. Marie-Claire has worked out the name of the black New Hudson bitch. 'What, Patricia, is the correct procedure in the case of a driver who knocks down a pedestrian?'

All the pencils in Patricia's pencil case rattle across the timber top of the desk and sail down onto the carpet as Patricia suddenly sits up at the sound of her name. Her eyes are as blank as her mind. She doesn't know anything about the correct procedure. 'Anybody? Wanda?' What *is* this procedure Old Olga da Polga is going on about? Eighteen pairs of eyes look vacantly at Olga. Wanda is silent since she has had a big night and is asleep, sitting upright in the corner. The correct procedure? 'You must stop, render assistance, call for help.'

This is news to the owners of the thirty-six eyes who are all on the brink of getting a licence to drive a motor vehicle. 'What? Why? Oh really?'

Stop, render assistance, call for help.

Myrtle Wilson was killed instantly, and the driver of the big yellow car, the death car, the car belonging to the Great Gatsby himself, put her foot down and drove swiftly on. To this information Olga's students register no surprise. So Daisy was driving the car and she killed Myrtle and left the scene at speed. So Myrtle had it coming. She was sleeping with Daisy's husband and she was only a slut anyhow. Daisy is Gatsby's girlfriend and long-time love, and she's as lovely as an ice-white blossom floating on a silver pool and her voice is full of money.

Wanda the Sleepy Giggler hears none of this. She is thought to be the richest girl in the school. Her father owns a city in the Middle East. Her mother is one of the Chicago van Cleefs. You might wonder what brings Wanda to Olga's classroom in the middle of leafy Leafland in the middle of the warmest autumn since time began. Well, for one thing one of her grandmothers went to Lisieux in San Antonio, Texas, and for another it's a matter of the miracle of modern marketing. Leafland Lisieux has come a long long way in cyberspace since Olga was a child in a great white collar. Wanda will in any case be Finished at a school in Switzerland where there are princesses of all descriptions and of every stripe, and where her down-under bloom will carry an exotic caché all its own. 'Drizabone Wanda Lust' they will call her, and they will wave a butter knife in her face gleefully crying '*This* is a knife!' But that is all in the future and does not concern us here.

'They were careless people.' Olga tells them to write that down. 'They disappeared into their money.' Learn that quote. A few pens quietly scrawl the short quotations onto paper. A number of silent laptops register the words as well. It's rather nice, really, disappeared into their money. Pieta was editing her photos and had no time for quotations; Marina was composing an email to Teddy Buchan who was never going to reply.

Well, you can see how things were, and I am not exaggerating in the manner of the guinea pig in the story. If anything I am being restrained and conservative and playing things down in the interests of fiction as against fact. But you can sense how this story is making its own bee-line towards a sharp and gleaming hot dry night in early summer when these girls have all closed their books and jettisoned their collars and have graduated from school with honours and accolades and laurel wreaths and stacks of valedictory books and higher school certificates and not a few glossy new cars. Pieta backed her lovely little Mazda into the muddy gurgle of the Merri Creek, and it is truly a miracle that she got out of it alive. Pieta is a survivor. Wanda is now on holiday in Florida with an aunt, so she is out of the picture.

So who, you wonder, is driving the death car in our story? Who is this speeding down steep Kennedy Hill Drive at three in the morning after a party to celebrate Teddy Buchan's eighteenth? It's Veronica Vale, deluxe dux of Lisieux, in her sleek green minty Volkswagon. And who should come tottering barefoot and unbelievably intoxicated and wickedly wasted from behind a leafy elm where lives a watchful owl? Look, it's Trinity Maxwell in a glittering slivery silvery slithery slice of a wisp of Armani silk and sequin which she bought on E-bay. Through drooping yellow fringes of sunny yellow hair, with large grey eyes that almost focus, Trinity sees Veronica coming and she calls and waves, imagining in what you might describe as a split second that Veronica will stop and give her a lift back to Leafland. But Veronica is on the bee-line of her cell, talking to Caro who is passing out in Teddy Buchan's mother's ensuite, and is about to get back in the pool with Teddy if he ever stops horsing around in the deep end with Charlie Beluga and a bottle of very expensive Bourbon.

So a teenager is killed on Kennedy Hill at three minutes past three, and the dogs in the vicinity howl as the sirens worry and wail their way to the accident, the fatality, the tragedy, the waste.

Choose Your Own Conclusion

The driver put her foot down and disappeared into her money.

She stopped. She rendered assistance. She called for help. Yes, she called for help.

Ploughing

Sophie Cunningham

He always wakes before dawn. Not just because his days are long, though they are – it hardly seems possible that a man can work as hard as he does without dropping dead of disease, or a stopped heart, before he turns thirty – but because there is a gentleness in the minutes between sleeping and wakefulness, which makes everything else seem possible. When he first arrived in this place Leonard had not imagined he could sleep through the crash and thud of the waves as they broke just a few feet below his verandah. But he slept well on his first night, and all the nights thereafter.

At around four every morning the roar of the surf intrudes on his dreams; slowly at first, then it is louder and louder, until there is no doubt about it, he is awake. There are other sounds too. The crow of the cocks, the chatter of waking birds and monkeys. But these sounds are faint under the waves. Suggestions only.

When he finally opens his eyes Leonard sees first of all the gauze of the mosquito net that he, as often as not, has become tangled in. Past that there are squares cut into the side of the bungalow that frame the leaves of the trees outside. Then the sea beyond. If it is still dark he might be lucky enough to glimpse stars or the moon setting over the ocean: sliver of silver-white against a velvet-black disc.

Often he chooses to keep his eyes closed for an extra minute, or two or three, and imagine that the waves below rise up and engulf him. It is not a terrible thought: this fantasy he has of the sea swallowing the coast and him being drowned. Afterwards, there will be nothing. He believes that with all his heart. The learning of this fact, his shedding of God, has bought him much tumult, and entailed its own kind of tossing and dumping in a wild ocean, but now the idea soothes him and the thud of the surf reassures him that death is near. He can choose it any time. Once he has done that, imagined his end, he can begin.

After sound, it is smell that comes to him. This day is different in that it is not salt he first smells, but smoke. It catches in his chest.

'Damn it,' his voice is raised loud enough that the mongrel Tom's ears prick up, and Minka wakes with a start and a screech.

Leonard pulls the net aside and swings out of bed. Why do the villagers insist on burning their *chenas* so close to where he lives? He tries, of course, to be reasonable. He insists that the *chenas* be measured out and the headman's initials carved into a tree at each corner of the piece of land, but even these rules are ignored. As far as the villagers are concerned the stakes are too high to care about recrimination. Drought reduces them, and the land around them, to a husk. The amount of rice the *chena* provides them with will be barely enough to feed a family for a year and then there will be starvation. Nothing but barren soil and barren women.

Leonard pulls on his trousers and steps onto the verandah. Tom follows close at his heels. The two of them stand together and sniff at the air. Leonard looks down at Tom – whom he loves, despite his nondescript beige coat and his unkempt appearance – and watches his nose twitch: the grimace of his snout as he bares his teeth at the ash that rains around them.

The *ayah* comes around the corner of the balcony with some tea. Leonard sips on the milky sweetness. Tom leaps the several feet off the balcony and trots down the beach. Minka calls to Leonard. She wants to be let off her chain. When he fails to come to her she picks up her chain in her tiny hands and tugs on it so that it rattles.

'Shhh.' Leonard steps back into the bungalow and releases the monkey, who immediately leaps onto his head as if she is some extraordinary furry hat. She rests her feet upon his ears and begins to pick at his hair. 'Stop it,' Leonard shakes her off. He turns his mind to the business of the day. He looks at his desk where the letter he is writing to Saxon lies. *I feel desolate & the horror of desolation.*

Ploughing. Today is the day Leonard will show the villagers what can be achieved with the use of a good plough. He has asked them all to be on the beach by nine that morning, despite the fact this will take them from their fields in the cooler hours of the day. It will be worth it, he assures them, in his hesitant Singhalese. He speaks it badly but there is some admiration for his efforts.

It is, in fact, close to midday before the crowd gathers and while Leonard grumbles to himself that these people have no idea of time, the truth is they had no intention of coming at the time specified but had been too polite to say so.

As Leonard walks down on to the beach he suddenly feels nervous, as if he is stepping onto a stage. Certainly he is wearing clothes suitable for a performance: white pants and jacket with a boater on his head to protect him from the sun. As if struck by stage fright he feels his tremor come upon him and tries to tame his left hand by holding it to his chest with his right. After a few moments he repeats the process, left holding down right. It is the mark of the Ashkenazi Jew. This is not a medical fact but one he intuits: his father shook; many of his relatives do. Leonard hates it. He thinks it makes him seem weak. He is a coward and his tremor is the proof. What did Thoby Stephen once say about him? *It was his nature – he was so violent, so savage; he so despised the human race.*

If only Thoby had known how savage he could be: that once he thrashed a horse until foam surged from its mouth and skin to fleck its entire black body white. The horse had almost died. Worse still, it refused to acknowledge Leonard again, its intelligent eyes registering him from a distance before it turned its elegant head to one side and moved slowly to the other side of the field. The disdain in that animal's gesture is one of the reasons Leonard no longer underestimates creatures' intelligence. *Every now and then I am amazed and profoundly moved by the beauty and affection of my cat and my dog.*

Thoby would never know how right his judgement was. He had died, at the age of twenty-six, just over two years ago. It makes no sense that Leonard survives typhoid, here, a thousand miles from civilisation while Thoby dies of it in a bed in London. Now his sister Vanessa has gone and married that pompous ass Bell. Leonard wonders for a moment where this has left Virginia, the younger sister. What has become of her?

Despite Leonard's hard-won love of animals, the black bull that his men bring to him now is in no mood to behave. Leonard spends half an hour trying to shackle the cumbersome creature to the plough but it keeps shaking its hump and throwing Leonard's concentration. This happens four times over. If the bull doesn't misbehave, Leonard's trembling hands do. The villagers, listless in the heat, watch this performance with something approaching boredom. Who is this crazy man who makes them farm salt and behaves like some kind of king? Their respect for him is grudging. Certainly there is not enough of it to stop the occasional giggle that Leonard can hear and that causes him to keep his back to them to hide the flush in his cheeks. He fixes his gaze firmly on the metal, and, if he lifts his eyes, the ocean beyond.

Finally it is done. Leonard stands back and takes the bull by the ring in its nose. He encourages it to walk in a line along the beach with loud clicks and hard tugs. He needs the line to be straight enough that the villagers can see the striations grooved in the sand.

'You see?' he yells. 'You throw the seed in here,' he gestures towards the furrow. 'It goes in deep. The soil protects it and keeps the seed safe.'

Leonard bends down and mimes sprinkling seed into the sand before, theatrically, covering it up. This seems to go well enough and he begins to 'water' the imaginary seeds. At this point the bull takes off. It moves as fast as it can towards the trees that line the beach, the plough rattling alarmingly behind it. Leonard chases the beast, cursing himself under his breath. *I should have practised this.* If only he hadn't come in so late last night, exhausted after his two weeks' tour of the district. When Leonard finally stops the animal he allows himself to look at his audience. He expects to see silent laughter in their eyes, or the formal staring at the feet that they undertake when they want to hide their contempt. But no, it is worse than that. Most of them have simply wandered off. It is time for lunch. Leonard tries, but fails, not to see himself as they must. An absurdly dressed *parangi*, who oversees absurd laws and stands in the heat of the midday sun. A heat that even a bull has the sense to get out of.

Meanjin

Lorraine Bracco

Frank Moorhouse

While in the supermarket last Saturday I took a phone call from my mother on my mobile. As it happened I was pushing a trolley and wondering if the bunch of bananas – the only thing I had in the trolley so far – was supermarket pick-up code and if so, for what? I could read the code of, say, one banana alone in a trolley, yes, but a bunch, well, maybe I could see a code winking there, but I'm not sure that it might not be conjuring up a personal fantasy rather than being a code, and if it were a code how widely understood would my hesitant hunch about *that* code be, and, if any encounter along those lines did develop how long would it take to iron out any misunderstanding without very acute embarrassment involving 'security,' that is, if my hesitant understanding, or that of the other person, was *very wrong.*

'Is that you?' my mother said. She had not yet accepted that a mobile phone as distinct from all other phones is answered only by the owner – at least, in the best of all relationships. I suppose in the case of suicide or murder (as we sometimes see in TV police dramas) the detective at the crime scene would answer having taken the mobile phone from our dead body.

'Yes mum, it's me,' I said, pulling a can from the shelf.

'I have something to tell you which I should've told you many years ago but your father and I think that now is as good a time as any,' she said. 'I suggest you sit down.'

It was one of *those* telephone calls, 'sit down' is a euphemism for 'someone has terminal cancer.'

I looked about me. I supposed I could hunch down in an alcove near the cleaning products.

'We are both OK – this is about you.'

'Have I won the Nobel Prize?' Maybe the rumour was about again.

It would not surprise me if the Nobel Prize committee called your mother and father first, Swedish old-world courtesy.

'It's not anything like that. Sit down!'

And the other thing the telephone call did, apart from *rebadging* my life, was that it caused me, for the first time in my life, to sit down in a supermarket aisle.

I slid down onto my backside, tucking in my legs gracefully together sideways – should boys sit that way? – was it a coded sit – out of the way, one hand holding my trolley although there is no point in anyone stealing a trolley inside the supermarket – unless, I suppose, they wanted to be relieved of the burden of choice. I have considered doing that myself, taking one of those huge, overfilled, abundant, family-provisioned trolleys, paying for it at checkout, and high-tailing it. When you got the load home there would be surprises, things you would never have thought of trying, treats. Or maybe I could sit myself on the child seat and go home to that abundant household. Note that down for my next therapy session.

My mother said, 'I would tell you to get a drink if I believed in drink, which you know I don't which reminds me, are you eating three meals a day?'

'I eat very well, I eat at the Rockpool most days.'

'A rock pool?'

'It's a restaurant, mum. A very decent restaurant.'

'I know it's a restaurant. But you said "at a rock pool." That must be expensive.'

I meant it as a joke but it was overrun by the conversation before I could explain it. 'It is but at least I get a square meal …' but as I thought about it this was not what my mother would call a 'square meal' although I have noticed that square plates are appearing in upmarket restaurants. 'But tell me the news which has required me to sit down in a supermarket.'

'You're in a supermarket?'

'It's Saturday morning, mum, every inner-city Playboy of the Western World is in the supermarket.' Buying the ingredients for a fabulous dinner party which will end in tears and screaming about foreign policy. Yeah, right.

A passing shopper asked me if I was OK. I smiled and nodded, and waved him on. Maybe he'd cracked the code of the bunch of bananas in the trolley and maybe, by sitting, I was becoming (in code) *rather obvious*. At least I had the mobile phone to my ear, having a mobile phone to your ear is an excuse for stationary standing or sitting anywhere at any time in public with your back to people. Perhaps sitting in a supermarket with your mobile to your ear is also *code*? Say, code for: *I-am-waiting-for-your-call, honey*?

She then asked, 'Maybe I should call you later at a more convenient time?'

I let out a very impatient, '*Tell me now* – if the news is so BIG tell me now, I'm seated.'

I wondered if at eighty she was pregnant. Anything now seemed medically possible in that area. Or were they splitting up? Or were they adopting a Bosnian child? Or had they rented my childhood room – mothballed from my last year at high school – to a Cambodian family of twelve?

'The news is this: I will give it to you as clearly as I can: your father and I are not your real parents.'

My eyes, obviously confounded by hearing what the ears were hearing, now became absorbed by the label of a cleaning agent for bathroom tile joints. Who worries so much about tile joints? 'You are not my parents?' My voice was calm. she will need palliative care, my brothers and I will need to get them into a home.

'We never have been.'

'Who, then, are my parents?' The milkman? I try to treat her statement as meriting of rational conversation. 'You mean my father did not father me with you?'

I found this appalling. My mother is so correct, so upright. But maybe way back then she'd been a wild thing. A flapper. A beatnik. Whatever.

'It's not like that – he was not the father and I was not the mother.'

'Who then were the father and the mother? May I ask?'

'Another couple.' This statement seemed to lack conviction but there was an inevitable logic to it.

'Which couple, may I ask?'

My eyes are still off there, studying the labels on packets in great detail as if my eyes were going on with the shopping not wanting *to know*, as if it were just 'ears business.' I became aware as my eyes did this reading, of how much of an agenda I had now with shopping – buy Australian first, no scented toilet-paper, no printed toilet-paper, low fat, which countries did I at present disapprove of, why *Italian* canned tomatoes? Careful about China. Which middle-eastern dates?

'Surely the hospital where I was born has a record of my parents.'

'Be that as it may, all that matters is that we're not your parents and you should write about that in one of the papers you write for – the *New Yorker*, maybe.

My mother: my agent. A little out of touch with my career.

'Your father – although he's not your father – thinks there might be a film in it. He said you should call Cohn in L.A.'

Cohn? Who the hell is Cohn?

'Now listen, mum, before we get into the magazine and film deal, this is shattering news, this turns my world upside down, we are not simply talking about a good subject for a deeply reflective essay here.'

'Your father and I think that you should get it into print as soon as possible. He's standing here with me. He says to say hullo.'

'Hullo dad – sorry – hullo "not-dad" – but why?' I heard my mother say to my father off-phone, 'He says hullo.'

'Why this rush to print?'

My mother answered for them both, 'he thinks it should go in the *New Yorker* but I said *Vanity Fair* because they've been good to you.'

I wondered tiredly whether this would mean more therapy work (when did therapy stop being self-knowledge and become 'work'?) For a start, I would have to rearrange my genealogy, in truth, I would have to start from nothing. I would have to move a lot of mental furniture around.

'You'll manage, I am sure there are many people who manage without a mother or father.'

'Hold it – hold it – all that's really changed is that you're saying that you and he – were a *surrogate* mother and father. For all purposes you were my parents.'

'I am sure there are books that will tell you how to go about it all and which word to use. Ask that therapist of yours.'

Her reference to the therapist was sarcastic, it carried the implication that my therapist was a know-all and in fact, she was the opposite, all she had was question-avoidance technique, endlessly returning the questions to me. I was always left panting and begging for answers.

I sat there in the supermarket waving away people who asked if I were OK and looked at the bananas and occasionally looked back at me with a lascivious movement of their eyebrows. Do I wish?

My mother put my father on the phone who said 'hullo' again and then said he would pass me back to my mother. Despite a satisfied certainty and a slight urgency in their voices, they both seemed surprisingly unperturbed by it all. But it had been part of our family style *never to panic.*

I told no one of this news over the weekend and on the Monday I went to the Office of Births, Deaths and Marriages and paid for my birth certificate which I would've expected – of all the government documents in my life – to be free, in fact, I would've thought I *owned* it and I was simply allowing them to hold it for me.

I suppose if you couldn't afford to pay for it you would be without any documentation of your existence and be released from life and all its legal obligations.

My birth certificate was quite adamant: my father was my father on the certificate and my mother my mother.

I rang them with this news. My mother said that they had rejected the certificate as null.

'How could it be null?' Were lawyers already involved? Should I have a lawyer before I said anything more?

'Your father and I discussed it. We rejected that certificate as null.'

I suppose when push came to shove, *they* would know. Or should know. I doubt, legally, that they could 'null' it unilaterally.

'You can't do that, you can't simply decide that an official document is *null.* This is a witnessed document, the matron of the hospital and the doctor present at birth witnessed it.'

'They must have been confused.'

'Why would they be confused?'

'Maybe they were intoxicated. Maybe they were rushed. Maybe they plucked our names out of a hat. It was a small town.'

This was ridiculous. They made the town sound like a frontier gold-rush tent settlement. Deadwood. Maybe I'd been born in Deadwood.

Over the phone came the sound of rustling paper, she seemed to be reading from a list.

I heard my father's voice off-phone saying, 'Tell him he could have a private detective search or put an advertisement in the paper which would be a good plot-move for the story.'

'YOU MEAN …' I said to him raising my voice to reach him off-phone '… that I should advertise for a mother and father?'

'Yes,' he said off-phone, 'a good plot-move – but remember that it'd be of no use. Waste of good coin. No one would want you at this point in time.'

'The private detective could adopt me, I suppose,' I said in a sotto-voce voice rife both with black humour and with hysteria.

'Now *that's* an idea, that would be a good development in the story,' my mother said, 'if he were a nice man.'

I heard my father say off-phone, 'Ask him if he has done anything about a film deal? Has he rung Cohn in L.A.?'

I heard them whisper, and she came back on the line, 'It was a sort of false upbringing, a pretend upbringing.'

All the wind and meaning had now gone from what had passed as my upbringing.

I heard my father say off-phone, 'It's null.'

During the conversation this time, I was seated in a comfortable chair with a strong drink, in fact the bottle of Jack Daniels was balanced on the arm of the chair, and I'd begun to think that I might never leave the chair.

'Your father and I think it might be best if you gave your name back to us. Put that in the story.'

By some sort of barmy Family Logic, it followed that I should return my name. If, that is, we had a 'family' logic anymore. I guess I was now outside the Family Logic. I was now part of the Family Illogic, if one were to get punctilious.

'And where then am I supposed to get a name?'

'Your father suggests that you buy one from a name shop.' I heard my father chuckling.

I heard my father say off-phone, 'Tell him to ask his damned Soprano woman therapist for a name. Or take *her* name.' Again, he chuckled away at this.

If my therapist were Tony Soprano's therapist I could perhaps wheedle Tony's telephone number from her and talk to Tony about this 'family matter,' Tony himself being big on Family and sorting things out. I am sure Tony would take my side and all that that would mean.

My mind left aside the barmyness of what was happening and actually took on board my father's idea. The idea had a sort of dark *therapy logic* to it. For a start, I wouldn't mind having Lorraine Bracco for a therapist. But taking the name of my own therapist was intriguing itself. It would certainly give the therapist and me a few more years of 'work.' I wondered if that breached the therapist–client (formerly 'patient') protocols, whether it had ever happened in the history of psychiatry? I knew that clients sometimes married therapists. Clients married prostitutes. I knew that the client (formerly patient) sometimes wants to become the therapist. Whether there was a damned thing she could do about it if I did take her name? Have me strapped to a bed, lock me away in a rural clinic with high stone walls, behind iron gates, with a gate house policed by uniformed guards, barred windows, and no visitors, might be one thing she could do about it.

'What about my brothers? What do they think? Or are they fraud children too?'

'Oh no, they're real enough.'

Oh good, good for them, bully for them. They made it into the inner circle of lifetime unconditional love and protection and support. And interest-free, non-recourse loans for holiday houses and yachts.

Three cheers for them.

I said, 'I suppose Dad's right. I could take the name of my therapist.'

I heard my father say off-phone, 'Now he's thinking – *for a change*.' I heard my mother say to him off-phone, 'in all these years, he never introduced us.'

Sweet Jesus. She's right – not in four years had I ever taken my parents to meet my therapist or vice versa. Never had her for dinner at our home, never invited her to Christmas. Never had her around for a barbecue. How dreadfully rude of me. That would have been fun, she could've stayed overnight, observed us all, listened to our toilet habits. Experienced our Family Logic. Analysed my father's jokes.

My 'mother' would probably be jealous if I took the name of my therapist. There's another four years 'work' – my mother's jealousy – my twisted motives.

'Or I could be like those trendy restaurants and call myself "No Name,"' I said, 'Writer No-Name.'

'Don't be silly about it,' my 'mother' said, 'that won't help.'

'I suppose not,' I said soberly.

'There's nothing much else to say,' my 'mother' said. I heard a slight pause, I swear I heard her folding paper – *all done*.

'I will come and get my things, my school things and so on from my room. My Biggles and Worral books.'

I heard my 'father' say off-phone, 'Those are not really, legally that is, *his* things. We paid for them.'

'Your father said that they are not really your things. Legally.'

What were they going to do with them? Sell them on the street? Give them to the incoming Cambodian family? Bring in a rubbish skip? I didn't want to know. And I didn't care, although the Biggles and Worral books were probably worth something.

I was beginning to have a feeling which didn't correspond with any feeling I'd had before in life. It was akin perhaps to the feeling after divorce, that relief and pleasant bewilderment when you step out of the courthouse into the sun, divorced, and find yourself not knowing which direction to turn as you stand there alone on the courthouse steps, avoiding your ex-wife's eyes, avoiding trying to pick her new boyfriend from among the huge bunch of our former friends and well-wishers crowding around her clutching bunches of flowers and bottles of champagne. But it was not quite like that either, it had a trying-not-to-be-sucked-through-the-hole-in-the-plane-when-the-door-had-blown-out feeling.

'Another thing,' my 'mother' said, 'your father said not to bother with birthday or Christmas cards. They are a waste of good forests anyhow.'

'Yes,' I said, 'that makes sense.'

'Bye now,' my 'mother' said, adding, 'at least I don't have to say those silly things like "I hope you're eating three square meals a day" or "don't forget Gran's birthday" or "Don't forget to take a cardigan in case it turns cold."'

I swear she sniggered. Had she ever meant any of that? Had she been an ironic mother all these years?

I heard my 'father' off-phone say, 'Ask him if he's rung Cohn yet.'

I said, 'Bye.'

I let her hang up first but it gave me no satisfaction.

Although somewhat estranged from my 'brothers' because, along with my 'parents,' they detested my writing, I conference-called them and asked them if our 'parents' had lost their marbles.

No, they didn't think so.

When I retaled the conversations I'd had and said that this turn of events sort of put me out in the cold, they said, almost in unison, 'Way out in the cold.'

One said that he'd always thought of me as a ring-in.

The other said, 'A martian, to be exact.'

I remembered then that I used to be proud when someone said, 'When I look at your family I think you must have been left on the doorstep.' Now I felt differently about it, not that I ever wanted so much to be *in* the family. There were now natural justice issues.

There was then a finger-drumming silence. My 'brothers' never really went in for a chat with me. Perhaps they were in on this with my 'parents.'

'I might take the name of my therapist,' I told them.

'Whatever,' one said.

'My therapist is Lorraine Bracco.'

'Whatever you say.'

'Whatever you want to believe,' the other one said.

'At least that means no more putting up with you at Christmas,' the older one said.

'And your dopey ideas on foreign policy,' the other one said.

I wished them and their families life joy and gently replaced the telephone, saying as I did, to myself, softly, experimentally, '*Lorraine Bracco.*'

I went to an agency called Peace of Mind Solutions. I asked if it were possible to run DNA tests to clear all this up or just to satisfy my own forensic curiosity.

They explained the technology and the legalities of the procedure and I returned with hair samples and my 'parents' combs and toothbrushes taken surreptitiously, my last use of the key to the 'family' home. My 'parents' would ponder and discuss the disappearance of these for many years, why of all things, it was these that I took for keepsakes. They would say to each other that I had always been strange. I left the key on the dining room table and after several attempts decided not to write a note. I took nothing from my childhood room, respecting their view that the possessions – the furniture for example – were technically not mine although it crossed my mind that my fencing trophies were legally disputable and gifts. They would probably argue in court about the lessons, the foils, the gloves, the mask, the glove grip-powder, and who paid for them and transport to and from venues.

The tests came back positive: my 'parents' were lying. I was *their* biological child. Not that it would make much difference, my 'parents' would just null the tests.

And my 'father' would say, this was all irrelevant, and '*that was that.*'

'I hope that gives you peace of mind,' the receptionist said, without conviction, writing the receipt for the whopping fee and handing me the file and the toothbrushes and combs in plastic evidence-bags.

'You wouldn't believe it if I told you,' I said, as I put away my wallet.

'Oh yes I would,' she said, tiredly.

I held up the toothbrushes and combs. 'May I throw these away here?' Without looking at me, she picked up the waste-paper bin and held it out. There were other combs and tooth-brushes in the bin.

I came to the conclusion that my 'parents' were putting on an act because they'd been influenced by the hundreds of 'I traced my biological father/mother' stories. Maybe they just wanted to get into the fashion or, sadly, to add drama to the years of hum-drum parenting. To be a 'discovered' parent made you a celeb-rity in the way that being a run-of-the-mill everyday parent never could be. They had reversed the fashionable story – they wanted to be the Unreal Parents.

It must all connect somehow to myths about abandonment and the 'lost child' and the 'found child.' Why didn't my thera-pist talk about those sorts of things?

Parents Disown. It was certainly a new form of celebrity from what I now realised – from dimly recalled biblical tales – was an old story.

My stronger conviction, though, was that they'd had enough of me and my writing and wanted to be well rid of me, the author–son, and my writing and that the 'not my real parents' story they wanted was a way of concluding the relationship between them and my writing and at the same time, cashing in on the celebrity. Having it both ways. Or as they would say in their folksy imagery, 'having a cake and eating it too.' Although my therapist would say that the Mother is always the central character, if she were ever to say anything.

Well, they and my 'brothers' can just put up with the embar-rassment they go through when they read what I write. Not being real parents or real brothers they are absolved from being held responsible or in anyway connected with it. 'He's not really our son or brother,' they could now say.

In turn I could say in answer to questions at literary festivals, 'I write under *that* name but my real name is *Lorraine Bracco.*'

Speak to Me

Paddy O'Reilly

Not all fantasy writers are geeks, I tell my friends. Most of us are normal people who like a good story with heroes and villains and right and wrong. We love to weave new worlds, grapple with the strange physical laws we have created and test the fabric of our new world for consistency. There is a single story in fantasy, I tell them, and it is the hero's journey, where ordinary people become extraordinary. It teaches us that every person has hidden talents, that we are stronger and more able than we know, and that one person can make a difference in the world. This is what I hoped I would find in myself one day.

I was typing on my computer in the dawn hours while the rest of the neighbourhood slept. An object the size of a thermos flew past my window, bounced like a football, and rolled into the yard. I switched on the yard light and ran outside. I stood there astonished, afraid, staring at the creature lying stunned beside its craft, which glowed white-hot before fading to grey and slowly crumbling to ash. When the ash had cooled, I bent over and took the limp creature into my hands. My glasses were fogging up. I took a deep breath and closed my eyes.

'Calm, Jules, calm,' I said. 'Slow breaths, relax the muscles, put the thing down.'

On the kitchen table the creature's limbs shivered and its skin, the colour of raw chicken, puckered in the chilly morning air.

With my hands encased in pink rubber gloves I carried it from location to location in the house. No matter where I put the creature down it squirmed, so I would lift it hurriedly, worried I was causing it distress. Finally, when I lowered it into my underwear drawer, it nestled into the silk fabric of an old petticoat like a puppy snuggling into a dog's belly.

Mouldy carrots and cheese from my fridge didn't tempt the creature. I raced to the supermarket and brought home everything from pig's liver to sesame seeds. Nothing made it stir until I brought out the broccoli. Slowly a suckered foot stretched out and closed around a broccoli floret. When the limb uncurled, the food was gone. It did the same with tiny portions of spinach, string beans, lettuce – anything green.

After it had eaten, I slid my hands into the new silk gloves I had bought and picked the creature up, careful to cup its spindly limbs. It trembled like a chihuahua for a few seconds before relaxing into my hands.

'Don't be afraid,' I whispered.

On the first day the neighbourhood was quiet, I took the creature out to the yard and placed it on the grass where it grazed, chewing the blades down to the earth. A white foamy slime trail, its waste I suppose, showed where it had travelled across the lawn. I heard my neighbour's car pulling into the driveway and hurried to scoop the creature into my hands and carry it back inside. A day later, when my neighbour, Denise, was watering her garden, she saw the network of silver trails criss-crossing the grass.

'I've got snail pellets if you want some,' she said, pointing to the trail leading toward the vegetable garden.

I shrugged. 'Live and let live,' I said to her and she laughed.

'You really are a strange one,' she said.

'Do these feel familiar?' I asked the alien, putting an empty water glass and a small volcanic rock in the drawer. The alien's limbs rippled over the surfaces and inside the rim of the glass. I tried an ice cube and a screwdriver, watching as it read the shape of the objects like a blind person.

The next day I borrowed braille books from the library and left them in the drawer. Each time I looked the pages had been turned. I bought a fountain pen and green ink and marked out the dots of the braille alphabet on a piece of paper that I also slipped into the drawer.

Every day I had to wash the silk petticoat of its slime trail.

'Imagine if someone saw this,' I said to the alien.

I bought two metres of expensive silk and lined the drawer. My petticoat went into a plastic bag. I knew that one day I would have to tell people about the alien and they would want all kinds of evidence.

'Why are you here?' I asked by writing a braille message in green ink on paper and leaving it in the drawer. The creature communicated with me by pressing the pads of its feet against the paper. Needle jets of green, a bright chlorophyll green, spurted from the pads and it answered me in braille dots on the paper. It wrote an odd broken English it had learnt from reading the braille books I had borrowed from the library. There were many Regency romances.

The reply said, 'Dear Lady. If you will allow. Express my feelings toward your home. This marvellous journey. A word in your ear.'

I took days to decipher the message because the creature's ink had bled into the paper. The dots were not spread evenly like printed braille but more like a finger painting or a Rorschach blob.

Next, I asked the creature's name.

'Viscount Ryland Pennington,' he answered.

I laughed and then wept. Viscount Ryland Pennington. Like the name of a romance hero. I realised that loneliness and isolation had finally broken me. The madness of writing.

'You seem so real,' I said to the Viscount. I stroked him with my fingertip.

I said that to the counsellor I booked into first thing the next morning. 'I'm having a nervous breakdown. I believe an alien landed in my backyard and is living in my underwear drawer. It's all so real.' Her eyebrows lifted when I said underwear.

'The alien,' I said, 'communicates with me in braille and is called Viscount Ryland Pennington.' By this time I was laughing, gasping for breath. 'He calls me Dear Lady, and My One Love.' The counsellor waited while my hiccups and snorting slowed.

'I think I have a problem,' I said.

'Yes, Julie,' she answered slowly. 'It's good that you recognise it's a problem.'

I giggled wearily. The counsellor looked down at my sheet.

'You're a writer?' she said. 'What do you write?'

All my laughter was spent. 'At the moment I'm writing about a universe with a fifth dimension. Like quantum physics.'

She smiled nervously and wrote a note. Her hair was pulled back into a tight bun and she wore a suit and held her head on one side like an experienced listener, but I guessed her age at twenty-seven or twenty-eight. She suggested medication to stabilise my anxiety.

'I know a good GP,' she said. 'You're obviously agitated. We'll get you a prescription and my receptionist will book some sessions so we can talk.'

I refused the drugs. I prefer to avoid even headache pills and, anyway, this problem was not anxiety. I understood anxiety.

'Would you like me to bring the alien in here?' I asked. 'Perhaps you could tell me it was a rubber toy or something and I'd be cured.'

'Does the alien speak to you, Julie? Does it tell you to do things?'

'Not really,' I said. 'He's written me a few notes.'

When I arrived home I found the next message from the Viscount in the drawer.

'Dear Lady. Our need to communicate. You alone My Love. Speak to me.'

Each spurt of ink left him pale and floppy, and after a bout of writing he needed several days of grazing to recover. The lawn was quickly shorn to dry nubs of chewed-off grass. Denise, calling over the fence, suggested the gardener was overdoing it.

'When did you get a gardener anyway?' she asked.

I wished she would stop watching me. Before her husband ran off, Denise had spoken about fifty words to me. Now she dropped in, she called over the fence, she left notes in my letterbox.

Wheatgrass seemed to give the Viscount more strength but the health food shop told me they couldn't grow it fast enough to meet my needs. I ordered deliveries from the wholesaler.

I imagined Denise inside her house taking notes. I thought she should get a job. Her children were away all day and sometimes I could hear her rattling around inside the house like a tin toy. The vacuum cleaner would drone for five minutes, a pop song would burst into the air followed by silence, the aroma of cakes and biscuits would waft across my yard before she brought them over in Tupperware containers. 'They'll keep for months in the freezer,' she told me.

'How's the new gardener?' she asked again, winking.

'He's quite charming,' I told her, knowing I was stupid to say it and that she'd be looking over the fence even more often. 'He writes me notes,' I said.

'Ooh la,' Denise squeaked. 'What's his name?'

'Ryland,' I told her.

'Ryland? How posh!'

The counsellor suggested that I attend sessions twice a week. Session Two, we discussed my childhood.

'Did you read a lot?'

'I'm a writer, what do you think?'

'I don't know,' she replied, deadpan, 'you tell me.'

'Look, I've never done counselling before. Is this what we're going to do – talk about my childhood? I think my problem's a bit more urgent than that.'

She recommended drugs again and I refused. She warned me that this kind of delusion could be the precursor to a full psychotic episode. I said she was on the wrong track.

'I feel calmer than I've felt in years,' I told her.

Session Three I brought in polaroid shots I had taken of the Viscount. She shuffled through the photographs, making odd little sounds.

'This looks like some kind of seafood,' she said.

I laughed. 'Well if it is, it should be pretty smelly by now.'

She reared back when I leaned toward her and took the snapshots from her hand.

'I'll bring the real thing in next time.'

The counsellor winced. 'I might invite my colleague to join us,' she said.

I stared at her. Did she think I would attack her with a rubber alien? If anyone was causing me anxiety it was the counsellor. The Viscount, real or not, had the opposite effect – he had given me a sense of purpose.

In the movies, when a UFO lands, the government always tracks down its whereabouts and sends agents to kidnap the aliens from the well-meaning citizen. No one came for the Viscount. On the day I was supposed to attend Session Four with the counsellor, I decided to give up the therapy. I was still washing the slime off the silk every day, I had an alien and a box full of notes at home and I had spent a fortune on wheatgrass. How deluded could I be? If I'd ingested that much wheatgrass I would have turned green.

The Viscount had things to tell me. I attempted to interpret his phrasing and syntax without prejudice but, perhaps because of the Regency romances, he did appear to be flirting with me while he imparted information about himself and his world. The flirting made me think about love. I thought about what love might mean to another species, how you could explain it when even humans can rarely explain it to each other.

At night I lay in bed imagining myself telling my friends about the Viscount. He comes from a very distant place, I would say to them. Where? they'd ask. But I couldn't answer. He calls it My Distant Estate. And his name. I would tell them, It's a translation. You know, like when someone from China called Xia Hue says, Call me Sadie. His real name is probably pronounced with pops and hiccups from some orifice we wouldn't even identify as a mouth, I'd say to them. And I knew they would laugh.

'Dear Viscount,' I asked him again, 'why have you come here?'

Two days later I had my answer. I noticed that he refused to use commas, although when I checked, the books he had learned from were filled with punctuation of all kinds. I wondered whether this was a sign about his own language. Perhaps even his thoughts were filled with long pauses that deserved more than the brief hiatus of a comma.

'Sweet One. I am charged with a duty. A chance encounter with fate. Your green milieu. My own Estate indisposed. My Dear Lady your charms ensnared me.'

He is on a mission, I interpreted. He comes from a planet of green that is dying. He is researching our green world. They want to colonise earth because they are running short of chlorophyll on their planet.

'Where is your estate?' I wrote. 'Can your people come to get you?'

I was so busy trying to nurture the Viscount when he first arrived that I was not thinking of the wider implications of his arrival. I am still amazed that we learned to communicate so easily – I have had more trouble understanding fellow human beings. But before long I became uneasy, knowing that I should give him to the world. Each day I told myself I would do something soon, as soon as he had explained to me what he needed, as soon as I had understood all I could about him, as soon as I was ready to lose him.

I waited for the Viscount's answer but none came. I opened the drawer and looked inside. The Viscount had barely moved. After three days I began to worry. I lifted the Viscount from the drawer and placed him on the lino floor of the kitchen, surrounded by the snipped stalks of wheatgrass he loved. He lay still.

At the veterinary hospital, a rambunctious golden retriever kept pawing at the cardboard box holding the Viscount. The dog's owner smiled and nodded at me and patted the dog as if such behaviour was cute. My name was called. Inside the surgery, I lifted the Viscount from the box and laid him gently on the stainless steel examination table.

'My God,' the veterinarian said. 'What is it?'

'I don't know,' I answered.

The vet was a thin man of Asian descent. His hands were slim and clean, and he lifted the Viscount's limbs gently. He inserted a thermometer into a body opening I had never noticed on the Viscount. I suppose I had been a little shy in my dealings with him – poking and prodding him, touching and squeezing his small body would have seemed like an assault.

The veterinarian retrieved the thermometer, examined it and shook his head. He stood opposite me across the shiny silver table. As he spoke, he fondled one of the Viscount's delicate limbs with one hand while stroking his body with the other. I realised this man must truly love the creatures in his care.

'Normally, an animal with birth defects this severe would not survive. How long have you had it?'

'Only a few weeks,' I said.

He shook his head again and squeezed his face into a sympathetic frown.

'I honestly don't think it will live much longer. Have you given it a name?'

'Viscount Ryland Pennington.'

The vet bent his head and leaned in toward the Viscount.

'Well, little fella,' he murmured, loudly enough for me to hear. 'Maybe it would be kinder to let you go, Ryland?'

The vet didn't look at my face. He was probably used to people crying in his surgery. While I tried to compose myself he kept stroking the Viscount, murmuring reassurances to him.

'Make it easy on you both, hey?'

'I can't do that,' I said when I had caught my breath.

I lifted the Viscount as gently as I could and laid him back on the silk bed in the box. I paid the vet's bill at the reception counter and hurried past the golden retriever lunging at the box.

At my front gate I met Denise. She stared at the box as she asked me over for dinner the next week.

'It's about time,' she said. 'I can't believe I haven't had you over yet.' She put her hand on my arm. 'I'll get the kids to bed early. We can have a glass of wine.' I noticed how thin she was getting.

'That would be nice,' I said. I wondered what we would talk about.

Three days later, the Viscount showed no more signs of life. His cool inert body felt different to my touch. I thought he had died, but how could I be sure? I left him in the drawer for another day, then I wrapped him, together with his notes, in silk and plastic and put him in the freezer.

That weekend, my writing group came to the house. One of them was rummaging in the freezer for icecubes when the Viscount's body, wrapped in its shroud, tumbled to the floor. We were sitting at the kitchen table and she turned to us with the package of the Viscount in her hands.

'Hey, Jules, is this octopus?' she asked. 'Are you supposed to wrap it up like this before you freeze it? Maybe that why mine's always so tough.'

I had thought I would tell the story of the Viscount to the writing group but that day I changed my mind.

'Yes, you should try it,' I said.

I got up from my chair, took the Viscount from her hands and put him carefully back in the cold dry freezer.

In a hero's journey the heroine is supposed to understand the clues. She overcomes obstacles with powers she never knew she had.

No special powers have manifested in me. Although I cared for the Viscount as best I could and tried to understand what I should do, he died. Perhaps my journey is supposed to lead on from here, but I have discovered that I am no heroine. I have no guide, the messenger is dead, and I am weak with grief.

The End of the World

To Genghis Khan, Oblivion and Holy Russia

James Halford

In a youth hostel in Ulaanbaatar, Outer Mongolia, a party was underway. Thin, miserable snow drifted down outside. A drunk weaved his way through the early evening traffic. A little distance down the road, a trio of street children lay curled up at the foot of a five-metre-high statue of Lenin.

There were about thirty people in all, crammed into the kitchen. A table was pushed against the wall. It was covered with photographs, used tea-bags, rolling papers, half-a-dozen empty cans of Korean beer, an overflowing ashtray, a sizeable bag of hash, a half-eaten tin of sardines and a small, plastic globe (made in China) on which Mongolia was marked as part of Russia. Beneath the window was a narrow bench, with a toaster and teapot placed where a thoughtful soul might gaze out at the locals shivering at the bus stop below, while buttering their toast and waiting for the jug to boil.

A bespectacled German was buttering now, chatting over his shoulder to a dreadlocked girl from Israel, who was cooking a vegetable curry on the stove.

'There's an exhibition at the modern art gallery,' he was saying, 'called *Eighty-Seven Renderings of the Sea.* Now, Mongolia is a landlocked country. None of these artists have ever seen the sea. And the interesting thing is, the sea always looks curved, and the waves always look suspiciously like clouds.'

'The thing I find strange is all this.' The Israeli girl gestured around the room. 'It's strange to be in a place, but feel you could be anywhere at all.'

The German nodded, moving to the stove and breathing the scent of her hair and that of the curry commingled.

'You come to the end of the earth,' he said, 'and find it full of people like you, doing exactly the same thing you're doing.'

By the cook-top sat a cheap, smug, copperplated Buddha (made in China), with two sticks of incense before it. A Canadian girl wearing a pink scarf knelt down and lit the incense with a cigarette lighter in the shape of a pig. It gave out two small but intense tendrils of flame, one from each nostril.

'I picked this up today at the black market,' she was saying to a barrel-chested South African in a tight T-shirt. 'It only cost me three Canadian dollars.'

'That's great,' lied the South African, eager to appear interested. 'What else did you get?'

'I'll show you,' she said, making for the dormitory. As she left the kitchen, she changed the channel on the television. She always changed the channel when leaving a room, to register how different things would be without her presence.

In the corner opposite the window stood an American in a baseball cap, watching the television soundlessly flicker. In his fist was a cup of fermented mare's milk. A thin line of the sour, white liquid coated his lips, droplets flicking to the floor as he spoke.

'Oh my God!' he said to no one in particular. 'I can't believe they get this here.' There was American wrestling on the television. He proceeded to film the action with a handheld video camera, stepping backward to get a clearer shot of the screen. As he did so, he bumped into a drunken Frenchman, whose thickly-furred eyebrows dipped and joined at the bridge of his nose. He had been about to take a swig from a bottle of Bulgarian red wine, but instead he glared at the American. For the past twenty minutes, the Frenchman had been sitting on an overturned milk crate staring at a photograph on the table. The image, propped against a bottle of Chinggis Khan vodka that he had already drained, showed a woman in repose beneath a cypress in Marseille.

'Sorry,' said the American.

'Fuck off American,' said the Frenchman. He returned his gaze to the photo, muttering under his breath as before:

Que tu es belle, ma compagne, que tu es belle!
Tes yeux sont des colombes
Derrière ton voile.

Then, switching his glass to the other hand as he switched languages: 'So beautiful. So beautiful.'

The American had also managed to spill his drink on the trousers of a thickly-bearded Russian. Before he could apologise, the other man clambered up onto the bench by the window. He tripped over the toaster (made in China), then regained his balance, then tried to stand upright, then finally bumped his tousled head on the ceiling.

'Atten-tion!' he roared, but was barely audible over an Irish girl in a striped beanie, singing a folk song about a mining disaster:

He woulda fought for Old Ireland with cutlass and cannon
But my love's lost in the black pits of Carrick-on-Shannon.

'Atten-tion!' the Russian shouted again, and this time the noise subsided. With a flourish, he twisted the lid from a bottle of vodka, barking: 'Glas-ses!'

The party crowded around, presenting their vessels. To speed up the process, a red-nosed Scot and a fur-collared Swede seized two more bottles and helped pour the drinks. When all glasses were charged, the Russian solemnly held his own aloft. He looked at the liquid as he spoke, never at his audience.

'Now, don't judge me,' he said in English, 'but the truth is I am not a good man. Ask anyone respectable and they'll tell you.' He cleared his throat noisily. 'My own mother attached a note with the last cheque she sent me.' He put on a shrill voice: '"This is for your tuition fees. If you spend it on booze, I shall know once and for all that you're a vagabond and a nihilist". Ladies and gentlemen, with that cheque, I bought the drink that now fills your glasses.'

A roar of approval went up.

'No no, I am not a good man,' he went on, extracting a mobile phone from his jacket pocket. 'But I am an honest one. Placing truth over virtue, I intend to call up that woman right now and tell her that I am raging drunk in Mongolia.'

More cheers. The Russian dialed the number and the crowd thrust their glasses toward the ceiling in anticipation. There was a pause as he waited for an answer. Then a small, shrill voice was heard at the other end of the line. The Russian interrupted it.

'To Genghis Khan, oblivion and holy Russia!' he bellowed into the receiver, draining his cup. The crowd drank with him, then watched as he wrenched the window open, and flung both phone and glass into the night. A moment later the sky was alive with blood-curdling cries and glasses plummeting to the pavement.

'Look out,' said a Japanese girl, blinking her false lashes. 'You hit someone.'

In the street below, the horse trader Yundensambuugiin Bathaan was in fine spirits. He had also been consuming fine spirits, stumbling about with a bottle in a brown bag, hollering words of his own composition to a traditional melody:

Little mushrooms, little mushrooms
In winter can't be found.
But in summer little mushrooms poke their heads out of the ground.
Little mushrooms.

The currency in Mongolia is the togrog, which roughly translates as 'small spherical fungus.' Today, though it was autumn and ten below freezing, the pockets of Yunden's overcoat positively bulged with 'little mushrooms.' He had had something of a windfall.

Early that morning, half-a-dozen Texan tourists had visited Yunden's home in the outskirts of the city – a domed yurt, comprised of a wooden frame wrapped in many layers of animal fur. Those beasts not yet turned into insulation grazed the surrounding pastures. Yunden's cousin, Dambadorj, who drove a taxi and spoke a little English, often picked up potential customers at the airport and brought them directly to him, while they were still jet-lagged and vulnerable. The group of Americans who had arrived that morning – a fast-talking oil baron with his two brothers and some buddies – wanted to take a horse trek out to Khentii Aimag to see Genghis Khan's home territory. Why did foreigners always say 'Genghis' instead of 'Chinggis'? Yunden wondered.

They had just stepped off the plane and were blithely unaware of local prices, but this didn't bother them, since their collective fortune was equivalent to Mongolia's gross domestic profit for the previous year. They'd bought six prime stallions, as well as riding boots, saddles and a spectacular collection of stylish, wide-brimmed hats. After yahooing about the property with their long legs almost dragging on the ground beneath the small Mongolian horses, the Americans had produced a mixed bundle of US dollars and togrog so enormous that Yunden could scarcely keep a straight face. Adding to the comedy was the fact that the local currency was nearly worthless. It took the men the best part of forty-five minutes to count out the agreed figure and Dambadorj kept smirking beneath his cowboy hat.

'Is very cheap horse for you,' he kept telling them. When they finally came to the serious end of the deal, things moved much more quickly. The oil baron handed over a smaller wad of American dollars, which was still of such imposing dimensions that Yunden completely forgot to count it. He took the money and stuffed it into his left boot, the safest hiding place he could think of.

'*Ba-yar-laa*,' he said quickly, to which his cousin added:

'This is meaning thank you much.' The two Mongolians watched in amused disbelief as the lanky foreigners rode east on their tiny horses, where the sun was still low in the sky.

Yunden and Dambadorj proceeded directly to a local gambling den, where they ate hot goulash and drank vodka and lost previously unthinkable amounts at roulette. They were ejected from the premises some hours later, for attempting to play the game with a meatball, both men light-headed and lighter in the pocket. Dambadorj disappeared to buy himself a Russian girl for the day, leaving Yunden alone to wander the streets.

Not long after, passing the monastery, he came across an old man playing a horsehead fiddle – 'The Dance of Ortos,' a haunting melody that floated up toward the eaves of the beautiful old wooden building. Listening to the old song in the shadow of the old walls made Yunden feel generous toward the world, so he took a note out of his pocket. He laughed with delight as the money fluttered down into the musician's upturned hat.

Flushed with happiness, he ran inside, plucking a stick of incense from a table by the door, lighting it and placing it at the altar. With the old man's song still resounding in his ears, he ran clockwise around the interior of the building, spinning the prayer wheels and flinging money at the bases of the many manifestations of Buddha that lined the walls, praying that his good fortune would continue. Back out into the street he ran, and he was singing now, making up the words and weaving through the traffic on Peace Avenue.

Little mushrooms, little mushrooms are what everybody needs.
Brought from foreign pastures
Exchanged for hardy Mongolian steeds.
Little mushrooms.

Then there was a whistling sound and a swift stabbing sensation in his temple. Yunden went to ground.

Up in the guesthouse, this was the cause of some consternation.

'He's gone down in the road,' said the German, flicking a piece of jam from his upper lip.

'Who is he?' demanded the Swede, further from the window.

'A drunk,' replied the Israeli.

'Drunks are easily knocked down,' said the Swede. 'No matter.'

'Is he OK?' asked the South African, eyeing the Canadian girl.

'You're not looking at my bag,' she said, showing an imitation pink Versace handbag (made in China) that she had purchased at the market. 'Isn't it cute?'

'He's not getting up,' said the red-nosed Scot.

'A bus is coming,' said the Japanese girl, with some urgency.

'I've got to get this on film,' said the American, shifting his camera from the television to the window.

'So beautiful,' said the Frenchman, still intent on his photograph. He switched his drink to the other hand. '*C'est une belle femme.*'

'Look at those people at the bus stop,' said the Israeli. 'Why don't they help him? He'll get run over.'

'This is called "the bystander effect,"' said the German. 'Everybody thinks someone else will help.'

'Why don't you do something then?' demanded the Israeli.

'I don't know the emergency number,' said the German. 'I don't even know if they have an emergency number in Mongolia.'

'The bus is getting quite close now,' said the Japanese girl.

'Tourism,' continued the German, 'is learning to look at something, without seeing it at all.'

'Damn, my zoom isn't working,' said the American.

The alarm went off on the stove. 'Shit,' said the Israeli girl, 'my curry's boiled over.' She rushed back to her cooking and switched off the alarm.

A car horn sounded in the street.

'The bus is not stopping,' said the Swede.

'I can't watch,' said the Irish girl, watching intently.

The bus stopped.

'Thank God,' said the South African, again glancing at the Canadian.

'You're not looking at my hat,' she said, modelling a furry, brown Russian-style hat with ear muffs (made in China). 'Isn't it cute?'

'They're picking him up,' said the Scot. 'Three of them, kids. They're moving him off the road.'

'That's good,' said the Israeli, tasting her curry, 'but it needs more spice.' She swung around at the sound of a general intake of breath. 'What's happened? What's the matter?'

'They dropped him,' said the South African. 'Quite hard. He landed on his head.' The Israeli continued stirring the mixture in the pot. The group gasped again and this time she left her cooking, rushing to the window.

'What now?' she asked.

'That little urchin in the blue,' said the Swede, 'has just stolen his boots.'

'Where's that Russian?' asked the South African. 'He's the one that's responsible. He's disappeared.'

'There he is, down there,' said the Israeli. 'What's he doing?'

'He's taking his pulse,' cried the Scot. 'He's shaking him. He's not moving.'

'Do you mean,' said the Swede, 'that one of us has ... I mean one of our glasses has ...'

Nobody spoke, except for the Russian's mother, whose voice squawked from a pile of icy slush in the gutter. The Mongolians below looked up at the bright window, and those in the hostel pressed against the pane, watching snow fall slanted in the street.

Voiceworks

Hemingway's Elephants

John Holton

I suppose I should have been more shocked to meet Ernest Hemingway on the Broadmeadows train – not least because he blew his brains out in 1961, three years before I was even born, when Broadmeadows was just paddocks of Scotch thistles.

You could tell he was embarrassed to see someone reading *Men Without Women*. This was 1988 – sixty years after its publication. It was published the same year my father was born on a kitchen table in Coburg. It reads like it was written yesterday.

'I'm reading the elephant one,' I said to Hemingway. 'Do you remember the elephant one? We all read it at school. I bet you never dreamed they'd be reading it in schools after you were dead.'

Hemingway looked confused for a moment and then said, '"Hills Like White Elephants?"' His voice was much higher than I'd imagined, but that could be a symptom of death.

'Yes, that's the one. I've always liked stories about elephants. I especially like Kipling – *The Jungle Book*. There were several elephants in that one.'

'I shot an elephant once,' Hemingway said with a certain pride. 'But it's not really about elephants.'

'But it says here about the colour of their skin through the trees.'

'Yes, but she's talking about the hills. It's about relationships. Not elephants.'

'But hills don't have skin,' I said dubiously. 'Why mention the skin if it's not about elephants?'

'Because it's suggestive of elephants,' Hemingway said. 'It's symbolic, don't you see?'

'Well, why mention elephants at all then? It seems a little strange – if they're not real. Aren't you just disappointing all the people who like to read about elephants?'

'Quite,' was all that Hemingway said.

'Quite, indeed!'

It was quiet for a moment, apart from the rhythmic clickety-clack of the train. Hemingway looked at his watch and scratched nervously at his beard.

'What about *The Killers*?' I asked, not letting him off the hook. After all, this elephant fraud was a man who'd won a Nobel Prize for literature.

'What about *The Killers*?' Hemingway said, sounding agitated.

'Well, is it about real killers? It seems to be more about sandwiches. Are the sandwiches the killers? I mean are *they* symbolic?'

'What sandwiches?' Hemingway was being downright aggressive now.

'He orders sandwiches. You wrote it – how can you forget the sandwiches? Are they like the elephants? Are they just symbolic sandwiches – is that what you're saying?'

Hemingway was wiping his brow with a handkerchief as the train pulled into North Melbourne station. He was out of the door in a flash – swept up by the rush-hour crowd – his camouflage hunting jacket fading into the jungle of commuters.

I didn't see Hemingway on the Broadmeadows train again. I looked for him every day, though. I had some serious questions about the opening page of *A Farewell To Arms.*

Allnighter

Bag Lady

Marele Day

I first noticed the bag lady around the time the ibises moved into town. I never feed those birds. The man next door does. He's on a disability pension though heaven knows what his disability is. He and his mates sit on the front verandah drinking beer all day. The birds loiter around the letterbox and the men throw them bits of their lunch – hamburger, fish and chips, whatever.

I never feed the ibises because it only encourages them. They'd hang around waiting for more like they do next door, hunched over like vultures. They shouldn't be in town in the first place, it's not their natural habitat. I don't mind the seagulls. They, at least, take pride in their appearance – cleaned, preened, every feather in place. The ibises have let themselves go.

They have forgotten their noble lineage. In ancient Egypt they were revered, sacred. Thoth, the god associated with writing, knowledge, and judging of the dead, was depicted with an ibis head. Mind you, some of those ancient Egyptians resemble ibises anyway. Take a look at Cleopatra's nose.

I can see the long curved ibis beak dipped in ink, writing messages on the banks of the Nile. When I told my boss about the link between the ibis and writing, she laughed and said perhaps we should call ourselves Ibis Office Supplies. It's a bit of a tongue twister, imagine answering the phone and having to say that. Worse still if it were Thoth Office Supplies.

I enjoy the job at Officeworld, the premises of which are not as grand as the name implies. I love the paper and pens, the satisfying weight of a ream of Reflex Pure White, Australia's top-selling office paper brand, 100% guaranteed for all printers and copies, sustainable timber sources only. On the dark blue packaging it doesn't say ream but 500 sheets, A4 80 gsm. A ream equals twenty quires. The only place you see those words nowadays is on a Scrabble board.

We also stock coloured paper, marbled and fine handmade sheets for people doing craft projects or connoisseurs who simply enjoy the pleasure of handwriting with quality pen and paper.

One of those connoisseurs is Keith. He's a small man with a pointed beard. Keith writes chick lit, under a pseudonym. 'Is it a name I would know?' 'Oh definitely,' he says. But he won't tell me what it is. Keith's favourite pen is an Artline 200 fine 0.4, made by Shachihata. He likes to write his first draft by hand. He buys different coloured pens so that he can keep track of the characters on the page, to make sure they are all getting roughly the same amount of words. 'Narrative space,' he calls it. If we happen to have run out of green, a colour for which there is not much call, he sighs and frowns, and stands in the shop not knowing quite what to do. I tell him the green pens are on order and will be here in a couple of days. 'OK, I'll wait.' He stands there for so long I'm thinking he intends to do the waiting here in the shop.

The bag lady hitchhikes between the town where I live and the town where I work, a twenty-minute drive away. All day, that's what she does, travelling backwards and forwards. I usually see her on my way to work but never pick her up. I don't want to start anything. If I give her a lift once she'll expect me to do it every time. Worse, she might come to my house. She must know where I live, recognise the car parked in the driveway, it's near one of her waiting points.

When I drive past her, I pretend to be distracted with something else – touch my hair, fiddle with the radio, examine something on the dashboard. I always wear sunglasses when I'm driving, she wouldn't necessarily know I've seen her.

She wears sunglasses too, those big Cancer Council recommended wrap-arounds. She is sensibly dressed for standing out in the sun – baggy trousers, runners, a loose long-sleeved top – red jumper in winter, plain grey cotton shirt in summer. She doesn't wear a hat. Her hair is tied back in a long plait, exposing her brave forehead, her tanned, weathered face. A hat would be a good idea.

One morning when there wasn't much traffic, I saw her looking up at clouds the shape of continents, with oceans of blue sky in between. She watched them move overhead, like the slow turning of the earth.

At first I didn't realise that she spent most of her time travelling backwards and forwards. I do too but I have a purpose – going to work in the morning, coming home in the afternoon. I thought she had a destination, a place she wanted to go, but when she arrives in the next town she crosses the road and starts hitching back.

My boss says she heard that for ten dollars the bag lady will give the driver a blow job. I'm shocked she's repeated such a thing. Keith gave the bag lady a lift once. She asked him for a couple of dollars but he didn't say anything about her making sexual overtures. See how rumours spread in small towns, how easy it is to get ostracised? Someone surmises something and the next thing you know, it's all over town. In the absence of facts people make up stories.

I did a bit of hitchhiking when I was young, footloose and fancy-free, when the contents of my backpack were all I owned in the world. My boyfriend and I slept in farmers' fields, on beaches, railway benches. Once we got a lift from London all the way to the top of Scotland arriving in Inverness at 2 a.m. We slept in the doorway of a cathedral, in the space between the big wrought-iron gates and the ornately engraved double doors. Even though we had all our clothes on and were nestled in a sleeping bag it didn't protect us from the stone-cold stones. We laughed about how freezing it was.

The bag lady has bags. About six of them. She can't carry them all at once, so does a relay, two at a time, moving her belongings from one place to another. One Saturday morning on my way to the shops I saw two of them, unaccompanied – the tattered green and white sports bag, and another made of canvas that was coming apart at the seams, revealing the lining but not the contents.

I'm not that curious about what's inside – clothes probably. The red jumper itself would take up one whole bag.

I could see her coming towards me, with another two, heading to where the first pair were waiting like obedient children. I had a bag, for my shopping. We were on equal footing – both carrying bags, both walking – so I said hello as we passed each other. It's a small friendly town, everyone says hello or good morning. She did something with her mouth that I took to be a smile, although it was a bit crooked, as if a visit to the dentist had left one side of her face numb.

When I looked back to where the bags were waiting, I saw three ibises on the strip of grass between the road and the footpath. They were poised, very still, like the pink flamingo statues that grace some of the gardens in town. The bag lady dropped crusts of bread on the ground for them.

You know, I think the ibises might actually like garbage and scraps. Our town is on a river, there are plenty of aquatic creatures, insects, worms, the food they should be eating. Ibises aren't the only ones who prefer junk. We have a very good health food shop, but some people, the man next door for example, get most of their meals from the take-away place.

One morning, when I'm out jogging earlier than usual, and the sun is only just beginning to make an appearance, I look up and see ibises in flight. I don't even recognise them at first, they are bold, majestic, a V-shaped flotilla planing through the air over the river, their wings tipped with light, their gleaming bodies out-stretched.

The ibises settle onto the dewy grass of the park, fold up their white breath-filled wings and become the familiar humped creatures poking in the grass with their ink-black beaks.

That same morning I see the bag lady coming from the direction of the service station, a bag in each hand. I jog by. On the footpath outside the service station are the rest of the bags, I go on a little further then stop, do some stretches, bending one knee and extending the opposite leg, arching my torso, surreptitiously watching the bag lady through the space between my thigh and elbow. She comes back for the remaining bags, bends down then lifts them simultaneously, like they are the handles of a wheelbarrow, and carries them to where the others are. Now she can begin her day.

Where does she go at night? I come home from work, make dinner, watch TV, go to bed. I am one of those light-filled windows, a house from which emanates the aroma of lamb roasting, garlic and fragrant herbs. I'm artificially illuminated, closed off from the outside, from the night the bag lady inhabits.

While I'm watching TV I think about possible places. In the park? Under a tree? Along the river you sometimes see remnants of a fire, a few empty beer bottles, but it would be damp and dewy in the morning.

I keep thinking about it, lying in bed in my warm pyjamas, wondering where she is. Discovering where the bag lady goes at night would fill me with as much joy as finding a bird's nest. Under a building? The community hall or one of the churches? They are built on stumps because the river used to flood. There's a space between the floor and the ground but it's boarded up. In my mind I range around the town. She has to sleep somewhere. Then it is obvious – the service station, where I saw her so early in the morning.

I get out of bed and put on my tracksuit and runners.

The town is eerie, deserted, a different place. The petrol pumps and service-station shop are lit up. She wouldn't sleep where she could be so easily seen. I go around to the back where there's no light. There's a corridor of space between the building and the paling fenced but it's too dark to see inside. I edge my foot in slowly, warily, I don't want to give the bag lady a fright. I continue on, one step after the other. I am in a long black tunnel. The air is thick as velvet. It's disorienting, I can't see. Mostly the path is smooth, but sometimes underfoot I feel a stick, the slipperiness of a plastic bag. Then I'm out, on the other side.

She's not here. Perhaps she knows I've been watching her and is deliberately staying away. Perhaps she is watching me. Even now. The thought catches in my throat. When I gasp, the night rushes in, cold, dry and black.

The nocturnal excursion has upset my bio-rhythms. I wake up late, so postpone the jog till after work. While it's still light I run along the bike path to the bowling club and the playing fields beyond, then I track back into town, take the footbridge across the river, jog along the bank till I reach the car bridge then cross back over. By the time it's properly dark I'm homeward bound, through the streetlights, past the pub and up the main road, Chinese restaurant on one side, take-away food shop on the other.

I go the next day after work as well. There's quite a tribe of people out at this time. Even if you don't watch the actual sunset there is something peaceful, transformative about jogging from day into night. Although it's the end of the day, the beginning of evening has the freshness of dawn. There's the cheery optimism of houselights coming on, the chirrup of crickets, kids being picked up from judo and jazz ballet, dinners being cooked. Various birds – mynahs, pigeons, lorikeets, sometimes even kookaburras – signal the passage, the change in the air. I've only once ever heard an ibis call. Apparently they don't do it very often. It was a dull croak, like a duck with something caught in its gullet.

On the third night I see the bag lady sitting outside the take-away, her belongings stowed under a bench. On the other bench are three teenage girls eating hamburgers. Perhaps the bag lady too has eaten, and is enjoying a quiet moment before retiring. There is a big bin on the footpath, ibises hang around here during the day, but they disappear at nightfall, cross the river and roost in the trees.

I could do it now – wait and see where she goes. It's all very well following someone in the city, where there are lots of people to hide behind, but not so easy in a town this size. I enter the shop, pretend I'm going to buy something, but I came out for a run and didn't bring any money with me.

Though I've lived here for several years this is the first time I've been into the take-away. The shop is from the old days, when the main road was still part of the highway, before the town was by-passed. It's a general store really. As well as take-away it sells cans of baked beans and spaghetti that have probably been there since the highway days, cartons of milk, butter, drinks, sometimes bananas or apples, newspapers.

I glance outside. The teenage girls have left but the bag lady is still there. The woman sitting at the cash register flicking through a magazine finally says: 'We're about to close. Can I help you?'

'I was looking for … capers.' Weirdo, she's probably thinking.

'Oh,' I say, patting non-existent pockets and confirming her suspicions, 'I've forgotten my wallet.'

The bag lady remains on the bench, even after the woman bolts the shop door and turns the sign around to read CLOSED. She just sits there as if nothing disturbs her, as if she is having her portrait painted.

I wait. It's starting to get cold. I could sit on the other bench but that would be too obvious. I move a little further along, towards the corner. A car comes along the side street, its blinker on, ready to turn left onto the main road. The driver slows down and stops, even though there is no traffic. He's giving way to me but I wave him on, I don't want to cross. He's waiting for me to do it. Finally I turn my back. Yes, that's right, I'm standing on the corner not going anywhere. Do you have a problem with that? I hear the car take off, the unnecessary revving. The driver probably thinks this is the gathering point for weirdos – me standing shivering in my singlet top, the bag lady on the bench staring into the night.

Her head turns slowly towards me, as if she has a stiff neck and moving it is painful. 'Piss off,' she says with her eyes, 'piss off.' I stand there a little longer, trying to be nonchalant, as if I haven't noticed.

She's on the road the next morning when I'm driving to work. I take my sunglasses off so that when I pass her she'll be able to see that I'm looking straight ahead, ignoring her. It's over. We grow apart, become more distant. It's getting too cold to jog in the evening now and I start going to the gym instead. I see the bag lady from time to time on my way to work but she is no more remarkable than the trees, the powerlines, the road signs I drive past every day.

It's a couple of weeks before I realise she is no longer on the road. In the evening I walk down to the take-away, but she's not there either. It might be a good thing, might mean she's found a place to live. Finally I ask.

'The bag lady?' The girl in the shop doesn't know who I mean.

'She used to sit outside. The lady with the long plait,' I want also to say, you know, the lady with all the bags, with the crooked smile. 'Usually wears a big red jumper.'

'You mean Evelyn? She died.'

For a moment I can't say anything, the breath has gone out of me, as if someone has thumped me in the chest. 'I'm sorry.' I finally find the words.

'Yeah. I think it was a stroke,' the girl comments. 'Mum said she died in her sleep.'

'Where?'

'Mum,' the girl calls out to the room in the back. 'Where did Evelyn sleep?'

'At the Catholic church. Who wants to know?'

The girl's mother comes to the counter. 'Are you a relative?' she asks. She obviously doesn't remember I was the one asking for capers.

'No, it's just that, well, I hadn't seen her hitching.'

I keep thinking about the bag lady all night. It's as if someone I knew died but I didn't know her at all, not even her name. Evelyn. I never once gave her a lift, that's all she wanted, just drove straight past.

I think about Thoth and now, instead of the ibis-headed god's link with writing, I recall his role in the judgement of the dead. Only if the heart of the deceased is as light as the sacred feather of Thoth's consort, Maat, does the soul enter the Blessed Land. If it is heavy with wicked deeds the person is damned.

The grass around the church is fresh and dewy. It is plain for a Catholic church, more like a Protestant place of worship – timber with a pitched roof, a modest cross on top. Evelyn could not have slept under the building because the space is boarded up. There are a few steps leading to the front door. It is locked. She couldn't have come in here at night.

Then I discover a smaller side door, three steps up to a landing with a dry sandy space under it. That door too is locked. On the way down the steps I notice markings in the sand and a stray feather. The markings resemble bird footprints but there's more – circles and lines around them. The pattern on the soles of shoes. The feather is a soft curved one, from a doona or sleeping bag.

I sit on the grass. I have brought wholemeal bread for the ibises, and watch the sky, waiting for them to land.

Uncle Jeremy Has Turned into a Tree

Patrick Lenton

After his wife died, Uncle Jeremy walked into the backyard and became a tree. It was strange, everyone in the family remarked, that Uncle Jeremy of all people would turn into a tree. In the highly mediocre extended Fredericks clan, Uncle Jeremy and Aunt Sue were known for being particularly boring.

Now there was cricket playing overloud in their TV room. It would have drowned out any conversation, if any had been desired. The older men just waited for their wives to collect them once the mysterious business of the funeral had been dealt with. None of them were overly sad about Sue's death, having had very little to do with her. Grandpa Fred recalled her excellent apple crumble and wondered if some may have survived in the fridge.

As the older men drank Uncle Jeremy's beer on his corduroy lounge, Grandma Beatrice and Great Aunt Mabel went through the cupboards, searching for clues to this strange shift in Uncle Jeremy's personality among the plates and the eggbeater. After every Fredericks funeral, it was custom for the women to clean the cupboards of the recently deceased's house. No one ever wondered about the practical purpose of this exercise, seeing as the dead rarely need clean cupboards. Its real purpose was to discover secrets. Evidence of used ashtrays in the pantries of supposed quitters. One too many bottles of whiskey in Cousin Henry's bedside drawer. Handcuffs in Aunt Heather's. However, the most suspicious item found in the back of a slightly dusty kitchen cupboard at Uncle Jeremy's house was a cake tray Great Aunt Mabel was sure used to belong to her.

'Nothing,' muttered Grandma Beatrice. 'Even kept her cups clean.'

'She made a lovely apple crumble though. If she'd just asked, she could have kept the tray.'

As Grandma Beatrice looked out the window and saw all the nieces and nephews playing around Uncle Jeremy, she was once again miffed at Jeremy's decision to turn into a tree. She worried it might upset the rest of the family's veneration for her own son, Harold. Harold was a qualified chiropractor, which, to the Fredericks, was as good as being a doctor. Every Christmas and Easter, Grandpa Fred would ask Harold about the pain in his lungs and the coughing that rattled his grey skin. Harold would say, 'Stop smoking those goddam cigars, Dad,' and Grandpa Fred would laugh and grip him around the neck, saying, 'Our son the medicine man, eh.'

Now Uncle Jeremy had gone and turned himself into a tree.

Aunt Cheryl talked to Aunt Myra out the back as they kept an eye on the nieces and nephews playing around Uncle Jeremy. As designated spinster aunts, Myra and Cheryl viewed the offspring of their married siblings as one amorphous mass of snotty noses and high-pitched voices. While their ovaries dried up and the cigarettes wrinkled their mouths into parched expressions of dissatisfaction, they had contemplated Uncle Jeremy and Aunt Sue. Sue, they felt, could have been a real pal, as she had never had children either, despite being married to Jeremy for longer than either of them could remember. They decided it was their marriage that was the oddest thing about them. Unlike anyone else they knew, they were very happy. In fact, too happy, they decided, nodding over newly lit cigarettes and the warm ends of their chardonnay.

'And now,' added Myra, 'he's gone and turned himself into a tree. Remember when Cousin Joe lost his Helen? Drank for two days straight and then turned up to play footy the next weekend. None of this tree nonsense.'

Jeremy had gone into the backyard almost immediately after the funeral, finding his house populated by the family he and

Sue had always successfully avoided. Each step off the back patio made him realise that, without Sue, he wasn't really alive. As though when they buried her, they had actually covered his torso with dirt as well, and now he was a pile of limbs that moved without explanation.

By the time he'd sat on a chair in the middle of the lawn, his skin was hard and brown and beginning to peel. He knew that many would contemplate suicide around now. So, closing his eyes, he thought back to his first memories of Sue and dug his feet deep into the earth.

The children watched as he began to lose shape, his legs and feet spreading into roots, brown and grey wood sheathing the chair. The memories turned into twigs, sprouting from his balding head, each strengthening and twisting higher, turning into branches, spiralling higher and higher. Jeremy became drier, evaporating and turning into thick, hard bark.

An hour later, Betty – mother of at least three of the assorted children who had ceased watching and started playing all over Jeremy – emerged from the house to give little Jai his ear medicine. She'd already fought with Bryan, her husband. He was anxious to leave, but she wasn't going until she'd collected all her Tupperware from Great Aunt Mabel, and the last thing she needed was another broken arm so soon after Cheine's fractured fibula. They all had little athletics tomorrow.

As she yelled at them to stop clambering over their Uncle Jeremy, the first of the birds started landing on his upper limbs and pecking at the white flowers that had appeared along each of the branches every time he remembered Sue. By noon he was covered in white blossoms that dropped onto the pristine lawn and blew into the house before the family shut the windows and left.

Voiceworks

Collective Silences

Sunil Badami

Feeling expansive, forgetting his oath and ethics, my father would gather us on the verandah after dinner and tell us stories of the various interesting cases he'd encountered in his long and distinguished career.

Nursing another whisky – or *digestif*, as he liked to call them – while our mother washed up, he'd tell us about the girl who grew a third ear in the back of her neck, the Siamese twins who'd fallen in love with the same lass, the man who was allergic to his wife, the woman who spoke in foreign accents despite having never left the district. As he always reminded us, he may have been terrible with names, but he always remembered patients' faces, and beneath their skin their *case histories*, as he liked to call them. Despite his preoccupations, he could still tell a good case history: and though my brother, by then in the grip of the hormones that had spoiled his face and soured his mood, had already lost interest, I always wanted to hear more, even as the mosquitoes became ravenous and our mother called us to bed.

Although you might find some of these case histories hard to believe today, my father, professionally dedicated to the facts, pure and simple, wasn't a man given to deliberate untruths. But although he told us lots of case histories, we didn't know much about his life before he met and married our mother. Nevertheless, he was well respected in the district ('a pillara the community' said the Mair), even if my brother sometimes failed to accord him the appropriate deference. I was always proud when people conferred on me the esteem of being in the Doc's Family. Every extra lolly from Matey down the Shops or a 'g'day' from Wally at the boatshed reminded me of the privilege of being in the Doc's Family, and kept me vigilant in protecting my father's hard-earned reputation – something my brother often neglected to do. I remember my father raising his voice in one of his 'little chats' to my brother: *I've worked too hard to earn a name in this town for a little lout like you to smoke it all away.* I think it only strengthened my brother's resolve to keep up that filthy habit.

My father was a man who had his own napkin ring when most men in town ate their 'tea' in singlets. He'd insist on drinks before dinner, and sometimes after as well, which is when we got to hear the case histories. *Shiny shoes show good character,* he always said, and nobody's shoes were shinier. It was only in regard to cleanliness that my father was strict with me (although he was forced by the hormones and my brother's own scuffed behaviour to take a harder line with *him*). I hope that it's due to my father's influence in matters of cleanliness, preciseness – sorry, I mean *precision* – and manners, that I've grown up to be what I am today. In later years, I often wondered where he ever found the intellectual stimulation his brilliant mind must have craved, let alone someone to share the interesting cases he encountered – apart from us, of course. Our mother wasn't much for talking.

Our town wasn't big like Borrigal. Everybody knew everybody else, and everybody else's business, though nobody said anything. Apart from school, the shops (or what was left of them), the boatshed and the servo, we had three pubs: Top, Middle and Doon. The itinerant workers who came for the summer to help bring in the prawns that got trapped spawning in the Spit or the jackaroos who worked with stock in the hills, drank and brawled in Doon Pub (the Lansdowne); the small land-holders off their selections, and the shopkeepers, would drink and gossip in Middle Pub (the Oak), looking enviously on at the shimmering lights of Top Pub (the Criterion Arms), membership of which was limited to my father, Mr Goodrich the Solicitor, Mr Horsley the Vet, and, when he came down, Mr Fulbright, the biggest squatter in the district. Even Constable Hudson drank down at

Middle Pub, though he did occasionally enjoy a complimentary lemon squash if he ever wandered into Top Pub while on duty.

It was a measure of the reverence my father enjoyed that he had his own bottle of Johnny Walker Black Label kept on Top Pub's top shelf. The 'Doc's Bottle' was only ever served to my father. The other patrons weren't necessarily bothered. Like everyone else, they usually only drank beer – unless their wives were away visiting relatives or shopping in the Smoke, and then they'd drink rum till their eyes watered.

My father was a big man, he had big hands. His arms, cabled with veins, were covered in thick black hair. In later years I'd often wonder how he was able to practise so competently with such big hands, despite their being so powdery-soft. Rushing to him when he arrived home from the surgery, I imagined I'd be swallowed up by his big boa arms and deep brown rumble. We're small like our mother, but I'm dark like my father. Maybe that's why he'd wink at me from time to time, reminding me that I too was 'shady.' *A touch of the tar brush*, he'd say almost proudly, and in a town like ours, it was no mean feat to admit it.

I didn't know much about our mother's life before she met and married my father either. She kept those details as closed as her bedroom door, which she locked with a key hung on a chain around her neck. Sometimes by the window near the sink, her hands steeped in washing, a lock of hair straggling her forehead, I'd watch our mother suddenly look out the window, looking but not seeing. Even then I knew she wasn't looking at the back garden or the shed, but somewhere else, somewhere I'd never visited. She wouldn't be aware of my standing there, and after a while, she'd begin to hum a soft, tuneless tune that I didn't recognise, and even now, despite hearing it so many times (and with increasing frequency that summer) I still couldn't describe it. Wisps of it flit through me, like angel hair on a windy day, and though I might grasp a note here and there, it's soon lost.

So anyway (*my father began, contemplating the ice melting in his glass*), there once was a woman who started speaking in a foreign accent, despite having never left town. It happened after she'd suffered a stroke that had left her unable to talk. At first I thought she mightn't talk again: she seemed like a blackboard with the words roughly rubbed out. She knew what she wanted to say, but the words were lost to her, as though they'd been misplaced under the couch or fallen behind the refrigerator. You could see the frustration in her face as she rummaged around in the empty corners of her brain for the simplest expressions or phrases. For a while all she could say was 'dog.' Imagine asking for a cup of tea and just coming out with 'Dog dog dog dog dog dog dog dog.' I thought she might be a lost cause, though her husband later said that he'd never understood her better than when she said nothing but 'dog.' He appreciated the eloquence of her silence.

When I visited her for a routine check-up, her husband was greatly excited, telling me that she'd started speaking again, but that she was 'torkin' funny.' I told him to expect her speech to be a little wrinkled after all that time away, her voice crackly and her teeth unwieldy around all those words. It had more than a few wrinkles in it, however: she sounded South African, even though she'd never been to South Africa or even left the district.

You know my own talent for accents (*my father continued, ignoring my brother's groaning. I always enjoyed his impersonations – he'd often interrupt his story to do the Indian or the cowboy to my delight*), but I was amazed at the accuracy of the patient's accent: her 'r's rolled like the Serengeti, her 'a's were flat and barren, her 'e's were clipped and ridge-backed.

My prognosis was that owing to some peripheral damage to her brain's speech and language areas, it was reasonable to expect some flattening of the vowel sounds. It was simply a case of lack of practice, after her silence all that time. But it was extraordinary: although she didn't use any Afrikaans words, she had all the inflections of an Afrikaner. I gave her some exercises to strengthen the muscles in her tongue and jaws, although I wasn't sure how they might work, and said I'd check on her the following fortnight.

You can imagine my surprise when her husband told me sadly that while she'd stopped speaking with a Boer accent, she'd started speaking 'like a frog, Doc.'

'What, croaking?' I asked.

'I *wish*,' he said, shaking his head. 'Like a Frenchie.'

I changed the exercises and told her I'd see her again in a fortnight. However, the only change the following visit was that she spoke in a clipped, precise German bark. It was as if her mouth had become the transit terminal of an international airport, and that while she spoke like a foreigner, she had also become one to her husband.

(*While my father didn't discuss his past, we sort of knew that he'd travelled before he met and married our mother. So it was natural that he would have been able to identify the afflicted woman's different accents, as opposed to those at the Middle or Doon Pubs who believed the world was divided into 'Us' and 'Wogs.' And 'Blackfellas,' if they were being charitable to the boongs down the Spit.*)

In the end (*my father continued*), the patient spoke in so many different accents that it seemed to her husband that the house had become like the Tower of Babel, filled with the cacophony of different voices, each stranger than the week before. When she started to speak in a Japanese accent he spent three days down Middle Pub, out of his mind with memories of the war. It was the talk of the town for a while, the way he sat at the Public Bar – talking to anybody, talking to nobody, just talking – immersing himself in a sea of drawls like a hot swimmer on a burning day, his eyes closed with the pleasure of those laconic vowels.

The patient, seeing he was falling out of love with her, stopped talking, afraid of the effect of her speech. Her husband returned to the comforting silence of their house to bring her cups of tea in the sleepy afternoon, undisturbed apart from the tick of the hallway clock and the occasional sound of the boards breathing beneath them. They decided they'd write each other notes on pads they wore around their necks – apparently you never heard them argue after that – but then, of course, you wouldn't. Matey down the Shops loved her because all she did was hand him her shopping list, never holding him up on busy mornings with gossip (apart from the odd discreet note from time to time).

The Collective Silences (as they'd become known round town) ended up celebrating their golden anniversary, more in love than ever. They had a big shindig at the school hall, which was filled to the rafters with descendants and lamingtons. You could see how close they'd become in all those quiet years together, as though their binding silence had helped them understand each other so much more. All their children and grandchildren, and even the great-grandson, clamoured for some words to mark the occasion, which the old man scrawled on the blackboard at the back of the hall:

'SILENCE IS GOLDEN'

They all applauded and cheered, thinking it the funniest thing they'd seen. But by all accounts, it wasn't a very rowdy party (*said my father, suddenly aware of clatter from the kitchen and our mother's stern shoulders as she washed up a little more loudly than usual*).

Meanjin

Albatross

Geoff Lemon

I've lost my poetic licence. I was caught reading the collected works of Coleridge after nine beers and a shot of chartreuse. The police were pleased.

'Thought you'd avoid us on the back streets, did you matey?' one said. 'Well you can't hide from us. We got you, matey.'

I wanted to tell him to stop calling me matey. I wanted to tell him that he wasn't a pirate captain. He wasn't even a police captain. Just a constable. But a pirate captain is a very romantic image, and I didn't have the licence to invoke it any more. The best that I could do was, 'Your head looks like … a head that's really ugly.' The best that I could do was emphasise the first syllable in constable. Repeatedly.

I denied everything, but he could smell albatross on my breath. He said I should be ashamed, that my alcohol reading was .16 and my poetry reading was incoherent. He said I'd put innocent infinitives at risk of being split, and could have left prepositions hanging dangerously at the end of sentences. I wanted to tell him I was sorry. As sorry as a prison cell, as sorry as empty bottles at 4 a.m. I was sorrier than a dying fire, or dinner for one, or a broken bike. I was as sorry as a three-foot coffin. But I couldn't use illegal metaphors in front of a cop. So I just said them quietly to myself when I got home, drunk, and sure I was alone.

Voiceworks

Reason

Jennifer Mills

One-two one-two: an owl cries out from the hidden branches of a ghost gum. One of the women jumps up, strides towards the tree and starts to shout. The other women sitting in the dust in a cluster rise more cautiously, but they raise both the volume and pitch of their chatter. I don't know their language, but I understand by the woman's tone that the owl is being warned.

I check my phone for the time. We should have left hours ago. I look over my shoulder, peer into the grubby window, but I can't make out the minister inside.

The women have all gone quiet now, their upturned faces fixed on the branches. As I watch, a young woman turns and meets my eye. She has a naked baby immobilised against her shirt. She walks toward my chair and I stand.

'That bird,' she says, 'she's telling him to leave us alone. That bird, *kuur-kuur*, he's the man who comes through our fence in the night.'

'What man?' I ask, looking around. There is no fence in sight. The woman smiles at me with pity, and I realise she is still in her teens.

'You can't see him, *kungka*,' she smiles. 'Spirit man.'

'Oh,' I nod, losing interest. I move back to my chair but she grabs my wrist. Her skin is rough, her grip like a vine.

'Kangaroo bone,' she says, and holds a fist to her throat. Her eyes are black with a glint of daring, though it could be reflected light. She lets go of my hand.

I smile faintly and step back toward the chair. My phone rests on top of it, a folder of paperwork leans against its unsteady legs. The night has cooled without warning, despite the stifling day, and I wish I had brought a coat.

It has been a productive day, I remind myself. A good meeting. In meetings I am useful. I keep the minister informed, hand him the appropriate paperwork. I don't participate in the discussion but it's my job that will go if this falls through. There's a lot at stake. Today we are brokering a billion-dollar deal between these people and an absent company. The minister is in the house of an elder, promising royalties. Even out here the real deals are made after the official meeting.

The woman puts a hand on my arm. 'He's gone,' she says.

It's true. The sound seems to have stopped. I nod and smile, trying not to show my disapproval. I am a rational person. I hate superstition. It's only a bloody owl.

She shifts the motionless baby with one hand and drifts back into her group.

After an age, the minister steps out of the house and loosens his tie. He smiles, unlessened by the lack of context. I nod tersely. I want to get out of here. It's been a long day and I crave nothing more than the comforting wax-coloured walls of my office, its ordered piles of paper, its calm wooden furniture. I even miss the heavy portraits in the halls.

'Let's go,' he says.

I dislike driving after dark, but we have an early flight. I have no choice but to spend the next two years obeying orders. It's a probationary sentence, I think, then remember where I found the phrase: the man who left the community today in the back of the police car, a battered four-wheel drive which looked as worn as any of the upturned vehicles we saw on the way here.

I get in the car and wait for the minister to fasten his seatbelt before I start the engine. As we pull out, the women watch us. Some laugh, a few wave, and the rest stand silent. The teenager with the baby stares beyond us into the trees, waiting for her moment. Our dust will not settle before we become her story.

*

Only a hundred or so kilometres of the road ahead is dirt, then it will be an easy run to town if we avoid the roos that will no doubt hurl themselves in front of our four-wheel drive. The car is hired. I miss the little flag on the bonnet.

'Did you reach an agreement?' I ask the minister.

'They'll be reasonable,' he says. 'We've done what we came to do – present them with their options.' He snorts. 'Didn't have to stand over them. They know we could cut them off in a second. Besides, those kids need shoes.'

I'm not sure this last is true, but I nod. 'I'll start on the report tonight.'

I hit a sandy patch and keep both hands on the wheel. To my right the moon has risen over the rocks, yellow and weak as though its batteries are running low. I concentrate on the road.

'You'll probably be tired from driving,' he says. 'Still, no harm making a start I suppose.'

I smile inwardly at the method of his pressure. Corrugations in the track keep us silent for a while.

He was in that last, unscheduled meeting for an hour at least. I sat on the old chair on the porch, going through my pile of papers from the day and checking my phone every ten minutes. There was no reception, but time still passed by the clock.

I half-listened to the women tell stories. With their babies asleep in their laps they were free to scare each other with ghost stories, like teenage girls at a sleepover. Some of the words were English ones. It's less jarring to hear them when I'm listening to Japanese or French, languages I pride myself on having and which are of little use in my own country.

I read over the draft agreements in my folder and checked the time. The sun had gone down an hour or so before he went inside. I would have objected to leaving so late, but it's a habit not to object to anything, and if I did it would be being left outside with the women during the real business.

I arrived here by following a trail of work I found myself good at. It was always obvious to me that I would get an internship and go on to Canberra. I have no real sense of lust, either for good or power. I am simply moving ahead in the most logical way. My father was a military bureaucrat, my mother his wife. I know there are paths carved out for us if we can hold to reason.

An erratic bat dashes in front of the windscreen and vanishes. Instinctively I press on the brakes, then remind myself about defensive driving techniques. The last thing we need is to be bogged out here. I shift in the seat.

'You have the stats I emailed you for tomorrow?' I ask, so that the minister will not offer to drive, not that he ever has.

'What? Oh, yes,' he says. His tone is distracted. When I look at him he turns away from me and faces straight ahead as if he has been caught lying.

'I can re-send them if you need me to.'

He yawns. 'Shame that airline went bankrupt. We could have chartered a flight.'

I don't remind him it was his idea to drive, to 'get to know the land up there' as he put it. I am too busy concentrating on the road. The dirt is turning half to gravel, so we must be near the tarmac. I slow for a wallaby that shoots in front of us and away into the darkness, safe.

After the owl, the women were quieter. They sat still and talked little, perhaps listening out for its reply. They got something else instead.

Without warning, a song crawled out of the night. From between the trees came a man's voice, atonal and pining. The women looked at each other and whispered, shook their heads. The tuneless song was like the drone of an insect. It crept into my body as if by stealth. My stomach tensed, then lurched dangerously.

There is an elevator in my office which does this. I sometimes stop the lift halfway down to prevent the sensation. The body, unused to sudden movement, tricks itself into thinking there is no gravity.

As spontaneously as it had begun, the singing stopped. The women immediately resumed their stories, as though the sound had been a brief, dull visitor. An encyclopaedia salesman, perhaps, or one of the charity collectors the minister refers to as 'can-shakers.'

I looked over at the group. The young woman with the baby against her shirt stood up and stepped over to me. She glanced back at her family before she spoke, reminding me of the careful, slow release of information common to politicians. Out of habit, I anticipated something I could use.

She tossed her head lightly at the darkness behind her. 'That man was singing out for somebody,' is all she said.

When we finally reach the paved road, I am so relieved that I let my foot relax on the accelerator. I open the window to let some real air in. The airconditioning has made my throat dry, but the dust is no less irritating. I close the window and stare into the dark beyond the headlights.

I see something. I squint and focus. There is a vague shape on the road ahead. As we approach, it grows into a man. He is not waving, simply standing in the dirt, one hand covering his chest. Must be an accident, I think, a breakdown. You can roll a vehicle out here as soon as blink. I scan the ditches either side for overturned cars. Nothing. When I look ahead again he seems to be the same distance away, just on the edge of visibility. I slow down.

'What is it?' the minister asks. He leans forward to look for an animal or interesting feature of the landscape.

'There's a man up ahead,' I say, 'I hope he's not in trouble.'

'Where?'

I refrain from mentioning his missed optometrist appointments, because I am his assistant, not his wife. Instead I raise a finger, but am forced to withdraw it. The road ahead is empty.

'He's gone. Must have walked off into the bush.'

The minister stares at me. 'There's nothing out here.'

'Must be an outstation or something,' I reassure him. 'The asphalt.'

Then again, maybe asphalt does not mean houses here.

'I'll call the office first thing in case any of those figures have changed,' I say. 'Accuracy is essential with these industry people.' I am speaking automatically, not really concentrating, because I am wondering how anyone could have gone so far ahead of us on foot.

Spirit man, the woman said. Just a teenager giving herself nightmares for kicks. But the imaginary bone in the fist at her throat. The pity in her voice: *You can't see him.*

*

As I come to a rare corner, the moon appears to grow brighter and dim again, a trick of the changing light. Town appears as an orange glow between the sudden hills. Canberra glows like that when you drive towards it in the night, and it means you're under half an hour away. Alice Springs is so small, we must be close.

I slow the car again, and this time the minister does not remark on it. He must think I want to admire the view of the ranges. They look dull and featureless to me, just dark lumps like the piles left by an earthmover on a kerb. I wonder what would possess someone to live out here.

My reverie is broken by a flash of movement, black and white and red like a bad joke. I feel something hit the bullbar and I press the brakes so fast that the minister grabs the glovebox with both hands. I do not have time to think, only to pray we will not flip over. The tarmac is kind, though, and the car the safest available. It is only after we squeal to a stop that I realise I have remembered not to swerve. We sit in the awful silence for ten, twenty seconds, clicked out by the hazard lights.

'I think I hit something,' I admit.

'I'll make sure it's dead,' he says, suddenly brightening. He wipes his hands on his knees. I imagine this is what he meant by getting to know the country: taking a story home to impress the gang with his outback know-how. It is all depressingly schoolboy, and he has forgotten the tyre iron. I unfasten my seatbelt and climb out of the car.

'Nothing,' says the minister, adjusting his tie. He bends to look under the car.

I walk back along the highway, checking both sides of the road. The moonlight is bright enough to see by. I follow the sound of flies and find the corpse of a big roo, but it's been dead for a long time.

When I give up and turn toward the car I see him again. He is standing in the middle of the road, beyond the minister. He is clasping something to his chest. His hand half-covers a red patch on his shirt. He looks solid enough. I slowly raise my hand to him in a greeting I realise must look a lot like surrender.

The minister is leaning on the car, bored now that he has nothing to club. He is staring at his shoes, probably thinking about getting them cleaned. I'm glad he's distracted. I might have time to assess the situation, deal with the injury, cover my tracks.

The man raises a hand to me from beyond the car. It is clenched. A sharp white shape grows out of his fist. A bone. The red shape is revealed on his chest. My heart races. I must have hit him hard. I think of broken ribs, and whether or not you are supposed to bandage them. I think of damage control, try to remember the name of the journo I met from the local paper. I am a good problem solver. I breathe. I walk slowly, without taking my eyes off him, until I can focus.

It's not blood. It's a shiny pattern on the shirt. I recognise the logo of a Melbourne football team. It is just some man out on the road for his own reasons. Maybe he's looking for something he dropped. There's a reason. There's a reason he's gone by the time I reach the car. He went somewhere.

'Mustn't have hit it hard enough,' the minister says when I get back into the driver's seat. 'Bounded off into the bush I'll bet.'

I start the engine. 'He went somewhere.' The problem seems to have solved itself. I drive carefully back to town, both hands on the wheel.

In my room at the hotel I open my laptop and my folder of papers. I stare at the notes from today's meeting until they swim. In one corner I have written the word PRACTICAL in small capitals and underlined it twice.

I step outside to breathe some non-conditioned air and blink the words from my eyes. Beyond the hotel's artificial oasis I can see the ranges, lit up by the moon. I stare at them for want of a horizon. They still look ugly to me, spoiled somehow, but there are arcs in the rock: patterns formed and broken over geological ages.

My hands are cold. I can hear drunks laughing in the riverbed. A bird lands in a tree nearby and rattles the branches. My desire to be outside evaporates without reason.

Alice Springs News

July the Firsts

Ryan O'Neill

It is July the first.

And Ernest Hemingway is cleaning his favourite shotgun, the one with the silver-edged barrel, which he will next day place in his mouth, and Charles Laughton is born and Thomas Moore is on trial for his life and I (1970 to present) am lying awake in Newcastle. On this day Vespasian was given the purple by the Egyptian legions and Napoleon captured Alexandria. The first television advertisement, for watches, was broadcast in New York City, costing the company nine dollars. It is 12.50 a.m. In 1971, in a Brisbane hospital, my wife Sarah has just been born. Four years ago at this time I lay in bed awake, listening to her stir beside me. She had wanted to make love, but I had said I was too tired. In truth I was bored of her. By then I already knew the history of her body, the provenance of every scar and blemish. I pretended I was asleep.

This year (2004) I have taken to sleeping in old piles of the *Newcastle Herald* which I bought from a pensioner in Charlestown. The past week I have been napping in the 1988 earthquake, but tonight I cover myself in a more recent pub brawl and the football results. For some reason, I find I enjoy most rest in December 1979. Yet just now I cannot sleep and so continue the introduction to my History of Newcastle (Newcastle University Press, 200?). One hundred and twenty notebooks filled with my handwriting are stacked on the floor around my desk, along with the dozens of history books and journals that are referenced in the ninety pages of footnotes. And still I have not arrived at the First World War. I once wrote a history of Africa that took less time and research than this history of a small Australian city. And yet still I believe I was born to be an historian, exiting from my mother backside first, in order that I might better understand where I came from. I take a new page in the introduction (p.104) and write: *Abraham Lincoln once said, 'We cannot escape history.'*

Then the Beatles start singing 'Paperback Writer' on the radio, number one today in 1966. There are more songs and I stop writing for a time and listen to them, 'My Foolish Heart,' 'Why Don't You Love Me.' Then I hear 'Guess Things Happen that Way' and I run barefoot to turn the music off, trailing a Lambton murder from December 14, 1983 on my heel. My feet are dirty. The floor is filthy with my dead skin and hair. Historians should not sit in ivory towers after all.

Now it is 4 a.m. on July the first and in 1993 I have just proposed to Sarah. We lay in bed together in an Edinburgh hotel. I had bought the engagment ring earlier that day at an antique shop – I wanted it to have history. She told me it was the best birthday present she had ever had. She told me of each of the men she had loved. She asked me about the women I had been with. 'I don't want our pasts to ever come between us,' she said. I had a cold that night, I remember.

My medical history: measles (1975), appendicitis (1984), a fractured left arm (1992), malaria (1990, 1991), and of course, clinical depression (2001 to present). Outside the house, a red and green and yellow bird is whooping in the dawn, but I don't know its name. I have no knowledge of natural history. It is a cool morning. I decide to go for a walk and dress in my second-hand clothes. I leave the house, cross the street, walk past the undertakers where an Australian flag is displayed against black curtains, as if the country itself is to be buried today. My house is near the harbour. The roof was destroyed by a Japanese submarine that fired thirty-four rounds at the city on June 8, 1942. Three drunken young men shout at me and I hurry past them and think of the first day of the Battle of the Somme. I could never fight. I have no history of violence.

I walk down to the foreshore and look out at the ocean where in the pale light I can see five identical coal ships spaced equidistant along the horizon, like a time-lapse photograph. Long ago today the French frigate *Medusa* sank and the survivors escaped in a raft which became stuck in the sea of the famous painting. There is a strong smell of seaweed. It is Estée Lauder's birthday. In 1998 at this time I was still asleep in bed, but not with my wife.

I walk back and forth along the sand for a while, and then return to the road. At this early hour I am surprised to see an old man reading on his front doorstep, with a faintly astonished look on his face, as if he had just seen his own name in the book. I pass him, then charge back up San Juan Hill with Roosevelt and take my street without casualties.

It is eight o'clock in the morning on July the first and I still cannot sleep. I return to bed and sit and watch old black and white films for some hours, looking for Olivia de Haviland to wish her happy birthday. Then it is midday and the postman rings the doorbell once and I wait until he rings again, in honour of James M. Cain, also born this day.

The postman is a Barbarossa of a man. Ink has come off on his large hands as if he has been making words with them. He has a package for me from Melbourne which I must sign for, and as I do so I entertain him with the history of my surname. He does not seem very interested. I take the package inside. Some history books, including one that I once wrote about the Mau-Mau rebellion. Years ago I lent them to Sarah's sister, but I need them now for my history of Newcastle. Sometimes I think I will need every history book, from the time of Thucydides to those yet unwritten, for my history of Newcastle.

When I open the book a photograph falls out. I stare at it for some time, for it has been so long since I have seen a photograph that was not stapled, captioned and dated. A man and a woman are standing outside a dark stone cathedral, smiling in a sunshower. The picture was taken on the July the first of 1989 in Glasgow, when I met Sarah for the first time. I could hear her in the next chamber in the cathedral before I saw her. She was leading a group of Polish students. Her Australian accent I noticed at once, but then certain other words that she pronounced differently, some rising unexpectedly, some falling. I imagined numbers over these words, leading to footnotes which explained that she had once lived in China, India, England. I watched her, fascinated. For when she spoke of the past, she threw her hand back over her shoulder, when she spoke of the present, she pointed in front of her, and the future was a sweeping gesture of both her hands. She had begun these motions to give her students visual clues for their tenses, but eventually they had become habit. She had sent her students away to look at a tapestry and she was finishing a book on a bench outside.

'What are you reading?' I asked her, and she looked up at me.

'A biography. Jane Austen,' she said.

'Oh. How does it end?'

'Well, she dies,' she said, and we laughed.

I remember how her hands moved when we arranged to meet the next evening. Later, I watched her students sing 'Happy Birthday' to her. The next year, we were alone when I sang it to her.

In 2004, now, I return to the 104th page of my introduction. Outside, above the houses, there is a picture of the sun in the sky that is already some minutes old. I wonder how it compares to the sun the Americans made in the Bikini Atoll, the fourth time of splitting the atom. It was on this day of course, years and years ago. After some time writing, I fall asleep and when I awaken I look at the clock. It is 5 p.m.

In 2001 the conference I was attending at Sydney University to discuss trends in African historiography had just ended. It was Sarah's birthday, and I was going to call her from the lobby, to tell her that I would be home soon. There was a black woman at the hotel bar. I recognised her accent as Burundian from the speech she gave about French colonialism. Her name was Clio Mbabazi. She was quite pretty and invited me to join her for a drink. 'It is July the first,' she said, 'and Burundi is celebrating its independence.' She looked at my wedding ring and my whisky. 'And so it seems are you.' I called Sarah at nine o'clock to wish her happy birthday and tell her that I would not be home that night, as we had planned. There was too much work to do.

And then I am hungry and I eat using November 23, 1997 as both tablecloth and napkin. The bread is four days old, the cheese is six days old, and I am 12,875 days old. It is evening and I go to shower off the history of the day. The ink, the sweat, the dirt. It is still July the first, still, and Marlon Brando has just died on television, though he is there in the screen screaming, 'Stella! Stella!' I sit on the floor. Something cuts into my leg. One of Sarah's diaries. She kept them from when she was fifteen years old. I have read them several times. In them I appear as an historical figure, like a Garibaldi or a Caesar. Herein, all my lies and my infidelities are recorded. 'For an historian,' Sarah wrote on July the first 1997, 'my husband is no good at fabricating the past.'

Suddenly, it seems, it is 9.02 p.m. In 2001 at this time I was in a Sydney hotel room. On the radio, Johnny Cash was singing. I kissed Clio Mbabazi and we took off our clothes. Afterward I could not sleep and I idly read the Gideon's Bible. Much later I learnt that the society had been formed on a July the first by some Wisconsin travelling salesmen.

It is 11.41 p.m. and in 2001 Sarah is dying on her thirtieth birthday, alone in our bed in Newcastle. A sudden heart attack. The doctors could not explain it. There was no history of heart disease in her family. If only someone had been with her, they said, she might have been saved. In Germany, Chekhov was dying too. They would take his body back to Russia in a crate marked 'fresh oysters.' Like Shakespeare, whom Chekhov greatly admired, Sarah was born and died on the same day.

Abraham Lincoln once said, 'We cannot escape history.' It is July the first.

Westerly

Nothing To Fear

Melissa Beit

When I catch up to the others and bounce through the wave at the bottom of the rapid, the pool is already jostling with kayaks, giant plastic jellybeans. My own is black and I have never liked it. Andy chose it not long after we started going out, for its sturdy lines and boxy shape; but to me it looks like a coffin. There is even a white cross emblazoned on the front deck, a Japanese symbol meaning something or other. It is late afternoon and Andy is already at the bottom of the next rapid, running safety. This means he is standing on a rock beside the river with a throwbag in his hand, waiting to toss a line to anyone who may need hauling out of the river.

Heidi is sitting in the right-hand eddy, crowded with three other boats, but she beckons me over. 'You have your kayaking face on,' she informs me. This means that my facial expression is an unfriendly mask of concentration, which she probably suspects is a scanty cover for pure terror. Once the look is there it will remain until I climb out of my boat at the take-out and know that I have lived through another river trip.

You can drown in an inch of water. My mother knows of several people who have. When I was five years old she shouted at me as I lifted up the lid of the washing machine, which was on. 'Don't you realise you could break your arm in an instant?'

She lifted me gently away and apologised for raising her voice.

I hadn't known that washing machines were unsafe. I backed away in a hurry, for I thought if you broke your arm you died.

We are at the top of a rapid called Devil's Cauldron Two. We have just paddled through Devil's Cauldron One and it is responsible for the appearance of my kayaking face. The first person to navigate their way successfully through a rapid gets to name it. Rapids the world over are called things like Lucifer's Leap, Big Mother, Sinkhole, Tombstone, and Trouble. They tend to be named by men.

It's very noisy. A man in a dark blue life-jacket, his helmet off for the time being, is standing confidently on a wedge of rock hanging out over the waterfall that leads into Devil's Two. From up there he can see the top and the bottom of the rapid, and his job is traffic control. When the previous kayaker has successfully negotiated the rapid and swung safely into the eddy below, he raises his hand to the next kayaker and blows on a whistle. The interval between turns is about thirty seconds if all goes well. If there is a particularly long wait between whistle blows, it usually means that someone has 'swum,' that is, flipped over mid-rapid and ejected out of their kayak to swim the rest of the way down. This is cold, painful and scary.

For my ninth birthday my parents took me to Legassi's, the best restaurant in Rockwell, population 3400. I wore my velvet dress. When the time came to order, I asked for steak Diane without consulting my family members or the menu. The waitress was impressed. When my brothers had gone outside to run around the restaurant grounds and my parents were dawdling over coffee, the waitress came back and asked if I wanted to see the kitchens. I followed her through the swinging doors and met the other waitresses, who were as young and beautiful as film stars. One of them gave me a chocolate frog. The chef was old, with a long droopy moustache and a small white hat. He was jointing a chicken and he demonstrated the order: legs, wings, breast, back. In some triumph I returned to our table. My parents listened to my tale in silence, and then my mother said, 'That's good, and it was OK because we knew where you were going. But just remember, Sweetheart, that some bad people might ask you to go somewhere with them and then cut you up with an axe or a knife.'

The crowd in the pool is thinning as people in boats disappear one by one over the horizon line into Devil's Two. I have seen this rapid from the riverbank, when I scouted it on the last trip. That day I made the decision to portage, and lugged my boat over the granite boulders and through the tea-trees all the way around the rapid to the pool at the bottom. Andy, sitting in the bottom eddy in his red kayak, had smiled up at me and said confidently, 'Next time you'll be ready.'

Heidi, ahead of me in the eddy, lets go of the tea-tree stump she has been clutching and paddles forwards and sideways, to ferryglide effortlessly over the eddyline and turn to face the rapid's entrance. From here she will paddle to a point slightly left of centre to avoid the large boulder at the top onto which half the river is rushing, forming the pillow of whitewater that is making all the noise. Then she will, all going to plan, race down the chute into the cauldron, the huge circulating hole that spills up the sides of a bowl of rock, before spurting out in a violent wash into the calm pool below. If the angle of a kayak entering the cauldron is just right, the boat will glide over the boils and whirlpools like magic and hurtle out the other side unscathed and still manned. If the angle is wrong the kayak will get caught in the cauldron and recirculate *ad infinitum*.

There is a man at the camp site next to ours called Brian who is a legend in the kayaking world. He is nearly fifty, Andy tells me, and has paddled rapids that no one even dreamed were navigable. Last year he flipped over in Devil's Two and disappeared. After a while his paddle emerged out of the whitewash, then his boat, an upside-down streak of purple; then after one minute, his life jacket and shoes appeared in the eddy downstream and the people running safety on the banks, their throw-bags ready, stopped laughing and shaking their heads and started to look worried and professional. When Brian emerged after ninety seconds, his nose and left leg were broken.

*

We were never allowed to dive into water, not even swimming pools, because you never knew if something was beneath the surface that could break your neck. Instead we had to perform a manoeuvre called a honey pot. We would huddle crouched beside the town pool, while kids all around us ran on slippery cement and leapt spine-first into the water, and then topple in sideways, falling all of ten centimetres through space. When we were older we graduated to the safety dive, and could plunge into water of any depth with our legs apart and our arms outstretched. My brothers and I were left unattended at a pool party when I was fourteen. I sat on the steps of the pool and watched as, after a brief hesitation, my brothers threw themselves into the water with our friends. They did bombdives, mickey-flips, pencil dives and backflips. I was so jealous I couldn't speak to anyone. My older brother clipped the back of his head on the side of the pool and it bled a little, but his hair hid the cut and none of us said a word to my mother.

Heidi has been gone maybe ten seconds when the whistle blows and that means it's my turn. There is a young man in a kayak behind me and our boats keep bumping into each other as the water in the eddy circulates. I can sense his impatience so I turn and say, 'I have to bail out my boat, you can go.'

He pushes off without a word and heads towards the lip, but his arms are travelling too high and his boat swings with each paddle stroke and I know he is going to swim. I pull my sprayskirt off the boat and crawl out into the tea-trees. I flip my boat over and watch the water, warm from my body and yellow with urine, drain into the river. It is a full five minutes before the whistle blows again, but by then more paddlers have arrived from upstream, and I wave them ahead.

When I turned seventeen and finished high school my mother encouraged me to go overseas. She suggested Scotland or Canada. 'Go wherever you like,' she said, but then added hastily, 'Just don't go to South America. Don't go to Peru. The Shining Path are killing tourists there.'

When I had been in Chile for three weeks and it hadn't stopped raining the whole time I caught the train up to Cuzco. Nothing happened. The Peruvians were friendly and helpful, although I was nervous whenever I had to catch a taxi by myself.

I met Andy at a bridge jump two years ago. I had my harness on and the rope in my hand and was about to jump when he walked up with Heidi. He wore a torn T-shirt and pink towelling pants, bare feet and a blue woollen beanie. I don't remember what Heidi wore, just that she was loud and energetic and hugged all my friends although I'd never heard of her. Andy grinned at me and called, 'Any last bequests?'

I smiled and shook my head and jumped. I could not have given him a more perfect first impression. Or a more misleading one.

I take my time in putting my sprayskirt back onto my boat, and spend some moments readjusting my chin strap and life jacket. My hands are wrinkled and white with cold, and clasped around my paddle shaft they look small and helpless. I move up the eddy as paddlers peel off and disappear one by one. Finally I am at the front of the queue again, having dawdled for maybe twenty-five minutes altogether. I know that downstream Andy will have figured out what has happened. 'You can't think at the top of a rapid. If you're going to do it, just do it. If you're not, don't. Walk.'

His world is simple like that and he doesn't understand the morbid lingering that precedes all of my more daring acts. Soon he will appear amongst the tea-trees from down below and meet my eyes across the river, shrugging his shoulders exaggeratedly and frowning as though perplexed.

Unless he is talking to Heidi.

I can see the picture they would make, her in her yellow kayak laughing up at him standing on a rock above her. It is this picture that brings about the epiphany. The whistle blows. I have had enough. I am going to run the rapid.

'Take care' is what my mother says instead of 'goodbye.' All my life she has bid me farewell thus; at school gates, bus stops, train stations, even at my friends' houses. 'Take care, Darling,' she says, as though anything could happen, anywhere.

*

As I reach the lip of the rapid, with Devil's Cauldron Two laid out below me, it is the people I notice, not the water. The traffic controller at the top yells 'Left! Left!' at me, his face frantic, but I know that I am on just the right line. Surrounding the cauldron itself are five or six people, poised with throwbags and expectant faces. Far away at the bottom of the rapid Andy stands with his arms folded talking to a man I don't know. With their helmets and sprayskirts on they look like Roman sentries, but not at all ridiculous.

Once, in a rare moment of intimacy, Heidi said to me, 'Some women get turned on by men in uniforms, but give me wet hair, bare feet and a life jacket. Anytime.' We were standing on the banks of Ellie Creek watching a group of men turning cartwheels in their boats in the smooth pour-over of Jackson's Rapid. Andy was amongst them and by far the best looking.

I slide down the chute and am in the cauldron. My boat is thrown about and almost tips over at every paddlestroke, but I am beautifully confident now that I am mid-rapid. I slightly exaggerate the casualness of my paddlestrokes, and move my hips fluidly to ride the jostling water. My boat is propelled towards the exit point through which all the river is rushing and I smile because I have practically made it.

When I had been going out with Andy for three months I said it for the first time. 'Take care,' I said, as he heaved his river-bag into his ute and climbed into the driver's seat. He turned to look at me and something like reproach flickered in his eyes. 'You mean, "Have fun, Andy,"' he corrected me and then started the engine and drove off.

At the last moment I am spun in a whirlpool and I broach. There is a crunch and grind as the boat pins itself sideways between two rocks and almost immediately I am under water, the whole river pounding onto my head. Then I am out of my boat and being sucked down. The light and air and the mysterious way a plastic boat glides over thousands of tonnes of moving water are a distant memory, a joke. We name rapids to tame them, to personify them, but the truth is that a river is just water moving over rocks and has no capacity for compassion.

*

Here is my most vivid recurring nightmare: I have been placed in a 44-gallon drum and someone has clanged the lid on and sealed it shut. There is a ray of light coming into the drum through a hole near the top. After a long wait, this hole is blocked by a hose being inserted into it. Water starts to pour into the drum. When the water is up to my neck, I wake up and the dream ends, but of course each time I don't know this is going to happen until it does.

I am far below the surface of the river and where I am is dark and cold and very quiet. My shoes are gently plucked off my feet, first one, then the other. My shorts are being tugged down past my knees. I think of Brian-the-river-legend and tuck myself into a ball. I know that somewhere downstream my boat will be surfacing like a small dark whale, and that my shoes, shorts and paddle may never be seen again. My hands make desperate dog-paddling motions near my neck and I wonder if ninety seconds is nearly up. I can't remember when my last breath was, or if it was a good one, but my lungs are taking over my body and I can hear Andy's voice in my head. He was drunk when he said it, and not talking to me. 'When you're just about to drown, you have a decision to make. You can hold your breath as long as you can and pass out, when your body will automatically take a breath and you will drown. Or you can take a huge breath of water and end it sooner.'

I can hear him saying it and I know that that time is now, but I can't decide what to do.

One of my earliest memories is of lying in our small blue above-ground pool supported only by my mother's hand under my head. There is a rain-tree shading us, and its leaves make a paisley pattern against the blue sky. We are alone in the pool, my older brother at school, my younger brother not yet born. I am only two or three, so my sister is still around somewhere, safe at school, or safely on her way home. I don't remember her, not at all.

'See?' my mother is saying, although her voice is muffled because I have water in my ears. 'Floating is easy. Bodies float all by themselves.'

*

The water around me is becoming less black and more tea-coloured. I see bubbles moving around me, then green and blue lights and realise that I have been flushed back to the surface. Before I can make sense of anything, someone barks my name and a yellow rope appears in the froth in front of me. The river is already changing its mind, and is propelling me back towards the base of the waterfall. I take the rope in both hands and am dragged down again. This is not right, and I remember that I am supposed to lie on my back. Flipping over is difficult but slowly I am pulled out of the maelstrom to where Andy stands on a rock shelf hauling me in hand over hand. I slide onto the rock, my bare legs still in the river. My throat has jammed shut and I lie choking for awhile, but then I roll over and vomit and can breathe again. I am still inside the circle of rock that contains the cauldron, and Andy is beside me, a trickle of blood running down his shin.

When I can talk I look up at him and say with some passion, 'I hate being cold and wet.'

He is panting, leaning against the rock wall. There is a long graze down his right arm and bloodless scratches on his knees.

'And I am afraid of water.'

He nods and looks at the sky.

'I have never liked kayaking,' I explain.

He nods some more. He knows this, I realise.

'I want to break up with you,' I say. 'I was coming down to tell you. I think you should go out with Heidi.'

People have gathered at the edge of the rock above us but it is so noisy in the cauldron that they can't hear us. I wonder how we'll get out. Andy has begun to coil the rope, the end of which I still clutch, and his hands shake just a little. He smiles down at me with sad blue eyes and says, 'It's going to be OK. There's nothing to worry about.'

Australian Women's Weekly

People Whose Names Bob Dylan Ought To Know

Tim Richards

'Remember that a person's name is to that person the sweetest and most important sound in any language.'

—Dale Carnegie

Grace says that I should stand up for myself. I've been playing bass for Dylan for thirty-two years, and he doesn't even know my name. Once in a while, Bob says, 'Man, what was that shit you played on Quinn?' and I tell him the amp crashed, and that's pretty much the sum of our conversations. When Grace says, 'You've got kids at college … If he doesn't know your name, how will he pay you?' I say that you don't bother a genius with trivia like back pay. Eventually, Bob'll see that I get my due.

Grace hasn't been with me all that time. Our paths didn't cross when she was on the catwalk, or singing 'Walking in the Rain' and 'I've Seen that Face Before,' and I guess she never imagined then that fate would fix her up with a plodder like me. If you check out the old photos, Grace looks so dangerous, really formidable, and you wouldn't believe she's quite petite, or that she would sing when she dried the dishes. Whenever she gets moody and tells me how fucking lucky I am to be living with Grace Jones, I remind her that Bob Dylan doesn't know her name either.

It might be easier for us to live in a city full of people whose names Bob didn't know, but geography's tricky like that. Our local school-crossing attendant is Jeff Lynne, who played with Bob in the Wilburys. His old band, ELO, sold container loads. I never heard them, but Grace says they were shit. Not that she'd say that to his face, because Jeff's a Wilbury, and a producer, and knowing a producer with clout makes a lot of difference when you're begging for a recording budget.

No question, Bob knows Jeff's name, and when the two of them tell their old stories about Roy, George and Tom, Bob uses Jeff's name maybe one sentence in a dozen. 'Well, yeah, that's what you say, Jeff. I don't remember that.' Dylan even sends him cards from different gigs, but that's the thing, when he sends him a postcard of a fat woman by the pool at the Bucharest Hilton, it's always 'Mr Geoff Lynne.'

Jeff says that Bob's just got the English Geoff mixed up with the more phonetically obvious American Jeff, and that's OK. An understandable mistake. With Jeff born in Birmingham, you'd expect him to be the English Geoff with a G, not the Cold War fighter-pilot Jeff with a J. Mr and Mrs Lynne got it arse-about trying to be fancy, and it's hardly Bob's fault that logic lets him down. But Grace says that not being able to spell someone's name is exactly the same as not knowing it. Best not to argue that point because it's something she gets strident about.

Maybe it's a Jamaican thing, but Grace has a two-directory view of the world. Most big cities have so many phone numbers that they split their directories in two, and she says that any decent authority would divide the volumes into People Worth Calling and the People Not Worth Calling. According to Grace, she and I would figure in the large volume of People Whose Names Bob Dylan Doesn't Know, and depending where you stand on the Jeff/Geoff controversy, our whole city probably squeezes into that category.

I guess other people never see themselves that way, as going through their lives as a name Bob Dylan doesn't know, and they'd prefer to see their names listed in the big volume, People Whose Names Bob Dylan Ought to Know.

For Grace, it might be different, but for me, it's glass half-full, glass half-empty. We know who we are and who we know, but we'll probably never know if the people we know want to know us, or if they give a shit about the spelling of our names. So fuckin' what if Dylan doesn't know my name. Should a friend choose to take that as an insult, or treat it as a sign that he and I communicate in a very particular way? I'm not like Grace. I'm not frightened to find my name listed among the names of the people in the fat directory. Those people wouldn't know my name either, but I'm happy to be one of them. I'm with them in spirit.

Meanjin

Some Kind of Fruit

Karen Hitchcock

> 'The day before I left Rome I saw three robbers guillotined … The first turned me quite hot and thirsty, and made me shake so that I could hardly hold the opera-glass (I was close, but was determined to see, as one should see everything, once, with attention); the second and third (which shows how dreadfully soon things grow indifferent), I am ashamed to say, had no effect on me as a horror, though I would have saved them if I could.' —LORD BYRON, 1817

It was medical school before the age of snuff-medicine TV. Before surgery and sawn-off-shotgun wounds hit prime time. I'd come into contact with live flesh, but the sick and infirm, the dead, I had only seen depicted by Old Masters. I wanted to be a psychiatrist, so I applied. My degree in fine arts, coupled with a new trend for the medical humanities, ushered me in. James and I made friends during orientation: two old hags who wanted to be shrinks, searching for unscorched coffee.

For a year both of our boyfriends lived interstate; we shared a ride to the airport every second weekend. He flew to Queensland. I flew to Melbourne. During the week we cooked dinner and studied at his apartment. He had an ocean view, my bed-sit didn't have a working stove. He always had cake: orange and spice, raspberry and coconut, chocolate, hummingbird. He was an English Lit graduate with a stomach as sensitive as my own.

There were three types of med student. Anorexic gym-bunnies who came from the School of Dietetics and Physiotherapy. Computer geeks with bad skin. And the majority: bland, clean-cut Christians; that sea of neat brown hair. James and I sat at the back, to the left, near the exit, so we could move out as fast as possible.

In first year we struggled with anatomy. The wet lab reeked of recirculated formaldehyde. Dissected body parts were stored in vats with texta signs: *Arms, Legs, Torsos. Heads with Neck.* The flesh hung from the bones in wet grey strings, the yellow tendons intact. We stood back, shoulder to shoulder, while students pretty as soap-opera stars huddled around the stainless-steel tables in lurid gloves. One of them pulled a tendon and made a finger curl. He looked at us sideways and said we'd learn nothing from way over there. I told him I was learning plenty. Under his breath James said *He must be what, twelve?* I bought Rohen and Yokochi's *Human Atlas*, the heaviest book on the planet. Its pages felt like cool water. They were printed on both sides with full colour, high definition photographs of newly dead bodies in perfect slices, red muscles deflected with steel forks. *Who needs tendons?* I said to James as we peered into its depths. *Yeah*, he said twisting his neck to get a different angle. *Who needs tendons?* The old man with the peeled face on page 165 taught us the muscles of mastication.

I looked at the atlas each night before bed. A drama of epic proportions. I got to know the bodies: their age, their sex, their race. The dissections were exquisite: so tender, the deepest layer of the neck with the spinal cord and medulla exposed. So vulnerable the chest when split, leaving heart and lungs bare. The Japanese man on page 320, his eyes closed, thick thighs open. Impressive. I would gaze down at my skin and understand what it held at bay. A story with the most intricate of plots.

James recalled a Cultural Studies lecturer claiming that the inside of a body was just a big mess. She'd said it was medicine that constructed the organs. That really, there was no such thing, in and of itself, as 'a spleen.' We scanned page 205 for her: *Posterior abdominal wall with duodenum, pancreas and spleen.* We signed it Anonymous Universal and sent it express mail. I found the whole thing amusing, but it made James really mad. *Cultural relativism*, he kept spitting. *Social constructivism*, he'd curse. *The body exists! The body exists!* He'd thump his chest like a madman and yell it at me, as if I didn't know.

We went to the national med students' conference to dance. Each night we took a pill some boy from Sydney Uni had cooked. He winked when we asked him what they were and told us to remember his name (some kind of fruit). James and I argued about whether the crumbly pills were amphetamines or E. We took each other's tachycardic pulse, we sweated, we laughed. James would scream *Science is truth!* from the dance floor while we boogied fury on muscles we knew the atlas's names for. We slept in the same bed from six till ten, then rose, cleared our throats and called our boyfriends: *Yes ... It's good ... You know. Just conference stuff.*

Towards the end of first year James's boyfriend moved in with him and my boyfriend decided we had drifted apart. He'd had a short story published in a journal and was hanging around people who wore interesting glasses. He said he didn't want to move and besides, he felt he couldn't go out with someone who'd joined an Ideological State Apparatus. *But I'm going to be a shrink!* I told him. He said those were the worst offenders. I felt gutted. The image of my future consulting room – with its leather couch, still air and abstract expressionist oil paintings – cracked up. But James rolled his eyes when I told him and made me mail the prick a copy of the spleen.

They assessed us relentlessly. Name. Define. Diagnose. Extrapolate and deduce. Examine, report, explain, memorise, tick-the-right-fucking-box. *I'm no scientist,* I'd threaten James. *I've always hated science,* I'd argue. He'd just nod and feed me bigger slabs of cake. We'd study hard then take a break. He'd go swimming, and I'd wander the National Gallery, visiting old friends on the walls, getting myself lost and found. I'd stand in front of Frankenthaler and squeeze and wring my hands. *I could have lived here, searching for words* I implored her dilute paint on un-primed canvas. Wring. Squeeze. Instead, I'd joined an Ideological Apparatus. James swam. I wrung my hands for answers. James's biceps hypertrophied. Security ushered me out at 6 p.m. each night.

*

There were little distractions: The intern named Fred with the skinny ties and stove-pipe pants who started off teaching me my heart sounds and ended up lifting my blouse right up over my head. The cardiologist – unnamed – who liked to torque me to the reserve in his ancient, silver Porsche. He'd lay a crisp white napkin over his Armani and I'd climb on board. He'd knead me and knead me, *You're so sexy, you're so sexy.* But what about loveable? I wanted to ask. I spent what money I had on make-up, shoe paint and vintage belts. I became obsessed with lip gloss and would test them out on James. *Whuddayathink?* I'd ask and pout, and he'd take his time to answer. I bought one called Strawberry Fields and told him to have a smell. He closed his eyes and leaned in close, almost touching his nose to my lips. *They smell like childhood* ... he said. *Your lips smell exactly like childhood.* And his eyes, when he raised them, were all out of focus.

Our Biochemistry lecturer was a psychopath. We tried to get interested, but lipids and amino acids and the Krebs cycle and DNA, although potentially thrilling, the very stuff of life, became monotonous chaff when ground through his mouth. If you asked him a question it only got worse, and the answers were certainly not English. I'd look at James and ask *Why?* He'd look at me and ask *Why?* We came up with a stock answer: so-we-can-be-psychiatrists-comma-so-we-can-spend-our-lives-exploring-the-mind.

By third year it had reched the point where I was no longer sure what was me and what was not. James too seemed smudged around the edges, like a line drawing smeared with wet fingers. It was almost mid-year exams. We took to dancing. Cheap red instead of dinner, studying over pots of espresso. In between sessions I would be gripped by terrifying questions: Does tricuspid incompetence lead to a murmur in systole or diastole? At what dose will hydralazine reach tachyphylaxis? I'd ring James. His boyfriend, if he answered, would call out *It's your girlfriend, James* and drop the phone on the floorboards. But James was ringing me too, breathing into the receiver, saying things like: *Science ... Truth? Knowledge? ... Foucault. Foucault!* Or: *I studied Culture ... And now I study Biology* ... I'd hang on the line waiting for his conclusion, but one was never forthcoming. Occasionally he'd ask me what I was wearing. Once he asked me if tonality was biological.

Tonality? I said.

Yes, he replied.

Biological? I said.

Yes, he replied.

I said I didn't know. Was making a flat canvas look 3-D biological? Was social realist writing biological? He told me not to argue.

I'm not arguing! I said.

We'd drink and then we'd dance, banging hips bone against bone. No one came near us. We were a universe. Something framed and perfect. Him and me.

On drinking nights we'd meet at my place and James would wait for me to get ready. I'd stand splay-legged in my bra and skirt flinging clothes from my washing basket. *It's in here somewhere. I know it's in here somewhere.* One time James said he would wait downstairs. I stopped mid-fling and straightened up with my palm on my back. *What's up?* I asked him. He ran out the door with his cheeks all red and his eyes in the carpet. I stared at the door, shuffling explanations. I looked down at my bra (a lacy black number the cardiologist had sent me from Paris). I laughed and shook my head. *I don't look that bad!* I beseeched the empty room, my arms stretched out wide.

Fag Hag is such an unappealing term but my distractions were now few and generally married. I did like the older man. But I also liked the younger man. The equi-aged man. And men in general. *I'm just not girlfriend material* I complained to James. Then my mouth ran riot about how girls with any cynicism scared men off; about brains and personal direction being taboo; about my refusal to play idiotic games. James started to laugh, his red lips pursed. *Is it perhaps because you're taken?* He asked. Then he laughed some more.

And we passed. Like diluted paint on un-primed canvas, the stuff had seeped in and spread; amalgamated, cohered with barely any willing on our part. But I was in the grip of a crisis I could no longer ignore. So in second semester I secretly overloaded my course and enrolled in the Philosophy of Science and Art. The lecturer was a quiet man who looked a lot like a jockey. Popper. Kuhn. Greenberg. Fry. What was science? What was art? What was I doing in med school at all? I wrote my essay on Rohen and Yokochi. On their aesthetic masterpiece of patience and technique. I split the essay in two: in part one I argued the book was science (they had a scary knowledge of where to cut; they found arteries no one knew existed). In part two I argued it was art (purity, light, form). I let the two rest side by side. Who ever said something had to be one thing or the other? James thought I was a genius. The jockey wasn't convinced.

I skipped the gallery and started swimming with James. I'd swim for fifteen minutes then sit in the stands watching him slice through the blue. I loved to watch him, that fierce stroke and muscular back, his regular gasps for air. I realised I'd rather look at him than 'Blue Poles,' than 'The Death of Marat,' than Frankenthaler, Kokoshka or Klee. I realised I loved to watch him; that he'd become my kind of aesthetic. Hopeless grief: my old familiar. If I loved a gay man what did that make me? A gay male? Confusion was just the beginning. This was worse than adolescence.

When his boyfriend was at work we'd hang out in the kitchen and James would bake us cakes. A shelf of mixed books hung above his kitchen bench: *The Thief's Journal*, Stephanie Alexander and *The Norton Anthology of Poetry*. I'd browse and he'd cook and sometimes I'd read to him, little snippets. One week it was chocolate and hazelnut and I tipped out a book on queer theory.

What exactly is queer theory? I asked, turning the glossy book over, looking for a summary.

Not what it used to be, he said and buried himself further in his recipe. *Can you pass me those hazelnuts? And line this pan with paper.*

Yes sir, right away ... I went to pass him the nuts, but snatched them back at the last moment. *I explained Neo-Classicism for you!*

It's a rancid can of worms, OK? An old, rancid, can of worms. And he looked so dark, like the blackest corner of an oil painting, one that might hide something or might not, and it was strange to see him pouring sugar with that look on his face.

In final year we did a semester of Obstetrics and Gynaecology. We had to attend three operations and three deliveries. I stood next to a young father and watched his face fill with horror as their daughter tore her way through his young wife's legs. I watched a seventy-year-old lady have a total pelvic evisceration and I subsequently missed my period. I remembered my pet guinea pig, with the ginger and white fur. It had what I thought was a period; left these horror-inducing little strings of blood and mucus all around its hutch and then, the next morning, I'd found her stiff, on her back, hunkered up next to the water dripper. And all I'd felt was relief. I was rid of her, she was gone; the bleeding thing was gone.

I told James about my missed period. He asked if I was pregnant. I raised an eyebrow. *Yeah,* I said, *with Jesus.* It had been a long time between distractions. *That's too bad,* he said. My head veered backwards. *Are you crazy?* He told me he desperately wanted a baby, a little tiny baby. I relaxed and I laughed. *I'm serious,* he said. My laugh flipped to stutter. *I'm serious,* he said, and his eyes followed suit. *With who, what? Are you crazy?* I asked, my stomach now something deranged. *I ... I've seen these women lose their gonads for Christ's sake James! I've seen them blown to bits.*

Blown to bits, he quietly repeated, some old sadness tangled in his eyes.

We studied for our final long-case. The wards were packed with students practising on all the available patients, so James and I had to use each other. My bed was for the patient and we took it in turns. *So, James, you are obviously in a critical condition,* I giggled. *Please remove your shirt, and your jeans, now lie back and just breathe.* I put my hand on his shoulder and pressed my stethoscope to his heart. It beat faster and faster and I could barely hear it over my own. I cleared my throat, looked to his face and proclaimed his heart normal. *Normal,* he repeated, and brushed his fingers across my lip gloss. I felt his breath on my face. He said, *You make me feel like a child in some endless playground* and then he kissed me, lightly, on the lips. Utter bewilderment didn't come close. *James*

… I said. *Well* … he answered. And, like the rest, he belted his jeans, and went home.

At the end of semester we had a lecture on transsexuality. They figured we were ready, and the content wasn't examinable. The professor of Gynaecology was an old-school fag who wore ties with insignia. He displayed a pre-op male-to-female like a rat in a cage. *This is Rachel,* he said in his clipped Oxford accent, pointing to a thin blonde in a polyester skirt-suit. One of the Christians in the class went berserk and turned on the professor. *You're treating a mental illness with surgery! You've forged a disease out of thin air! We are born male or female, it's chromosomally determined!*

The professor stretched his neck ever so slightly. *These people,* he replied, *are not easy to treat. These people,* he replied, *have a high rate of suicide. These people attempt the surgery on themselves.*

The professor spoke about the intersexed, about hormones and their disregulation. He explained that the removal of the penis was a procedure covered by Medicare, but the subsequent construction of the vagina was not.

I leaned over to James, *All of my boyfriends have turned out to be cunts.*

He looked at me and smiled, *Well, that makes you a lesbian.* He raised his eyebrows up and down. *And must have saved them a bit of cash.*

The professor projected slides of removal and reconstruction; of penises made from abdominal flesh.

You know, I knew a lot of doctors were frustrated sculptors, but this, this is ridiculous! I whispered.

The professor cleared his throat.

I continued, *I mean, does anything go? What if I decide that I'm actually a goat trapped in this body? Can I get a hide graft, a horn graft? Give up language altogether and hang out in a paddock bleating?*

James frowned and turned to the front of the auditorium. He looked at Rachel, he looked at the professor and then he turned back to me. That look took the smile from my mouth. He wasn't laughing, was no longer playing along. He curled his lip like a queen, closed his folder, stood up. He left me sitting in the back row, alone.

Pre-emptive Strike

Will Elliott

OK. So well basically the gist of it is Claude's nothing but trouble, which I've known for some time. Part of it's not his fault, given the whole slight-retardation thing, a.k.a. booze in the womb, whereby he's stuck at age sixteen. Believe me I was real sad when I found this out, and even wrote a two-page poem called 'the boy trapped in ice' which used really innovative rhyme schemes, and definitely didn't overdo the echoing of the word 'why' if you want my opinion. But that was then. There comes a point one must swallow one's lumps and forge paths onward through the murk.

He's my brother, I should point out, Claude is, which I had no say in at all. And you name it: pot, beer, crystal meth, those goddam pills, yes he's into them. It breaks my heart: there he is still at my folks' place, age twenty-five for God's sake, sitting there on the couch with this sagging dead face after a weekend binge.

And the man has no standards. Doesn't matter what's on TV at the time: those fucking puppet shows or whatever, romance soaps, daytime talk-shows where these bucktooth people screw each other's wives and fight. He just sits there absorbing it like a sponge and staggering outside to smoke now and then and that's that. Lifting a finger around the house? Forget it. Meanwhile my parents' hair has gone white and they're at that age where stuff starts to happen, in terms of cardiovascular surprises. Like they need the stress, if you get me.

And it's not like I don't ask the hard questions, e.g. 'Get a job, fuckhead.'

Then he's all: 'Are you my dad or something?' This all angry and aggrieved and I cannot reply, mind boggled. It just brings the Rage out and I have to walk away clenching and unclenching my fists, and set down expensive items e.g. mobile phones or else there's a real chance of hurling them hard at the wall in sheer Rage. And OK, I know I'm not entirely Mr Angel, in terms of Claude, in that maybe when we were kids I kind of occasionally whaled on him a little, and perhaps am therefore partly a part of what made him modern-day Claude. But I apologised over beers, sincerity levels through the roof, the whole 'Let's Start Over' bit. To any avail? None.

So yeah he's a wreck in slow motion and like I said to Louise, get ready to haul serious weight through life because of Claude? Baggage, babe, forget it, is what I said. Dead weight. It kills me. Picture this guy who just rather than walk home on his own legs, lies across the train tracks so other people have to carry him. They do every time, he knows this, a vampire of other people's decency is the basic deal. Even if this time there's a train coming, he just lies there waiting for us to turn back around and rush over to pick him up and haul him over our shoulders, and he's saying all along how sorry he is and he broke his ankle, but he's smiling inside, which just makes this curtain of blood-coloured Rage descend whenever I see him sitting there, opening another tub of Pringles while Oprah smiles and nods and eggs him on. While here I am busting my hump at the firm, you get me? Man those phone calls never stop all day and my assistants couldn't find a turd in a sewer and I get back spasms from the computer chair I have to sit at plus goddam conjunctivitis from the monitor made in the '80s and I can't lay across any train tracks and get people to carry me along since little Kenny was born and Louise kicked me out of the house after that night of extended Rage, for which of course I'm truly totally sorry.

Oh so let's talk friends then. Who's Claude hang with? Could it be freaky shits who literally have no soap in the house of any kind and keep animal skulls on their walls as decorations? Go on and guess. The type who shoot endangered wildlife with crossbows, yes CROSSBOWS and keep the skins? And would they indulge in drugs, these people? Check. Would they be full of stories about pillowcase beatings, whereby you slip a pillowcase over someone's head as he gets out of the car so he can't see, then pummel hell out of him with blunt items in the twilight, silhouettes frantically lashing to the backdrop of passing headlights as the victim's body sinks to the ground? Check. Would he have actually invited to my parents' house one time these dudes who were connected with the leading organised-crime family in the city? Check again, and my God those shifty glances, creeping over Ma and Pa's household goods like some dude's fingers feeling up a woman on a crowded train ... I still dream about those glances and sweat profusely, sometimes sitting up very suddenly and gasping words like, 'No, no.' These people he hangs around with, they keep pet snakes! There's rubble ankle-deep in their living rooms. Is Claude the type of guy you want hanging around with little Kenny or your dear old Ma and Pa as they approach retirement?

And well basically the first time it occurred to me that sometimes an untimely death is not so untimely? Yes, shocked. And I would never have done anything to make it happen, because how would you live with yourself etc., but just once in a while would find myself wistfully hoping for a car smash on the news and a glimpse of footage of a mashed-up old light blue '86 Astra, or a photo in the paper of same with the headline NO SURVIVORS. Then of course as you can imagine I felt (approx.) level-three guilt and did the whole standing-in-front-of-the-mirror thing with the head-shaking and the whispering 'You Monster' at self, sincerity levels moderate/heavy, eyes with a kind of pleading look which, even now looking back, moves me almost to tears (BUT I could also kind of see my point).

So like, I've been reading about serial killers. And I wouldn't go as far as to say I've made a comprehensive diagnosis, but there are dots: early life head injuries? Check. Occasionally traumatic childhood with, say an older relative, for e.g. sibling, maybe once in a while doing stuff with a billiard ball swung in the end of a sock hypothetically? But only when he really fucking deserved it, like that time he broke my new CD player I got as my only birthday present when dad was unemployed and times were tough?

Check. Cruelty to animals as a kid? Like that time he hit poor loyal Snuffy with the basketball or when he let his fish starve by being too pot-focused to feed them? Check check. And there was that fixation he had with *Silence of the Lambs* don't forget, when I caught him rewind-playing that scene over and over where the chick is trapped in a well and the dude is saying, 'You don't know what pain is,' plus once I think I overheard him saying that line before the bathroom mirror. And I have definitely found things that could possibly pass for souvenirs from victims, mostly cigarette lighters and maybe key rings, which he has far more of (both) than any person would ever need.

Look I'm not saying for sure I know Certain Things but what's with all the disappearances for days at a time to his friend's house, only he wasn't actually there, as phone calls revealed? And the time he thoroughly cleaned out his car's interior for the first time in years after coming back? These key rings and lighters all over the damn place and once this thing of lipstick on the back seat of his car? What was I supposed to think? So yes while open minds are handy no one can deny there are dots to connect, oh yes indeed there are dots.

But what topped it for me I guess was that conversation my old man had with us about making a will, now that we're adults and all, not that Claude has shit to leave to anyone but a bunch of $2000 phone bills, I kid you not two-grand phone bills, plus no one in their right mind would rent to him after all the drama. Scum, human scum is the only word for it. Anyway, re. the convo, dad was saying how we should make a will and I was carefully watching Claude's face, as I did those days because I was frankly growing more and more wary of what he's capable of. Without scruple? You bet. And lies? My God, I have never seen someone lie with Claude's skill. And when you know he's doing it right to your face it basically invites the Rage to seep from your pores in heated waves, I swear.

At the mention of wills, you could see Claude's face kind of brighten up for a moment as some new tidbit hit his reptile brain, for later sucking and digestion. Something just occurred to him in a very major way, it was clear. Then the shutters closed and his face went deliberately back to showing nothing.

The whole process: visible. It doesn't take Sherlock to figure out he was thinking then: yes, Ma and Pa's will, oh ho ho, shiver me timbers. Their estate, he was thinking, and how many coloured pills and bags of green stuff and powder his half of it would fetch, plus porn/hookers no doubt, and no more getting up early to ride garbage trucks around the block. He was thinking, if Ma and Pa were to croak as of tomorrow, why, it's party time, he's thinking. And I swear it was all I could do there not to scream and lunge across the dinner table, the whole chopsticks-in-the-eye thing. The Rage came again most powerfully and I had to turn a kind of snarl sound into a cough, like I'd choked on my sushi, and poor unsuspecting Pa made that gag about being too late for me to make my will and that dirty 'garbologist' fucker had the audacity to pretend to laugh, like he wasn't contemplating where he'd hide the bodies (for e.g. with the OTHERS?).

And that look kept replaying over in my head for like the next two weeks, just that shutters-closing look, poker face. And the way he glanced at the knife-rack as he left his plate by the sink, it gave me the chills and more sweaty dreams with the murmuring 'No, no,' as I lunged up, awake.

And my God, then Claude's suddenly moping around the house, slinking, no shit genuine slinking, and this air of lurking in every room he's in like some dude behind the bushes outside a girl's bedroom, and a sudden thoughtful look on his face when he sits there absorbing TV, and every time you speak to him he has this calculated lack there, like someone doing an innocent whistle when they're up to no good at all. And I know the people he hangs around, how they could arrange a hit for just a few grand, and how I saw him talking on his mobile way out in the backyard away from where we could maybe overhear, and how when he came back to the house again with that poker face, that thoughtfulness, eyes darting around the room and such, that moustache on his upper lip like a bit of dirt he's refused to wipe off, that godawful stink he makes, that stink of corruption, and all this combined I guess in sum kind of explains why I went ahead and did it, and of course I'm truly totally sorry.

Hanging On

Michael Wilding

In memory of David Myers, 1942–2007

Henry sat despondent in The Golden Bowl. The restaurant was empty because he was early, and he was early because he had nothing much else to do. By noon Henry was hungry: hungry for food, hungry for company. Thirsty too. Most of the customers came in for lunch at one or one-thirty, civilised Italian style. But Henry was there when the doors opened at noon, and sometimes before. He sat there browsing through the paper. A bottle of wine stood on the table, already opened, breathing, Henry already stuck into a glass, and still breathing too.

Dr Bee came in not much later. They grunted at each other, greetings of a sort, of a sort given when breath was short and civilities eroded with familiarity.

'Keeping busy?' Henry asked. 'Prowling the shopping malls?'

Dr Bee claimed the shopping malls were the site of contemporary erotic adventure. The *flaneur* of Franklins. The *boulevardier* of Bi-Lo.

'Too sick,' said Dr Bee. 'I lay in bed and planned my own funeral.'

'Alone?'

'Just a funeral,' said Dr Bee. 'Not a suicide pact.'

'Ah, well,' said Henry. 'I suppose it's something to pass the time.'

'Churchill spent the last decade of his life planning his funeral.'

'There you are then,' said Henry. 'It gives you an interest in life.'

'True,' said Dr Bee.

'Though it sounds pretty terrible to me.'

'It may sound terrible but you're still going to need one,' said Dr Bee.

'Face that when I come to it,' said Henry.

'Somehow I doubt you will be able to.'

'We shall see,' said Henry.

'Most likely you won't,' said Dr Bee.

They picked desultorily at the marinated olives. Dr Bee poured some olive oil on to a plate and dipped his bread in it.

'Olive oil reduces cholesterol,' he announced.

'Ah,' said Henry. 'So you're not leaping into this funeral. You're still attempting to stave it off.'

'It has to be cold-pressed olive oil,' said Pawley, joining them. 'And extra virgin.'

Dr Bee gave a lascivious laugh, lapping his lips round the phrase. 'Extra virgin.' Retirement had not reduced his lasciviousness, as he kept reminding them.

Henry had leapt at it. Early retirement. The alternative had been an increased teaching load. Worse than that, his old personalised courses had been scheduled for termination – the few that were left. The future was group teaching. Or first-year tutorials. It appealed to none of them. 'If it had been group sex?' Dr Bee pondered. But it hadn't.

They had all taken it. Early retirement. Various incentives had been dangled before them, which they took. But they would have gone anyway.

And they did.

And now Henry felt bereft.

He reached down and rubbed his leg, swollen and painful from deep vein thrombosis. The industrial disease of international writers and airport academics.

'How's it going?' Pawley asked.

'Bloody nurse,' said Henry.

'Which nurse was that?' Dr Bee asked.

'The one who did my blood test. She waved the needle at me and said, "Little prick." So I said, just as a joke, you know, "It's not that little." And she jabbed me. Viciously. Look at that bruise.'

He rolled up his shirt sleeve to reveal a large, purple haematosis.

'Nothing changes,' said Pawley. 'Enticement followed by humiliation. Just like the old days. But without the sexual act in between.'

'I'll pass,' said Dr Bee. 'I have no more wish than the nurse to gaze on your anatomy.'

Dr Bee was depressed. He glowered malignantly at the world around him. He picked up Henry's newspaper and turned to the obituaries.

'I remember the first thing my parents used to turn to in the local paper was the death notices. It gave them some satisfaction. Indeed, the only satisfaction they ever had, as far as I could see. Somebody else off the board. Somebody else's funeral you could make a point of not going to.'

There was a certain satisfaction in funerals. Especially of former colleagues. Either in refusing to attend, or in attending and catching a sight of the wives and mistresses and boyfriends and partners and offspring that had been concealed over the years. Hearing the ambiguous tributes delivered by other former colleagues who would hopefully soon be following them. But even they were getting less frequent, funerals and former colleagues, as one by one the former colleagues dropped dead.

'In the past,' Dr Bee said, as he found himself saying more often since there wasn't much future to talk about, 'in the past when I felt like this, I would go out and buy new clothes. Raise my spirits that way.'

'You still can,' said Henry.

'No point,' said Dr Bee. 'I wouldn't get the wear out of them.'

'Wouldn't get the wear out of them?'

'Before I died. It would be a waste of money.'

Henry poured a drink with shaking hand. Shaken. 'That's a defeatist way of looking at it,' he said.

'Doesn't mean it's not true,' said Dr Bee.

'Exactly,' said Pawley, who had taken his early retirement up the coast. 'Got to face reality. A few weeks back there was a pair of pied oyster-catchers on the beach. They just sat on the sand near the water's edge. I looked at them and they looked back at me.'

'Perfect communion,' said Dr Bee.

'They're an endangered species,' Pawley added.

'Like us,' said Henry.

'Exactly,' Pawley agreed. 'I got to wondering if they knew they were posted as endangered. I know that we are, though it's not been posted anywhere.'

'Oh, it has,' said Henry. 'At the university. Dead white males. Spelled out loud and clear.'

'Posted for extinction,' said Dr Bee lugubriously. 'Open season.'

'Nature tells you these things,' said Pawley.

'We already know,' said Dr Bee. 'We don't need nature telling us.'

Pawley shrugged.

'I do,' he said. 'It's calming. We could be scheduled for extinction and no one would raise a murmur till we'd gone. Been eliminated. Then they could express a certain satisfied sadness about it. But we'd be gone. Like all those other vanished species. We were nowhere. Then we were here. And then we were gone again.'

'I don't find that at all calming,' said Henry.

'Realistic, though,' said Pawley. 'At our age you've got to be realistic. Keep the house clean. Do the dishes before you go out. Don't wear ragged underwear. You don't want to be found dead on the beach and have everyone discover how squalidly you lived.'

'I have no intention of being found either dead or alive on a beach,' said Dr Bee. 'Anyway, I can't see that it matters once you've dropped dead.'

'Reputation,' said Pawley. 'How you wish to be remembered.'

'I wish to be forgotten,' said Dr Bee.

'You won't be if they see your ragged underpants,' said Pawley. 'I think it's worth buying new ones even if you're not going to get full wear out of them.'

'And how will you be remembered? The man with feet of clay?'

Dr Bee snapped, glowering at Pawley's R.M. Williams boots, mud-spattered and unpolished. The rural life.

'I don't want to be one of those sad old men with highly polished shoes,' Pawley explained. 'You see them, desperately keeping up appearances, blazer, cravat, golf jacket, polo shirt, trying to look like anyone still cares whether they live or die, trying to look like they're walking purposively somewhere. But they're not. They've nowhere to go. Nothing to do. The shoes are the giveaway. Nothing else to do but polish shoes. Who would ever polish their shoes unless they had nothing else to do? Anyway, people mainly wear trainers these days.'

'Hideous,' said Henry.

They looked through the menu. They read the specials board. They read through them again and tried to figure out what they could eat without ill-effects. Except for Dr Bee who was on a new medication. He showed them the pill packet. 'I take a couple every night. Prophylactic measures. They give me the stomach of a twenty-year-old.'

'They don't,' said Pawley.

'I can eat anything without any ill-effects.'

'That you know of,' said Pawley. 'But they're just suppressing the symptoms. You don't have the stomach of a twenty-year-old any more. Or any other organs. They're all clapped out.'

'I no longer have indigestion all night.'

'Indigestion is nature's warning,' said Pawley. 'It lets you know you're eating the wrong things. You suppress the symptoms, you'll end up poisoning yourself. Give yourself ulcers. Diabetes. Colon cancer. It's the same as sexual appetite. Better be nauseated than …'

'Than what?' Dr Bee demanded.

'Than all those terrible things that happen to you when you think you have the genitalia of a twenty-year-old.'

'Safety in numbness,' said Henry.

The new female wait-person came over, all cheeriness and lack of reverence.

'So what is it today, boys?'

'Boys!' Henry said, hollowly. 'Oh that we were!'

'Good old boys,' she offered.

Dr Bee glowered, giving his best shot at being a bad old boy.

He ordered garlic prawns followed by veal parmigiana. Henry went for linguine vongole. Pawley ordered sardines. Entrée size.

'That it?' she asked.

'That's it,' Dr Bee snapped.

'Just piss off and leave you alone?' she asked.

'Got it in one,' Henry assured her.

'Given up the vegetarianism?' Dr Bee asked Pawley.

'Up to a point. Got to stay alive. Can't be a vegetarian if you're dead. Sardines are a source of Omega-3. Natural health. Better than taking pills.'

'I threw all my pills away,' said Henry. 'I couldn't stand it. Every morning. Realising I was going to be doing this every day until I died. Just to stay alive. Counting them out. Breaking the soluble aspirin in half. Trying to remember which I'd taken. I bought a medicine box and within weeks it wasn't big enough. In the end I got so depressed I threw the lot away.'

'And became immediately better,' said Pawley, all New Age therapies from his coastal retreat.

'I damn near died,' said Henry. 'Doctor had a fit when he checked me out.'

'He damn near died too?' Dr Bee asked.

'He's not that well,' Henry agreed. 'We compare symptoms. Everything I've got he seems to have had.'

'And you still go to him?' said Pawley.

'He's still alive,' said Henry.

'Even if in ill-health.'

'But I figure he knows how to stay alive.'

'Or to stay ill,' Pawley persisted.

Henry shrugged. He poured a glass of mineral water and took a couple of warfarin tablets. Pawley produced his CoQ10. Dr Bee showed them his packet of Pariet.

'Oh, that it should come to this,' Henry said. He poured the wine. An Italian Pinot Grigio. Now they were having to drink less they once in a while went for something more expensive than the house white from the Riverina. And Henry claimed Italian wines had fewer allergens than Australian wines. Anything to reduce the negative impact of lived experience.

'Here's to life after retirement.'

'Don't call it retirement,' said Pawley. 'Never use the R-word.

No point in letting people think we're finished. Once they think you're finished you're out of the game. Never another invitation. No more international visitors. No one taking you to lunch. No more overseas travel. No more domestic travel. No, Henry, never surrender anything. You mightn't like the university.'

'Couldn't stand it,' said Henry.

'Doesn't matter. You don't have to actually go to it anymore.'

'Never went there that much anyway,' Dr Bee remarked.

'Exactly,' said Pawley. 'So keep up the connection. Ask them to make you an honorary associate. Or an emeritus chair. Whatever you can get. Never say you're retired.'

'I never thought I'd hear you say this,' said Henry. 'You were always dying to get out.'

'True,' said Pawley. 'But no need to make it easy for the buggers. Don't want to make it look as if we're ready for the knacker's yard. Call it a change of emphasis. Focused on writing, now.'

'I don't know,' said Henry. 'It would be like taking one of those adjunct professorships they hand out to clapped-out bureaucrats and disgraced politicians.'

'Still time to disgrace yourself,' said Dr Bee, 'if you feel your novels haven't sufficiently done that.'

'Anyway, they don't mean anything.'

'Your novels?'

'Adjunct professorships. It would be embarrassing to have one. Mark of obloquy,' said Henry. 'No, I am a writer. Free at last to write what I want.'

'What's the point of trying to write a best-seller now? At your age?' Pawley asked.

'Fame, recognition, wealth,' said Dr Bee, derisively.

'He's far too old for that. It would kill him. Sex, drugs and air-travel. All the perils of celebrity. All the things he thought he wanted. At Henry's age they'd prove fatal.'

'I don't know about that,' said Henry. 'I'm no older than you.'

'Exactly,' said Pawley. 'My body can only just handle the drugs I can afford on my superannuation. If I had unlimited wealth, can you imagine what would happen?'

'I'm willing to take the risk,' said Henry.

'AIDS, heart attack, thrombosis, syphilis, blackmail, divorce, alimony, palimony, addiction, madness,' Dr Bee listed.

'Nonetheless,' Pawley persisted, 'don't give up the university, otherwise you'll end up with nothing. It's like fishing.'

'Fishing?'

'A good spot on the river. Don't let it go. Don't let someone else grab it. The point is not to give the impression we've given up.'

'Why not?'

'Why let the administrators and accountants and time-servers take over?'

'They already have.'

'Don't surrender to them, Henry. Don't give it away.'

'They're welcome to it.'

'You're making a mistake. You don't want to be seen to moulder.'

'I'm not mouldering.'

'You don't want to look like you're past it.'

'I am past it. As far as the university is concerned.'

'So am I,' said Pawley. 'And have been for years. Decades. Longer even. Way past it. The world has passed me by. Hopefully. But there's no need to draw attention to that fact. I'm keeping my honorary associateship and my library card. And my shared room. Even if I never go into it. Can't fit into it anyway, there's five of us sharing. But the point is, we don't want people thinking we're old and finished and washed up. As they will if we say we're retired. They'll dismiss us.'

'Dismiss us from where?'

'From notice. From participating. From life's grand designs.'

A chill wind blew along the street, driving leaves and blossoms and plastic bags before it.

'Personally,' said Dr Bee, 'I can see little point in going on. Except to make sure I get more back from the pension fund than I put in. That gives me a certain satisfaction.'

'The secret of staying alive is to do something every day,' Pawley said. 'It doesn't matter what. As long as you do something. It doesn't need to be a lot. Just sticking a stamp on an envelope. You don't even have to write a letter. Do that another day. Address it another day again. Just as long as you retain an interest in staying alive.'

'I'm not sure I do,' Dr Bee said.

'I was asked to write an article on staying alive,' said Henry.

'How far have you got?' Dr Bee asked. 'It could give a new meaning to the concept of a deadline.'

'My acupuncturist said: "Coming alive, Henry, not staying alive. Take the opportunity to come alive."'

'She's quite right, of course,' said Pawley.

'She also said: "The gift the dead leave with us is the message to live."'

'Jesus,' said Dr Bee.

'Jesus especially,' Pawley agreed. 'But other teachers, too. Come alive, Henry. Let the dead bury the dead. Reorient yourself. Abandon the negative. Love life.'

'It's hard to imagine what for,' Dr Bee said.

'That's the challenge of it,' Pawley assured him. 'To discover the meaning of life. To live it to the full.'

'Golf?' Dr Bee inquired. 'Kayaking?'

'Enjoy, as the wait-people say,' said Henry, holding up his glass.

'That's the spirit,' said Pawley.

Griffith Review

Love and Honour and Pity and Pride and Compassion and Sacrifice

Nam Le

My father arrived on a rainy morning. I was dreaming about a poem, the dull *thluck thluck* of a typewriter's keys punching out the letters. It was a good poem – perhaps the best I'd ever written. When I woke up, he was standing outside my bedroom door, smiling ambiguously. He wore black trousers and a wet, wrinkled parachute jacket that looked like it had just been pulled out of a washing machine. Framed by the bedroom doorway, he appeared even smaller, gaunter, than I remembered. Still groggy with dream, I lifted my face toward the alarm clock.

'What time is it?'

'Hello, Son,' he said in Vietnamese. 'I knocked for a long time. Then the door just opened.'

The fields are glass, I thought. Then tum-ti-ti, a dactyl, end line, then the words *excuse* and *alloy* in the line after. Come on, I thought.

'It's raining heavily,' he said.

I frowned. The clock read 11.44. 'I thought you weren't coming until this afternoon.' It felt strange, after all this time, to be speaking Vietnamese again.

'They changed my flight in Los Angeles.'

'Why didn't you ring?'

'I tried,' he said equably. 'No answer.'

I twisted over the side of the bed and cracked open the window.

The sound of rain filled the room – rain fell on the streets, on the roofs, on the tin shed across the parking lot like the distant detonations of firecrackers. Everything smelled of wet leaves.

'I turn the ringer off when I sleep,' I said. 'Sorry.'

He continued smiling at me, significantly, as if waiting for an announcement.

'I was dreaming.'

He used to wake me, when I was young, by standing over me and smacking my cheeks lightly. I hated it – the wetness, the sourness of his hands.

'Come on,' he said, picking up a large Adidas duffel and a rolled bundle that looked like a sleeping bag. 'A day lived, a sea of knowledge earned.' He had a habit of speaking in Vietnamese proverbs. I had long since learned to ignore it.

I threw on a T-shirt and stretched my neck in front of the lone window. Through the rain, the sky was as grey and sharp as graphite. *The fields are glass* … Like a shape in smoke, the poem blurred, then dissolved into this new, cold, strange reality: a windblown, rain-strafed parking lot; a dark room almost entirely taken up by my bed; the small body of my father dripping water onto hardwood floors.

I went to him, my legs goose-pimpled underneath my pyjamas. He watched with pleasant indifference as my hand reached for his, shook it, then relieved his other hand of the bags. 'You must be exhausted,' I said.

He had flown from Sydney, Australia. Thirty-three hours all up – transiting in Auckland, Los Angeles, and Denver – before touching down in Iowa. I hadn't seen him in three years.

'You'll sleep in my room.'

'Very fancy,' he said, as he led me through my own apartment. 'You even have a piano.' He gave me an almost rueful smile. 'I knew you'd never really quit.' Something moved behind his face and I found myself back on a heightened stool with my fingers chasing the metronome, ahead and behind, trying to shut out the tutor's repeated sighing, his heavy brass ruler. I realised I was massaging my knuckles. My father patted the futon in my living room. 'I'll sleep here.'

'You'll sleep in my room, Ba.' I watched him warily as he surveyed our surroundings, messy with books, papers, dirty plates, teacups, clothes – I'd intended to tidy up before going to the airport. 'I work in this room anyway, and I work at night.' As he moved into the kitchen, I grabbed the three-quarters-full bottle of Johnny Walker from the second shelf of my bookcase and stashed it under the desk. I looked around. The desktop was gritty with cigarette ash. I threw some magazines over the roughest spots, then flipped one of them over because its cover bore a picture of Chairman Mao. I quickly gathered up the cigarette packs and sleeping pills and incense burners and dumped them all on a high shelf, behind my Kafka Vintage Classics.

At the kitchen swing door I remembered the photo of Linda beside the printer. Her glamour shot, I called it: hair windswept and eyes squinty, smiling at something out of frame. One of her ex-boyfriends had taken it at Lake MacBride. She looked happy. I snatched it and turned it face down, covering it with scrap paper.

As I walked into the kitchen I thought, for a moment, that I had left the fire-escape open. Rainwater gushed along gutters, down through the pipes. Then I saw my father at the sink, sleeves rolled up, sponge in hand, washing the month-old, crusted mound of dishes. The smell was awful. 'Ba,' I frowned, 'you don't need to do that.'

His hands, hard and leathery, moved deftly in the sink.

'Ba,' I said, half-heartedly.

'I'm almost finished.' He looked up and smiled. 'Have you eaten? Do you want me to make some lunch?'

'*Hoi*,' I said, suddenly irritated. 'You're exhausted. I'll go out and get us something.'

I went back through the living room into my bedroom, picking up clothes and rubbish as I went.

'You don't have to worry about me,' he called out. 'You just do what you always do.'

The truth was, he'd come at the worst possible time. I was in my last year at the Iowa Writers' Workshop; it was late November, and my final story for the semester was due in three days. I had a backlog of papers to grade and a heap of fellowship and job applications to draft and submit. It was no wonder I was drinking so much.

I'd told Linda only the previous night that he was coming. We were at her place. Her body was slippery with sweat and hard to hold. Her body smelled of her clothes. She turned me over, my face kissing the bedsheets, and then she was chopping my back with the edges of her hands. *Higher. Out a bit more.* She had trouble keeping a steady rhythm. 'Softer,' I told her. Moments later, I started laughing.

'What?'

The sheets were damp beneath my pressed face.

'What?'

'*Softer,*' I said, 'not *slower.*'

She slapped my back with the meat of her palms, hard – once, twice. I couldn't stop laughing. I squirmed over and caught her by the wrists. Hunched forward, she was blushing and beautiful. Her hair fell over her face; beneath its ash-blond hem all I could see were her open lips. She pressed down, into me, her shoulders kinking the long, lean curve from the back of her neck to the small of her back. 'Stop it!' her lips said. She wrested her hands free. Fingers beneath my waistband, violent, the scratch of her nails down my thighs, knees, ankles. I pointed my foot like a ballet dancer.

Afterward, I told her my father didn't know about her. She said nothing. 'We just don't talk about that kind of stuff,' I explained. She looked like an actress who looked like my girlfriend. Staring at her face made me tired. I'd begun to feel this way more often around her. 'He's only here for three days.' Somewhere out of sight, a group of college boys hooted and yelled.

'I thought you didn't talk to him at all.'

'He's my father.'

'What's he want?'

I rolled toward her, onto my elbow. I tried to remember how much I'd told her about him. We were lying on the bed, the wind loud in the room – I remember that – and we were both tipsy. Ours could have been any two voices in the darkness. 'It's only three days,' I said.

The look on her face was strange, shut down. She considered me a long time. Then she got up and pulled on her clothes. 'Just make sure you get your story done,' she said.

*

I drank before I came here too. I drank when I was a student at university, and then when I was a lawyer – in my previous life, as they say. There was a subterranean bar in a hotel next to my work, and every night I would wander down and slump on a barstool and pretend I didn't want the bartender to make small talk with me. He was only a bit older than me, and I came to envy his ease, his confidence that any given situation was merely temporary. I left exorbitant tips. After a while, I was treated to battered shrimps and shepherd's pies on the house. My parents had already split by then: my father moving to Sydney, my mother into a government flat.

That's all I've ever done, traffic in words. Sometimes I still think about word counts the way a general must think about casualties. I'd been in Iowa more than a year – days passed in weeks, then months, more than a year of days – and I'd written only four and a half stories. About seventeen thousand words. When I was working at the law firm, I would have written that many words in a couple of weeks. And they would have been useful to someone.

Deadlines came, exhausting, and I forced myself up to meet them. Then, in the great spans of time between, I fell back to my vacant screen and my slowly sludging mind. I tried everything – writing in longhand, writing in my bed, in my bathtub. As this last deadline approached, I remembered a friend claiming he'd broken his writer's block by switching to a typewriter. You're free to write, he told me, once you know you can't delete what you've written. I bought an electric Smith Corona at an antique shop. It buzzed like a tropical aquarium when I plugged it in. It looked good on my desk. For inspiration, I read absurdly formal Victorian poetry and drank Scotch neat. How hard could it be? Things happened in this world all the time. All I had to do was record them. In the sky, two swarms of swallows converged, pulled apart, interwove again like veils drifting at crosscurrents. In line at the supermarket, a black woman leaned forward and kissed the handle of her shopping cart, her skin dark and glossy like the polished wood of a piano.

The week prior to my father's arrival, a friend chastised me for my persistent defeatism.

'Writer's block?' Under the streetlights, vapours of bourbon puffed out of his mouth. 'How can you have writer's block? Just write a story about Vietnam.'

We had just come from a party following a reading by the workshop's most recent success, a Chinese woman trying to emigrate to America who had written a book of short stories about Chinese characters in stages of migration to America. The stories were subtle and good. The gossip was that she'd been offered a substantial six-figure contract for a two-book deal. It was meant to be an unspoken rule that such things were left unspoken. Of course, it was all anyone talked about.

'It's hot,' a writing instructor told me at a bar. 'Ethnic literature's hot. And important too.'

A couple of visiting literary agents took a similar view: 'There's a lot of polished writing around,' one of them said. 'You have to ask yourself, what makes me stand out?' She tag-teamed to her colleague, who answered slowly as though intoning a mantra, 'Your *background* and *life experience*.'

Other friends were more forthright: 'I'm sick of ethnic lit,' one said. 'It's full of descriptions of exotic food.' Or: 'You can't tell if the language is spare because the author intended it that way, or because he didn't have the vocab.'

I was told about a friend of a friend, a Harvard graduate from Washington, D.C., who had posed in traditional Nigerian garb for his book-jacket photo. I pictured myself standing in a rice paddy, wearing a straw conical hat. Then I pictured my father in the same field, wearing his threadbare fatigues, young and hard-eyed.

'It's a licence to bore,' my friend said. We were drunk and wheeling our bikes because both of us, separately, had punctured our tyres on the way to the party.

'The characters are always flat, generic. As long as a Chinese writer writes about *Chinese* people, or a Peruvian writer about *Peruvians*, or a Russian writer about *Russians* …' he said, as though reciting children's doggerel, then stopped, losing his train of thought. His mouth turned up into a doubtful grin. I could tell he was angry about something.

'Look,' I said, pointing at a floodlit porch ahead of us. 'Those guys have guns.'

'As long as there's an interesting image or metaphor once in every *this* much text' – he held out his thumb and forefinger to indicate half a page, his bike wobbling all over the sidewalk. I nodded to him, and then I nodded to one of the guys on the porch, who nodded back. The other guy waved us through with his faux-wood air rifle. A car with its headlights on was idling in the driveway, and girls' voices emerged from inside, squealing, 'Don't shoot! Don't shoot!'

'Faulkner, you know,' my friend said over the squeals, 'he said we should write about the old verities. Love and honour and pity and pride and compassion and sacrifice.' A sudden sharp crack behind us, like the striking of a giant typewriter hammer, followed by some muffled shrieks. 'I know I'm a bad person for saying this,' my friend said, 'but that's why I don't mind your work, Nam. Because you could just write about Vietnamese boat people all the time. Like in your third story.'

He must have thought my head was bowed in modesty, but in fact I was figuring out whether I'd just been shot in the back of the thigh. I'd felt a distinct sting. The pellet might have ricocheted off something.

'You could *totally* exploit the Vietnamese thing. But *instead*, you choose to write about lesbian vampires and Colombian assassins, and Hiroshima orphans – and New York painters with haemorrhoids.'

For a dreamlike moment I was taken aback. Catalogued like that, under the bourbon stink of his breath, my stories sank into unflattering relief. My leg was still stinging. I imagined sticking my hand down the back of my jeans, bringing it to my face under a streetlight, and finding it gory, blood-spattered. I imagined turning around, advancing wordlessly up the porch steps, and dropkicking the two kids. I would tell my story into a microphone from a hospital bed. I would compose my story in a county cell. I would kill one of them, maybe accidentally, and never talk about it, ever, to anyone. There was no hole in my jeans.

'I'm probably a bad person,' my friend said, stumbling beside his bike a few steps in front of me.

If you ask me why I came to Iowa, I would say that Iowa is beautiful in the way that any place is beautiful: if you treat it as the answer to a question you're asking yourself every day, just by being there.

That afternoon, as I was leaving the apartment for Linda's, my father called out my name from the bedroom.

I stopped outside the closed door. He was meant to be napping.

'Where are you going?' his voice said.

'For a walk,' I replied.

'I'll walk with you.'

It always struck me how everything seemed larger in scale on Summit Street: the double-storeyed houses, their smooth lawns sloping down to the sidewalks like golf greens; elm trees with high, thick branches – the sort of branches from which I imagined fathers suspending long-roped swings for daughters in white dresses. The leaves, once golden and red, were turning dark orange, brown. The rain had stopped. I don't know why, but we walked in the middle of the road, dark asphalt gleaming beneath slick, pasted leaves like the back of a whale.

I asked him, 'What do you want to do while you're here?'

His face was pale and fixed in a smile. 'Don't worry about me,' he said. 'I can just meditate. Or read.'

'There's a coffee shop downtown,' I said. 'And a Japanese restaurant.' It sounded pathetic. It occurred to me that I knew nothing about what my father did all day.

He kept smiling, looking at the ground moving in front of his feet.

'I have to write,' I said.

'You write.'

And I could no longer read his smile. He had perfected it during his absence. It was a setting of the lips, sly, almost imperceptible, which I would probably associate with senility but for the keenness of his eyes.

'There's an art museum across the river,' I said.

'Ah, take me there.'

'The museum?'

'No,' he said, looking sideways at me. 'The river.'

We turned back to Burlington Street and walked down the hill to the river. He stopped in the middle of the bridge. The water below looked cold and black, slowing in sections as it succumbed to the temperature. Behind us six lanes of cars skidded back and forth across the wet grit of the road, the sound like the shredding of wind.

'Have you heard from your mother?' He stood upright before the railing, his head strangely small above the puffy down jacket I had lent him.

'Every now and then.'

He lapsed into formal Vietnamese: 'How is the mother of Nam?'

'She is good,' I said, loudly – too loudly – trying to make myself heard over the groans and clanks of a passing truck.

He was nodding. Behind him, the east bank of the river glowed wanly in the afternoon light. 'Come on,' I said. We crossed the bridge and walked to a nearby Dairy Queen. When I came out, two coffees in my hands, my father had gone down to the river's edge. Next to him, a bundled-up, bearded figure stooped over a burning gasoline drum. Never had I seen anything like it in Iowa City.

'This is my son,' my father said, once I had scrambled down the wet bank. 'The writer.' He took a hot paper cup from my hand, 'Would you like some coffee?'

'Thank you, no.' The man stood still, watching his knotted hands, palms glowing orange above the rim of the drum. His voice was soft, his clothes heavy with his life. I smelled animals in him, and fuel, and rain.

'I read his story,' my father went on in his lilting English, 'about Vietnamese boat people.' He gazed at the man, straight into his blank, rheumy eyes, then said, as though delivering a punch line, 'We are Vietnamese boat people.'

We stood there for a long time, the three of us, watching the flames. When I lifted my eyes it was dark.

'Do you have any money on you?' my father asked me in Vietnamese.

'Welcome to America,' the man said through his beard. He didn't look up as I closed his fist around the damp bills.

My father was drawn to weakness, even as he tolerated none in me. He was a soldier, he said once, as if that explained everything. With me, he was all proverbs and regulations. No personal phone calls. No female friends. No extracurricular reading. When I was in primary school, he made me draw up a daily ten-hour study timetable for the summer holidays, and punished me when I deviated from it. He knew how to cane me twenty times and leave only one black-red welt, like a brand mark across my buttocks. Afterward, as he rubbed tiger balm on the wound, I would cry in anger at myself for crying. Once, when my mother let slip that durian fruit made me vomit, he forced me to eat it in front of guests. *Doi an muoi cung ngon*: Hunger finds no fault with food. I learned to hate him with a straight face.

When I was fourteen, I discovered that he had been involved in a massacre. Later, I would come across photos and transcripts and books; but there, at a family friend's party in suburban Melbourne, and then – it was just another story in a circle of drunken men. They sat cross-legged on newspapers around a large blue tarpaulin, getting smashed on cheap beer. It was that time of night when things started to break up against other things. Red faces, raised voices, spilled drinks. We arrived late and the men shuffled around, making room for my father.

'Thanh! Fuck your mother! What took you so long – scared, no? Sit down, sit down– '

'Give him five bottles.' The speaker swung around ferociously. 'We'll let you off, everyone here's had eight, nine already.'

For the first time, my father let me stay. I sat on the perimeter of the circle, watching in fascination. A thicket of Vietnamese voices, cursing, toasting, braying about their children, making fun of one man who kept stuttering, 'It has the power of f-f-five hundred horses!' Through it all my father laughed good-naturedly, his face so red with drink he looked sunburned. Bowl and chopsticks in his hands, he appeared somewhat childish sitting between two men trading war stories. I watched him as he picked sparingly at the enormous spread of dishes in the middle of the circle. The food was known as *do an nho*: alcohol food. Massive fatty oysters dipped in salt-pepper-lemon paste. Boiled sea snails, large grilled crab legs. Southern-style bitter shredded-chicken salad with brown, spotty rice crackers. Someone called out my father's name; he had set his chopsticks down and was speaking in a low voice:

'Heavens, the gunships came first, rockets and M60s. You

remember that sound, no? Like you were deaf. We were hiding in the bunker underneath the temple, my mother and four sisters and Mrs Tran, the baker, and some other people. You couldn't hear anything. Then the gunfire stopped and Mrs Tran told my mother we had to go up to the street. If we stayed there, the Americans would think we were Viet Cong. "I'm not going anywhere," my mother said. "They have grenades," Mrs Tran said. I was scared and excited. I had never seen an American before.'

It took me a while to reconcile my father with the story he was telling. He caught my eye and held it a moment, as though he were sharing a secret with me. He was drunk.

'So we went up. Everywhere there was dust and smoke, and all you could hear was the sound of helicopters and M16s. Houses on fire. Then through the smoke I saw an American. I almost laughed. He wore his uniform so untidily – it was too big for him – and he had a beaded necklace and a baseball cap. He held an M16 over his shoulder like a spade. Heavens, he looked nothing like the Viet Cong, with their shirts buttoned to their chins, and tucked in, even after crawling through mud tunnels all day.'

He picked up his chopsticks and reached for the *tiet canh* – a specialty – mincemeat soaked in fresh congealed duck blood. Some of the other men were listening now, smiling knowingly. I saw his teeth, stained red, as he chewed through the rest of his words.

'They made us walk to the east side of the village. There were about ten of them, about fifty of us. Mrs Tran was saying, "No VC no VC." They didn't hear her, over the sound of machine guns and the M79 grenade launchers. Remember those? Only I heard her. I saw pieces of animals all over the paddy fields, a water buffalo with its side missing – like it was scooped out by a spoon. Then, through the smoke, I saw Grandpa Long bowing to a GI in the traditional greeting. I wanted to call out to him. His wife and daughter and grand-daughters, My and Kim, stood shyly behind him. The GI stepped forward, tapped the top of his head with the rifle butt, and then twirled the gun around and slid the bayonet into his neck. No one said anything. My mother tried to cover my eyes, but I saw him switch the fire selector on his gun from automatic to single-shot before he shot Grandma Long.

Then he and a friend pulled the daughter into a shack, the two little girls dragged along, clinging to her legs.

'They stopped us at the drainage ditch, near the bridge. There were bodies on the road, a baby with only the bottom half of its head, a monk, his robe turned pink. I saw two bodies with the ace of spades carved into the chests. I didn't understand it. My sisters didn't even cry. People were now shouting, "No VC no VC," but the Americans just frowned and spat and laughed. One of them said something, then some of them started pushing us into the ditch. It was half full of muddy water. My mother jumped in and lifted my sisters down, one by one. I remember looking up and seeing helicopters everywhere, some bigger than others, some higher up. They made us kneel in the water. They set up their guns on tripods. They made us stand up again. One of the Americans, a boy with a fat face, was crying and moaning softly as he reloaded his magazine. "No VC no VC." They didn't look at us. They made us turn around and kneel down in the water again. When they started shooting I felt my mother's body jumping on top of mine; it kept jumping for a long time, and then everywhere was the sound of helicopters, louder and louder like they were all coming down to land, and everything was dark and wet and warm and sweet.'

The circle had gone quiet. My mother came out from the kitchen, squatted behind my father, and looped her arms around his neck. This was a minor breach of the rules. 'Heavens,' she said, 'don't you men have anything better to talk about?'

After a short silence, someone snorted, saying loudly, 'You win, Thanh. You really *did* have it bad!' and then everyone, including my father, burst out laughing. I joined in unsurely. They clinked glasses and made toasts using words I didn't understand.

Maybe he didn't tell it exactly that way. Maybe I'm filling in the gaps. But you're not under oath when writing a eulogy, and this is close enough. My father grew up in the province of Quang Ngai, in the village of Son My, in the hamlet of Tu Cung, later known to the Americans as My Lai. He was fourteen years old.

Late that night, I plugged in the Smith Corona. It hummed with promise. I grabbed the bottle of Scotch from under the desk and poured myself a double. *Fuck it*, I thought. I had two and a half days left. I would write the ethnic story of my Vietnamese father. It was a good story. It was a fucking *great* story.

I fed in a sheet of blank paper. At the top of the page, I typed 'ETHNIC STORY' in capital letters. I pushed the carriage return and scrolled down to the next line. The sound of helicopters in a dark sky. The keys hammered the page.

I woke up late the next day. At the coffee shop, I sat with my typed pages and watched people come and go. They laughed and sat and sipped and talked and, listening to them, I was reminded again that I was in a small town in a foreign country.

I thought of my father in my dusky bedroom. He had kept the door closed as I left. I thought of how he had looked when I checked on him before going to bed: his body engulfed by blankets and his head so small among my pillows. He'd aged those last three years. His skin glassy in the blue glow of dawn. He was here, now, with me, and already making the rest of my life seem unreal.

I read over what I had typed: thinking of him at that age, still a boy, linking him with who he would become. At a nearby table, a guy held out one of his iPod earbuds and beckoned his date to come and sit beside him. The door opened and a cold wind blew in. I tried to concentrate.

'Hey.' It was Linda, wearing a large orange hiking jacket and bringing with her the crisp, bracing scent of all the places she had been. Her face was unmaking a smile. 'What are you doing here?'

'Working on my story.'

'Is your dad here?'

'No.'

Her friends were waiting by the counter. She nodded to them, holding up one finger, then came behind me, resting her hands on my shoulders. 'Is this it?' She leaned over me, her hair grazing my face, cold and silken against my cheek. She picked up a couple of pages and read them soundlessly. 'I don't get it,' she said, returning them to the table. 'What are you doing?'

'What do you mean?'

'You never told me any of this.'

I shrugged.

'Did he tell you this? Now he's talking to you?'

'Not really,' I said.

'Not really?'

I turned around to face her. Her eyes reflected no light.

'You know what I think?' She looked back down at the pages. 'I think you're making excuses for him.'

'Excuses?'

'You're romanticising his past,' she went on quietly, 'to make sense of the things you said he did to you.'

'It's a story,' I said. 'What things did I say?'

'You said he abused you.'

It was too much, these words, and what connected to them. I looked at her serious, beautifully lined face, her light-trapping eyes, and already I felt them taxing me. 'I never said that.'

She took a half-step back. 'Just tell me this,' she said, her voice flattening. 'You've never introduced him to any of your exes, right?' The question was tight on her face.

I didn't say anything and after a while she nodded, biting one corner of her upper lip. I knew that gesture. I knew, even then, that I was supposed to stand up, pull her orange-jacketed body toward mine, speak words into her ear; but all I could do was think about my father and his excuses. Those tattered bodies on top of him. The ten hours he'd waited, mud filling his lungs, until nightfall. I felt myself falling back into old habits.

She stepped forward and kissed the top of my head. It was one of her rules: not to walk away from an argument without some sign of affection. I didn't look at her. My mother liked to tell the story of how, when our family first arrived in Australia, we lived in a hostel on an outer-suburb street where the locals – whenever they met or parted – hugged and kissed each other warmly. How my father – baffled, charmed – had named it 'the street of lovers.'

I turned to the window: it was dark now, the evening settling thick and deep. A man and woman sat across from each other at a high table. The woman leaned in, smiling, her breasts squat on the wood, elbows forward, her hands mere inches away from the man's shirtfront. Throughout their conversation her teeth glinted. Behind them, a mother sat with her son. 'I'm not playing,' she murmured, flipping through her magazine.

'L,' said the boy.

'I said I'm not playing.'

Here is what I believe: We forgive any sacrifice by our parents, so long as it is not made in our name. To my father there was no other name – only mine, and he had named me after the homeland he had given up. His sacrifice was complete and compelled him to everything that happened. To all that, I was inadequate.

At sixteen I left home. There was a girl, and crystal meth, and the possibility of greater loss than I had imagined possible. She embodied everything prohibited by my father and plainly worthwhile. Of course he was right about her: She taught me hurt – and promise. We were two animals in the dark, hacking at one another, and never since have I felt that way – that sense of consecration. When my father found out my mother was supporting me, he gave her an ultimatum. She moved into a family friend's textile factory and learned to use an overlock machine and continued sending money.

'Of course I want to live with him,' she told me when I visited her, months later. 'But I want you to come home too.'

'Ba doesn't want that.'

'You're his son,' she said simply. 'He wants you with him.'

I laundered my school uniform and asked a friend to cut my hair and waited for school hours to finish before catching the train home. My father excused himself upon seeing me. When he returned to the living room he had changed his shirt and there was water in his hair. I felt sick and fully awake – as if all the previous months had been a single sleep and now my face was wet again, burning cold. The room smelled of peppermint. He asked me if I was well, and I told him I was, and then he asked me if my female friend was well, and at that moment I realised he was speaking to me not as a father – not as he would to his only son – but as he would speak to a friend, to anyone, and it undid me. I had learned what it was to attenuate my blood but that was nothing compared to this. I forced myself to look at him and I asked him to bring Ma back home.

'And Child?'

'Child will not take any more money from Ma.'

'Come home,' he said, finally. His voice was strangled, half swallowed.

Even then, my emotions operated like a system of levers and pulleys; just seeing him had set them irreversibly into motion. 'No,' I said. The word shot out of me.

'Come home, and Ma will come home, and Ba promises Child to never speak of any of this again.' He looked away, smiling heavily, and took out a handkerchief. His forehead was moist with sweat. He had been buried alive in the warm, wet clinch of his family, crushed by their lives. I wanted to know how he climbed out of that pit. I wanted to know how there could ever be any correspondence between us. I wanted to know all this but an internal momentum moved me, further and further from him as time went on.

'The world is hard,' he said. For a moment I was uncertain whether he was speaking in proverbs. He looked at me, his face a gleaming mask. 'Just say yes, and we can forget everything. That's all. Just say it: Yes.'

But I didn't say it. Not that day, nor the next, nor any day for almost a year. When I did, though, rehabilitated and fixed in new privacies, he was true to his word and never spoke of the matter. In fact, after I came back home he never spoke of anything much at all, and it was under this learned silence that the three of us – my father, my mother, and I – living again under a single roof, were conducted irreparably into our separate lives.

The apartment smelled of fried garlic and sesame oil when I returned. My father was sitting on the living room floor, on the special mattress he had brought over with him. It was made of white foam. He told me it was for his back. 'I made some stir-fry.'

'Thanks.'

'I read your story this morning,' he said, 'while you were still sleeping.' Something in my stomach folded over. I hadn't thought to hide the pages. 'There are mistakes in it.'

'You read it?'

'There were mistakes in your last story too.'

My last story. I remembered my mother's phone call at the time: my father, unemployed and living alone in Sydney, had started sending long emails to friends from his past – friends from thirty, forty years ago. She'd told me I should talk to him more often. Not knowing what to say, I'd sent him my refugee story. He hadn't responded. Now, as I came out of the kitchen with a plate of stir-fry, I tried to recall those sections where I'd been sloppy with research. Maybe the scene in Rach Gia, before they reached the boat. I scooped up a forkful of marinated tofu, cashews, and chickpeas. 'They're *stories*,' I said, casually. 'Fiction.'

He paused for a moment, then said, 'OK, Son.'

For so long my diet had consisted of chips and noodles and pizzas I'd forgotten how much I missed home cooking. As I ate, he stretched on his white mat.

'How's your back?'

'I had a CAT scan,' he said. 'There's nerve fluid leaking between my vertebrae.' He smiled his long-suffering smile, right leg twisted across his left hip. 'I brought the scans to show you.'

'Does it hurt, Ba?'

'It hurts.' He chuckled briefly, as though the whole matter were a joke. 'But what can I do? I can only accept it.'

'Can't they operate?'

I felt myself losing interest. I was a bad son. He'd separated from my mother when I started law school and ever since then he'd brought up his back pains so often – always couched in Buddhist tenets of suffering and acceptance – that the cold, hard part of me suspected he was exaggerating, to solicit and then gently rebuke my concern. He did this. He'd forced me to take karate lessons until I was sixteen; then, during one of our final arguments, he came at me and I found myself in fighting stance. He had smiled at my horror. 'That's right,' he'd said. We were locked in all the intricate ways of guilt. It took all the time we had to realise that everything we faced, we faced for the other as well.

'I want to talk with you,' I said.

'You grow old, your body breaks down,' he said.

'No, I mean for the story.'

'Talk?'

'Yes.'

'About what?' He seemed amused.

'About my mistakes,' I said.

*

If you ask me why I came to Iowa, I would say that I was a lawyer and I was no lawyer. Every twenty-four hours I woke up at the smoggiest time of morning and commuted – bus, tram, elevator, often without saying a single word, wearing clothes that chafed against me and holding a flat white in a white cup – to my windowless office in the tallest, most glass-covered building in Melbourne. Time was broken down into six-minute units, friends allotted eight-unit lunch breaks. I hated what I was doing and I hated that I was good at it. Mostly, I hated knowing it was my job that gave my father pride. When I told him I was quitting and going to Iowa to be a writer, he said, *Trau buoc ghet trau an.* The captive buffalo hates the free buffalo. But by that time, he had no more control over my life. I was twenty-five years old.

The thing is not to write what no one else could have written, but to write what only you could have written. I recently found this fragment in one of my old notebooks. The person who wrote that couldn't have known what would happen: how time can hold itself against you, how a voice hollows, how words you once loved can shrivel on the page.

'Why do you want to write this story?' my father asked me.

'It's a good story.'

'But there are so many things you could write about.'

'This is important, Ba. It's important that people know.'

'You want their pity.'

I didn't know whether it was a question. I was offended. 'I want them to remember,' I said.

He was silent for a long time. Then he said, 'Only you'll remember. I'll remember. They will read and clap their hands and forget.' For once, he was not smiling. 'Sometimes it's better to forget, no?'

'I'll write it anyway,' I said. It came back to me – how I had felt at the typewriter the previous night. A thought leapt into my mind: 'If I write a true story,' I told my father, 'I'll have a better chance of selling it.'

He looked at me a while, searchingly, seeing something in my face as though for the first time. Finally he said, in a considered voice, 'I'll tell you. But believe me,' he continued, 'it's not something you'll be able to write.'

'I'll write it anyway,' I repeated.

Then he did something unexpected. His face opened up and he began to laugh, without self-pity or slyness, laughing in full-bodied breaths. I was shocked. I hadn't heard him laugh like this for as long as I could remember. Without fully knowing why, I started laughing too. His throat was humming in Vietnamese, 'Yes ... yes ... yes,' his eyes shining, smiling. 'All right. All right. But tomorrow.'

'But– '

'I need to think,' he said. He shook his head, then said under his breath, 'My son a writer. *Co thuc moi vuc duoc dao.*' Fine words will butter no parsnips.

'*Mot nguoi lam quan, ca ho duoc nho,*' I retorted. A scholar is a blessing for all his relatives. He looked at me in surprise before laughing again and nodding vigorously. I'd been saving that one up for years.

Afternoon. We sat across from one another at the dining room table: I asked questions and took notes on a yellow legal pad; he talked. He talked about his childhood, his family. He talked about My Lai. At this point, he stopped.

'You won't offer your father some of that?'

'What?'

'Heavens, you think you can hide liquor of that quality?'

The afternoon light came through the window and held his body in a silver square, slowly sinking toward his feet, dimming, as he talked. I refilled our glasses. He talked above the peak-hour traffic on the streets, its rinse of noise; he talked deep into evening. When the phone rang the second time I unplugged the jack. He told me how he had been conscripted into the South Vietnamese army.

'After what the Americans did? How could you fight on their side?'

'I had nothing but hate in me,' he said, 'but I had enough for everyone.' He paused on the word *hate* like a father saying it before his infant child for the first time, trying the child's knowledge, testing what was inherent in the word and what learned.

He told me about the war. He told me about meeting my mother. The wedding. Then the fall of Saigon. 1975. He told me about his imprisonment in re-education camp, the forced confessions, the indoctrinations, the starvations. The daily labour that ruined his back. The casual killings. He told me about the tiger cage cells and connex boxes, the different names for different forms of torture: the honda, the airplane, the auto. 'They tie you by your thumbs, one arm over the shoulder, the other pulled around the front of the body. Or they stretch out your legs and tie your middle fingers to your big toes– '

He showed me. A skinny old man in Tantra-like poses, he looked faintly preposterous. During the auto he flinched, then, immediately grinning, asked me to help him to his foam mattress. I waited impatiently for him to stretch it out. He asked me again to help. *Here, push here. A little softer.* Then he went on talking, sometimes in a low voice, sometimes smiling. Other times he would blink – furiously, perplexedly. In spite of his Buddhist protestations, I imagined him locked in rage, turned around and forced every day to rewitness these atrocities of his past, helpless to act. But that was only my imagination. I had nothing to prove that he was not empty of all that now.

He told me how, upon his release after three years' incarceration, he organised our family's escape from Vietnam. This was 1979. He was twenty-five years old then, and my father.

When he finally fell asleep, his face warm from the Scotch, I watched him from the bedroom doorway. I was drunk. For a moment, watching him, I felt like I had drifted into dream too. For a moment I became my father, watching his sleeping son, reminded of what – for his son's sake – he had tried, unceasingly, to forget. A past larger than complaint, more perilous than memory. I shook myself conscious and went to my desk. I read my notes through once, carefully, all forty-five pages. I reread the draft of my story from two nights before. Then I put them both aside and started typing, never looking at them again.

Dawn came so gradually, I didn't notice – until the beeping of a garbage truck – that outside the air was metallic blue and the ground was white. The top of the tin shed was white. The first snow had fallen.

He wasn't in the apartment when I woke up. There was a note on the coffee table: *I am going for a walk. I have taken your story to read.* I sat outside, on the fire-escape, with a tumbler of Scotch, waiting for him. Against the cold, I drank my whisky, letting it flow like a filament of warmth through my body. I had slept for only three hours and was too tired to feel anything but peace. The red geraniums on the landing of the opposite building were frosted over. I spied through my neighbours' windows and saw exactly nothing.

He would read it, with his book-learned English, and he would recognise himself in a new way. He would recognise me. He would see how powerful was his experience, how valuable his suffering – how I had made it speak for more than itself. He would be pleased with me.

I finished the Scotch. It was eleven-thirty and the sky was dark and grey-smeared. My story was due at midday. I put my gloves on, treaded carefully down the fire escape, and untangled my bike from the rack. He would be pleased with me. I rode around the block, up and down Summit Street, looking for a sign of my puffy jacket. The streets were empty. Most of the snow had melted, but an icy film covered the roads and I rode slowly. Eyes stinging and breath fogging in front of my mouth, I coasted toward downtown, across the college green, the grass frozen so stiff it snapped beneath my bicycle wheels. Lights glowed dimly from behind the curtained windows of houses. On Washington Street, a sudden gust of wind ravaged the elm branches and unfastened their leaves, floating them down thick and slow and soundless.

I was halfway across the bridge when I saw him. I stopped. He was on the riverbank. I couldn't make out the face but it was he, short and small-headed in my bloated jacket. He stood with the tramp, both of them staring into the blazing gasoline drum. The smoke was thick, particulate. For a second I stopped breathing. I knew with sick certainty what he had done. The ashes, given body by the wind, floated away from me down the river. He patted the man on the shoulder, reached into his back pocket, and slipped some money into those large, newly mittened hands. He started up the bank then, and saw me. I was so full of wanting I thought it would flood my heart. His hands were empty.

If I had known then what I knew later, I wouldn't have said the things I did. I wouldn't have told him he didn't understand; for clearly, he did. I wouldn't have told him that what he had done was unforgivable. That I wished he had never come, or that he was no father to me. But I hadn't known, and, as I waited, feeling the wind change, all I saw was a man coming toward me in a ridiculously oversized jacket, rubbing his black-sooted hands, stepping through the smoke with its flecks and flame-tinged eddies, who had destroyed himself, yet again, in my name. The river was behind him. The wind was full of acid. In the slow float of light I looked away, down at the river. On the brink of freezing, it gleamed in large, bulging blisters. The water, where it still moved, was black and braided. And it occurred to me then how it took hours, sometimes days, for the surface of a river to freeze over – to hold in its skin the perfect and crystalline world – and how that world could be shattered by a small stone dropped like a single syllable.

Overland

I See Red

Shane Maloney

Everything was going great until that maniac with the axe burst through the door.

Let me tell you, when you're not expecting it, something like that can really throw you off your stroke. Scared the crap right out of me, I don't mind telling you. Makes the hairs on the back of my neck stand on end, just thinking about it.

There I am, right in the middle of the job, really cruising. Then, bam! The door flies open and there he is, some huge guy in work boots and a flannel shirt, never clapped eyes on him in my entire life, going at me with a fucking axe.

No way was it just a coincidence. You can't tell me he happened to be passing, was overcome by a sudden fit of curiosity, took a peek through the window and just reacted spontaneously. That's plain unbelievable. No, he must have been outside the whole time, just waiting to make his move. The whole thing's got set-up written all over it. There's no way it wasn't a sting.

For starters, it's not like there's any passing traffic, way out there, middle of nowhere. That's how come the joint caught my eye in the first place. There it is, standing all by itself, no other houses around, way out on the far side of the trees. No road, just a dinky sort of little path that comes winding out of the woods, going nowhere in particular. You can't tell me the guy just happened to be passing by. Absolutely no way.

And it's not like I didn't check out the whole area before I made my move. I'm a professional, after all. This is what I do for a living. You put in the time, do your homework, sniff the wind, stalk around, get a very clear picture of the situation, the comings and goings. And believe me, this was just about the perfect scenario. One of the sweetest I've ever seen. The old biddy lived by herself. Not even a pet. And there'd been nobody near the place for days.

Getting inside was a cinch. The doors on those old-fashioned cottages, most of the time they're not even locked. On top of which, the woman was sick, so I knew she wasn't going to give me any trouble. Old and sick, sort of turns your stomach when you think about it. But, hey, I'd been having a lean time of it. You do what you have to.

And the girl turning up in the middle of things, that was pure gold. The way I played it, I don't mind saying myself, it was inspired.

She was a pretty sharp cookie, too. Just a slip of a thing, but sharp as a tack. Nobody could accuse her of being a few sandwiches short of a picnic. So I knew it wouldn't be long before she twigged, but it's amazing how trusting people can be, especially kids.

My disguise was crap, of course, but I was improvising. And the voice, Jesus, the kid would've had to have been a halfwit not to pick up on the voice. Still, I had her there for a minute, hooked in, just toying with her. *All the better to hear you with. All the better to see you with.* Priceless, eh?

A few more seconds and that would've been it. One quick lunge and voila – goodnight sweetheart. But then the bozo with the axe arrives and it all goes down the toilet on me.

An axe, for Chrissake! What sort of a lunatic walks around with an axe?

What's really got me beat is how he got onto me in the first place. I work alone. I improvise, go with my instincts. No equipment, no trail, no fancy stuff.

Or maybe, and this is the only thing that makes sense, he wasn't after me at all. Maybe it was the old lady. Or more likely, the chick. Maybe he'd followed her. Yeah, that adds up. Bastard was stalking her. Trailed her though the woods, saw her go into the house, just went for it. Me, I just happened to be in the wrong place at the wrong time.

I was damned lucky to get out of there alive. Nearly chopped my head right off, he did. Blood and fur everywhere, great chunk of my tail gone.

Well it sure as shit won't happen again. I've learned my lesson. From now on, I'm picking my marks a lot more carefully. Targets nobody else'd be interested in, not in a million years. Make sure 100% there's nobody lurking around with a weapon.

I've been thinking about those three new places going up on the far side of the mountain. The guys building them, there's nobody else checking them out, I'm pretty sure. Not unless it's some total weirdo with a thing for hairy chins. These guys, believe me, they're real pigs.

Soon as my wounds heal up, I'm taking a closer look. I've got a real good feeling about this one.

Big Issue

9.7 Milligrams of Heaven

Barry Cooper

I watched the movie *Praise* while bombed off my face on codeine tablets late the other night. I like the codeine tablets. They make me laugh at things, and when I get real tense in the shoulders they help me relax. I am worried about my kidney or liver though, and my piss in the morning is real yellow. Sometimes I get a pain in the right side of my body down near my stomach, but I don't know if that's because of the codeine tablets or not. You can't wank with the tablets in you because you don't feel like it. You go around the next day with real red eyes that have a glassy surface to them too.

I island-hop between chemists to get the packets of tablets. The chemist-brand ones are the cheapest, but I can't seem to find them lately. I don't know if they are still making them or what. The next cheapest brand has a blue and yellow cover and have 9.7 milligrams of codeine in them, and 500 milligrams of paracetamol, too. The doctor told me the paracetamol is more dangerous than the codeine for the liver or kidney. I tried taking codeine and Nurofen, but the Nurofen gave me stomach cramps.

Sometimes I go into a big song and dance about why I need the tablets at the chemist and tell them something about having lower-back pain or whatever. Sometimes I realise it's better if I don't say anything because they will probably think I'm making a big show for a reason. I do have lower-back pain, and it is sometimes so bad that I have to take the tablets, but mostly I just take them to bomb myself out of the place.

It's nice taking them in the afternoon because they work well with the afternoon sun going down. The outside and inside light mix well and everything looks yellow and golden. The sunlight coming off the window panes of the big office buildings looks absolutely amazing. The sunlight coming off chrome chairs and hand railings and the marble looks amazing, too.

The only drawback I can see is that one day my liver or kidney might explode, but I don't feel it happening soon. The tablets taste a bit dry going down and are best swallowed with a sweet soft drink with ice. It takes fifteen minutes to half an hour for the initial six tablets to kick in, and if you want to keep going till midnight, another six to eight tablets will do the trick. It's not the recommended dose, but it hasn't harmed me yet.

I used to go to uni but I couldn't handle being around the cheeky white cunts there, even with the tablets in me. Everywhere I looked there was some young, smart-ass white cunt and his woman walking around looking like they owned the world. If me and my cousins ever cornered them in our neck of the woods we'd wipe the smiles completely off their fuckin' faces, that's for sure. We'd complete their education for them, all right – HECS-free with honours!

And the subjects were fucked there, too. I had to write an essay about a magic ring that makes you invisible when you wear it. Well the cunt wouldn't make you invisible if you didn't wear it, would it? *Invisible!* I thought to myself and looked around the room. The cunts can't see me as it is. What the fuck do I need a ring to make me invisible for? I wrote the poxy piece anyway, bombed outta my mind on my talcum-tasting tablets, and handed it in thus …

> The Ring of Gyges would add sweet legitimacy to my existing invisibility. From birth until now I have been living under an assumed identity, sentenced to a cell in the minds of white people to serve my time as a human being bereft of complex feelings and thoughts. I would happily wear the ring every day for the blessed relief of being stared through by shop assistants, bank tellers, teachers and policemen – for good reason!
>
> So enthralled by my new-found freedom – at being able to walk around in the land of my ancestors free from the mental

construction of others – I wouldn't feel the inclination to rape, murder, maim, annoy, tickle, tackle or fight with anyone at all.

Oh please give me the Ring of Gyges. And could I have one each for my grandmother and grandfather too? God knows they've waited long enough to be stared through with good reason. Though my grandfather may want to decapitate a few cow cockies and the owners of timber mills and bean paddocks, and my grandmother may lift clothes from the Salvo's and Vinnies, I'm sure they would escape conviction. They've lived so long with social invisibility that no jury would find against them simply because no one would be able to locate them! In fact, their legal indiscretions would crystallise their existence in the eyes of the jurors.

Maybe I should do all manner of nasty stuff with the Ring of Gyges? Perhaps I could rape, pillage and plunder, destroy and rip asunder all manner of goods, laws, customs, men and women, so that I too could be brought before a judge and jury to argue my case: though not one of guilt or innocence – but of existence!

'Here I am, your Honour,' I'd plead. 'I've read everything from Ernest Hemingway and Ralph Ellison to Bret Easton Ellis – and not only do I lead a fictional existence which would do justice to the above authors, I still can't get courteous counter service at the Niagara Café in downtown Bega!'

The café staff can't see my existence because I always present a profile similar to that of a single page turned side-on. With only a hair's breadth to work with they never get a chance to actually see me. Could you imagine what they would see if a whole legal judgment was devoted to me? Especially if I appealed all the way to the High Court of Australia!

How silly I've been in thinking that my newfound invisibility would separate me from prejudice, fear, loathing, hatred, misrepresentation, horror, agony and ugliness. I have my real identity to worry about, and that depends on making myself visible at all costs – doesn't it?

And the simple, institutionalised professor gave me an HD for it, too! He said he had never read anything like it before. I told him he's never met anyone like me before. I also told him that there's a whole army of us invisible ones out there to contend with, and just because we're bombed out of our minds most of the time doesn't mean we can't see. Hell, I think the reason we get so wasted is because we see too much! We've read all about Carl Jung's concept of Individuation and Oscar Wilde's little theory on Individualism and all the other little theories put together, but we don't buy it. And the reason we don't buy it is because no one else is investing their spiritual capital in it, either. Everyone seems to be spending their other capital on mobile phones, wide-screen TVs, hair-removal techniques, microdermabrasion technology and footwear that Starsky and Hutch wore back in the seventies. So why follow those poor, lost lemmings over the consumer cliff?

Actually, none of the brothers I know have read Jung, or any other psychologist for that matter, but most of them do go wild a lot of the time – especially when they get the drink and the drugs in them. I'm the only simple black idiot in the whole family who's read as widely as the whites. So much so that I find myself bored shitless whenever I go back home and have a yarn with my mob. What a predicament: education that leads not to personal emancipation – but to greater alienation! A person might as well run down the road and never come back, as my mum would say.

And that's why I like my crazy codeine crunchies: it sets my black sense of humour free because it's the only thing left in me that's truly mine. Everything else has been overthrown. Don't we now walk and talk like our white brothers and sisters and wear the same clothes as well? Hell, even our desires have been colonised! I wonder how much internal territory we have surrendered over the years and how much we have kept for ourselves. How much is truly ours? (You can imagine how this sort of talk goes down with the mob back home).

So let my kidney blow, I say, and let the other organs follow as well. I'll become an organ donor tomorrow just to make sure of it. I'll even donate my eyes to some young clone from the suburbs. I'll make sure they are glazed over before the transplant takes place. No one will know the difference.

Meanjin

Passion Fruit

Vivienne Kelly

When we children had grown into adults and had children of our own, our parents divorced. They uncoupled as smoothly as train carriages, shunting with dispassionate ease into the newly separate platforms of their lives. My sisters and I were astonished and injured.

'What about all those years together?' I asked my mother. 'What about your commitment to each other?'

She looked at me slantwise, foxlike as ever.

'Your father's in fact been living on his own for most of all those years. I'm just letting him have more space for it. As for commitment, it's what I should have done to him a long time ago, had him committed.'

It was true that my father was eccentric. He was an amateur historian with a great passion for cemeteries, and used on wintry Saturday afternoons to go for agreeable rambles among plastic flowers and corroding headstones. At these times I often accompanied him, my mother and sisters having bundled themselves, waterproofed and trailing scarves, off to the football. I did not much like graves, but I liked football less, and I enjoyed my father's company. So as a child I frequently sauntered after him through the graveyards, developing what I considered a connoisseur's attitude. I watched him pause before the lucid heavy sweep of an angel's stone wing, or the crumbling tracery of a Celtic cross. I heard the tiny troubled click his tongue made upon pausing by a baby's grave, and saw the calm concentration on his face as he copied down details from tombs into his little notebook, the quarry for his painstaking essays for historical societies.

If my father was eccentric, my mother was not far behind. Acid of tongue, ginger of hair and temper, she reserved her warmth for the grandchildren we produced and her energy for her vegetable garden and the long treks she undertook with her local seniors' hiking club. Wiry and sharp and hungry for something after the separation, she bought proper boots and haversacks and set off for day-long bush tramps which left her exhausted and full of satisfaction.

'You girls aren't fit,' she said smugly.

We tried persuasion and mediation. We spoke to my father about mending his ways and to my mother about tolerance. The word reconciliation ('something you do to a bank account,' said my mother, impatiently) recurred ineffectually in our conversations. My father listened with weary courtesy but ignored us; my mother became so exasperated that eventually she refused to let us into the house unless we promised not to raise the subject.

My mother was so infuriated by my elder sister Louisa's proposal of counselling that she refused to speak to her for a fortnight. So Louisa turned the hose of her attack on my father. He listened to her and sighed. 'We don't really speak any more,' he said, lamely.

'But you never did!' she wailed. 'You've never spoken to each other, so long as any of us can remember. but you've always been perfectly happy, haven't you?'

It was true: none of us remembered conflict between our parents during our childhood: a small hum of distant civility connected them. We vexed and frayed my mother, not because we misbehaved but because we were children, little and unpredictable and irrational: irrational and unpredictable herself, she chased us in shrill staccato attacks to the corners of the house. My father was not subject to the fiery minor battles erupting so incessantly between his wife and her daughters: her abraded personality channelled itself into smoother moulds for conversation with him. She was not at all tender to him, but the edge dropped from her voice in their discourse. It wasn't strange at the time (since children expect adults to adopt in their behaviour with each other different patterns from those governing their interaction with children), but now it seems so. In the mild detachment with which they parleyed there inhered a permanent stand-off which was courteous but not communicative. (We were amazed, in fact, when she became a grandmother, by how patient my mother was with our babies. Gone were the piercing battle cries and the ferocious skirmishes: in their place was a soft pliancy, a doting willingness to compromise or indeed to concede, which unsettled us badly until we became accustomed to it.)

Their only common interest appeared to be gardening, but even there my mother was intent on beans and zucchini and small sweet new potatoes; my father focussed on azaleas and roses and finely-manicured wheels of herbs. The depths of the fissure between them first appeared when my older sister married. My mother wanted my father to wear a dinner suit: his refusal was implacable. We had previously observed silences between them: lipfolding and averted glances, but this was the first proper quarrel we knew of. Even so, it was something of a fizzer in terms of participation: my mother did all the shouting. My father simply refused. Nobody knew why he opposed her so fiercely on this trivial matter. He simply said that he had never worn a monkey suit in his life and he wasn't going to start now. But one quarrel in twenty-five years didn't seem to indicate incompatibility.

We decided eventually to let them take their course. There was no option, of course, but by deciding to let them do as they wished it was as if we had taken control, a little. The old family home was sold and each of them bought a bright, modern unit, not too far from where they had always lived. ('I know the shops hereabouts, and they know me,' said my mother with snappy assurance.)

They settled happily. Each followed established pursuits and adapted undramatically to solitude. My mother gardened and walked; my father visited more cemeteries. He diversified, broadening his investigations to the goldfields, and wrote a great many careful and loving little monographs about family histories in goldrush regions. The change had a different effect on each, though: whereas my mother's edges seemed to sharpen and harden, making her movements and her shadow quicker and cleaner, my father seemed to blur, to draw around him a fine fog. Presenting an increasingly opaque outline to the world in general, he became gentler, vaguer, more withdrawn.

Most people do not have cheeks like apples, despite peasant stereotypes in fairytales, but my father's cheeks late in his life really were like apples – hard and round and rosy-veined. His eyes were bright blue, and his face was benign and surrounded by unruly white ruffs of hair and beard. When he was wearing his gardening gumboots, he looked like a prototype fisherman from a nursery-rhyme book. Once, when we were young, he was asked to be the primary school Santa Claus. He agreed, but it was a great agony to him. We crouched outside the bedroom door and heard him practising his *ho-ho-ho*: it rang hollow with despair. He looked jovial and gregarious: it was a deeply misleading image. He was an intensely shy man and the genial assurance of his packaging concealed an interior landscape whose dimensions were vast and whose nature was contemplative. He carried with him a quality of dogged inner repose. His communicative style was sparse, but he cared greatly about us and used from time to time to demonstrate this by buying us small gifts for their usefulness and ingenuity. He was scrupulous about equality in the distribution of these gadgets, which he would pick up in bunches of three in the local hardware or supermarket. Can-openers devised on new principles, long-life torches, cunning gardening implements, screwdrivers with replaceable blades: all these caught his attention and were gravely delivered to us. Diffidently he would point out to us the extra ratchet or the inner compartment or the unexpected angle of the lever. His enjoyment in the cleverness of these articles was evident and disarming.

My father announced his impending death to me one afternoon, with such nonchalance that I nearly missed it. I had dropped by to give him some petunia seedlings: as I kissed him goodbye (my lips landing somewhere in the air near his cheek) he said, abruptly, 'I might not be around, in a little while.'

'Are you going away?' I asked, looking at my watch and heading for the door. We are never prepared for the great moments.

'No,' he said, flushing with apparent embarrassment. 'I saw the doctor yesterday, and things aren't good. I don't want any fuss, mind you.'

I stared at him.

'What do you mean, things aren't good?'

'Seems to be a problem with my liver.'

'What? What problem?'

'A problem. Does it matter?'

'Dad,' I said carefully, 'are you telling me you're dying and you don't want any fuss?'

'I can't think of a better time not to have fuss,' he said.

My sisters and I fussed. We especially fussed over my mother and her sturdy resolve to avoid rapprochement.

'Don't you want to reach proper closure?' I asked her.

She breathed in sharply. 'Proper closure is what happens when you diet a lot and finally you can do up the zip on your skirt. This zip bust a long time ago.'

'You must love him,' I persisted. 'You must have loved him, anyway.'

'Love is a tennis score,' said my mother, crisply.

'But you can't hate him. You lived with him all those years; you're the mother of his children; he's such a sweet harmless person: you can't hate him.'

'Remember,' said my mother, with the careful speech of one who is exercising forbearance: 'remember I told you this, when you're older and have more sense: it isn't hatred that destroys a marriage. It isn't even boredom, though God knows that's bad enough. It's sheer bloody irritation. When that sets in, there's nothing can be done about it.'

'It's so dysfunctional,' wailed my younger sister.

She got one of those glittery green sideways looks. 'I don't know where you girls get your vocabulary from. Dysfunction is when the washing machine stops working,' she barked.

The problem with the liver turned out to be carcinogenic and in an advanced stage. My father died with the emotional economy and tranquil consideration we had come to expect of him, and more swiftly than we had imagined possible. Perhaps my mother did visit him in hospital towards the end; but neither mentioned it to us.

My mother did come to the funeral. We expected opposition and had half decided not to argue, but she said it would be seemly for her to attend, and she did.

'Seemly!' said my older sister Louisa furiously. 'When has she ever cared before about what was seemly? Why couldn't she care about seemliness while he was alive, for goodness' sake?'

It was a modest, desolate funeral, to which my mother seemed to pay little attention. Her composure was absolute and her gaze rested untroubled on my father's coffin as it disappeared, gliding like a large slow arrow with eerie certainty through indigo velvet curtains to the crematorium flames. Having been anxious that she would refuse to come, we now wished she hadn't: we would have preferred her absence to the stony equanimity of her presence.

A month or so after the funeral, I was rung by a hospital at the other end of the city, reporting that my mother had been admitted there in a state of exhaustion. I found her in bed, dull-eyed and startlingly passive.

'Have you seen the bunions on your mother's feet?' a young doctor asked crossly. I did not say that my mother did not encourage inspection of her feet or of any other part of her, only that I hadn't seen them. He showed her feet to me and I saw that they were severely deformed.

'She walked here,' he said, accusingly. 'She walked here from her home. It seems to be more than sixty kilometres, you know, from where she lives. She just walked. And then she collapsed.'

'She's an independent adult,' I said, marvelling as I heard my own words at how ungenerous I sounded, how cold and ungentle. 'We can't stop her doing as she pleases. She likes walking. She always walks.' I chafed her poor feet distractedly, and she paid me no attention. The bunions thrust out as if they were part of an additional alien skeleton, bones projecting outside her without any reference to the shape of the rest of her body.

'How often does she do this?'

I didn't know. None of us did. As the doctor pointed out, and as we all realised, solitary lost escapades through the northern suburbs were different from supervised hikes with the jolly seniors' club of bushwalkers. We questioned her, and got about as far as we expected.

'I walk when I please,' she said, spiky as a new toothbrush when she had recovered from her first exhaustion. 'When, and where, and how I please.'

'But you got lost.'

'Lost is what happens to dogs,' she said. 'I knew where I was.'

It happened seven or eight times more over the next couple of years. The last time she was found walking barefoot: her feet were torn and bleeding and her state was almost catatonic. I can hardly start to imagine the strenuousness of her long marches, one of which was in the fierce heat of midsummer, some through winter rain, one through a violent storm. The arid tenacity that fuelled her through these expeditions collapsed at their end, leaving her spent and shuddering. Her behaviour bizarrely mingled aim and aimlessness: she was so grimly determined on the one hand, so bereft of motive on the other.

She spoke openly of her walking only once. This was after the last time, when she stayed for four days in the hospital to which she had been taken. (My older sister – who had inherited more than a little of her astringency – commented at the time that my mother's stays in hospital could be represented like a batsman's strokes on the television: around the central pitch of her home the spokes stretched out all over the city.) I drove her home. I think I was a little more annoyed than usual: we all disliked having to submit to the reproachful glances of hospital staff, and moreover there had been some emergency with one of my children from which I had had to disengage myself in order to attend to her. So I felt resentful and cross and inconvenienced, and added to all of that I felt mean-spirited because I was so unable to respond in what I suppose might have been a more appropriately daughterly spirit. She, on the other hand, had been (I think) for once a little frightened by the state to which she had brought herself, and by the length of time it had taken her to recover. So the dynamic between us had altered subtly, and this perhaps explains her unusual readiness to confide in me.

'Why do you do it?' I demanded when we reached her house, putting a kettle on and knocking one of the teacups inadvertently. 'It's so mad. It makes all of us miserable, and to look at you

I can't believe it makes you happy. I mean, please. What's the point?'

'I hear him,' said my mother.

It took me a moment to understand.

'Dad? You hear Dad?'

She took a breath.

'He speaks to me. When I walk.'

'Only then?'

'Only then.'

I stared at her.

'You hear Dad's voice when you walk?'

'Only if I walk alone.'

'What does he say, Mum?'

She sighed.

'He speaks to me as he used to do. When we were courting, when we were first married. I can tell you think I'm quite insane, but it's true.'

'No, no,' I said, and in fact I meant it. Any reason for undertaking these lunatic adventures was better than none. 'Tell me, Mum. What does he say?'

She shook her head.

'You think I'm mad,' she repeated. 'I won't say any more. You'll have me put away.'

There was no question of having her put away, but shortly afterwards her doctor advised her to move into a home. When she told us of this suggestion, we expected a fight of feral dimensions, but there was none. Nor did she try to escape for another walk. It was as if something in her had been finally defeated. As she aged further she did not exactly soften, but her warlike charges weakened to random flurries and she became forgetful. Her absorption with her grandchildren remained intense, and grew in inverse proportion to her interest in us. It was as if we no longer mattered very much, as if the baton had passed to the younger generation and carried the purpose of everything with it.

After she died, my sisters and I shared the sorting of all the things she left behind – the clothes, the books, the bills, and so on. She was an organised person, so the task was not difficult.

At the back of a drawer we came across an old packet of letters, tied neatly in a faded red ribbon. We gawked at each other, eyes rolling and imaginations running riot. My older sister held the bundle up, dangling it by the ribbon.

'What should we do?' she asked.

But it wasn't possible not at least to look at them. They were written by my father during a separation enforced early in the marriage. We recognised the handwriting (which was angled sharply and hard to decipher) but not the language, nor the sentiments.

'They must have loved each other after all,' said my younger sister, weeping slightly. 'And she left the letters there so we'd find them, and know.'

'Perhaps she just forgot them,' Louisa suggested.

'And then again, perhaps not,' I said.

I took the letters home with me and read them alone, properly, carefully, late that night. They were fifty-three years old and were the letters of a young and ardent man who could almost not endure this separation from the woman he had married less than a year before. He wrote of my mother's beauty, of her breasts and her eyes and her smile. He wrote of how his love for her was the greatest and the best thing that had ever happened to him, of how it had illuminated his existence and convinced him that life was worth living, that he was a person who mattered, that God existed and that the world shone with apocalyptic planetary splendour. He wrote of nights alone, longing for my mother's naked body to fit curled spoonlike into the contours of his own body, and for her fluttering ginger hair (he called it golden, which it was not) to tickle his nose and his chest. He wrote of the sweetness of courting her, the unbearable craving of loving her and the mad happiness, the cumulative frenzied joy of their marriage and their first night together. I had an old photograph of their wedding day and re-examined it: my parents stood watchfully apart from each other, holding hands as they stared glassily into the camera, nerveless and frozen, apparently as strange to each other then as they now were to me.

He wrote to her – my tart, sallow mother – as if she were a love goddess, an earth mother, a cornucopia of sexual exotica. He wrote of her spare frame as if it were voluptuous and divinely seductive, and of her taciturn ungivingness as if she were a fountain of erotic bounty. The tenderness of the letters was as great as their passion; their desire as deep as their gentleness.

Were these the words, I wondered, that my mother had heard in her long painful hikes alone? Had my father's voice from these letters drifted down the years to her in this flood of extravagant and inventive ardour? As she strode unmindful of her bleeding soles along distant suburban streets, were these the phrases that had preoccupied her? Why had this earlier phase of their relationship returned so compellingly, so late? And what had caused it to dissolve with the passing years? And had his voice truly come from the past, or had something of his gentle spirit gathered itself newly about her, enfolding and supporting her in his love, after his death?

> *You are my flower, my fruit, my passion fruit. I taste your creamy inner shell, your golden nectar: I am dying in the creaminess and goldenness of you. I swim in the sweetness of you; I long to taste and savour you, to lick my lips (and then yours) over you, to sink myself in you over and over and over again. My love, my love, I will be with you soon, and we will waltz naked in the moonlight and twine together like vines and ski to the clouds and back again on the fresh deep mountain of our love.*

Where was my father – that sober contemplative man, that intent roamer of cemeteries, that dilettante of hardware stores – in all of this? In nothing in these letters, in nothing he said of himself or of her, did I to the faintest degree recognise either of my parents. I could detect or imagine neither of them in these heady words: the string of recognition did not twang. He wrote out of the deepest core of his heart directly to her, without pretence or dissimulation, wrote with unselfconscious confidence and appetite and will; and all was as foreign to me as if I had never known them. I had no knowledge at all of what had caused their lives to blend and then to divide. I found I could not comprehend their blazing golden youth any more than their savagely private and separate old age.

I lived with them for twenty-three years, and knew them upwards of fifteen years after that, and I have no knowledge of the dark bright places in their souls. I have no knowledge of their demons or their heroes, of what made their hearts chant or their blood course. I am the immediate result of their fusion; I am if you like the fruit of their passion. I inherit their stock and carry their genes, but I did not try properly to know them when they were alive, and now they have slipped away and I will never know them, never comprehend them. This is a part of my life that should not have passed from me, but it has slid away entirely, as if I were nothing but water over which a boat skims, leaving behind it a brief wake which quivers and melts, leaving no imprint.

Suckered into a Perfect Line

Bill Collopy

Listen, this is how it is. I don't want to be Mr Popular. Doesn't worry me what people think. But nor do I fancy being the bloke standing in a flat-bottom skiff firing both barrels at his mate. Over he goes and so do I, recoil shoving me into the drink.

Underwater I watch a ribbon bleed from Andy's chest, limbs twisting slow-motion as he tumbles. Once I'm certain the body is debris, I climb back in our boat, tossing his gear over, glancing around and checking for witnesses. Then my eyes open.

The river licks its banks. Crouched in reeds, I shudder, a gun cold in my hands. Breathing steam, Andy fiddles with reloads. Idiot.

He keeps on tinkering. The dead Andy was better company. Am I a bad person to get sucked into daydream? You have to understand. I'm tired. Been tired a long time.

Jesus it's cold. Can't think about that. Can't.

Between my teeth I find apple bits, like rubbish floating in the current. Empty stubbies and cans catch first light as it spills above trees to prod the birds awake. I try not to think about Andy and Nicole either. Instead I'm running an oil rag over my weapon, resting it on the bank. Got to keep working.

From the bore I pass through the breech, like I did two nights ago, crouched on a crate in my garage, smoothing the barrel with solvent, over and over until dawn, massaging metal with oil, over and over in smearing motions. I could have been hypnotised – only I was shit-faced.

You don't need to tell me that drinking isn't recommended before a shoot. But I couldn't help myself, getting angrier with each glass, gripping tight enough to shatter it, watching Andy and Nicole kissy-kissy in the bar. She must know how long I've wanted her, even back in the days when Lyn was around, when the four of us used to go camping together. I know Lyn sussed it. She reckoned she had me figured out, doing her psychology at uni.

'I don't really know you,' she said one night, after another bedroom fizzer.

'Not surprising, lady. You're never here.'

'And you're always wanting what you can't have.'

'Spare me the Freud. I got actual work in the morning.'

OK, maybe I was jealous. Left school at fifteen. Not an educated man, I'd be off to do a twelve-hour workshop stint while my wife went to lectures, spending her day with friends. For talk, I just had the men I hire. We don't say much. Meanwhile I was paying Lyn's bills. I ran the motel of her life. Lying in darkness, I would listen to her snore, thinking of words I should've said.

Nothing comes to me at the right time. If I crack a joke at work, the men might smile but they don't ask me to join them for a beer later. I work right through most weekends – except during autumn, when I head for the wet. For company I usually take Andy. My old mate.

He and I did our apprenticeship together. He finished. I've known the bloke twenty years, so you'd think I could discuss stuff with him. But how can I? Fact is, lately I've been imagining how to bump Andy off. I'll be thumping my wheel in traffic or stuck behind some retard at the lights, or at home fingering the neck of a drink. I can feel heat in my fingers. I can hear myself doing it, plugging him with both barrels. And then I'm racing back to snatch Nicole. I would be doing her a favour. Andy's a moron.

Proof positive. The moron makes a Velcro rip, alerting waterfowl and mudlark for miles around. Swearing under his breath does not count as an apology.

Jesus, it's cold out here. My back hurts. I've got a headache the size of Bendigo. Sliding and cramping inside the waders, my legs chill. Eucalypt-coloured water seems to seep in, icing up my skin. The river slurps against tree roots. Gives me the creeps sometimes. Earlier it sounded like girls laughing. That's dumb, I know. But my balls aren't all that shrinks. The brain goes numb. You might think it's pathetic for a grown man to go on about a Grade Four accident so many years ago. Get over it, you could say. Trouble is, I don't. I get pulled in.

Another time our little girl walked in during my shower and laughed at my privates. Embarrassment maybe. I couldn't ask. Trouble is, I don't forget stuff, like that time I had to sack an apprentice for mimicking my limp. He was a troublemaker anyway. I had no choice. Only way to regain respect from the men.

So maybe I'm full of it but out here there's nobody laughing. It's just birds and water. No one around. I find it weird what being in the wetlands can do to you. By half-light, the Murray oozes like sump oil. Scraps of scum ride the rim, quiet as my bedroom. Thing is, it's more complicated than that. There's the sky. Hanging low, it feels close enough to stroke. Like a woman's hair. And there's a drop of dew bending back a grass blade right in front of my eyes on the bank. An ant crawls up my nose. I don't move. That's a skill Andy needs to learn. Horizon clouds might be swollen, and your gut twisting from the strain of keeping still, but this is what you've got to do.

Watching the leaves fall, tracing a line of treetops crooked as a punk haircut, seeing eucalypt branches form an arch. It's hard to explain. And I'm sure my shooting mate wouldn't understand. Isn't it what women complain about, how we're so thick about all that?

Two nights ago, I sat next to Andy's girl at the movies. Her leg rubbed mine by semi-accident. She plays with fire.

'Popcorn?' she said, touching my arm.

Even in the cold water, the memory of it stirs me. Got to slam on the reality brakes. Supposing I did put myself forward – she'd freeze me out in an instant. As her boyfriend's mate, I'm a safe tease. Jesus, that rips me up. I can't keep away from her but when I sit beside Nicole I burn from the effort. She radiates heat like she's got a furnace inside. And her perfume odours. Combustible. Have to force myself not to touch her. Lyn knew it. She could read me that easy.

I haven't forgotten Lyn's skin, how she started to turn clammy as she got older. Thin in our wedding photos, she fattened up on chocolate. Then she went vegan. Losing kilos, she deflated. Her neck and arms sagged. Her mouth shrivelled. Uphill battle, as she tried to look young again, bleaching her hair, squeezing into jeans: diet pills and sleep pills. Despite all that mineral water she sucked down, Lyn dried.

Where did the years get to? We shared a bedroom and a daughter. Then she went back to uni, to finish what she left behind for marriage. Lyn found other people to talk to. At home, she had nothing to say. After sex I'd try to make a comment but none came. I blanked, just rolling back on the wet spot to stare at light fittings, like a storm had crashed through the house and chucked around our furniture, then disappeared, leaving things where they fell. I couldn't explain it. One time I nearly managed but she did her cross-examination thing. I hated her for that. No way could I get words out.

I started hunting again. I took Andy. These last few years I get hungry for next season, never skipping, even if the forecast is for sheeting rain. You might think it's only a blood sport. But you'd be wrong. Out here, there's no bullshit: just bag limits and Hardhead and Pacific black. I can get legless. Nobody cares. I can make mess. Nobody cares. No customers or suppliers, and no bullshit.

Home tomorrow night, I'll buy groceries and sweep up – though my daughter won't. I will find pizza boxes, cereal bowls and a spill near the toilet where some kid has missed – and Bethany in bed with the current boyfriend. But I can't comment. If I open my mouth she'll only slam doors, threatening to leave, like her mother.

On our front lawn I was staring after Lyn, feet soaked but not feeling anything. I hosed the grass long after her cab went. When Bethany got home from school she didn't say anything, just slammed her door. Six months later, at the funeral, she refused to hold my hand. A stupid P-plate driver had put Lyn out of her misery. My eyes stayed dry. Nothing left. I looked at her coffin and chucked in a scoop of soil. Apology stuck in my throat.

'What're you doing ...?'

Andy is fiddling again, mucking with the load. Amateur. For black duck, he should use one-and-a-quarter ounce of number four.

'Try smaller shot.'

'Matter of opinion, mate.'

There's nothing he can do about being thick. I might try coming up to the Murray alone but it wouldn't be the same. Even Andy's better than no company.

Not a sign of other hunters yet. Early in the season, I often hear young clowns bragging about 'woodies' and 'spoonbill,' showing off with their shithouse long-range shooting. They use the wrong loads and skyblasters. They cripple birds. Rather than wear camouflage gear they slosh around in jeans and Nikes, holding their guns like cricket bats. A kid drowned, season before last. He didn't respect the river.

I need at least one barrel with full choke at maximum range. Depending on forecasts, Andy and I sometimes bring the skiff, or climb into mud for improved control – still the best way to get forward clearance – but it's always me that does the thinking. Andy's a passenger, and no oil painting. Why do the women go for him?

'No one else up yet.'

And a master of the bleeding obvious. There's not even a do-gooder trying to rescue wounded birds. That lot ought to be trying to save the whale or hug a spotted gum. They mean well but there's more going on up here than they know. I'm caught on a nail. I'm walking a tightrope over a gorge. Duck rescuers don't get it.

The Murray swells, grey as a bruise, but I'm pumped just to be wading through it, loaded and ready. Blood beats in my ears, like it did for ancestors. Flannelette smells of dried sweat. It's just me – us – in the water, waiting.

'Could move closer.'

I've told Andy it's a good spot, better than a blind. He mocks.

'Hey, not using your old pumpgun, mate? Crap recoil.'

Imbecile.

'Next time we'll bring the boat,' says Andy.

Moisture drips from our waterproof caps. I spot the floating rubber shapes we staked yesterday.

'You get better swing-through here,' I explain. 'Plus a view of the decoys. With more gear it'd be just a nuisance.'

At daybreak's edge I can feel the juice going through me, not only to smear teal from the sky but ... how can a man find words? Away from fumes and powder coating, the wetlands call. It's like the floodwater and swamp need us. You should see the night sky, sprinkled with salt. Frogs make a song noise that rinses the town away. If I could write songs, they'd be the sound of this water.

First light twitches down each hair on my arms, heating the muscles of my back, swelling the chest. That could be us, all the way up there, instead of birds, skimming clouds before we get caught. It's how we're supposed to feel, how it used to feel before the duck became more important than the gun.

OK, I'm no hero. Memory shoves me into corners I'd rather not see, like when Andy introduces me to his girlfriend in a see-through singlet, hair bouncing on her bare shoulders, with that husky laugh like she's coming up for air, and a black coffee voice that makes me wild. But I can't tell Andy she's the kind that men kill for. He wouldn't understand.

Lyn used to pretend that she and Nicole would become great pals. We were living in a High Street flat, five minutes from the market. During that hate phase, Lyn hated her skin and her hair, plus having to share a bed with me. I no longer felt hitched to her like a water tank on the back verandah. I hadn't even noticed her getting older. One day I noticed wrinkles on her cleavage, like a tide was going out.

The swampland gurgles then goes quiet. Moments later, a squeak of mynahs. On with the gloves, earmuffs and safety glasses. I check my ammo.

From the pack I pull a flask, and knock one back. Bourbon floods me, heating the cold corners. Breakfast was apricots and cold sausage with Andy. Watching him chew I noticed that his sideburns aren't cut the same, like he does his shaving in a bathroom that needs reblocking. Tiny veins crack his cheeks. He's got eyes the colour of beer. What do women see in it?

Even my wife found him interesting. But then nothing I did was good enough for Lyn. I should've finished school. I should be running a real business, not a glorified toolshed. I shouldn't eat eggs or meat. I should make an effort to understand wine. I shouldn't make love like I'm changing a tyre.

'You don't enjoy it,' she told me. 'You'd rather I lie still so you can get it over with. Do you kill birds because they don't hit back ...?

Sometimes she would scream, not caring who heard. I took to sleeping in the spare room.

Slipping off my gloves, I stand. Spread my feet. Loosen my hips. I mount the stock against one cheek, fitting its self-pump action to my shoulder.

A noise.

'Greenhead.'

No point in hushing Andy. I concentrate my aim down a line of decoys: ready for trigger slap, hand supporting the fore-end.

Up they soar, heading somewhere better, suckered into a perfect line that wags only at the end. I'm ready to wipe sky, bead on the muzzle, tracing a line of flight to take my shot.

Wuh-bang ...

Then the recoil, ripping through earmuffs. My nose throbs from flake powder.

But something's wrong.

A lapse in concentration maybe, or thinking about Nicole.

Shit.

My mouth hangs open. I see spiralling teal. Worse than a miss – I've tail-feathered one.

With swing-through, I've got time to hit another dead centre. Hurrying the third, I go wide. I am buggered.

Sloshing through reeds, my legs squish inside the waders. Got to make sure nobody's about. I don't want witnesses.

Swinging my stock, I hit hard. The bird thrashes. I whack again. Would you believe tears? I'm actually blubbing. In a stink of scorched feathers I feel sick, tasting a spasm of vomit. The bird's beak hangs open, as if to criticise.

From my pockets I fumble, pulling gloves over wet hands to begin the plucking. My thing might still be edible. Flies nag and buzz. I yank out its feathers, washing as I go, removing the crop and pulling entrails from its body cavity – not skinning or cutting off wings, like Andy would. As I return, he's about to say something. But I shut him.

'Not a bloody word.'

He has bagged four, each a work of art.

Rinsing and drying, I fold up the carcasses. My nose swells with shot, guts and singed feathers. Flies cluster. I flop on the bank, waders bloody, pumpgun beside me mud-caked: the weapon that missed. I point the barrel at Andy.

'What do they see in you anyway?'

But I'm full of crap. The gun in my hands is a crock. Andy has heard nothing. I swipe at the air – a mosquito or wasp. What is the thing I'm trying to grab? I can't seem to get hold …

On my feet, I gather up gear. Tomorrow night, I will stack carcasses on the kitchen bench. I might kick out Bethany's latest boyfriend but how can I lay down the law when I've pissed off for a weekend? Beth will shuffle in, belly button hanging out, and the top of her knickers peeping. I can't comment.

Something snags my thinking. I'm trying to figure it. Up ahead looms an old bluegum, thick as a pylon but twisted at the trunk like it's got stress fracture. Then I see a colour, parrot green. Tied to one branch there's a rope hanging, hacked off just beyond a man's reach. Somebody has slung it there. Question is – did that someone have to be cut down?

I really am full of it. The rope must be left over from a camping trip, some kid's tyre-swing maybe. No reason why it should scare the shit out of me, a frayed end swinging in the breeze. Except.

A moment before seeing it, I was rubbing my old gun, thinking how easy it would be to open up and slide the muzzle in.

Twitch of finger. Couldn't miss. About time someone else did the cleaning up.

'Let's give it another crack later,' Andy says, 'at sunset.'

Brushing away feathers and blood, I join him for the trek back. Tomorrow night Bethany will sneer at me, like her mother used to, but she won't leave. I'm what she comes home to, when school is over and she breaks up with her latest. We'll reheat pizza, or something. I'll wash. I'll mop the kitchen.

'You bring any coffee?' Andy is asking.

The Age

Désincarné / Disembodied

Meera Atkinson

'... the lover's discourse has been replaced by its simulation ...'
—Roland Barthes, *A Lover's Discourse*

We met in 'Books and Literature.' It was a quiet room; just us and a smart-arse from Delaware. I said I was new to chat rooms. He said, get out now. I typed lol (laugh out loud). He said he was serious. I asked if he'd been chatting long. He said longer than he cared to remember. We identified locations (him Manhattan, me Milton Island) and talked books (*Finnegan's Wake, White Noise, By Grand Central Station I Sat Down and Wept*) and poets (Anne Sexton, Gregory Corso, Octavio Paz). We exchanged some pointless repartee. After a while he asked my age. I said I was thirty-three. He told me he was fifty-two; an editor in the Big Apple, born and raised in the Bronx. He said he hated journalism, that he envied me being a poet. I paused and asked him why. Journalism is the opposite of writing, he wrote. Yes, I said, the opposite, the facts without the truth. But – I reminded him – poets don't get salaries. That's right, he said, except in communist Russia. He told me he was writing a novel. He was quick and his words were good and I liked him straight away. I drew a bold breath and sent him a private message.

We talked for two hours that night.

He asked what my cyber name meant. It's the meaning of my real first name, I said. I asked what his cyber name meant. He said ghost of a long dead French anarchist. He asked me what my real first name was. I told him it was Emalia and he told me his was Alex.

I can't remember how it came up, but at a certain point he said something about national boundaries being stupid. I asked if he thought such things would change as a result of global economics. He said that frankly, he didn't really care. I started, said I was only making conversation. He said it was just that, as he got older, he cared less and less about politics. I said, well, it's a free country. We both wondered about that. There was an awkward silence. He wrote that he did believe certain things. I asked what things he believed in. I wasn't prepared for what came next. I didn't see it coming. The word love flashed up on the screen. Good answer (smiles), I wrote.

That might have been the start. A sharp, invisible hook pierced my corporal flesh. I could feel it.

Out of the blue he asked, did I want to read his novel? I panicked, said something like, what's it about? Suddenly he turned New Yorker and said hey, I only offer once. Don't back off, I said, it's just that I get nervous. We swapped email addresses. He said he'd send the first chapter and if I liked it he'd send some more. I said I'd send him a couple of recent poems. He said he had to go, that it was four in the morning his time, and that by the way I had a lovely name. We said goodbye a couple of times using words like 'later' and 'ciao.'

Later I mailed him two poems.

Date: Sun, 26 Mar 2004 07:53:24-0800 (PST)
From: flirtinlatin <flirtinlatin@yeeha.com>
To: proudhoneysghost <proudhoneysghost@yeeha.com>
Subject: swap

alex,
hi there. i really enjoyed talking – it's refreshing to connect with someone among the fractured thought of chat. poems following, as promised. can't help feeling they're a little weighty for this sort of swap, but i don't do light poems and don't do stories so …

as i said before, i get nervous showing my poems to, or

reading the work of, people who are neither trusted friends nor total strangers (it's that pesky middle ground that bothers me), so bear with me if I seem a little guarded.

i do appreciate your suggesting it though and a riskless life is not a life worth living, or even really an option, so i'll leave them with you and say bye for now.

emalia alias flirtinlatin

That night I couldn't sleep. Watched the curtains billow above my head. Worried about his chapter. Maybe I wouldn't like it. Maybe I'd get trapped in that tight crack between the discomfort of lying and concern for another's feelings. In the morning I logged on.

Date: Sun, 26 Mar 2004 14:00:06-0800 (PST)
From: proudhoneysghost <proudhoneysghost@yeeha.com>
To: flirtinlatin <flirtinlatin@yeeha.com>
Subject: Re: swap

Dear Emalia – I liked your poems very much. I enjoyed talking to you too, though I'm afraid I was half unconscious due to the hour, and far from at my best. Here is the first chapter to repay you.

A.

The chapter was good. I was relieved I liked it.

Date: Mon, 27 Mar 2004 04:02:10-0800 (PST)
From: flirtinlatin <flirtinlatin@yeeha.com>
To: proudhoneysghost <proudhoneysghost@yeeha.com>
Subject: story

dear alex,
loved the chapter, really, an excellent beginning. feel like sending some more of your novel through?

i'm in an interesting situation here on the island, lifestyle-wise, which means i'm mostly home and work or not when i want so i'm flexible about meeting times, let me know if and when you feel like chatting again.

hope you've caught up on the sleep, emalia

Date: Mon, 27 Mar 2004 11:37:53-0800 (PST)
From: proudhoneysghost <proudhoneysghost@yeeha.com>
To: flirtinlatin <flirtinlatin@yeeha.com>
Subject: Re: story

Dear Emalia – thanks for your kind words about the chapter. I'm attaching the second chapter. What is this island you live on? I'm not entirely clear where in Australia you are.

Would love to chat more. How about the weekend? Send more poems.

Love, A.

The 'Love, A' didn't escape my attention. It was an unavoidably significant moment in our relationship. I stared at the text like a fortune-teller staring into a crystal ball, trying to determine it's precise resonance. After a while I decided that it was a friendly 'Love,' rather than a frightening or lecherous 'Love.' Merely the healthy expression of a sense of mutually developing warmth. Still, I cowered. I could reciprocate the messages but not yet the 'Love.' I hoped this wouldn't hurt his feelings.

I hoped any sting felt by the absence of a 'Love' would be soothed by a gentle sense of humour.

Date: Mon, 27 Mar 2004 14:55:55-0800 (PST)
From: flirtinlatin <flirtinlatin@yeeha.com>
To: proudhoneysghost <proudhoneysghost@yeeha.com>
Subject: situation

dear alex,
weekend is good. re the island – it's a long story but basically i was living in melbourne, lecturing in english lit at monash university, when i left my partner of 5 years. my father, who lives alone on the island (northeast of brisbane, in queensland), took ill at the same time, so i took sabbatical and moved

in temporarily to care for him. i'm taking the opportunity to work on a new collection of poems.

so here i am. the island is like a tame, miniature, australian version of florida. aside from tending to my father, i spend my time reading and writing, with little else to do besides, apart from taking long walks. i hope to be back in melbourne in two months if my father's recovery runs on time, but this surrealistically suburban interlude with goldorangepink sunsets and dolphins in the bay has turned out to be quite lovely.

emalia

I read the next chapter and liked it. I liked it a lot. As I read, I felt myself drawn to him, drawn into his pulsating textual body.

It's hard to describe the way the intoxicating to and fro of messages caused me to start falling in love, the way their rhythm beat like a pair of clever feet that swept me into a dance. It's hard to explain the strength of feeling that gestated in a womb of words and words alone.

It was an embryonic admiration, tender, young, buoyant in the medium like so many miraculous cells bubbling in a body.

Date: Mon, 27 Mar 2004 17:37:33-0800 (PST)
From: flirtinlatin <flirtinlatin@yeeha.com>
To: proudhoneysghost <proudhoneysghost@yeeha.com>
Subject: chapter

this correspondence is running thick and fast isn't it? i just logged on again to tell you that I really liked the chapter. really.

on another note – i don't quite know how to put this … be assured i'm not sizing you up with any particular agenda in mind but … now that we're becoming friends i'm curious to know certain things: what you look like, your style as a person, if you're jewish – an obvious question arising from reading your novel and i hope not an offensive one. please don't feel pressured to respond.

i imagine you're wondering the same about me so i'll oblige a little first: I have straight shoulder-length honey-brown hair, fair skin, am five-six and a half, don't know my weight but i'm curvy. don't do dior suits or round the clock make-up. hate sporty casual. i wear vintage clothes. I love the cut and fabric of old dresses. i'll leave it there for now as i have a tendency to run on in email and you have enough of my words to be getting on with.

send more novel please.

emalia

Date: Tues, 28 Mar 2004 17:10:25-0800 (PST)
From: proudhoneysghost <proudhoneysghost@yeeha.com>
To: flirtinlatin <flirtinlatin@yeeha.com>
Subject: Re: chapter

>what you look like

Six-one, 170 pounds (on a good day), still have hair (gone grey), wire-rimmed glasses.

>your style as a person

19th century anarchist.

>if you're jewish

Son of Russian Jews.

>send more novel please.

Am back at work after a week's leave and swamped. Chapters attached.

A.

I noted that he had deleted his 'Love' and felt bad about it for a moment. Had I been mean in withholding it? I now had plenty to ponder. Nineteenth-century anarchist was interesting. Six-one was good. Glasses could be cute. Still has hair.

As to the gone grey, well, I was partial to older men. I convinced myself I would find Alex attractive. I had reached a time of life where I could see beauty in an older face. How could a map of wrinkles erase the lure of lingua? How could I not love the nakedness of a body when I longed to strip that body of its words and reach the nakedness of its mind?

Overnight, I imagined various shapes of glasses on an amorphous identikit face. Formlessness and fear. Language and love. If the body could not be touched and seen it would be imagined into being. I had a sudden impulse to sign my next message with a 'Love.' In the end, I held back on the 'Love' but, filled with compassion for a fellow artist strapped to the wheel of material life like some tortured literary butterfly, I took a risk in making physical, if bodiless, contact.

Date: Tues, 28 Mar 2004 18:17:13-0800 (PST)
From: flirtinlatin <flirtinlatin@yeeha.com>
To: proudhoneysghost <proudhoneysghost@yeeha.com>
Subject: p.s.

dear alex,
i'm moving through the chapters quick so you can keep sending them through. sorry to hear about the back-to-work demands. sending you a comforting shoulder rub.

emalia

Date: Wed, 29 Mar 2004 04:25:39-0800 (PST)
From: proudhoneysghost <proudhoneysghost@yeeha.com>
To: flirtinlatin <flirtinlatin@yeeha.com>
Subject: Re: p.s.

>please send more through.

More chapters attached. You are very sweet.

Love, A.

The 'Love' was back. The rub had called it back.

It tormented me. I wanted a clear vision of Alex. My cat prowled into the room complaining in long meows. I closed my eyes and she licked the salt off the back of my hand with her raspy red tongue as I tried yet again to pin down a picture of him. I wanted to be patient, to not ask too much too soon. But I couldn't wait. I had to know more.

Date: Wed, 29 Mar 2004 14:00:50-0800 (PST)
From: flirtinlatin <flirtinlatin@yeeha.com>
To: proudhoneysghost <proudhoneysghost@yeeha.com>
Subject: my still burning curiosity

dear alex,
height, weight, hair is too vague. say something more about your physical presence. are you homely? menacing? wildly attractive to women? do you, in the spirit of a 19th century anarchist, wear any form of frockcoat?

for my part (i'm assuming you're curious too), i'll put it this way. i'm not a raving beauty but i have a certain, delicate, appeal. to a stranger i probably look like a cross between an intellectual and ... something not intellectual for which i can't think of a word. does that give you a better picture?

love, emalia

There it was in black and white. I had written 'love.' It was done. It felt like a weight had been lifted.

Date: Wed, 29 Mar 2004 18:42:33-0800 (PST)
From: proudhoneysghost <proudhoneysghost@yeeha.com>
To: flirtinlatin <flirtinlatin@yeeha.com>
Subject: Re: my still burning curiosity

>are you homely? menacing? wildly attractive to women?

Homely? Certainly not. Menacing? Only to people who confuse being ill-barbered with lunacy. As for actual looks, when I was younger I was very attractive to women, though – owing to modesty or hopeless stupidity – I never wrung from this the advantage I could have. I suppose I'm still reasonably attractive now, if your taste runs to the geriatric. I don't seem to myself to look as old as most people my age, but no doubt I'm deluding myself. In the spirit of truthfulness I should also add that I'm thrice and currently married and the father of three children ranging in age between 16 and 25.

>do you, in the spirit of a 19th century anarchist, wear any form of frockcoat?

No frockcoats in my closet.

You on the other hand sound quite delightful and I'm sure you would turn my head if I saw you.

You are – in case you didn't know it – quite a fascinating individual.

Love, A.

So he was married. Of course he was. I was seized by a sudden urge to cry. I had not been looking for a lover or husband and yet …

Married. For how long? Twenty years? Longer?

We had established a certain frankness, and I was in no mood to play pretend.

Date: Wed, 29 Mar 2004 21:52:50-0800 (PST)
From: flirtinlatin <flirtinlatin@yeeha.com>
To: proudhoneysghost <proudhoneysghost@yeeha.com>
Subject: curiosity killed the cat

sigh. just as well you told me you were married. i was beginning to fall for you. i know, it's ridiculous, under the circumstances, having known you in cyberspace all of four or five days. you probably think i'm desperate for love but i'm not. perhaps you just enjoy a spot of cyber flirting. if so, no hard feelings. but i haven't even thought of this as flirting, just as two people getting along obscenely well.

sigh again.

wistfully yours, emalia

Not long afterward I grew embarrassed about my confession, concerned that he would think I had, all along, been courting him. I went back to my computer and logged on again.

Date: Thurs, 30 Mar 2004 00:46:27-0800 (PST)
From: flirtinlatin <flirtinlatin@yeeha.com>
To: proudhoneysghost <proudhoneysghost@yeeha.com>
Subject: qualifying statement

dear alex,
i realised after that last message that it must seem to you that i was doing exactly what i said i wasn't doing – sizing you up with an agenda. not so. i guess i just don't hit it off with many people. just wanted to qualify my last message.

emalia

Date: Thurs, 30 Mar 2004 01:59:30-0800 (PST)
From: proudhoneysghost <proudhoneysghost@yeeha.com>
To: flirtinlatin <flirtinlatin@yeeha.com>
Subject: Re: qualifying statement

Dear Emalia – I'm not at all offended by your curiosity. But didn't you say you're rather new at chatting? You'll find as you continue – and it's the reason why I warned you against it – that it's a very seductive medium and that almost everyone you meet is looking to fall in love in one way or another. Why not? It's so easy to fall in love this way, with no inconvenient bodies attached to complicate matters. I'll tell you frankly I've had my share of these cyber romances, and if you like I'll cheerfully fall in love with you, too.

Love, A.

I reeled. So he'd known others? How many? Four? Fourteen? Forty? Was I being taken advantage of? Was I being toyed with by some ruthless internet Lothario who preyed on cyber virgins like me? My father knocked on the door, opened it, asked a question. I snapped a reply and turned my back on him. I was concentrating, scanning my memory for proof of deception, of less than honourable intent.

I was held in the mercurial field of his utterances, the invisible glow that bounced off them, that was uniquely his in all the world. Had it all been a performance of language trancing me into the void? Was I, after a few short days, addicted to his words?

His having cyber lovers bore more jealousy than the existence of a wife. The wife was fleshed in some unthinkable space, some alien domestic world. But cyberspace was our space, our human, non-human orb. It was as if he'd had others in our bed.

The labyrinth of ego takes unthinkable routes and leads to impossible destinations.

I had guessed it, certainly, but this admission rebounded in my mind. It was the exact sentence I hated most, that 'share of these cyber romances.' *Share of these cyber romances.* Did he mean to include me? Was it possible that another's words had seized him more than mine? I stared indignantly at the screen then looked out of the window at the night and a swaying branch.

Deranged as it was there was no escaping it: I wanted to be placed above all others. I wanted my words to burn so bright in his mind and to slice so deep into his heart that another's would pale and disintegrate before his eyes.

Date: Thurs, 30 Mar 2004 15:20:44-0800 (PST)
From: flirtinlatin <flirtinlatin@yeeha.com>
To: proudhoneysghost <proudhoneysghost@yeeha.com>
Subject: metaphors

dear alex,
yes, i did imagine that, you being a long time chatter, i could hardly have been the first to notice your charms ... and, yes, it is a strangely safe medium – intimacy without the discomfort of intimacy – the perfect plan for our human disease of fearing intimacy and desiring it in equal violent measure.

however the issue remains that, oddly, through our disembodied touch, i can't help but get a palpable sense of you. i could be dreaming it up, i know, but regardless it *feels* real and it's alluring. if you like i'll try to be un-allured, to turn the attraction off, like a tap. all the same i can't promise that, to stretch the metaphor further than it wants to go, it won't continue to drip.

you should know that i'm sulking about you having other lovers. i'm not good at feeling not special and by nature i am not suited to life in a cyber harem (the medium might not admit 'inconvenient bodies' but the inconvenience of bodies – feelings, jealousy, sensitivities – slips through sure enough).

in the meantime, while we ponder this development, please send more chapters.

love, emalia

Date: Fri, 31 Mar 2004 08:57:40-0800 (PST)
From: proudhoneysghost <proudhoneysghost@yeeha.com>
To: flirtinlatin <flirtinlatin@yeeha.com>
Subject: Re: metaphors

Dearest Emalia,
Yes, the foil of intimacy. No other creature on earth is like us in this respect. Other animals mate or they don't mate. They eat each other or they don't. Some species have great intelligence and demonstrate love, but they don't engage in this elaborate life-long psychodrama that we call relationships.

And once you reach my age you begin to truly understand the 'inconvenience of bodies.'

Please don't sulk. There is no harem.

Love, A.

But I would not be placated. It was not enough.

Date: Fri, 31 Mar 2004 10:21:12-0800 (PST)
From: flirtinlatin <flirtinlatin@yeeha.com>
To: proudhoneysghost <proudhoneysghost@yeeha.com>
Subject: others

no harem you say. there is still the matter of your wife. tell me about her. what does she look like? do you still love her? if so,

why are you in chat rooms seducing young women?
p.s. do you still want to meet this weekend?

emalia

Date: Fri, 31 Mar 2004 21:16:58-0800 (PST)
From: proudhoneysghost <proudhoneysghost@yeeha.com>
To: flirtinlatin <flirtinlatin@yeeha.com>
Subject: Re: others

You are a hard woman to ask such questions of a vulnerable old man. What would you like me to say about my wife? She is a middle-aged woman, once beautiful, ageing not so well. She has black hair (which she dyes to keep that way) and blue eyes. She is an alcoholic. Do I still love her? Marriage is a complex union. After a time the answer to that question no longer comes in a simple yes or no. In regards to seduction, one could argue about who is seducing whom.

As to chatting, I can meet you tonight 11 p.m. my time.

Love, A.

Date: Fri, 31 Mar 2004 18:46:29-0800 (PST)
From: flirtinlatin <flirtinlatin@yeeha.com>
To: proudhoneysghost <proudhoneysghost@yeeha.com>
Subject: tonight

you're right. that was mean of me. sorry. i don't know what's come over me. must be the isolation. this island is like something out of a fellini dream sequence. the people are enormous and grotesque and sweaty. or half-dead in that mothball, tight-lipped, walking sock way. i recognise no one here and am too alone. my father is my only company and he is frail and depressed, my friends are thousands of kilometres away, and i don't like the humidity.

anyway, will see you tonight at 11. i'll be in better spirits then.

love, emalia

We talked until the sun rose in New York. I went to bed imagining our encounter in an East Side hotel. I had conjured his voice, his accent, so fully it was as if I'd been hearing it all my life. We agreed to meet again same time next night. I slept for a few hours, dreamt about the wife. In the dream she humoured me, blew smoke in my face from her long, thin cigarette. I woke in a state at 2 a.m. and logged on.

Date: Sat, 1 Apr 2004 06:36:18-0800 (PST)
From: flirtinlatin <flirtinlatin@yeeha.com>
To: proudhoneysghost <proudhoneysghost@yeeha.com>
Subject: last night

did you mean it when you said you daydream of meeting me? what would you do if i showed up? i'm going to look into flights today. why not? my father's improved and could cope for a week or two.

btw: i have the money so don't think i won't do it.

emalia, x

I checked my mail thirteen times throughout the night but there was no reply. By 9 a.m. the silence had put me into a frenzy.

Date: Sat, 1 Apr 2004 17:00:18-0800 (PST)
From: flirtinlatin <flirtinlatin@yeeha.com>
To: proudhoneysghost <proudhoneysghost@yeeha.com>
Subject: hello?

i wonder what your wife would think of all this.

I regretted it as soon as I hit send. I wished I could reach through the ether and retrieve it, but it was gone, shooting down the wires and sparks. Language is a virus, just like William Burroughs and Laurie Anderson said, and I was sick with it. A threat. Me, a stalker.

Date: Sat, 1 Apr 2004 17:08:18-0800 (PST)
From: flirtinlatin <flirtinlatin@yeeha.com>
To: proudhoneysghost <proudhoneysghost@yeeha.com>
Subject: last night

alex,
please forgive me. i didn't sleep. you're under my skin. i'm not usually like this.

emalia, x

It was a painful wait. I paced the house. Checked my messages too often. Finally it came.

Date: Sat, 1 Apr 2004 17:36:18-0800 (PST)
From: proudhoneysghost <proudhoneysghost@yeeha.com>
To: flirtinlatin <flirtinlatin@yeeha.com>
Subject: Re: last night

Dear Emalia,
Just got in. I've been out all day with the family. I do daydream of you. Often. But I'm not sure if a visit is a good idea. Going to take a nap now so I can meet you tonight. Let's talk about it more then.

Love, Alex

At 3 p.m. I logged on to 'Books and Literature' and waited. We had come to a punctuation of sorts. A full stop. There was no telling what sentence would come next. I counted on my fingers and worked out the time difference. It was 11.15 p.m. his time. I sat and listened to the cicadas as they slowly faded with the day's heat.

At 11.30 I knew he wasn't coming. I closed my eyes and crossed the sea. I flew over Californian rooftops, soared above mid-western fields of corn, flew east, east, to Manhattan's iconic streets. I found his house still and solid in the windy spring night. His youngest slept as the city hummed and tree arms flailed outside their windows, and I was drawn toward the dim light of a room. I looked in and watched as he led his wife to the waiting bed. I clenched my eyes tight but I was forced to see that desire needs the body like a baby needs the breast.

I watched as their two ghosting shapes linked in the darkening room. I would not feel his whispery pant at my ear, would not read the wordless scripture of his body as it blessed me and left me breathless.

I looked at the screen. There was yet another conversation about Ayn Rand taking place. I looked down the list of chatters: bunnyfoofoo, david_2000, rightersblock. I was just about to click out of the room when a new name flashed up: Marcus_De_Sade. I smiled and started typing.

Etchings

A Chinese Affair

Isabelle Li

I dream of my mother again. She is sitting in front of the sewing machine, crying.

I press on the wooden blue door and it opens quietly. My father asks me to come in. He is lying in bed, looking at the ceiling, where cobwebs dangle at the corners. He is murmuring, but his voice is loud, echoed by the whitewashed walls. It is a winter morning before dawn. The fluorescent light tube is black on both ends, casting white light on my father's dark skin.

My mother wears a thick cotton vest. She hunches over the sewing machine, holding a piece of cloth with one hand and rolling the sewing wheel with the other, sobbing. Her tears are trickling down her plump face, her nose red. She grimaces in silence.

I cross the room and spread my arms to hold her, and I am woken up by a stabbing pain in my heart. My hands are on my stomach, sweating.

My husband is in his third stage of snoring, loud but even. The first stage is when he has just fallen asleep. He snores suddenly, waking himself up. He then turns on his side, starting the second stage, soft and varied. The third stage is now, when he is deeply asleep.

I get up and steady myself, feeling the soft hair of the carpet between my toes. I have become used to this – waking up suddenly in the middle of the night, as sleepy and as alert as a snoozing owl.

The hall is lit by the moonlight through the ceiling windows. Maybe moonlight has a slightly cooler temperature. I tighten my dressing gown.

On one side of the living area is an antique Mongolian chest in dark green and two Ming dynasty antique chairs in burgundy. Above the vase of artificial white roses and between two cast-iron golden candelabras, my husband's deceased wife is smiling at me. She is surrounded by other family photos, her eyes following my movements. I sit down on one of the antique chairs, feeling dizzy.

I told my mother I live in a house next to the beach. On sunny days I open the window and the white curtains blow in and out, depending on the direction of the wind. I sometimes put on a straw hat and a pair of sunglasses to take a walk among the beach-goers. I wear various shades of grey and blend into the surroundings. I become two dimensional, a moving shadow, walking under the sun like a grey cat walking under the moon. On rainy days, I close all the windows and peep into the yellowish-grey sky and the greenish-grey ocean. Raindrops knock on the roof urgently like visitors keen to come in. I told my mother I live happily in an expensive house.

I told my mother I am an interpreter. When I was young, she hoped I would one day live overseas and work for the United Nations. I told her as an interpreter, I attend meetings, where people from different countries negotiate important matters. I interpret for businesses, educational institutions, and government agencies. I learn the jargon for macroeconomics, banking, insurance, fashion, medicine, including cochlear implants and IVF. I create Chinese names for expatriates going to China, and their wives and children. I find beautiful Chinese words from the dictionary, and explain the meanings to them, quoting Chinese poetry.

At night, I may be called in to interpret for counselling hotlines, when young mothers speak about losing their children to illnesses, middle-aged wives speak about losing their husbands to younger women in China, and old women speak about their loneliness at having no one. The counsellors sound as tired as I am, but they diligently ask the Chinese-speaking callers open-ended questions, reflect back the situations by paraphrasing, and name the callers' feelings. I hear 'What should I do? I cannot see a solution,' and I say 'What should I do? I cannot see a solution.' I hear 'Are you feeling trapped?', and I say 'Are you feeling trapped?' I speak for both parties as if I am having an internal dialogue, as if I am comforting myself, being simultaneously the suffering child and the hand that's combing through her hair.

I told my mother I was the interpreter at an international conference on a neurological condition in which two or more bodily senses are coupled. So I was not playing games when I told her the colours of people's surnames. I cornered our neighbour's youngest boy, not to bully him, but only to teach him the colours of numbers. I met a Chinese artist who painted lotus in crystal blue. In another painting he painted raindrops in yellow and he titled it *The Shower of Gold.* He painted me too.

I met my husband when I was interpreting at a writers' festival for a Chinese poet in exile. What the poet said did not make much sense but I tried my best to make it sound logical. At the request of an earnest audience, he read a poem from his latest volume. People applauded, not so much for his poetry because he read it in Chinese, but for his long hair and his animated voice. My husband came to talk to me afterwards.

I was in my Chinese costume, Prussian blue with gold and silver bamboo leaves. There seems to be some decorative value in a Chinese costume, which makes me feel like a porcelain vase, exquisite and brittle, to be treated with care, by others and by myself. So that day I walked with my chin high and my chest out.

My husband used to be a carpenter, known for his impeccable craftsmanship. After his wife's death, he studied a real estate course and worked in the property industry. After he retired, he started to learn to paint, visit art museums, and go to writers' festivals.

He has the look of a well-maintained and respectable gentleman. His jaw, once square, has lost its sharp edge. Like the furniture he made decades ago, he now looks subdued and reliable.

My husband's first wife died twenty years ago. She has large eyes, a prominent nose and a sensitive chin. She smiles contentedly in every photograph. Her last photo was taken on her forty-fifth birthday. She smiled from behind the elaborate square cake and the orange glow of the birthday candles, oblivious to the accident to happen a few days later.

My husband had been progressively reducing the number of her photographs in the house, until I noticed it and asked him not to. Instead I reframed some of them. My favourite is in an oval-shaped ivory frame displayed in a corner amid fine china. She wears a Chinese top and looks straight out of a 1920s movie. I also like an old photo of her mother and her six aunts sitting on the fence of their family farm. Seven young women, squinting under the sun, cheerful and relaxed, their frizzy hair and floral skirts flowing in the wind. I spend a lot of time walking around the house, feeling accompanied and blessed by the dead. I am safely buried in someone else's family history.

My husband's eldest son is a contractor for telecommunications projects. The second son is an accountant for a large chain of funeral companies. His daughter is a nurse in a mental-health hospital. She is the only one younger than me.

They are generally kind to me. Just like their father, they share a collective comical affection for me. My comments are exotic, amusing, controversial and not to be taken seriously. Once I told them an old neighbour of mine could read characters written inside folded paper. They all laughed. It has since become a standing joke.

I can afford to be controversial. I can blink my almond-shaped eyes and make provocative statements to peoples' faces. I once said, 'The world is made of strings of energies. A brick and I are made of the same basic elements. The strings vibrate differently to form different particles.' My husband stared at me, shaking his head, sighing, speechless. He did not speak to me for the rest of the evening, but he made me Masala Chai tea.

The next day coming back from the church, he said he was going to save a space for me in heaven. I looked up from my book and said, 'How do you know we are not in heaven already? Every realm has the same problem of increased population.' We were sitting in the garden under a weeping maple. The sunlight was filtered through the new leaves. My husband shuffled his newspaper but he did not turn the page for a long time.

My husband likes to think of me as coming from the middle of nowhere. He often mixes up my hometown with Inner Mongolia and he once believed I rode a camel to school.

I go back to China less often now. After each trip, I would be depressed for some weeks. I read Chinese books, browsed Chinese websites, listened to rock music from the pirate Chinese CDs, and talked to my friends in China on Skype. My husband asked why I did not listen to the equivalent rock music in English. I said rock is about anger and there is nothing to be angry about in his society. When probed further, I said I cannot explain because it is a Chinese affair. He was satisfied with my response; it confirmed me as his inscrutable oriental muse.

Going out with me is not without challenges for him. We walk on the street, and people look at us, older men with envy, older women with contempt, Chinese women with curiosity, and Chinese men with disgust. Those that are English-speaking talk to me in simple sentences. Those that are Chinese-speaking pretend to whisper knowing that I can hear and I understand. The funniest is when we see other mixed couples, mostly older white men with younger Chinese women, and we look into each other critically as if we are looking at ourselves in the mirror.

My husband took me on holiday one day. When we came back, we went to his house and it was repainted in crimson. A local landmark, it used to be called the white house. It is now called the red house. I accepted his proposal for marriage and the fact that he had a snip done years ago. I told my mother I am married to an older husband, just like Jane Eyre to Rochester, and we do not plan to have children.

I tell my mother many things, but I do not tell her everything. I do not tell my mother that I dream of her and the dreams are my worst nightmares. I dream of her being sick, being hurt, losing her way home, or falling. Even her smiles make me worry.

My mother is losing her memory. She hardly speaks and if she does it would be questions about the children or remembrance of the distant past. She walks very slowly and has great difficulty climbing up to their apartment. On winter afternoons, she often sits on the sofa in front of the television, and if asked, she says she is waiting for the weather forecast. She looks like a chubby child wrapped up in too many layers of clothing.

I have not written to my mother lately. I have not told her that I am nearly three months pregnant.

My mother once told me she was very hungry when she was pregnant with me. The only treat she had was three hardboiled eggs a day. She could not endure the intervals between peeling the eggs, so she always peeled them all before eating them in one go. She said she longed for fried rice during those days.

I have been hungry too, sometimes feeling a surge of hunger in the middle of a meal, and I have to start afresh. I often feel like a wolf wandering in the winter forest, tormented and isolated by my hunger. I feel like smashing the table when food is late and kissing the waiter or waitress when my food is carried down the aisle. When other people's food arrives ahead of mine, I regret every order I have not made. During the day, I give up my usual Vietnamese roll or sushi and go straight to chicken kebab. At home, my husband is delighted to see his hearty stew suddenly in demand. I pity the North Koreans – no one should suffer from hunger like that.

Sometimes I feel I am being eaten from the inside. Other times I feel like a ripe fruit, about to burst into something pulpy.

My nose seems sharper than usual. I walk by men on the street, and I account in my mind: beer; cigarette; Indian curry; onion; perspiration. What I consider natural smells are still better than some deodorants that smell like blunt knives, and some perfumes that hit me like broken glass.

I search the internet for articles and images. I know which day the egg was fertilised. It should have turned into a foetus this week with its sex apparent. I try to imagine a world where sound is muted. The blood flow the spring creek, the heartbeat the distant thunder, a rub on the tummy the autumn branches swaying in the wind.

I find myself talking to her, apologising for any stress I have put on her. I have become careful. As the bearer of a secret, I avoid stepping on manholes or walking under roof edges, I wait patiently for the lights to turn green at pedestrian crossings, and I move away discreetly from people who sneeze or cough. At home I keep away from the microwave oven when heating up soy milk and I wash my hands excessively.

I have put on weight, particularly around my mid-section. I have outgrown my pants and since the weather is warm, I wear skirts and dresses. Loose long tops with ruffles in front are the most deceiving. My body temperature is higher and I feel like a mini steamboat. My hands are warm and my forehead feverish. My husband says the extra weight I have put on suits me.

My husband is an experienced gardener but the only thing I can help with is the weeding. He mows the lawn, trims the rosemary hedge, applies fertiliser for the gardenia and cuts back roses, while I squat picking weeds from the garden beds or between the pavements and the gravel.

Every Saturday morning, when we are working in the garden, I wait to find the perfect moment. This is the time when I most want to tell, to confess, to unburden and expose. The calming new green, the fragrance of the spring flowers, the primitive labour, make me feel innocent. Sometimes I feel so tense that I almost cannot breathe. I have prepared a whole speech, but still I wait behind the curtain for the lights to dim and the spotlight to turn on. The audience will stop their polite conversations and turn their heads to the stage. Then I will go up, ready to be executed.

I did approach my husband once while he was cutting back the citrus trees. He was in his shorts and T-shirt, his knees and elbows looked dry, he was panting from manoeuvring the heavy-duty scissors. I asked him to follow me and sit in front of the lattice screen with star jasmines. The flowers had not opened but already the perfume was leaking from the rosy pink buds. I was in a green floral dress, a pair of sandals, my feet crossed at the ankles, my hands held together on my lap. I focused my eyes on the pavement, where a group of ants were carrying a dead bee. Just as I was about to start, he took my hand and held it between his palms. He said he had not been able to squat for a long time and luckily I could and it was very nice of me to do the weeding.

Maybe we could use a gardener so we did not have to do everything ourselves. Then we would have more time to smell the roses.

The night air is damp and heavy, the moon has gone behind the cloud. The wind chime makes a timid sound, as if it too is afraid of breaking the silence.

I open the bedroom door as loudly as I can and switch on the light.

My husband raises his upper body on one elbow and squints under the sudden brightness. What is left of his hair is sticking up. His face is more wrinkled than usual, red from pressing on the pillow.

'I have something to tell you.'

'Come back to bed. You'll catch a cold. And turn off that light.'

I turn off the light and lie down. He reaches out his right arm under my neck and holds me from behind.

'We'll talk about it tomorrow,' he says. His left hand is on my belly.

UTS Writers' Anthology

The Seventh Letter

Sean Williams

The stroke hit him like a thunderbolt in front of the whole board. The world vanished as if a shutter had been drawn. Later, he remembered the feel of his left hand at his temple, where a knife seemed to enter his brain and twist, before all consciousness was snuffed out. He didn't remember the blow that left a deep, purple bruise above his left eye, where his head struck the table so hard it would've knocked him out cold if he hadn't been already.

Then … shadows, shapes, distant conversations. He wasn't truly aware for some time. Forever, it seemed to him, when he could think at all. He was a puzzle in its box, with all the pieces tumbled and unlikely to fall into place on their own.

When he returned to himself, he was flat on his back in a well-lit, white room, loomed over by an ashen-haired woman with protuberant ears.

'What happened?' he croaked.

The woman looked pleased but not unsurprised. 'Welcome back, Mr Jameson. How are you ——?'

He blinked. 'How am I what?'

'——,' I said. 'Is there any pain? Can you move? I'm Doctor Harrod. We put you on —— within an hour of your stroke and the scans seem mostly clear now. The devil, however, is always in the details. Can you feel it when I do this?' The doctor lifted his hand and manipulated the joints.

He pulled it back. 'Yes, I can feel it, but ...'

'What?'

He didn't want to say it. He knew what a stroke was. Everyone in their fifties knew. If his mind was broken, would it be better or worse to see the cracks?

'Talk to me, ——. If you describe your symptoms fully, there's a chance we can see to them.'

'What did you just call me?'

The doctor lost some of her bedside cheer. 'Your name, Mr Jameson. I used your first name. Don't you remember what that is?'

He shook his head, and the full force of his mortality struck him in that moment.

'Excuse me, Mr Jameson, just for a second. I will be back.'

Unlike me, he feared, as the doctor swept out of the room. Unlike me.

A battery of tests consumed the next few hours. He clearly wasn't entirely well, despite the full recovery of his physical functions. He could sit, point, eat, and excrete to the satisfaction of the therapists summoned to examine him. The problem was more subtle than that. He had trouble with some instructions, particularly those specific to one side of his body – a problem of comprehension, not volition. If he couldn't understand what was asked of him, how could he comply?

The disability was thus isolated to the speech centres of his brain, where words were formed. Even so, its exact nature still proved stubbornly elusive. Some words were simply absent, excised from his brain with a semantic scalpel. There seemed to be no pattern to the excision. Nouns, verbs, adjectives and adverbs were victims, but not all nouns, verbs, adjectives or adverbs.

His wife came to visit, flamboyant in sombre tones. She too called him by a name he could not understand, and looked appropriately dismayed when he could not say hers.

'Oh, pumpkin. What's happened to you? Do they think you'll recover? The board is anxious. They can't keep the —— on hold forever.'

He suppressed a flash of irritation. Who cared about the board when his life had been shattered?

'Please don't call me "pumpkin,"' he said, aware of a nurse by the door. His circumstances embarrassed him sufficiently as it was.

'Well, what am I to call you, then? You've already made it clear you won't hear your name, and you won't use mine either.'

'It's not that I won't. I can't. They don't sound like any words I've heard before.' He searched for an appropriate metaphor in his oddly truncated vocabulary. 'There are times when we're not in the same country. I'm here and you're in Paris. You speak French and I speak ...'

He couldn't finish the sentence. The name he needed wasn't in his mind any more, escaped like so many other words. There had to be a way to talk about such matters, but all too frequently he found himself road-blocked.

The expression on his wife's face was one he would come to know well, in the days ahead.

More tests. Flash cards and electrodes taped to his scalp. Extended, self-conscious conversations with psychiatrists and speech therapists. Occasional incarcerations in claustrophobic tubes in which every neuron of his brain was untied and examined. The lesion proved difficult to isolate, and without isolation a cure would be impossible. He endured it all, keenly aware that with every day his case became odder, strayed further and further beyond the medical norm. Sometimes it was difficult to tolerate, the awareness that the puzzle he represented was more important than who he was. His condition was to be defeated, not cured.

In the end, an intern achieved what all the experts had not. Sam was affable, warm-natured, and had taken to him despite the difference in their years. He came frequently to chat. The topic of Jameson's condition could not be avoided, but Sam seemed interested in a personal capacity, as well as professional.

It was Sam, the intern, who had proposed that he, the patient, use his middle name, Lee, in place of his first. That worked. Lee Jameson was acceptable to his inconveniently broken mind.

'I had an idea, Lee,' Sam said on another occasion. 'You can turn left but not ——. You can run but you've never been ——. You can say "Lee" but not ——. Has anyone asked you about the alphabet?'

Lee shook his head. 'What about it?'

'How many letters there are, for instance.'

'Twenty-six. Everyone knows that.'

'Tell me them, then.'

He felt like a child but did as instructed. 'A B C D E F H I J K L M N O P Q R S T U V W X Y Z.'

'That's twenty-five.'

'Nonsense. Don't mess with me, Sam.'

'I'm not. You missed a letter.'

'I'm sure I didn't.'

'Try once more.'

'A B C D E F H I J ...'

'Stop there, Lee. What comes between F and H?'

'There's no letter between F and H.'

'Then that's your problem.' Sam beamed. 'You've lost ——.'

Lee shook his head. The sound Sam had made bore no relation to any in his lexicon. It didn't exist. It didn't exist to him.

More tests followed. Sam's theory was upheld. Odd as it seemed, one letter out of twenty-six had utterly vanished from Lee's life. Any word spelt with that letter was therefore incomprehensible to him, whether written or said aloud. The extraordinary plasticity of the brain enabled him to fold his speech around that absent letter so effectively that its absence was invisible to him, but the consequences remained dire. His name, which contained that letter, had vanished into the blind spot, as had his wife's. Whole sections of the dictionary and the phone book now meant zero to him. Some suburbs seemed like lands more distant than Denmark. Entire tenses were denied him.

The only consolation he could see was that he hadn't lost one of the vowels – E would have been very difficult to live without – or a common consonant like S. How could he have coped without plurals?

'So you can say Jameson but not ——, and Jesus but not ——?'

'Yes.'

His wife looked at him in a way that revealed she didn't quite believe him. Her scepticism hurt less than he could have expected. They still hadn't decided what he should call her, now her name was off-limits. That worried him. Now that his condition had been defined and declared no immediate threat to his life, he was free to return home.

Perhaps the condition would be named after him, he speculated. His last name, he hoped, not his first.

After Sam had finished his shift and when the shadows were thickest in the ward, Lee dressed in the clothes his wife had provided for him to wear home the next day. She had booked a car for him, under his new name. The clothes didn't quite fit. He had become thin in hospital, older. His hair stood up in a wild, ivory wave when he looked in the mirror. The bruise above his eye had turned yellow. He pulled at his cheeks and blew himself a kiss that looked more final than he had intended.

Somewhere behind that skull was a tiny scar, one that had thus far utterly eluded the finest of science's searches and could remain undiscovered for years, perhaps forever if he was unlucky. He would wait all that time for his name to be returned, for the lexicon to be restored. Wouldn't it be better to accept who he was now and move on?

Move on to what? He could be a carpenter, or a teacher. No, not a teacher. He was a card short of a full deck. His pupils would matriculate with a one-letter deficit, innocent inheritors of his own fundamental flaw. His choices were limited to ones he could pronounce and therefore think of, such as carpenter, mechanic, postman, scientist.

It would be unwise, too, he decided, to pick a field in which communication was essential, such as politics or the priesthood. How could he be a priest, when he couldn't even say the word most people used for 'deity'? He lay awake in search of the absent letter and the hole in his head that it had fallen into. That was an entirely different sort of existential mystery, one he was already tired of.

He tore his stare from the mirror and put a hand on the doorknob. At that moment it turned. The door opened to reveal a tall man in the corridor outside. His cheeks were hollow. The hat he wore was broad and old-fashioned, his suit conservative and uncreased.

'Mr Jameson?'

Lee stepped backwards, filled with an unaccountable shame

at his planned escape. It was his life; he could do with it whatever he wanted, even run off into a new one if required.

'I'm sorry to startle you at this late hour.'

The hat came off with a practised sweep. The man's shoulders were stooped, as of one ill-accustomed to his superior stature, but his manner was confident. 'I came the moment I learned of your condition from Doctor Harrod. Here.' A business card issued forth from an inside pocket, proffered with an economical motion of one hand. 'My name is Simon Le Hunte.'

The card said: 'Treasurer, Royal Society for the Semantically Impaired.'

'My condolences,' Le Hunte offered with his hat held to his chest. 'May I talk with you for a moment?'

'I ... yes, of course. Come in.' Lee retreated to the bed, concerned that a sudden pins-and-needles sensation in his extremities heralded a new neuronal assault.

'I want you to know, first and foremost, that you are not alone.' Le Hunte stood at the end of the bed, his hat now at his side. 'Neither is the injury you have suffered completely unknown to science, even if it is often misdia ... ah, that is, often overlooked in the normal rounds of medical treatment.'

He understood then that Le Hunte's word-choice was carefully considerate, so Lee could understand every word. The rest followed naturally.

'Which letter have you lost?' he asked.

'Alas, I cannot tell you. I can only refer to it as the seventeenth letter.'

A quick count revealed that to be Q.

'We are fortunate, you and I,' said Le Hunte. 'With a more inconvenient overlap, we could barely converse. That's why I am often chosen to introduce the Society to new recruits. I am pleased to be here about that service today.' He executed a small bow.

A joke occurred to Lee then, but he could not put it in words. In his mind's eye he saw an assembly of the Semantically Impaired, all with different letters lost and forever stuck in the attempt of conversation. It could be impossible for them to communicate except by morse code or numbers or even semaphore. But he could not find the words to describe such an assembly. He had attended many such as chair of the board of his company, but he could not name them now because those words were lost.

Words lost like those of the man before him and who knew how many others? Words that had never returned.

For the first time he wept, not just for himself, but for his wife whose name would remain forever unspoken by his lips – and for people without the letter L who could not speak of love, those denied M and the word 'mother,' and others whose incapacities he could barely conceive of. Even Le Hunte would never toast the queen, which had never before seemed an important part of life. To be denied any aspect of speech and perception was unbearable. Inhumane.

Le Hunte made no move to physically reassure him, but he did speak.

'It's perfect all ri ... I mean to say, you shouldn't feel ashamed. We've all felt this way at some point. It is not easy to be as we are, alike and yet profoundly unlike. It's not amnesia; it's not aphasia. It's entirely too difficult to explain to those without our particular lack. And to lose your name ...' Le Hunte's expression became mordantly sympathetic. 'I would have you know that you're not alone in that circumstance, either. There are others on our books in the same straits.'

'Is that supposed to cheer me up?'

'Perhaps not. But there is a chance of recovery, if that is what you need. Science has made terrific advances in recent years. Doctors cannot yet repair the lesions that cost us our letters, but there is talk of prostheses – artificial letters, if you like, rather than ones that have been reversed or distorted as offered to us in the past.

'I was born with this condition and remember all too well the awkward spectacles and lenses forced upon me. Now, there is none of that. Society has learned of our condition, however slowly, and makes adjustments. For instance, there exist translations of classic novels that permit even the most unfortunately impaired to read as others do. There is hope, you see, Mr Jameson. There is always hope.'

'Really?'

'Yes. And – well, I don't wish to be harsh, but people survive far worse disabilities. We are fortunate, you and I. There is much we can still say – and limitations, some believe, only make us more creative. For every common word denied, an old one is revived. Shakespeare and Chaucer would be pleased, I think, with some of our more inventive members.'

Lee reached into a pocket for a handkerchief and blew his nose rather messily. 'Has anyone else lost my letter?'

'The seventh? Not anyone I have met.'

'I'm unique, then.'

'You are what?'

'Oh, sorry. I'm one of a kind.'

'I see. Yes. That's certainly true. Is that a comfort?'

He wanted to say, no, not really, but that wasn't entirely true. He did feel somewhat better for the joint awareness that someone else had his condition too and that he wasn't just another in the herd.

'Well,' said Le Hunte, hat atop his head once more, 'you have my card. Call me any time. We meet weekly. Please join us. You are most welcome.'

Lee stood to shake Le Hunte's hand. 'Thank you. I really am terribly ...' He floundered, at a momentary loss for the correct word.

'Appreciative?'

'Yes.'

For the first time, Le Hunte smiled. 'I believed you would be. Farewell, Mr Jameson,' he said with a wave. 'Au revoir. See you anon. Until next time!'

When the sound of his visitor's footsteps in the corridor outside had faded to silence, Lee took off his street clothes and returned to bed. Prostrate in the darkness, with his hands behind his head, he considered all that Le Hunte had said. How peculiar that his condition could be so common that a Royal Society existed to assist its sufferers – and more peculiar still that all across the world were dotted people whose alphabets deviated from everyone else's! Did such exist in China, Russia, Israel? He supposed they must. He hoped they had the equivalent of a Royal Society to cater to their needs, too, to help them find a new path in their oddly contracted but expanded worlds.

No more did he feel the need to run away. There could be no escape from his condition, even if it was one that he would find difficult to explain to people. He had no visible symptoms. He could, with a little practice, function. Yet he had lost his name, which in every society had a symbolic and undeniable effect on his sense of self. He was Lee Jameson now, and who that was remained to be seen. His old self certainly wouldn't have resolved to tell his wife that 'pumpkin' would be fine, provided he could call her that in return. And he wouldn't have spoken to the duty nurse to put in a recommendation for Sam the intern. He would have been too busy with the board and his other responsibilities.

Lee Jameson had new responsibilities, new demands. His relationship with the world had been turned upside down by a purloined letter. Never before had he suspected how complicated words could be. They were for much more than mere description. What one can't find the words for, he decided, cannot exist in one's experience – and what is the world, after all, other than the sum of one's experience?

Reassured that he had found a level of comprehension sufficient to survive the days and weeks ahead, he let his eyes drift shut and sleep take him away.

And his dreams, like those of the blind who dream in colour, were full of mergers, board meetings and gun-fighting guinea pigs riding stagecoaches of pure gold.

Bulletin

Venetian Glass

Amy T. Matthews

We made ourselves one person. It was easier than being separate. Our names contracted, we built ourselves from scratch on the MySpace page. We chose Linda's smarts, but my creativity, Linda's fear of empty rooms and my fear of pain. The photo was of Linda, there was no question it would be of Linda, but I was in it too, a black silhouette reflected in the mirror behind her, the flash glaring from my left eye like a star.

The suture began the night she ate the aspirin. It was the night my father left, taking all of his clothes and the plasma TV, while my mother smoked on the back deck, pretending she didn't care. I sat in the dark of my room, with the music turned up loud so I wouldn't have to listen to the sound of his car pulling out of the drive, and I thought of death. Swallowing Mum's sleeping pills; running a kitchen knife the length of my tubular blue veins; submerging under hot water, sucking it in, letting it swish through me like a living river. It wasn't the first time I had thoughts like these – they didn't lead to the cabinet, or the kitchen, or the bathtub. They led to tears and restless sleep, and to a headache when I woke up the next day.

Linda's father hadn't left. He was never going to leave. He was just going to sit bitterly at the dinner table, wishing his life had happened to someone else. Linda hated him. Or said she hated him. Her mother wasn't much better. I thought she was beautiful but Linda said she'd been 'done' and that nothing was real anymore. She was walking talking plastic. So Linda said.

The night my father left was the night Linda ate the aspirin. Nothing dramatic led her to the cabinet. Dinner as usual with plastic mum and bitter dad, followed by her heading up to bed, the aspirin packet tucked into the sleeve of her jumper. She ate the whole packet and I know why she did it. Every bitter little pill ground, crumbling, between her teeth was meant for them. She finished the packet and lay on top of her bedclothes, fully dressed, arranged like a still life. I guess she thought they'd find her and be driven to ... something. But no one found her, she woke up the next morning with the same headache.

I had seen myself at the cabinet, she had gone there. It meant something – we knew right away it meant something. The same hulking darkness lurked in the corners of our bedrooms when we were alone at night. Between us was recognition, abating the fear.

Belinda became the key – a person who was both of us, neither of us and no one. Belinda's fingers were easy on the keys. She could talk about school, parents, anything, with ringing irony, with none of the specific shame we felt. She was not alone.

I was the first to drift to the sites. Morbidity. Curiosity. Compulsion. The 'how to' lists of poisons raised no terror in me. How could it? It wasn't me looking at it. Who cared if Belinda looked – she wasn't real.

She read that poison causes vomiting and it's best to take an antihistamine an hour or so beforehand. A full stomach can delay death. Most poisons cause pain. I didn't want pain.

We didn't sit side by side. One didn't speak and the other type. Physically, I was alone in my room. Linda was implicit, part of Belinda, her photo before me on the page, haloed by the light from the star in my eye. Sometimes I'd log on and find a trail of sites Belinda had visited while I slept. The sites about jumping from buildings I found second-hand. (Ten stories at least for the jump to be fatal – too much time to think on the way down.) And I wasn't there the night Belinda joined the Common Aim Community.

I'd been having dinner with my mother. It was a new thing of hers, since Dad left. I think she found the silence frightening –

she always had a radio on talkback, up loud so the voices rang through the kitchen and down the hall. I took my sketchpad to the table and sketched her eating, which she hated. Her thin faced emerged in charcoal, strained and more sour than was accurate. At the hollow of her neck I drew in her pendant, the one my father bought her on their honeymoon. A night sky, in midnight blue Venetian glass. Long before my birth, when the glass was hot and liquid, the glassmaker swirled white stars into the blue; then plunged it, screaming, into icy water. When it cooled the stars were trapped, flat and hard and cold to the touch.

She didn't like the picture. She said she looked too old.

I hung it on my wall and switched the computer on, leaving a charcoal smudge on the button. Belinda had been online, discussing the problem of heights with the Community.

I could do it if it were five stories. HardSlut.
Won't work. Spook33.
I like heights. They make me feel like I can fly. Linda. Belinda. Us.

I saw the words on the screen and wasn't entirely sure I hadn't typed them myself. Spook33 and Belinda chatted for a long time. They continued to chat over the coming nights, mostly when I slept. He was a font of wisdom.

The neck break is best. Instant.
What if the neck doesn't break?
Five to ten minutes. Not so bad if you just strangle but if you've busted your jaw it'll hurt more.

It gave me gooseflesh. I could picture the knot, solid as a fist, and hear the whoosh of air past my ears. When I thought about it there was no pain. Hanging for me was a moment frozen like glass, suspended like the stars, caught mid-flight, hair streaming. I thought of the moment before the pain. Freefall.

It wasn't planned but it was no surprise. She came for me in the night, when my mother was on the deck, cigarette in hand, listening to talkback through the open kitchen window.

'Come on,' she said breathlessly when I opened the door. She said no more than that. She didn't have to.

We got into her car and drove. I felt as though the world around me had thickened and slowed, the orange streetlights like amber closing in around us. There was no sense of hurry. We went to the beach. It was August and cold, cloudless and moonless; a night full of stars. Cold stars like ice chips. We walked through the dunes, down to the edge of the black water. There was a sharp breeze that was clean in my lungs. I felt alive and I know she felt it too – we were connected. She took off running and I followed. We pounded along the hard packed wet sand and I could hear the rasp of my breath join the whistle of the wind and the rush of the surf. I felt powerful, strong, endless.

We stopped a long way from where we began. I felt her calm seep into me, felt the slowness returning, heard the surf overwhelm my fragile breath. We walked back to the car and she drove. There was no hesitation. She took us to a construction site, where the steel frame of a house loomed out of the darkness – the skeleton of a house, all possibility, with emptiness where its heart and flesh should be.

She had two ropes, already tied. I let her lead, she was the steel and I was the emptiness. We climbed scaffolding to the second floor and she fixed the ropes to the frame.

That was the first time we looked at each other, as she lowered her noose, hangman's knot at the base of her neck. It was like looking into a mirror. I thought of the flash, like a star in my skull.

The rope wasn't rough like I expected but smooth, shellacked. I looked down. Below us was a concrete slab, glowing in the moonless darkness. She took my hand and I startled. Her hand felt wrong – warm, damp and fleshy, like a handful of raw sausages – and immediately I felt the wind in my ears, heard again the pounding of my own feet and the rush of the surf.

'Ready.' She gave my hand a squeeze and let go. It wasn't a question and I didn't answer. Everything had sped up, from slow liquid glass to whistling steam. She leapt.

The rope caught her and she swung, snapped, the rope creaking and singing in the cavity of the house.

We'd made ourselves one person.

On a MySpace page.

But, here, in the hollow of the house, we weren't. Because, in the end, I stayed on the steel girder, my heart hammering in my ears, the stars cold and wheeling above me, not trapped in glass but exploding, burning, dying.

Reading the Signs

Laurie Clancy

My wife has had to 'let go' another employee in the company. My wife never speaks of firing people or giving them the sack, the boot, the Khyber or the flick. She always says that she let them go. Presumably not of their own free will. As if they were an endangered species of wildlife and she had released them back into their natural environment, to join their fellows in the nest. In the last three months she has 'let go' five of her disoriented staff.

My wife is the managing director of Flamingo Business Services. Flamingo Business Services is the only company in the state which specialises in creating business profiles of particular industries and making forecasts for the government and for private enterprise. When people ask her why it is called Flamingo, she laughs and says because the company hardly has a leg to stand on. My wife has a wonderful sense of humour.

Last year my wife created one hundred and eighty-two business profiles and was paid $1,178,000. Or was it the other way around? Meanwhile, I stay at home, work, clean the house, do the cooking, potter among the pot plants in the garden, and try to write. Over the past twelve months or so I have been writing scripts for movies that are never made and lyrics for songs that are never recorded. This is much more satisfying than writing novels that are never published.

*

At the moment I am writing a number of songs for a band called The Boys with Green Hair. I have great faith in the Boys and believe they will become the most successful band in Australia. At the moment they are doing gigs for free in Ballarat. I write songs about love and the absence, frustration, denial, deprivation and betrayal thereof. This seems to be what they want. At the moment I am writing a song called 'Reading the Signs':

> You'll be my lover if you've got the time.
> You'll fit me in between five and nine.
> What's mine is yours and what's yours is mine,
> Baby, I'm reading the signs.

The Boys are very pleased with this song. They think it is amongst my best work.

My wife has no respect for my work. For that matter, she has no respect for me, either. She tells me I am feeding mindless pap to the masses – or rather, that I am trying unsuccessfully to feed it since, as I point out, the masses show no inclination to swallow. I am pandering to the lowest common denominator. I am sacrificing my undeniable talents, squandering my undoubted gifts, selling my soul and betraying my birthright for a mess of pottage. I don't even know what the hell pottage is.

I tell her she is practising a sophisticated form of voodoo under the pretence of using science. She tells me that last year her company earned $1,780,000. She tells me that my declared income over the last twelve months amounted to $6,149. End of argument.

My wife Stephanie – she hates to be called Steve as the boys at work call her – sees me as a kind of glorified houseboy and to my chagrin that is what she sometimes calls me before her guests when we have dinner parties. Still, that is better than being called a nagging housewife, which is the lowest point to which she once descended, on a memorable day on which three rejections arrived simultaneously in the mail.

I am good at cleaning and tidying up. In between trying to write songs I clean the house immaculately and struggle for inspiration over the kitchen sink. I compose:

Don't say it's the song, and not the singer,
If you no longer want me, I don't want to linger.
Used to count your lovers on the fingers of one finger,
But now I'm reading the signs.

Inspiration does not always come.

My wife, who studied German briefly at the University of Melbourne, says that my lyrics sound like badly translated Brecht poems. I am not sure whether or not this is a compliment but am inclined to think it is not.

She does, however, appreciate my cleaning efforts. She also calls me her Mr Cleen. (Have I mentioned my wife's sense of humour?) Sometimes she shows her appreciation in thoughtful little ways, bringing me home flowers or a box of chocolates, or inviting me out to our favourite restaurant. I put on aftershave lotion before she comes home.

I am careful how I clean, and take pride in using the correct materials. For washing the dishes I use Sunlight. Power at a sensible price. For cleaning the stove I favour Jif. Powerful cleaning without harsh scratching. For glass I employ Windex, extra-strength, streak-free glass and household cleaner. I use Scotchgard Carpet Cleaner for high-traffic areas and spot-stain removal. I polish the furniture with Marveer, scrub the pots with Steelo for those stains that simply won't go away and deodorise the toilet with Pino-Cleen.

Every morning I brush my teeth in champagne.

Lately I have started to become bored with this routine. I have begun to think of adventurous alternatives. Wiping the windows with Nugget boot polish. Washing the dishes in Draino. Stephanie would not be pleased. She does not have a great sense of humour.

Modern man – and woman – is obsessed with hygiene. How many cleaning products are there on sale? Hundreds? Thousands? Last week I went down to the local Safeways and began to count them. For the hygiene-minded it was a feast, a smorgasbord, a cornucopia. I reached one hundred and thirty-seven before the girl on the checkout desk asked me to leave. She thought I was a spy for a rival chain.

*

Stephanie is now my wife but in fact it took a great deal of persuasion to make her that. Although we have been together for nearly six years, we have been formally married for only two of them. Stephanie could not see the point. It was the second marriage for both of us and, as she put it in one of those mysterious metaphors she was very partial to, we'd both been to the well before. Neither of us wanted any more children and there was no pressure on us to marry but I became irritated with the lack of a satisfactory term with which to refer to her and this finally led to marriage.

If I said 'wife,' which seemed to me to be the most logical, my friends would smile with conspiratorial satisfaction and say, 'Ah, you've done it at last!' I tried 'de facto spouse,' 'companion,' 'mistress,' and 'lover' but none seemed satisfactory. 'Fuck' was demeaning and in my case only rarely accurate anyway. A friend suggested 'partner,' which she said was becoming fashionable, but I felt that made us sound like a couple of cowboys or cops, or perhaps members of a law firm. Stephanie started calling me her live-in companion. I retaliated by calling her my c.c., which I had heard on the radio and which means constant companion and she began calling me shithead. When a truce was finally declared, she agreed to marry me. She says it is (and I quote) a '*mariage de convenance*.'

Apart from flowers and chocolates, my wife is constantly bringing home what she calls little knick-knacks for the house – pot plants, vases, small tapestries, dining tables, baby elephants she says she has found in the Botanical Gardens. Last week she brought home a reproduction of a painting by an English artist, Sir William Orchardson (1835–1910), titled 'The First Cloud.' It is one of a series. Another one is called 'Marriage of Convenience.' It is hung in the National Gallery of Victoria. My wife always prefers handsome reproductions to obscure originals, like me. The painting depicts a tall, patriarchal figure, standing on the carpet in front of a fireplace, hands aggressively in his hip pockets; he is addressing his wife, who has her back to him, so that we see her only dimly reflected in the window she is looking out of. Even so, we can tell she is very beautiful and probably only about half his age. 'The First Cloud.' I have been examining this painting all week since she brought it home.

'It is the little rift within the lute/That by and by will make the music mute.' This is not one of my lyrics. It comes with the painting.

For my wife, the world is full of signifiers and signifieds. Human intercourse for her consists of an incessant transmission and reception of signals, an uninterrupted translation of codes. She even talks like that. At work she says things like 'I get your message,' 'I read you,' or 'You're on my wavelength.' Sometimes in telephone conversations with her I have to resist the temptation to say 'Roger. Over and out.' It is like living with a human powerhouse incessantly emitting messages. In the meantime, I hum quietly to myself over the Draino:

> Loving might fill your life.
> It still doesn't fill your day.
> I fell in love with my wife.
> I saw her drift away.

She also believes passionately in the unconscious, to the point where she has dismissed the conscious itself almost completely as a source of reality or truth. This makes for strained and difficult relations at times. Nothing one says can be taken at face value, so that now I have learned to express the opposite of my real desire or opinion in order to have her ferret out the real one. We have conversations like this:

'Would you like to go to the pictures tonight?'

I think quickly. No, I'd hate to. 'Yes. I'd love to.'

'No, you're just saying that to please me. Really, you'd rather stay home and work on your music.'

Perfectly correct. 'No, I'm mad keen to go to the pictures.'

'You can't fool me. We're staying home.'

Whew! But it doesn't take long for this to become exhausting. I have had to tell her I vote Liberal, am a believing Christian, and think there are too many refugees coming into the country. If she ever stops second-guessing me and takes what I say at face value, I will be a disgraced figure in front of all her friends. Even now, I wonder what she tells them about me.

*

Stephanie has not come home again tonight, the third night in a row. I light the fire with 'the spitting wood,' as she likes to call the kindling, eat a slice of bread and a piece of cheese, and drink a glass of claret. Passing Clouds. I put on a CD, Sinead O'Connor, one of what my wife likes to call my 'whining women.' I wash my plate, knife and fork – in Morning Fresh dishwashing fluid. Extra-strength, economical, gentle on the hands, freshens the kitchen. I gaze again at the painting hanging on the living-room wall.

I would like to be a patriarch, I decide, and live in an age of comfortable certainties and clearly defined roles. I thirst for hierarchic privacies. Grow eight or ten inches in height, perhaps. Double my weight. Stop using Vaseline Intensive Lotion and try Oil of Ulan. Allow my skin to grow swarthier and darker and develop sideburns. Drop my voice several octaves and become booming and peremptory. Thrust my hands into the pockets of my double-breasted suit, take my watch and chain out of my fob pocket and consult it.

When Stephanie came in guiltily, I would glower at her and say nothing. She would take off her hat and gloves. She would be wearing a long white frock and not those mannish, square-cut suits she affects at the office. She would walk over to the window, waiting for me to speak, intimidated as I allow the room to fill with the silence of my accusation.

'Well,' I would finally demand. 'And just where have you been, young lady?'

She turns. There are tears in her eyes. She looks modestly down at the ground as a blush fills her cheeks. 'I'm sorry, Jules,' she says. 'It won't happen again.' She comes towards me and I take her in my arms, bending protectively over her.

Bystander

The White Peacock

Marion Halligan

He is a nice man. He asks me to do things with him. I say no. Every time. He doesn't ask all that often, he's quite timid, but he is also dogged. As though he has dares with himself, and must go through with them. I decline with politeness and almost excessive regret. I'm so sorry Vaughan, I can't ... I'm going ... they are coming ... I've promised ... I said I would ... It is probably this excessive politeness that allows him to go on asking me.

There are never many women in the bar. The women in this town are mostly mothers and at this after-work hour are at home with the tea and the children. There are some older women who are free, mostly the young leave. I have reversed this process, having come. I'm the schoolteacher. I have my own house beside the school, rather larger in fact than the school and after one or perhaps two glasses of wine will go home to it and light the fire and make a meal. Dan who runs the pub opens bottles of red wine for me though normally he wouldn't sell it by the glass. The men drink beer. They stand at the bar and hitch their bellies. I sit at a table by the fire and sometimes they pause and talk to me. They don't sit down, only the card players sit down.

Sometimes lean men in worn tight jeans come into the pub. They prop booted feet on the bar rail and push their Akubras to the backs of their heads. Brad and Rod and Marvin and Joe. From the farms and the mill. Nino and Hughie from the garage on the main road. Gerhardt from the bakery. He wears a baseball cap. The kids at school wear similar caps but with big flaps round their necks to save them from the sharp high-country sun. I lean on the bar for a moment and have a word. Some of the men have children in the school. Some are just passing through.

I sit with the glass of red by the fire and stare into it. The fire is a friend. A present companion, silent but always fascinating. You can gaze into the fire and think and not feel lonely. When the men address their remarks to me it can feel like an interruption. Today the topic is the snow, a very good thing, it will melt and gently soak the poor droughty ground. I think they are shy, not that it shows among themselves but they do not believe they have anything to say to me. They know my name is Jess but don't call me by it.

Vaughan is not tall or lean, he's stocky. His bottom is too big, it's plump, not hard. The men with their huge beer bellies tight and taut as drums – I imagine walking along and playing them, different notes booming out as I beat my hands against them – these men have neat buttocks, their jeans hang under their stomachs and fit firmly around their bottoms, whereas Vaughan is generally rather full in the hips, though his belly is flat enough, and his jeans bunch around his middle. Have I come here to this forsaken country on the cold rind of the world to look at men's bums? When I was married to one I did not pay so much attention, it was a pleasant part of a body that I loved and lusted after. When a man says he does not care in that way for you any more, the marriage is over though we can still be friends, why not, good friends as we have been lovers and partners over the years, you have to put away loving and lusting and get on with another life and coming here to this cold rind of the world seems a good idea. You can look at men's bums or stare into the fire and drink your glass of red which is half-way decent and remember the article in today's paper which said people especially women who drink wine, a lot of wine, five or six bottles a week, think better, their brains work better. And come to think of it I suppose I think quite well, I certainly do a lot of it.

Vaughan has shining clean brown hair that flops around his head in a messy silky fashion and rosy cheeks in a plump soft face. His skin is very pale brown and then there are these two patches of flaming red on his cheeks. He speaks gently and looks as though his clothes are ironed. He lives with his parents and works on the farm. I suppose his mother irons his clothes for him. He looks very young, and even allowing for the fact that he's probably not as young as he looks, he's not very old, not rugged and weather-beaten like the other men, even the younger ones. Certainly a good bit younger than me.

He is a nice man, Vaughan. Who wants to be nice? In my day the mothers of girls wanted them to be nice but the daughters didn't. I think the mothers of sons probably didn't care about the boys being nice. Mothers of daughters say, he seems a nice boy, and the daughters don't think that's a good idea either, who wants a nice boy, and anyway what would mothers know. The men with the big bellies, the lean rugged cowboys (sheepboys?) are probably very nice men too, but somehow it isn't what you think of them, and with Vaughan it is.

That day Vaughan sat down at my table. He said, A fire is like the sea. You can look at it and never get tired.

I thought this was a good thing to say. I smiled. He said, Jess? I am going to the sea. Would you like to come? On Saturday.

Oh Vaughan, that's a nice idea. Except, I'm sorry, I've got ...

There's a peacock garden.

A peacock garden?

A garden with peacocks.

Peacocks ... the sea ...

I found I had said yes.

I'll pick you up at eight o'clock. Get a good start. He finished his beer, waved to the blokes at the bar and left. I wished I hadn't said yes. Down the mountain in his dusty old ute. What if it didn't have good brakes? I was going to stay home on Saturday and sit in front of the fire and read. Lorna gave me Patrick White's *Twyborn Affair* when I told her I was coming here. The Monaro plateau, she said, it's so important in that book, you have to read it. Well, Patrick White's not really my thing, we had to study some awful boring full of incomprehensible-abstract-meaning novel of his in one of my courses and I swore off him forever. But being here, I thought I should. One day. This Saturday. Now another one day.

When he came it wasn't the old ute but a shiny four-wheel

drive. The parents', he said, they lent it to me so we could be comfortable.

Did you mother also inquire whether I am a nice girl, I wondered, but then I am hardly a girl, having wasted eight years of my life on a marriage that failed. Not me, not Sam, it wasn't us that failed, it was the marriage. Like a baby that didn't thrive, grew sickly, died. But then we would have blamed ourselves. Whereas a marriage that fails, it's somehow its fault. So Sam would have it. The car was white and cosy with leather seats and good heating. I hate four-wheel drives but I have to confess it was fun sitting high up looking at the world. I thought, this isn't a date, this is going to the sea with a nice man. I said, I was planning to stay at home and read Patrick White.

I don't know why I said it. To put him off perhaps. Telling him you've got a clever one here. Making myself a formidable woman, a terrifying woman. Not a woman to take on dates. Provided he knew who Patrick White is, of course, he might think he's the latest thriller-writer. In which case I would already have read the book, I can never resist thrillers.

The Twyborn Affair? Haven't you read it yet, he said. You must, living here.

You've read it then?

I reckon. It was one of the family farms he came to, over the way a bit, I could show you some time. It's still a family story. The blooding of young Patrick. And of course, you have to ask, did he do those things.

Did you like it?

Yeah. Not so much as *Riders in the Chariot*. Or *The Vivisector*. But I liked it. He knows how to make you feel the Monaro.

The cold rind of the world …

Where the wind wuthers, said Vaughan.

There was a lot of snow still, heaped by the side of the road, lying in striations across the bare paddocks, caught in the serrated tussock, and when we started the descent from the plateau, where there were sparse forests of trees, the ground between them was covered with a thick blanketing fall. It's like Germany, said Vaughan. I know the trees are different but the way the snow piles on the ground, and drifts over the bushes, and powders the branches. And you can see how quiet it is.

Waiting for a fairytale to happen. Grimm, or someone. A wicked stepmother.

Hansel and Gretel and the birds pecking up the bread.

He pressed a button and a CD started playing. Elton John. That line, lovers like children, it gets to me, I don't know why. I didn't say much, as the car wound down the mountain, just listened to Elton.

We crossed the river, going into Merimbula. It's a very wide river, I said. He explained that ships used to come right up, big ships, loading and unloading, the granite for the harbour bridge pylons came from the Merimbula quarries, he said. I imagined great blocks of stone loaded on to ships, sailing up the coast to Sydney.

We had coffee by the water at Merimbula and looked at the big game fishing cruisers with their towering wheelhouses and massive rods, the chairs fitted with harnesses and fastened to the deck. And the whale boats tied up at the wharf. The whale boats being whale-watching boats, not whale hunting any more.

We got to Eden by lunch time and bought fish and chips at the wharf and drove up to the beach and ate them at a table on the edge of the sand. Vaughan had brought a bottle of red wine and some long-stemmed glasses. I hope you don't mind red wine with fish, he said. I think it's OK with fish and chips. Oysters, now ... he shook his head. Out in the bay a pod of dolphins swam up and down, cleaving through the water, not showily jumping up and curving down in their playful disporting way, more serious, fishing. Vaughan was right, you can stare at the sea and never grow tired, especially when there are dolphins threading through it.

The sun shone down on us, the air was cool but balmy, the red wine was beneficent, especially as I was getting more than my fair share, since Vaughan was driving. I told him about wine-drinking improving thinking. He pointed out Ben Boyd's tower, which Boyd meant for a lighthouse but was never allowed, because he wanted to do it only when he wanted to, and lighthouses have to be all the time or not at all. He talked about the killer whales who were called that because they herded the other whales into the bay so the whalers could kill them. Like dogs with sheep, he said. Most of the time we just sat, watching the birds, the maimed seagulls, the brown speckled ducks that looked like eagles when they flew, the water that stretched smooth between the arms of the bay like a piece of taut blue silk. I said that and he laughed. I know it's a cliché I said but sometimes clichés are just right.

After lunch we walked through the cemetery which was a kind of paddock sloping gently away from the sea and all its headstone facing towards it, tall and upright and as if staring out at it. I suppose, I said, they are all sailors, gazing out at the sea they spent their lives on. Mariners at rest, though still paying attention. But they were mostly the town's fathers, and mothers, the mothers often dead young and the children too. One small grave was enclosed by a fence of elaborate ironwork like a cot for the child who slept there. Some of the headstones were too old and worn to read, just the occasional stroke of a letter remaining. I like cemeteries, they are melancholy places but full of lives. The fathers, the mothers, the children, the families, deaths in childbirth, in accidents, in safe old ages, they are all stories, some of them sad, some tragic: that is the human condition. And the human connection, clearer in death. It's comforting that it's all been done before. I think of never having a baby, but at least I would not have to suffer from its dying.

We pottered about, sometimes calling to one another to come look at some poignant thing, some piece of bad poetry about the afterlife, some lengthy tender message, some pompous worldly claim. I remembered a strange movie I'd seen, very late at night and years ago, the kind that was made to be second rate, to accompany the main picture, about a man who somehow went back in time and fell in love with a woman, a doomed love since he had to return to his own time, and over the sad kisses of their parting she promised that when she died she'd have her headstone cut very deep, so the words would last, and the final scene is him back in his own present and going to the cemetery and finding her tombstone among all the other half-obliterated ones, and tracing the deeply carved letters with his fingers. So silly really, and hopelessly romantic; some impossible notion of love beyond the grave, love there in those deeply etched letters, and yet I remember it, and what does that say, that I want to believe in eternal love, love as permanent as words deep in stone? I gazed at the worn stones in this graveyard with their obliterated words and it seemed particularly sad that the stone should remain but the message that was its reason for being was entirely lost. Time stealing what was meant to defeat it.

A wind came in from the sea, ruffling its silk, worrying its fishy grey surface into scurrying waves, fanning Vaughan's rosy cheeks brighter red. His jeans were still baggy but you couldn't see his bottom under a heavy parka.

We got into the car and made our way to the peacock garden which turned out not to be public but the property of some friends of his who were away, he called in from time to time, to cast an eye, he said. There was a long drive from a locked gate through rich forest and the slow falling notes of bellbirds, then a grand house with shuttered windows and dry stone walls forming terraces covered with leaf litter, dropping down to a dam. The peacocks strutted the mulchy slopes of the terraces and cried their terrible cries like abandoned children. I don't think I could live with peacocks, there is too much pain in their voices, I know that isn't so for them but I couldn't bear such anguished meaningless cries. Vaughan prowled round the house and I sat quietly on an iron bench. After a while he came and stood behind me and then the peacocks began to dance. Three magnificent males and a small brown peahen. The males spread their tails and danced, and I marvelled that such gorgeous heavy swathes of feathers could be supported on such small bird bodies. They arched and stepped and fluttered their tails and the small brown peahen took no notice. What *peacocks,* I murmured, so extravagant, so spectacular. So vain. And the peahen such a small dull thing.

Yes, said Vaughan, but who has the power? Look how she ignores them.

Just then a bird came down from a small copse, its tail folded behind it like a fan, drooping towards the ground but held proudly out of the dirt. At a little distance it unfurled its tail and began to strut too, rattling its feathers in a shimmying dance. It was pure white and I breathed a sigh, it was so astonishingly beautiful. So much more beautiful than the brilliant blue birds, who now seemed gaudy, vulgar, over-painted. This white was so pure, so dazzling, so angelic. White was magic, white was desire.

The peacocks danced, their tails shimmered, the peahen took no notice. Occasionally one moved towards her and nonchalantly she stepped away. Suddenly, as one approached, she turned her bottom to him and he sprang upon her, shimmered violently several times, and the act was done. They all folded their tails and strolled off, making small pecks at the leaf litter.

All that display, said Vaughan, for one little dull brown bird. And she chooses. They're gorgeous but she chooses.

I'd have chosen the white one, I said. He's by far the most beautiful.

She never will. However beautiful he is, however well he dances, she will never choose him. He is not right. It's the shimmer of the blue, that's what turns her on. He might as well be white washing on a line. He's not sexy.

You mean, no peahen will ever have him?

No. He's a sport. He's an albino. Peacock is blue. You know that. If I say peacock you think blue, these particular rich cobalts, turquoises, indigos. That's what a peahen needs to see. The white bird cannot breed, his kind will die out. Until another sport appears.

Nature is very cruel.

Of course. You know that.

And of course I do. I thought of the cemetery. Of the young women who die in childbirth. Of the babies that survive for days or months or maybe a year, and then are called, their parents want to think and write it on their tombstones to help them believe it, to a better place. God wanted another angel, the stones say. The child was too good for this sinful world.

Yes, I said, I do know that. But somehow I have to keep realising it.

Do you think, I said, that the white peacock knows he will never make it.

I wonder, said Vaughan. They're not supposed to be very clever birds. Maybe he lives in hope.

Being beautiful.

There was a peacock feather with its single glittering bronze and indigo eye lying on the leaf litter. Vaughan picked it up and bowing slightly presented it to me. I was reluctant. Peacock feathers are bad luck, I said.

Are they? In China they bestow honour. They indicate the emperor's regard.

Do they? You're making that up – ?

Would I do that? And think of the land of the peacock throne. Why would they be bad luck rather than honour, when they're so gorgeous?

He opened the door of the four-wheel drive for me and waited while I climbed in. He put on a CD of Bach, that's what he said it was. Bach! I thought I should have brought my own. Savage Garden. Silverchair. But it was OK, pretty, really, tumbling somersaulting notes with a very pure energy to them. It was dark twilight, with snow clouds bunching. The car filled with the Bach notes singing, and Vaughan drove us up the mountain.

The Easy Way Out

Patrick Cullen

Ray went down the hall to the kitchen at the back of the house. His wife sat at the small square table in the corner of the room.

'Where have you been?' Pam asked.

'Just putting the bin out,' he said and went to the sink to wash his hands. He stood a while with the water going. It was getting dark outside and he saw fruit bats making their way over the city. They were there in the corner of his eye and when he looked hard at them, they disappeared into the night.

'Your dinner's probably cold,' Pam said, nodding at the plate of food on the table. 'And I'm almost done with mine.'

Ray sat at the table and began to eat.

'I don't know why you take so long,' she said, working the last of the meat away from the bone. 'You always do.'

'Not always.'

'More often than not.'

'I ran into Paul again,' he said, 'and we just got talking.'

'Talking?' Pam laid her knife and fork across her plate. 'For that long?'

Ray nodded.

'Talking about what?'

'Just, things,' he said, reaching for his drink.

Pam leaned back in her chair. 'I haven't seen Paul for a while,' she said. 'Is he working again?'

'No, he's been busy though.'

'What's he up to?'

'Sorting a few things out.'

'You know what?' she said. 'I think it's weeks since I last saw Carol. She doesn't seem to get out anymore. I've heard her in there though. Calling out to him like she does. I started to think they had a kid in there the way she called after him.'

Ray got up and went to the tap. He filled his glass and sat back down.

'You know something?' Pam said. 'I didn't think that they'd last without kids of their own.'

He looked up at her.

'You know what I mean,' she said. 'Usually one person wants them and if the other doesn't then it's something big between them.'

'What about us, then? Which one of us didn't want kids?'

She leaned forward on her elbows. 'We both did.'

Ray looked to the window above the sink.

'We did, didn't we?'

He nodded and looked back at her. 'But would we have lasted this long without the kids?'

'I don't know,' she said, looking at the space between them. 'I really don't know.'

'Heard anything from Lucas?'

'No, not for a couple of weeks. You could call him,' she added.

'He'll call if he wants to talk.'

'And he's probably saying the same thing about you,' Pam said and got up from the table. She took her plate to the sink and rinsed it. 'Claire's doing well?'

'Sounds like she's enjoying herself at least,' Ray said, chewing a mouthful. 'Let's just hope she still manages to get some study done.'

Pam stood at the sink and watched him while he ate. It was dark out the window behind her. 'Do you really think that we wouldn't have lasted without the kids?'

'I don't think that. I was just wondering what you thought about it.'

'Well I think that you are wrong anyway. We're still together for a lot of other reasons.' He looked up at her and smiled. 'I just can't think of any of those reasons right now,' she added and they laughed. She went back to the table.

Ray stopped eating. 'Would you ever leave me again?'

Pam laughed then, when she saw that his face hadn't shifted, stopped herself. 'When did I ever leave you?'

'When you went to your sister's.'

'That was only for a couple of days,' Pam said. 'And you were painting our bedroom.'

'But you said that you wouldn't come back until it was finished.'

'That doesn't mean that I left you.'

'You said that you wouldn't come back. You were willing to not come back.'

'Until it was finished,' she added. 'I said that I wouldn't come back until it was finished. And you finished it.'

'But what if I didn't? What if I never finished it?'

She reached out under the table and put her foot on top of his.

'I would've come back,' she said. 'I'd never leave you. I wouldn't.'

He stared at her and she reached out to touch his wrist. He nodded and went back to eating.

After they'd both finished with dinner and the dishes were done they went into the lounge room.

'Has Paul ever mentioned why he and Carol don't have kids? The last time I talked to Carol she asked me how the kids were and I asked about her and Paul and why they didn't have any of their own.'

'What did she say to that?'

'She said that they couldn't. They'd had it looked into, she said, and they were told that they just couldn't.'

'It happens, I guess.'

Pam shook her head. 'I think there's more to it though, Ray. It seems to me just from talking to her that there's something missing.'

'They've got each other,' he said, patting her knee and getting up to switch on the television. 'And sometimes you've just got to be happy with that.'

*

The movie ended with a man and woman standing in the terminal of an airport. The woman took a suitcase from the man and started to walk to the check-in counter. The man stopped her and looked at her without saying anything and she just kissed him and walked away.

Pam turned to Ray. 'I still get the feeling that something missing over there.'

He looked past her to the television, the camera had pulled back to show the man in the crowded terminal. People moved passed him and the camera pulled back further still until the man was lost in the crowd.

Pam got up and turned the television off. 'What did you mean when you said that Paul's "sorting a few things out"?'

Ray looked to the doorway. 'I shouldn't say anything.'

'Why not?'

'Because he asked me not to.'

Pam sat beside him on the lounge again.

'What's he got to sort out?'

Ray leaned forward with his head in his hands. 'He's been seeing someone.'

'Oh, Ray. Why?'

'He has a daughter from a previous relationship.'

'Does Carol know?'

Ray nodded. 'But she doesn't know that the girl and her mother are back in Newcastle.'

'So what's he going to do about it?'

'He doesn't know. He's not sure what he wants. He doesn't know what the woman wants either. He's been seeing his daughter but ...' he worked his fingers into his temples. 'It's complicated.'

'What? That's not complicated enough? Paul just told you that he's going to leave Carol.'

'He won't leave her,' Ray said. 'He won't.'

'Why not?'

'She's got cancer,' he said. 'She's had it taken out and they've given her a good chance. But, you know, they never really know with these things, do they?'

*

In bed they lay in the dark talking about whether or not to keep out of it. Pam thought that they should do something but she wasn't sure what that something was.

'Let's just see what happens,' Ray said.

'That's just the easy way out.'

'Does it feel like it's the easy way out? Does it feel like the easiest thing to do in the situation?'

'Please don't raise your voice at me,' she said. 'I wish you'd never found out these things, Ray. If you hadn't have been out there so long maybe he'd have never gotten around to telling you these things.'

'He just came straight out with it. I was out there so long because he wanted to talk about it.'

'What did you tell him to do?'

'I didn't tell him to do anything. I told him that it was his call. I told him we could talk about it whenever he wanted to.'

Pam was quiet for a while, and then her voice lifted. 'We should have them over,' she said. 'We've been neighbours for years and we've never even shared a meal together. Did you know that? Never.'

He thought about it for a moment and had to agree. 'OK,' he said. 'I'll ask Paul about it the next time I see him.'

'No,' she said. 'I'll go and see Carol tomorrow. I haven't seen her for so long.' She felt Ray go tense beneath the covers. 'Don't worry, I'm not going to say anything. We should just keep out of it. That's what we should do. Just keep out of it. We've got enough of our own stuff to sort out.'

Ray lay still beside her without speaking.

'Call him tomorrow, will you? Please call Lucas. You need to talk things through.'

'I will,' he said, and the bed rocked a little with his nodding. 'I will.'

Pam turned away from Ray and he moved over and lay on his side behind her. He put his arm over her waist and buried his face in her hair. He said, 'Please don't ever leave me.'

Sleepers Almanac

In That Crowded Minute, That's Where it Began

Davina Bell

Out on the skin of this world, I was the youngest member of a large band of players – two siblings, ten pseudonyms, twenty-three alter egos, an invisible cast of seventy-six imaginary friends. We were like magnets kept in a small bag, at times attached firmly, at others, repelled.

Five years my senior, my sister directed the theatre of our lives, often in a bathing suit, with mini hands on skinny hips. Dictator, mimic, chanteuse; choreographer, critic, pianist and ham. My brother – the 'poor middle child' – was spoiled and volatile, at turns willing captive and simpering victim. Absorbed in a role he was princely and regal, but secretly craved my sister's control and often abandoned productions mid-script, in a copper rage that matched his hair.

And then there was me, dark-fringed and big eyed, bumbling behind in ecstatic attendance, grudgingly kept for stage props and bit parts. My eagerness was often met with disdain, my dedication annoying, my suggestions ignored. But to me, it was enough just to be there, a happy Pluto to my sister's Sun. To be near her was my present, to become her, my future. With fierce, fearful love, I lived for rare drops of her praise and attention and, like a desert cactus, stored up just enough on which to survive.

And so, when the curtains closed on that life, I was a wistful nine, an imaginative nine, a sheltered nine. Only just nine.

My sister matured late and soured quickly. At fourteen, she grew sulky and silent with unveiled contempt at our countless offences, unknowingly committed. She shut us out with the force she had drawn us to her. The theatre closed down, the actors dismissed. I consoled Eggbert Birdseed (imaginary botanist) with my own private re-runs, which sadly lacked plot drive and narrative force. I was aimless, though not entirely downtrodden. From under the telephone table, I frequently heard the expression 'passing phase,' my mother's wry laughter and deep, resigned sighs. It seemed we must wait. It was not always easy.

'Cheery' was now a heinous crime, punished with door slamming. Earnestly home-baked treats (packed in wobbly craft baskets) were 'disgusting,' 'unhealthy,' 'ugly' and 'vile.' Homemade cards, secretly popped in her bag before school, were held up as 'invasions of personal space.' For five solid nights, I praised her piano practice, pointing out progress, improvements, perfection. On the sixth night, she quit the piano, and would not reconsider. My insides cried for her 'Theme Song to *Bagdad Cafe*,' its lilting nostalgia and ache for things gone.

I sought solace in books, reading deep into nights by cracks of hall light that split through my door. In imitation, I started to 'study' ('You're, like, only just learning the *alphabet – MUM – she just copies me!*'). I won maths competitions and spelling bees, but they didn't seem to matter, those small hollow wins, like little tin soldiers marching beside the crevasse of my loss.

And then came that day, that particular day, when my doe-eyed teacher came to class, softly sad.

'Girls' (beautiful, uniformed, posh little girls; girls sheltered from heartache and hardships and things that are broken). 'Pip won't be coming to school today, girls. Something … has happened. Her sister has … died. Samantha, her sister …'

We are captive and fidgetless. My stomach feels squeezed. Her doe-eyes are teary. She is suddenly quivery. We are confused. Pip's sister's a Big Girl. We've seen her at play time. Her hair's long and shiny. She's lively, alive-ly.

'Sometimes … when people feel … very sad … they don't want to … be alive any longer. They … I mean, at times, there are times when people feel they … can't cope …' (Perhaps this is like my mother and ironing?)

'And that's the way that Samantha felt. And her friend … they … just couldn't cope. And so they made a deal …' (*To share doing ironing?* But deep down I know that is not what they did. I'm old for my years and don't need to be told. I stop listening. Start thinking.)

'… and the word for that is *suicide.* Sue-iss-ide. It's a sad word, girls. And a very sad thing for Pip and her mummy and daddy, and Ben. So I thought, girls, we could make them some cards, so they know we are thinking of them. Is that nice?'

Blue-ribboned pigtails nod gravely. It is sad. Cards will help. The monitors set out the paper and glue. And it starts, our vocabulary practice of 'who-what-when-whys,' as they flash around tables in Chinese whispers.

'How did they do it?'

'They hung themselves, on the trees on that spare block. Like this.'

'Don't do that, that's not nice.'

'But they did! On the trees.'

'Why didn't they snap?'

'Their necks?'

'No! The branches.'

'Maybe they did. Who was the friend?'

'Alice, the Big Girl.'

'The one with the freckles? You shouldn't be drawing a smiley face.'

'But I want them to smile.'

'I don't think they're happy.'

'My mum says they were naughty. Please pass the purple.'

'When did they find them?'

'In the morning I think, they did it at night-time so no one would see them.'

'Did what?'

'Died, I s'pose.'

'Oh. Grandpa died once. In the night.'

'How'd you spell it? That word that she used.'

'S-o-o-i-s-i-d.'

'Thanks. Is it two "r"s in sorry?'

'Yep. I have a Kit Kat today, in my lunchbox.'

'Lucky.'

I just listen.

Later that night, allegedly bed-tucked but slid between bookshelves, I see these tattle tales confirmed on the news. I feel heavy with sick, my whole body beating. Because I have a sister. A Big Girl sister. A Very Sad sister. And I know now what happens to that kind of sister. I am nine, and convinced it's unchangeable fate – what has happened before must of course be again. That is logic.

Mum's after-school pikelets round the kitchen table (raspberry jam).

'Everything alright at school today?'

Nod and smile.

'Anything happen?'

'Nup, same as normal.' Pause.

'Was Pip Higgins there?'

'Away. Got a cold.' Downcast eyes.

'Teacher say anything about that?'

'No, nothing.' (A little too quickly?)

'I see.'

My drumbeat heart tells me she knows, but she mustn't know that *I* know – I know she would worry. Mine aren't thoughts for her baby. I'm not sure how I know this. I nibble edges of pikelet and squint through my fringe to Check On Things.

'*Stop STARING at me. Mum, she's staring ... I said STOP.*' And she's gone, flounced off to her room. To do what? I put down the pikelet to stop it from shaking.

'Never mind,' says my mum. But I mind – so should she – doesn't she see?

'She just needs some alone-time, some space.'

And that's when I realise – Mum's missed it. 'Space' is for stringing up nooses to trees.

[Just there – did you catch it? In that crowded minute, that's where it began.]

We are taught to 'be normal' when Pip comes back to school, to smile in a certain way, and say 'Hullo Pip! Nice to see you.' My classmates forget in a couple of days, and I feel I am watching their take-off to a faraway planet. For I don't think my friends see those girls like I do, in the corners of eyes and bedroom ceilings. In turns they are glassy-eyed, wall-eyed or pop-eyed;

sometimes they're staring, at others they groan. Necks crooked like snapped chickens, limbs heavy and greying, rhythmically swinging, or stock-still like they are playing dead. Sometimes light through the leaves of the trees snags on gold freckles and long, glossy hair. At times they are smiling, through rope-burn and bruises and zombie-red-lips. And sometimes (read 'often') it's Her, my enchantress, hung on our gum tree from the rope swing we used to call the 'Ladder to God.' Graffitied on top of the endless montage, there's That Word. And every time I hear That Word or think That Word or live That Word, something shoots through me and grabs all my insides and winds them up tighter on bone-cracking racks.

It is not just my sister – there are bigger Big Girls. At each school assembly I count the school prefects' perfect blue blazers as they file onto the stage. Who is missing? The sports captain – *where has she gone?* In agony, I sit through awards and await the announcement, the sad sad announcement, the hugging, the tears. I see her, fair-haired and strapping, strung from the bridge near the railway tracks, bronzed skin pale and face purple, eyes popping. Mrs Briggs clears her throat.

'... and today the cross-country team are away at the inter-school carnival, led by sports captain Fliss Marshall. Good luck to the girls! In diving news, our very own state champion ...'

I don't understand why I want to cry. I start savagely folding my hymn book pages into a flower, to follow the craze.

I learn to dread Home Time, the final school bell, the ending of all it contains and restrains. When it rings, I'm on guard, watchful and shadowing. At first my attentive new presence is noted with hysterical shrieks of 'snoop,' 'weirdo' and 'freak.' Doors are slammed with new vigour. Glares are much colder. But I become artful, and silent, and subtle. I can slip between pillars and realign things just so – papers I rifle through, searching for notes, drawers I shut quietly, looking for ropes. And all the while acting the part of a child, which feels now like pulling on too-small skivvies and pretending the necklines don't gag me and scratch.

But it is the drawn-out dawns that bleach me away. They begin when my parents shuffle to bed and I'm suddenly holding all the world's happiness, like a thorny ball I mustn't drop.

I wait until my bedroom buzzes with my brother's next-door snores, tummy buzzes with terror, mind buzzes with That Word dangling from trees. At that stage, I'm prepared to forget I'm afraid of the dark.

I set off. The passageway is a gauntlet of creaking boards that could each draw my father from bed – curt, gruff and crusty with not-enough-sleep. So I balance my weight on my out-stretched arms – just wide enough to span the walls – and tiptoe across, one board at a time, pausing between them for nervous forevers. The naked bulb bounces white light off high ceilings, back into my headachey eyes. My breath sounds like traffic.

At the lounge, I peer through frosted-glass doors to check she's not dangling from the light fitting. And finally, past my granny's antique desk, the floorboards end and my cramping toes grope for the concrete kitchen floor. It is soundless, and cold against my cheek, pulse bouncing off its hardness as I lie to catch my breath. Post recovery, the next bit is easy, bathed in the extraterrestrial lime of the microwave clock. And just beyond that I take up my nightly post at my sister's door.

I make my breaths shallow and short, until they burn in my chest with the tension of not wanting to wake her, but wanting to know she can wake. Do I make a sound to stir her and risk her wrath, or do I wait in the half-light, not knowing, and every second becoming more certain of what she has done. My knees hurt from kneeling, but I am good at that. I knelt with her on the car floor eating sweets every Sunday, aglow with our heroic Sunday-school escapes from happy-clap songs and teachers with terrible haircuts and sensible shoes. I knelt when she made me bark on all fours and stamped on my paws. She demanded I whimper, and then stroked my head, so very softly. 'Poor doggy! There there.' And I lived for those pats.

My neck strains as I press my ear, ever flatter, against the hole in her plywood door. Two summers ago, in a petulant rage, my brother attacked it with the butcher's cleaver, which sprouted out the other side, inches from my sister's temple. '*I could have died*,' she had shrieked, '*I could have died*.'

And my thoughts whisper to me, *Just stand up and go in, she is already dead*, for I can't hear her breathing. *She's not breathing*.

But I don't.

I shift my weight and hug my shivery knees, picking tiny fluff-balls off my worn pyjamas. Turquoise birthday pyjamas, requested on loop; they are just like hers. She stopped wearing them the day I opened mine – she did things like that.

Dark treacle minutes ooze past, and still nothing. The refrigerator starts to click and hum, and I start to panic, trapped-moth panic. I stand up too quickly, and squint against prickly light and shudder-breathed bile. My hand is on the doorknob and then off it, and then on. And then in my mouth, clamping in tears. If I go in now, I will see her up there, swinging, but maybe I could cut her down in time? I am not allowed to use the big kitchen scissors (an unfortunate prior self-barbering incident) but maybe just once? I reach up to the kitchen bench – and knock off a glass from the draining board. I watch it, backlit in green, fall to the floor, where it clatters and rolls.

And she rolls over. I hear the bedsprings mutter. She's alive. I stifle a whimper. But maybe she has woken up? Alone, in the dark, with dark dark thoughts (*They did it at night-time so no one would see them*). And outside, the wind taps the trees on the window, boughs perfect for bending suspended bodies. Taut with duty, I take on the next shift, resolving to stay till the sun can play sentry. On a normal day, as soon as I saw its orange pyjamas, I would dart back to bed for my pre-school nap, abuzz with superhuman fatigue. Having cheated fate, I'd clasp my reward of dreamless sleep.

But tonight, for the first time in three months, I fail.

My forehead hits the floor when she opens the door that I've slept against, and she screams. My eyes are pasted closed against the streaming morning light.

'*Oh my GOD. What the HELL are you doing??*'

I can't open them up. I'm just too tired. I hunch into a ball, awaiting a blow. I don't care. She is there – that's all that matters. But then I feel her kneel down. I tilt my head up and half open one eye from under my fringe. Intently, she's gazing into my face, with a look I think I've seen somewhere before, like she might reach out to pat my head.

'No, really, tell me – what are you doing?' It's a calm voice, a normal voice, maybe even a caring voice. No dark desperation, no tint of depression. It is not a noose voice. "Cos you've been acting nuts for weeks now. Mum thinks you have worms. I'd watch out.'

'I just ... I thought maybe ...' On the tip of my tongue, the words in my head sound silly – no, crazy.

Closer to her than I have been in months, it strikes me quite plainly she's not a noose girl. Grumpy, perhaps, what with growing lots taller, and homework, and such. But nothing beyond that.

'I was lost,' I confide.

'Well, I'd get back to bed before she wakes up.' She flicks back my fringe and looks into my eyes. 'You look tired.'

Sleepers Almanac

Gulag

Shane Strange

In the morning we woke and it was like all the mornings we'd imagined. The sun brushed the edges of the heavy, dark drapes of your bedroom and the air held us softly on the bed. I looked at you in the moments before you woke and I saw you then as I always wanted to see you, as I've always imagined you in my mind. The perfect you – asleep, and free.

Our clothes lay in a pile on the floor – a dirty collaboration of grey and black. The khaki hat that you bought me sat on the low bench underneath the window and as the sun came upon it, it looked proud. I felt the back of your hand rub my shoulder, and I knew that you were awake, but I waited a little longer, looking at the room. You let your finger run down my shoulder, across the long scar on my back and onto the tattoo on my arm, tracing its outline.

I turned to you, and saw you in the half-light, and we smiled. I remember we smiled like children.

There we were on that first day. After the work was over, and our bodies felt tired. But that didn't matter, because we were, after all this time, where we wanted to be.

It was like all the mornings we'd imagined. Exactly like it.

We held hands as we walked together across the plaza in front of your building. The streets were smoky and the planes flew overhead from time to time. Explosions echoed from the distance, perhaps from the hills. There were rifle shots that sometimes seemed close to us and sometimes far away, but we were safe with each other. In the plaza the air was heartening; warm, but with an undertone of winter passed. It felt like soft hands upon us, holding us, pushing us forward.

We kissed on the corner of George and Ann Streets. Drunken soldiers sat on the stairs of an office building and they jeered at us good naturedly. I waved to them and you smiled and gave them a curtsy, which made them jeer louder and laugh and slap each other.

You turned and looked at me and I could see you felt something that couldn't be said. I knew what it was. I always knew what you were thinking. You reached up and opened a tear on the shoulder of my uniform. I took your hand in mine and looked at you.

We said goodbye, until that evening, back in your room. We both stopped then, because we could make those plans and they would be true plans and we would have a place to meet and be, and it would be the same place night after night. You laughed at me and told me to stop looking at you so. There was much to be done, you said, and I love you. You turned to walk down Ann Street, to the railway station, where the soldiers were coming in. You had your backpack over your shoulders and your head held high. And though it was stained, your uniform made you look magnificent. As the soldiers spied the bright red badge on the shoulder of your black shirt, they became quiet and looked down at their boots.

I felt certain that I would see you in the evening. I would bring home bread wrapped in a newspaper, and you would have found some fruit, perhaps a pear. We would eat and listen to the radio and kiss and fall into your bed. And I would get up and draw the heavy drapes before I undressed.

I heard the noise of the crowds coming up from King George Square, and the burbling of a loudspeaker. There were speeches, punctuated by cheers from the crowd. It was early, but the speeches would last all day and into the night.

I continued on past Queen Street, where hundreds of people pressed in from the Victoria Bridge. I jostled with them as I tried to get across the mall. Some were dancing and drinking. An old man had an accordion out on the steps of a building and I smiled and wondered how long all this would go on for.

As I crossed the street, I was caught in the swirl of the crowd and became lost for a minute, until a guard came over from where he'd been standing and led me out by the arm. I thanked him, but he returned to his place against the wall, saying nothing. I could see from his eyes how life would be for him now. Too many were affected this way.

A group of soldiers had broken into a pub on George Street and were handing out bottles of beer to all who passed by from cartons stacked on the sidewalk – it was the day for this sort of thing – everything was acceptable.

A few hundred metres from Old Parliament House, the guards had placed a roadblock and were checking papers. I dug into my pocket and showed them my card and my orders and they let me pass. Beyond the roadblock, the streets were quieter, industrious. Some of the rubble had been cleared from the road and men and women bustled along the street, stepping into doorways and office buildings. Soldiers and black-shirted guards stood on every corner and in every doorway. Suddenly I had the feeling that there were things of consequence yet to do. What a feeling. To be there at that time and to have believed in it all.

Our offices were in an old building beside the square. I saw Connor as he walked up Alice Street and went to him. We hugged and smiled. I hadn't seen him in six months. Then suddenly there was Hughes and Boyle, and even Luxford had come, though he leaned heavily on a stick. We stood in a group and smoked our cigarettes on the footpath and told our stories. We were dishevelled, unkempt, rough, but we were happy to be alive. If someone had told us all even a month before that we would be here we would have marvelled, I'm sure, like a child marvels at the sun.

An old truck pulled up on the corner and unloaded some of the accused. More accused were standing in lines in the square. A perimeter of guards paraded the edges, walking up and down the lines, pushing and hitting. We all tried not to look. Luxford told a joke, and I laughed nervously. Then a guard came and told us that it was safe to enter the building.

Do you remember, in the early days, when we would all meet in wooden lounge-rooms dotted around the city? Of course you do. Someone would put music on, and there would be wine and dancing. Or we'd sit around a kitchen table, a small group of us, and lean in and look deep into each other's eyes as we *espoused.*

I remember we met that night at O'Neill's place in St Lucia. We'd all come back from a march where we'd taken on the police and everyone was happy but exhausted. You were new. You'd come with that dullard Jaco (he was shot quite early on, wasn't he?). I knew that I had to get you away from him, if only for your own good. Jaco was aiding O'Neill in boring people in a corner with some speech or other. Someone had taken their shirt off and was dancing in the middle of the room with a beer bottle balancing on their forehead. I don't know from where I received the courage (I had not been drinking) but I crossed the room to the small group and took your hand and led you onto the front verandah. There was something about your hair, about the way your eyes looked strong. You told me for the first time in your life you felt alive, really alive and I believed you.

There was much talk in those days about who should go and who should stay. We'd make a game of who we'd send away: this politician, this lackey, this union leader, this celebrity. 'To the gulag!' we'd say, drunk, and point outwards, beyond the room we occupied, to somewhere out there, to our imaginary gulag. We didn't know what a gulag was. For us it was a way of saying 'rubbish bin' or 'place of no return' or 'place where we don't have to think about you anymore' or 'place of the righteously punished.' It felt like a weapon in our arsenal.

Everything on that first day was makeshift except our anger; that was solid, well practiced and refreshed. There was some uncertainty about procedural matters and an amount of chaos: overcrowding, people being sent to the wrong tribunals, paperwork. There was tonnes of paperwork. Where had it all come from? And we, in our torn uniforms, hardly looked the part.

I was assigned as sub-commissioner on the fourteenth tribunal. The commissioner was Hallewell. We were placed in a small room on the fourth floor. We sat behind tables facing the accused, who sat on a chair in the centre of the room. Clerks filed in and out of the room all day, with papers, files and photographs. There was a projection screen behind us where slides and film could be shown.

From inside the tribunal room we could hear the rifle shots clearly. At that time they performed the shootings by the riverbank, so the bodies would float away downstream on the tide out to sea. Later, they stopped when they found the bodies getting caught in the mangroves around Kangaroo Point and New Farm. They started using cattle trucks and ditches on the outskirts of the city soon after.

The main trials were downstairs in the Great Hall; the big cases – the decadent politicians and generals. Our transgressors had less profile, but were no less dangerous.

The procedure would always be the same. Guards would drag the accused in and sit them down. The tribunal clerk would pass us the file and we would review the evidence, as it was. The intelligence officer would make his case. There was not much in the way of deliberation. We weren't great legal minds, that was true. I remember it was my job to stamp the verdict papers with the seal of the commission. Hallewell would make a little speech. The accused would be led away, and the next case brought in.

I don't remember many of the cases of that day. The faces have blurred with the hundreds that followed in the weeks and months afterwards. I do remember one fellow, however. His name was Strange. Believe it or not, he was a few years ahead of me at school. The guards brought him in and sat him on the chair. He was thin, with glasses and a fresh cut on his forehead; a dirty bandage wrapped around his foot. I'm not sure he recognised me.

He was a writer, a minor intellectual who'd come out against us. The evidence was clear, undeniable. As the intelligence officer made his case, I looked up from my papers to find Strange staring at me. His eyes didn't move. Rivulets of spittle hung off his shabby beard. His eyes were dark behind his glasses.

Hallewell began his little speech: 'Your life is over. You shall never be free again. You are condemned to die. The only point of contention is whether it is now, or later. Later, we think, will be harder. So, the sooner the better, would you agree?'

'So I shall be shot,' Strange said without emotion.

With this Hallewell gave a wistful smile and gestured to the guards and they led Strange away. I brought the stamp down on his papers.

Later that day I snuck down to see O'Neill being convicted. Hughes came up to me while I smoked in the courtyard. He'd heard that they were building a gulag on the edge of the desert, near the coal mines and gas fields. When they cleared out the hills, they would send the enemy combatants there. 'Good,' I said.

That evening I came back to you. You were asleep on the chair in the living room, but you stirred as soon as I entered. The radio was on. I had only managed to get half a loaf of bread, but you had brought home a bowl of tomatoes and two apples. And from your backpack you produced half a bottle of gin, a packet of cigarettes and some chocolate. The soldiers, you said, are good and generous.

I came over and we kissed. We ate and drank and went to bed. You stood behind me and unbuttoned my torn shirt and I felt your hand run smooth down my back. And as I drew the heavy drapes across your window, I looked out across the city and in the darkness it was like a quiet world, filled with silence and unspoken promise.

Griffith Review

I Am So Sweet and Truthful and Once I Was Betrayed

Maree Dawes

When I caught the betrayer out, I was filled with wild revenge. It was as if revenge had lain dormant in me, strands of it seeded through every cell, waiting for the right season, the moisture and the sun or the early thunderstorm and heat and there it was, mushroomed complete.

Me and my betrayer and my revenge, together we walked in the dusk at the edge of the sea. I told him I would tell his wife. We would go there immediately and tell her, or if he preferred he could tell her and I would listen. After that he could do as he liked, I would do what I liked and his wife as she liked and my revenge would be spent and its spores laid down. And we saw that we had him, my revenge and I. He argued it was not in my nature. Why involve her, his innocent wife? If I hadn't known of her, and if equally, she hadn't known of me. She needs to know, said my revenge, and I am just the woman to tell her.

Punish me he said, not her, punish me he said, because he was desperate. I was adamant, then with persuasion weakened, you are right I said, it's you I want humiliated. If you do what I say, then I won't tell her. If you do what I say for the next half-hour I won't tell her. And you know I never lie. So he agreed, knowing me, knowing my sweet nature, perhaps thinking I wanted to make love one last time, and I smiled, knowing he was desperate, for her not knowing.

We walked on the edge of the sea and through the night and onto the jetty until we were surrounded by liquid. The stars above in the cosmos soup, the seaweed and fish in the lap of the tides. We stood on the jetty and I gave him the task, the chance to keep his secret. Yes, I said, you must leap into the ocean and swim to the shore. I will see you wet and cold and be satisfied.

It's too cold he said, be reasonable, just let me tell her myself (but we didn't believe him, revenge and I, who would?). No, I said, you have the bargain, you swim or we go and tell her. He went to kiss me before he jumped – a kiss or a plea for mercy? I stepped back. I heard his gasp over the splash as he entered the water, the watery world of my revenge, and I ran home through the streets in my blue and white sneakers, feeling so light, and inside my door with the sweat still dribbling on my warm skin, I called his wife, just to let her know that in his distress, when I ended our affair, after I found out about her, he had slipped into the sea and been unable to climb back onto the jetty, and I wanted to let her know, sweet as I am, that he was swimming back in the wild wet and would then come home all sodden, well I hoped he would be coming back, but the sea was rough and I just thought that if he wasn't back soon, someone would need to raise the alarm, and I didn't really want to be the one to make the call.

Then across the communication ducts and lines I could feel the strands of betrayal infect her. I could hear her sucking in outrage with every breath. I am so sweet and truthful, but once I was betrayed.

Indigo

When You Hold Me ...
(The Bra Monologues)

Beth Spencer

With a bra, I don't need you. I feel feminine. I can keep remembering (watching television, doing the dishes, leaning over to pick up the paper) that I have breasts. That these are desirable objects. That *I* am desirable.

I feel contained, defined. Firm, solid. A woman, not a girl.

And when I take it off at night I feel all the fleshiness and softness of my inside form, my private body.

*

I like wearing a bra around the house. I am wearing one now as I type. It is like a tight band holding me around my chest, just under my breasts: the underwire circles and defines them, points them out to the world, to you, myself, reminds me of who I am.

*

My favourite bra is black with underwiring, like two half-moons that shape and lift, and it has a black eyehole-cotton-lace bodice, with old-fashioned vertical boning going all the way down to my waist, keeping it in place, keeping me upright, graceful, reminding me of my bondage, my servitude, my exquisite place in the world, my fragility, the delicate whiteness of my bones and flesh underneath all this wire and lace and fabric, my suppleness, my flesh, my skin, the blood that is faintly constricted, my breath that comes more as a slight pant, my incredible strength and resilience that I can wear such a thing and survive, that I can still be free inside of it, that inside I am private, myself, a secret self that you don't know about, and that you might want.

I am protected, behind bars. I am safe. I am ...

*

I am an exotic hothouse flower, take off these clothes and I will fall down, bruise easily. I am tough, because I can wear these garments which would make you faint.

*

I feel suffocated, I want to scream. I feel like someone is pulling at me, reined in when I want to move and run, I want to tear at the bit and struggle against these straps and tiny finger-defying hooks. I am furious, white foam at my lips. I am mad! I want to run till my heart bursts ...

*

When I take off my bra at night, my flesh sags out, my form dissolves, my breath expels, my shape disintegrates. I deflate, become a formless mass. A fleshy blob of tissue and skin and fat fat fat. I am shapeless. I am everywhere. My breasts shrink, they float back against my ribs, dissolving like a moon in water. I am so indefinite now. I am no longer Jane Russell (in miniature), I am just me. Nobody.

*

I look at myself in the mirror when I wear my bra and suddenly I no longer like the thickness of my waist. I am part way there to being the shape that is fashionable, but the rest of me is out of place. The wrong shape. The new breasts don't match the old waist and hips (I need a girdle. I need a New Body).

*

I look more professional in my new silk shirt when I wear a bra, not soft and nipple-showing and formless, but hard-lined and definite, a woman who can safely take on the men, mix with the boys. Protected, armour-plated, secure, phallic with the best of them.

My new bra is called a bombshell, and it has a miniature metal bomb sewn onto the valley between my breasts. My sports bra is called Sports Jock.

(My Joan of Arc)

My bra gives me balls.

My shoulder pads give me muscles.

My high heels give me stature.

My red mouth is moist and ready, signals that I am what I make myself, my brave face, my lucky amulet, my mouth which can hiss, sneer, pout, smile, laugh, kiss, bite, sting, and speak.

My bra makes me feel feminine, powerful.

My red lips make me feel sexy.

(You make me so weak)

Hold me tight. I need you.

*

When I take off my bra at night, for a long time afterwards it feels as if I have someone's arms wrapped around me, cupping my breasts in strong palms, thick hard fingers holding me in place, imprinting on my flesh, making me real.

*

I keep thinking of your fingers unclipping my suspenders, running your hands along the inside of my thigh where it is soft and white.

I want to gasp, but I can hardly breathe.

I put my knee between your legs as we dance. I know what you're thinking.

*

I feel breathless.

I feel afraid. Choking. Delicate and weak. Strong like iron, like steel wires, impenetrable.

To get access to me you have to take off something first. You have to do some work, learn to manoeuvre the delicate tricky hooks and eyes that are so foreign to your sex, you have to learn some of my secrets. You have to be patient.

You are so clumsy.
Here, let me do it.

*

I unwrap myself from your embrace, my breasts fall forward to try to touch you as you move away, my muscles expand and shudder, the skin tingles where your bones bit into my flesh, the blood begins to circulate all over again like new life, my body joins up with itself, I take a deep breath. I put on something slinky. I slide in between the sheets.

I fall asleep with your silhouette watching over my bedside chair. The shape of me, vigilant. My vigilante.

*

And I will wear a black wonder-bra, and black suspenders, and lavender knickers and purple lipstick. And I will cut off one of my breasts to fire the arrow. And I will carry a big stick.

*

And I keep your love letters in my favourite bra, tucked close to my heart, the pulse at the lip, the white crease – the red bra with the satin stitching and the bow in the middle. It is almost midnight! The party is about to begin. I can hear the fireworks over the river. (Shh shh, let me think…)

*

And I will wait for you
by the shore.

Purchase

John Kinsella

They had their hearts set on purchasing a piece of land up north, but not too far north. Coastal – or as near coastal as they might afford. Close to a town for supplies, but not too close to a town: they wanted privacy and a sense of having 'got away' from it all. This wasn't really a 'sea change' (as the trendies and media would have it) – going down to the city had been that, for them. They were country people who'd retired from the farm early and given the city a go. Now they wanted out. But not a place on a large scale. A small property of, say, thirty acres. Grow a few olives, keep a few sheep for hobby shearing, nothing more.

A suitable block came up not long after their search began. They visited a small town close to the Batavia Coast, and had a chat with the local real-estate agent. There was nothing up in the sales window, but she had her ear to the ground, as real-estate agents do, and knew of a property about to go on the market. The owners had only had it for a year, so it was good luck they were selling – land in the region was at a premium and much sought after. There was a waiting list but, recognising like minds – she was a farmer's daughter – and the prospect of cash on the button, she 'juggled' her list.

The boy watched his dad's car emerge out of the setting sun and speed down the gravel driveway, the back end dropping out in clouds of dust, then pulled back into line. Perched on his trail bike on the hill, he glanced across at the people walking the neighbouring property with the real-estate agent. He revved the engine and dropped the clutch, spinning the back wheel and kicking dirt and stones out towards the newcomers. They were too far away to be hit by the debris, but not too far to sense some kind of aggression. They stared at the boy zigzagging over the crest of the hill – that bare property next door ... not a tree on it.

For a moment, the couple basked in the neat mixture of clear space and white gums they were buying. And they had (for in their minds it was already theirs) a small hill as well – looked like an old mine on the far side, to the east, but it'd been filled in or blasted shut. The estate agent said she didn't know much about it, but could guarantee it was entirely sealed and there was no risk of sheep wandering in and being lost. An ex-farmer, the man – or Darl, as his wife called him – took a close look, and agreed. *Perfectly safe!* At the access road end of the property – to the west – there was a creek, dry mid-summer. Plenty of water too: a well had been sunk and there was a dam in the western corner which would catch the entire flow off their hill, and off their neighbour's. The couple was going to sign off on the deal that evening – one last wander around and chat with the agent.

The boy's dad had only had a few drinks after work, and was in a sardonic yet almost pleasant mood. The boy had to tell him now. If he left it, his dad would go spare. It was the boy's job to keep a look-out. And then, if Dad was really pissed when he discovered for himself – because he would, because all the blokes at the pub were his dad's spies and they'd know quick as lightning – he'd give him a good kicking for holding back the info.

Dad, I saw that bitch real-estate agent with some new people. The boy steadily ripped open a Coke and kept his eyes to himself. The fizz of the can would be the prelude to ... *Jeez! What now?! Can't get any privacy round this fucking place. Get rid of one lot and another rolls in. Bitch! Fucking bitch! I've got her number ... give it time, give it time.* His dad stopped there and the boy knew the silence meant his dad did have a plan for the real-estate agent. She'd keep. And when his dad fixed things, he really fixed things. In the meantime, he sensed his dad switch attention to the problem immediately at hand.

Taking a bottle of spirits from the cupboard, the bearded miner called the boy to get his lazy carcass into the kitchen and cook him a steak. That was the night Dad was supposed to eat at the pub before getting home. The boy looked after himself on these nights – he was good at that. Even though he only had his dad – his mum had gone a long time back – he liked it out on the block alone. He was never scared … only when his dad got back from the pub. The boy started to walk towards his room. *Hey, where do you think you're going? Cook your dad a steak!*

To get their new place started, the couple went south to Batavia and picked up an old donga from a construction company. It was to be delivered in a few weeks – enough time to clear a pad for it, and sort out the details of their move from the city. The plan was to live in the donga for as long as it took to get their new house established. They'd always wanted to build.

Though Batavia was much further away than the small town where the real-estate agent plied her trade, they stayed in a motel down there because it was easier to get things done. They arranged for workers to go up and build the pad – being on site to ensure it went in the right place, of course. Choosing to work with an architect to design the plans themselves, they shopped around builders for the best product. It was an exciting time, though – somewhat ironically – one during which they barely had a chance to be at the new place.

The couple was out there to see the donga set to rest. And it was then they met the boy on the trail bike … heard his dad yelling in the distance. A stream of abuse they were unable to interpret. They thought the dad drunk and best avoided. Nonetheless, it was an exquisite day, and it reminded them of their best times on the farm. After the harvest cheque was in, and they didn't have to worry about money for a while. That kind of feeling. And the pressures of the city were gone. Down there, drunks were never far away either – it was no big deal.

But what the boy had to say bothered them a little. Darl more than his wife. *Pet,* he said to her, *these neighbours aren't all there.*

They're a few planks short of a jetty. He enjoyed sayings like that. He always smiled after using them, even when concerned. To be honest, Darl thought it bullshit and was suspicious of the kid anyway. Looked like a dope smoker. You get them on small properties – Darl hadn't come down in the last shower. But given the place next door didn't have a bit of green on it, he reasoned the boy wasn't growing it there, and that was all he cared about.

The boy was nervous, even frantic around his father. *So I told them like you said, Dad. I told them it was an old lead mine and that the tailings are all over the block. That the place is poison. That there's lead in the well-water. Just like I told the other people.*

And what happened? his dad growled.

I think it worked. The old girl looked scared and the bloke with a pole up his arse stared at me without saying anything. Their names are Pet and Darl. I've heard them call each other that.

The boy's dad laughed and then repeated to himself, *Pet and Darl … Pet and Darl … bloody dickheads.*

Then, dead quiet. The boy watched his father, trying hard not to tap his foot or do anything else that'd set the burly miner off.

Bastards, the drunken miner muttered. *Bastards … sticking that eyesore there without so much as a by-your-leave. Who do they think they are? Squatters? The landed fucking gentry?* He then started yelling again, punching a fist into a hand: *No neighbours! No neighbours! No neighbours!* The corellas, scratching at the dirt and eyeing the neighbours' spread, squawked en masse and plumed into the air, settling on the other side of the fence.

Pet rang the real-estate agent just to check about the abandoned 'lead mine.' The voice hesitated only slightly on the other end: *Don't worry about it, the kid's got a mental problem … He's known in town for making up stories. Always being suspended from school. My daughter knows him … says he's weird. Don't worry, though. I think he's harmless.* Pet could tell the agent was clutching at straws.

The prospect of coexistence – even distantly – with a drunkard and a weird kid distracted them from the lead business. Darl did say, though, *I should probably get the place tested.* And Pet carried out a quick internet search at a Batavia café, and found that there were in fact lead mines throughout the area, and that lead had been detected in local well-water. Dogs had died from it. She insisted. He said: *Well, we haven't got any dogs and we haven't got any small children* ... She could hear that he was becoming a farmer again.

But Pet wouldn't let it go. She couldn't. And as they stood in their donga looking out at a blood-red sunset, the drunk next door screaming across the distance, in ragged bursts that punctuated lulls in the fresh sea-breeze: *No neighbours! No neighbours! No neighbours!* She caught Darl's eye twitching – a sign that he was reaching the end of his tolerance. He wasn't a violent man, but still he had a temper. He'd give that drunken neighbour a run for his money, then there'd be real trouble. Pet felt it in her waters. *Well, the town has been drinking the water for a hundred years, so I think we'll survive,* Darl said suddenly, and calmly. As if that was that, and there'd be no more talk about the matter. Gradually they both decided they couldn't care less about the lead. Even if it were true, they'd live there. They had once been farmers. Back then, they had saturated their paddocks and animals in poison every year. *What was the difference? Real-estate agents will say anything.* They remained proud of their purchase.

The donga had been there for a few weeks and workers were already laying the house-pad. The boy's father was mumbling something about the next phase of the operation. The night before, he'd fired rifle shots into the air and played the stereo extra loud.

Funny thing was, the boy had watched the donga being set in place with a dull excitement – almost creeping skin – as the crane hoisted the donga from the semitrailer. Overwidth, overlength. The cops were there – a car out front, a car behind the load. That'd cost them. And he'd watched in amazement as the ground was levelled for the pad. The boy liked how *precise* it all was. The old couple – *Pet and Darl* he drawled their names sarcastically, mimicking his father – weren't there much, but when they were he rode along the fence-line on his motorbike, revving the shit out of the engine as per his dad's instruction. Darl would watch him doing this for an age, and the boy thought he saw the old bloke shaking as if he were really angry once, but it might have been the easterly that had whipped in, hot and burning though it was only spring.

When the truck and workers and new owners were gone, the boy rode his trail bike up to a tear in the fence and wormed the bike through. He rode over to the mine, got off, and threw tailings at the crumpled and suffocated entry. Phase two of his dad's plan to cleanse the district of invaders. Then he mounted up and raced down to the creek. He leant his head so far back he nearly fell off his bike – he was looking up at the sun through white gum leaves, the oil of the trees headier than dope. His dad was a smart man.

It was an 'earthquake-proofed' house. A steel frame with single brick and plasterboard walls, built on a sand pad. The boy was fascinated. He rode over and asked the builders about it. Dad was at work and he was wagging school, so it would be OK. He was bored. *Earthquake-proof, eh? We haven't had an earthquake here, I don't think*, he said to them. A gnarled and bearded builder with tobacco stains around his mouth and moustache, said:

Well, some people like to be prepared, matey. The builder asked the boy to pass him his beer, cool in its foam holder. *Yep, nothing like working in the bush, he said, no problem drinking on the job.* He hacked and spat as he laughed.

The builder paused as he set a string for a new line of bricks, and said to the boy, who was rocking his bike back and forth so its wheels bit into the dirt, *So you've been a bit of a bastard to my employers?* The boy looked away and said: *My dad doesn't like neighbours.*

Yeah, well your dad's being an arsehole. The boy shot a look back at the builder and sized up the opposition: the guy was built like a brick shithouse. Ten axe handles across. Sunburnt and milky-eyed with drink. But still sharp. The boy wanted to say something back, but hit the kick-start with his boot and throttled up, spewing sand all over the place as he raced back to the hole in the fence.

The boy stared at his dad spread-eagled on the couch, watching television. *What are you staring at, you little bastard?* his father half-asked him.

Nothing. They're putting the roof on the place next door.

Who gives a damn, his dad muttered, taking the boy by surprise. Dad looked strange. It worried the boy.

Darl and Pet were living in the donga, waiting for their house to be completed. It wouldn't be long now. The summer had set in and it was getting pretty hot even through the nights – they craved the ducted airconditioning they'd had installed in their dream home. The power was through, and they'd made the massive outlay to have scheme water put on. Darl said: *It's not because of this bull about the quality of groundwater around here, just that it's more reliable.* It was late, and in the cramped space they were watching television, doing dishes and talking over the plans when there was a knock at the door. The husband called out: *Who's there?*

It's me, from next door ... The couple looked at each other.

Don't open it, Pet said. Darl looked at her for slightly too long, then shook his head and went to open it. The boy was standing on the step shaking. His hair was slicked to his forehead with sweat. *What's happened?* asked Darl. Pet was behind her husband's shoulder now, and seeing the boy, pushed her way through and placed her hand on his arm. *What's wrong, son? What's happened?*

It's my Dad. He's sick. I mean he's really sick. I think he needs a doctor and the phone isn't working. I mean, Dad broke the phone when he got in from work.

Darl didn't mind paying the extra for scheme water to be piped out to the place. Cost thousands, but peace of mind is peace of mind. Probably nothing wrong, but why go through the worry? The real-estate agent's sister – a nurse at the hospital – said tests showed there was nothing wrong with the groundwater. That's what the real-estate agent reckoned. But what the hell. And when Darl suggested to the boy's dad he connect his place to the scheme for a few thousand, the ex-drunk surprisingly said yes. *I can taste the bloody water now,* he mumbled. *When we ran out of rainwater, the well-water tasted pretty bad, didn't it boy?*

Yes, Dad.

His dad stared at his boots and then added, *Nothing wrong with it, though ... just that my tastebuds are shot, like my liver.*

Darl spent a lot of time at the old lead mine. Sometimes the boy would come over on his trail bike. He'd dismount and they'd squat near each other without saying a word. It smelt strong, even heady up there in the heat … assaying the lead tailings, listening to the pasture crackle with the dryness, watching oddly-coloured sunsets. Sometimes Darl would ask after the boy's dad. *Oh, he's OK, the boy would say. He keeps saying his liver's shot and that's why he got sick. When one of his mates rings and tries to get Dad to go out on the piss, he just says, can't mate, doc says my liver's shot.*

After a while, Darl and the boy would hear Pet calling up from the new house – or the 'mansion,' as the boy called it: *Hey, boys, come down and have something to eat and drink.*

It was as if they were the only people in the world. It would always be like that.

Griffith Review

The Plumber

Tracy Crisp

Veronica wishes she had picked the underwear up from the bathroom floor. He is probably used to it. But still.

He says that a washer will fix the hammering in the wall and he will put a new something in the cistern to stop the drip.

He seems less certain about the stormwater drain.

'A tennis ball?' he asks. He is on his knees at the inspection point.

She knows he does not have children.

'I've screwed it down,' she says when he tries to lift the plastic grille. 'So they can't put anything else in.'

He nods without looking up, then stands.

She starts talking again. 'I'm sorry. I should have thought. I should have done it before you arrived. I can get a screwdriver. There are tools in the shed.' Her voice is dry. She does not know why.

'I'll get it off,' he says. He is looking at her now. 'When I've brought my things in from the van.'

He stands up. He has his hands on his hips as he looks around the yard.

'D'you know which direction it goes?' he asks about the drain. He turns to the left and looks at the side of the house.

The earring he wears is silver. It shines when his head is turned that way and it is only because of the sun that she notices the slope of his neck. It is bristly under his chin and she wonders if he is the kind of man who has to shave every day.

Veronica thinks of her first boyfriend.

'I've always assumed it's that way.' She wonders why she is even pretending to know.

His head turns and he looks at her again. The sun is on his face and his hands are still on his hips. He blinks a little and narrows his eyes.

'I'll work it out,' he says. 'It shouldn't be too hard.'

He sniffs and shakes his head as he looks around. He looks at her. She waits for his smile.

It was not my child who did it, she wants to say. *I mean I should have been looking, I should not have been inside while they played. I know, I know.*

Not looking has been her problem for too long.

'I'll start with the toilet,' he says.

They walk back inside.

She says, 'Would you like a cup of tea?' and he says, 'Yes.'

'Do you want normal tea or would you prefer herbal?' she asks. It is a household joke made before she can think.

'I'm not usually too fussy,' he says.

His voice is soft and leaves a trail across her soul. His hair is blond and he wears boots which look like they have never been cleaned. Because of the way his eyelashes curl she does not make the usual jokes about chamomile and blokes.

'I'm having spearmint,' she says with an offer in her voice.

He nods, and then he will not look away, so Veronica must.

'I don't have milk,' he says. 'Not in spearmint tea.'

'No,' she says, 'of course.'

He leaves the tap running as he walks back and forth to his truck.

Veronica chooses a white cup for him, one without stains, a brown one for herself. She stands next to the kettle while it boils. She pours the boiling water into his cup, but not to the top, then, after she has taken the teabag out, she puts cold water in.

She carries the cup to the bathroom and stands in the doorway holding it. Do plumbers mind drinking in bathrooms that have toilets in them?

She thinks of the nights she puts the lid of the toilet down and sits, with a glass of wine in her hand, watching the children in their bath. She should not have glass in the bathroom, but without the wine, the children's voices are too loud, the bathroom is too cold, and when the splashes reach her she yells. It is better to drink than to yell.

'Here's your tea,' she says.

'Thanks.' He speaks, but he does not look up.

'Where would you like me to put it?'

He looks at her now.

'On the sink is fine.'

She moves to the sink and sees that the lid is off her body cream. The cream is Moroccan Rose and new. It is thick and rich and coloured gently pink.

She scoops it on after she has towelled her hair and before she powders her face. Left arm, right arm, left leg, right.

The lid and the label are black and after only a week they are showing her fingerprints.

It has the kind of smell which wafts in and out of her day and makes her reach for memories that haven't been made.

She puts the cup on the sink and the lid back on the cream.

She waits for a moment, and when he doesn't speak, Veronica leaves.

Veronica stands at the kitchen sink while she drinks her tea. She wraps her hands around the cup, right fingers over the left. She has never liked the feel of this cup in her hands. She thinks of blackboards and fingernails and of balls of cottonwool squeezed and rubbed until they squeak.

She has told herself that she will not throw anything away until James has been dead for a year.

She only ever says *dead* to herself. It is *passed away* to everyone else.

The bloody black cat jumps onto the fence. It looks at her, then slides, front feet first down the fence. She watches it strut across her yard. She does not throw things at it any more.

Veronica hears the clink of metal against the bathroom sink. The toilet flushes, the shower runs.

She goes into the study and sits at her desk. She puts the cup on the coaster, adjusts her chair. There are no new emails.

She opens the report. She has promised them it will be finished this week.

He stands at the doorway and says, 'That's done. I'll just go out and look at that drain.'

She looks up as he speaks. She takes her glasses off with both hands. She smiles at him and nods, but he says nothing more. She wishes she had put mascara on.

She hears him put the cup on the sink before he goes outside.

He finds the ball, plastic pliers and a chopstick in the drain. He has lined them up on the lawn.

'Give them a wash before you give them back to your kids,' he says. He is holding a thin brass pole in one hand, and his other is on his hip. He licks his lips. She does not look away.

'I thought you might have to use some kind of machine,' she says. 'A pump or something like that.'

'No. You just have to fish around,' he says. He lifts the pole a little, then lets it hit the ground. The metal grates against the cement. He shakes his head a little bit. 'Plumbers cost ninety dollars an hour.' He clears his throat. 'Plus parts.'

She nods. 'I know. They tell you when you ring up.' She thinks *I can't be blamed for everything.* And she says again, 'I thought you might have a machine.'

Neither of them looks away.

'I do the lawns myself,' she says and there is an emphasis on the *self.*

His are the kinds of silence she needs to fill.

'It's therapeutic, isn't it?' she says. 'Mowing the lawn.' She waits only a moment before she speaks again. 'I do it in a square, not in lines. I start at the outside and work my way in.' She thinks of telling him of the way she watches the green grow dark as she mows. Of how it feels to reach the middle and see that your square is not quite square. She thinks of describing the smell of the clippings compost bin to him. She would call it *rich.*

He looks at the lawn, nods, looks around again.

She doesn't say anything more.

'Not many people have still got tomatoes this time of year,' he says.

'I always plant some late,' Veronica says. 'There's not many there now. I'll probably pull them out this weekend.'

He nods.

'I'll put in some peas. The kids like shelling them.'

He nods again. She can think of nothing more to say.

'I'll go and do the paperwork, shall I?' he says.

He walks through the house, picks up his things and goes to the van. It has taken him at least three trips to bring everything in, but only one to take it out.

Veronica puts the kettle on again while she waits. She does not want another cup of tea and she has had two coffees already today. She flicks the kettle off before he can come back inside. She uses a cloth to wipe the sink down. She rinses the cloth under the running tap, then wipes her hands on the tea towel. She moves the fruit bowl from one end of the bench to the other. The banana is black and the onion has started to sprout.

He comes back into the house without knocking on the door. He stands on the other side of the island bench and holds the clipboard out to her. His pen is blue and chewed. She uses her own which is felt-tipped and black.

He does not say *Sign your life away* or even *I just need an autograph.*

She writes him a cheque.

Neither of them speaks.

The cheque book is still printed with both their names. He clips the cheque to his folder without looking at it.

He rips her copy of the receipt from the top of his folder, puts it on top of the bench and pushes it towards her.

'There you go,' he says.

'Thanks,' she says without picking it up.

She walks behind him along the passage and down to the front door. He opens the door, steps on to the verandah.

He turns and he gives her the kind of smile which could mean anything.

'Hopefully for you, you won't be seeing me again,' he says. 'But just in case ...' He pulls a card from his top pocket and hands it to her.

She takes it from his hand and can't stop herself looking at it. Jeremy is a lovely name, she thinks. She looks at him, he smiles again and she thinks, if he were a friend she would walk him to the gate.

She has a shower at nine o'clock that night.

The children are asleep. She has only had one glass of wine.

She has taken new pyjamas out of the washing pile, changed the sheets on her bed, put out fresh towels. One for her body and one for her hair.

She has the heat lamps on, but not the fan, and clouds of steam fill the room. She faces the shower, closes her eyes, lets the water run down her front. She holds her arms at her sides so that she cannot touch herself.

She washes her hair, puts the conditioner in, shaves her legs, then under her arms. She washes her face and all of her neck and almost down to her chest with the deep-cleansing soap. She rubs it in using small, circular strokes.

She rinses the conditioner out and even when she is sure it is all gone, she stands with her back to the shower and she holds her head back. She holds her arms at her side again.

The water is nearly too hot.

She dries herself, towels her hair, scoops the body cream on. Left arm, right arm, left leg, right.

She looks at herself in the mirror and she practises the smile she will use at dinner parties in months to come. She will joke about the plumber and say *He's the kind of boy would make any mother proud.* She will use her own mother's inflections when she speaks and two of her friends will know exactly what she means.

Island

Publication Details

Meera Atkinson's 'Désincarné/Disembodied' appeared in *Etchings 1*, Ilura Press, Melbourne, 2006.

Sunil Badami's 'Collective Silences' appeared in *Meanjin,* vol. 66, no. 2, 2007.

Melissa Beit's 'Nothing to Fear' appeared in the *Australian Women's Weekly*, November 2007.

Davina Bell's 'In That Crowded Minute, That's Where It Began' appeared in the *Sleepers Alamac 2007: The Family Affair*, Sleepers Publishing, Melbourne, 2007.

Sally Breen's 'Mac Attack' appeared in *Griffith Review 13: The Next Big Thing*, Spring 2006 and *Allnighter*, Cardigan Press, Melbourne, 2006.

Laurie Clancy's 'Reading the Signs' was commissioned by the National Gallery of Victoria as one of a series by Australian authors on paintings in the gallery. It subsequently appeared in *Bystander* magazine and in his collection *Loyalties*, Ginninderra Press, Canberra 2007.

Bill Collopy's 'Suckered into a Perfect Line' appeared in the *Age*, Melbourne, 20 January 2007.

Barry Cooper's '9.7 Milligrams of Heaven' appeared in *Meanjin*, vol. 65, no. 4, 2006.

Tracy Crisp's 'The Plumber' appeared in *Island 108*, Autumn 2007.

Patrick Cullen's 'The Easy Way Out' appeared in the *Sleepers Almanac 2007: The Family Affair*, Sleepers Publishing, Melbourne, 2007.

Sophie Cunningham's 'Ploughing' appeared in *Meanjin* vol. 66, no. 2, 2007.

Maree Dawes' 'I Am So Sweet and Truthful and Once I Was Betrayed' appeared in *Indigo*, vol. 1, Winter 2007.

Kate Grenville's 'Humble Pie' appeared in the *Bulletin*, 19 December 2006.

James Halford's 'To Genghis Khan, Oblivion and Holy Russia' appeared in *Voiceworks 66*, Spring 2006.

John Holton's 'Hemingway's Elephants' appeared in *Allnighter*, Cardigan Press, Melbourne, 2006.

John Kinsella's 'Purchase' appeared in *Griffith Review 16: Unintended Consequences*, Winter 2007.

Lee Kofman's 'Floating above the Village' appeared in *Island 105*, Winter 2006 and in *Allnighter*, Cardigan Press, Melbourne, 2006.

Nam Le's 'Love & Honour & Pity & Pride & Compassion & Sacrifice' appeared in *Overland 187: Gatekeepers*, Winter 2007.

Geoff Lemon's 'Albatross' appeared in *Voiceworks 66*, Spring 2006.

Patrick Lenton's 'Uncle Jeremy Has Turned into a Tree' appeared in *Voiceworks 69*, Winter 2007.

Isabelle Li's 'A Chinese Affair' appeared in the *UTS Writers' Anthology 2007: What You Do and Don't Want*, ABC Books, Sydney, 2007.

Shane Maloney's 'I See Red' appeared in the *Big Issue*, 26 December 2006.

David Malouf's 'Mrs Porter and the Rock' appeared in *Every Move You Make*, Chatto & Windus, London, 2006.

Roger McDonald's 'The Concern' appeared in the *Bulletin*, 19 December 2006.

Michael Meehan's 'Repossession' appeared in *Meanjin* vol. 66, no. 2, 2007.

Jennifer Mills' 'Reason' appeared in the *Alice Springs News*, 7 June 2007.

Ryan O'Neill's 'July the Firsts' appeared in *Westerly*, vol. 51, 2006.

Paddy O'Reilly's 'Speak to Me' appeared in *The End of the World*, University of Queensland Press, St Lucia, 2007.

Tim Richards' 'People Whose Names Bob Dylan Ought To Know' appeared in *Meanjin*, vol. 65, no. 3, 2006.

Shane Strange's 'Gulag' appeared in *Griffith Review 18: In the Neighbourhood*, Summer 2007–2008.

Michael Wilding's 'Hanging On' appeared in *Griffith Review 17: Staying Alive*, Spring 2007.

Sean Williams' 'The Seventh Letter' appeared in the *Bulletin*, 19 December 2006.

Robert Williams' 'From the Wreck' appeared in the *Age*, Melbourne, 6 January 2007.

For more information about these publications, please visit:

ABC Books: www.abcbooks.com.au

The *Age*: www.theage.com.au

Alice Springs News: www.alicespringsnews.com.au

The *Australian Women's Weekly*: www.aww.com.au

The *Bulletin*: www.thebulletin.com.au

The *Big Issue*: www.bigissue.org.au

Cardigan Press: www.cardiganpress.com

Ginninderra Press: www.ginninderrapress.com.au

Griffith Review: www.griffithreview.com.au

Ilura Press: www.ilurapress.com

Indigo: www.indigojournal.org.au

Island: www.islandmag.com

Meanjin: www.meanjin.unimelb.edu.au

Overland: www.overlandexpress.org

Sleepers Publishing: www.sleeperspublishing.com

University of Queensland Press: www.uqp.uq.edu.au

Voiceworks: www.expressmedia.org.au

Westerly: www.westerlycentre.uwa.edu.au

Notes on Contributors

THE EDITOR:

Robert Drewe is the author of ten works of fiction and the editor of four collections of short stories. His novels and stories have been widely translated, won many national and international awards, and been adapted for film, television, theatre and radio around the world.

AUTHORS:

Meera Atkinson is a Sydney-based writer. Her short stories, essays and poems have appeared in many publications including *HEAT*, *Salon.com* and *Griffith Review*. She has a website at <meera.atkinson.googlepages.com>.

Sunil Badami has an honours degree in communications from the University of Technology, Sydney and a Masters with distinction in creative and life writing from Goldsmiths College, University of London. He has written for the *Sydney Morning Herald*, *Good Weekend*, the *Australian*, *Australian Literary Review*, the *Cultural Studies Review* and *Meanjin*.

Melissa Beit lives in Alice Springs. She was born in Cairns in 1974 and spent her childhood in the sugar-mill towns of far North Queensland. She has worked as a matron in a Scottish boarding school, an outdoor instructor, a counsellor, and a full-time mother of two. 'Nothing to Fear' was runner-up in the 2007 *Australian Women's Weekly* short-story competition.

Davina Bell is a West Australian who currently lives in Melbourne. She is a co-founder of the city's newest literary quarterly, *Harvest* magazine, and is establishing a not-for-profit organisation that will send books to orphanages and schools in Australia and Africa.

Carmel Bird is a novelist and short-story writer. Her most recent novel is *Cape Grimm*, and her latest story collection is *The Essential Bird*. In 2007 she published *Writing the Story of Your Life – The Ultimate Guide to Writing Memoir.*

Sally Breen is a creative and non-fiction writer based in Brisbane. Her work has apperared widely in Australia. She lectures in creative writing at Griffith University and is associate editor at *Griffith Review.*

Tom Cho is writing a short-fiction collection that explores the themes of identity and popular culture. He is writing this as part of his PhD in professional writing at Deakin University. His stories have been published widely, with recent publications in the *Age* and *HEAT.* Hise website is at <www.tomcho.com.>.

Laurie Clancy is the author of twelve books of fiction and literary and cultural criticism and many reviews and articles. His most recent work is a collection of short sotries, *Loyalties*, published by Mockingbird Press in 2007. He lives in Melbourne.

Bill Collopy works and writes in Melbourne. His stories have been published in a variety of fiction anthologies, literary periodicals, newspapers and on-line magazines. His first novel, *House of Given*, was published in 2006.

Barry Cooper is an Indigenous Australian and a descendant of the Yuin People from the far south coast of New South Wales. He currently lives in Canberra and has been studying Aboriginal art and cultural design at Reid CIT. He has been writing for about three years.

Tracy Crisp lives in Adelaide. She writes shorts stories, essays, reviews, stand-up comedy and blogs. Her novel manuscript *Black Dust Dancing* was shortlisted in the 2006 South Australian Festival Literature Awards, and she was a national finalist in the 2007 Melbourne International Comedy Festival Raw Comedy competition.

Patrick Cullen is writing a collection of stories as part of a PhD at the University of Newcastle. These stories have been broadcast on ABC Radio National and published in *The Best Australian Stories* in 2005 and 2006, and in the *Sleepers Almanac* in 2006 and 2007.

Sophie Cunningham has worked as a publisher at McPhee Gribble/Penguin, Allen & Unwin and Lonely Planet. Her first novel, *Geography*, was published by Text in 2004 and her second, *Bird*, will be published in 2008. 'Ploughing' is the beginnings of her third novel, *This Devastating Fever*, about Leonard Woolf's time as a colonial administrator in Ceylon.

Maree Dawes is a nationally and internationally published poet based in Albany, Western Australia. She is fascinated by the internal workings of people and the natural environment and has an enduring interest in naming and words.

Marele Day is the award-winning author of four crime novels, as well as the internationally acclaimed novel *Lambs of God*, and most recently *Mrs Cook: The Real and Imagined Life of the Captain's Wife*. She lives and works on the far north coast of New South Wales

Will Elliott's novel *The Pilo Family Circus* won the inaugural ABC Fiction Award and the Aurealis, Golden Aurealis, Australian Shadows, Ditmar and *Sydney Morning Herald* Best Young Novelist awards. It is presently short-listed for the International Horror Guild award, up against Stephen King. He is twenty-eight years old and lives in Brisbane.

Peter Goldsworthy's most recent book was *The List of All Answers: Collected Stories* (Viking Penguin). The State Theatre Company of

South Australia's adaptation for the stage of his novel *Honk if You Are Jesus* won the Ruby Award for Best Work, the Curtain Call Critics' Award for Best Comedy, and the *Advertiser* 'Oscart' award for Best Play. He is currently working with his daughter Anna on a stage adaptation of his novel *Maestro.*

Kate Grenville is the author of seven books of fiction, including *The Secret River,* which has won prizes both in Australia and internationally. Her most recent book is *Searching for the Secret River,* a memoir about the writing of the novel.

James Halford studied creative writing at the Queensland University of Technology and received honours in literature from the University of Queensland. In 2005 he travelled throughout China and Mongolia. A short story written during this period won the 2006 Queensland State Library Young Writers' Award. His work has appeared in *Griffith Review, Voiceworks* and the *Courier Mail.*

Marion Halligan has published eight novels, including *The Fog Garden* and *The Point,* as well as collections of short stories and *The Taste of Memory: An Autobiography in Food and Gardens.* Her most recent novel is *The Apricot Colonel*; a sequel, *Murder on the Apricot Coast,* will be published in February 2008.

Karen Hitchcock's fiction has been published in *Meanjin, Griffith Review,* the *Sleepers Almanac 2007: The Family Affair* and *The Best Australian Stories 2006.*

John Holton is the author of the short-story collections *Snowdropping* (runner-up in the 2001 Steele Rudd Award) and *The Affairs of Men,* and a collection of children's stories, *Teacher Free Day* (2001). His most recent book is *Caring ... And Other Highwire Acts.*

Vivienne Kelly has worked as an academic, a public servant and a university administrator. Her PhD thesis from Monash University examined myth, history, and theatre in Australia. She lives in Melbourne and works as a freelance researcher.

Cate Kennedy has written two collections of poetry, *Signs of Other Fires* and *Joyflight*; a travel memoir, *Sing and Don't Cry: a Mexican Journal*; and a collection of short stories, *Dark Roots*. She is writing a novel, to be published by Scribe in Australia, Grove Books in the US and Atlantic Books in the UK. She lives with her family in north-east Victoria.

John Kinsella's poetry and prose have been widely published in Australia and internationally, and his poetry has won major prizes in Australia. His most recent publications are *The New Arcadia* (poetry: FACP, 2005) and *Fast, Loose Beginnings: A Memoir of Intoxications* (autobiography: MUP, 2006). A new collection of poetry, *Shades of the Sublime and the Beautiful*, will be published internationally in 2008.

Lee Kofman is an Israeli-Australian author of three books (in Hebrew). Her English publications include short fiction, non-fiction and poetry in *Griffith Review*, *Island* and *Cordite*. She is a recipient of an Australia Council grant, the Varuna Flagship Fellowship, the Emerging Writer in Residence at KSP Writers' Centre and an ASA mentorship.

Nam Le's debut collection of short stories, *The Boat*, will be internationally published in 2008. Penguin will be his Australian publisher. His fiction has been awarded the Michener-Copernicus Society of America Award and the Pushcart Prize, and has appeared in *Overland*, *Zoetrope: All-Story*, *A Public Space*, *One Story*, *Harvard Review*, and *Best American Nonrequired Reading 2007*.

Geoff Lemon is a writer and performer, poetry editor of *Voiceworks* and *Harvest* magazines, and convenor of Melbourne's Blue Velvet Readings. In poetry slam, he currently holds the New South Wales State Slam, the Melbourne Slam, and the Melbourne Writers' Festival Poetry Idol titles. His first collection of poetry will be published by Picaro Press in 2008.

Patrick Lenton is currently finishing his double degree in creative writing and English literature at the University of Wollongong. He writes prose, script and poetry, and he is one quarter of Australia's only Poetry Boyband, The Bracket Creeps.

Isabelle Li was born and educated in China and now lives and works in Sydney. She is currently studying for her Master of Arts in professional writing. Her short story 'The Floating Fragrance' appeared in the 2005 *UTS Writers' Anthology*. 'A Chinese Affair' is her second published work.

Roger McDonald is the author of seven novels and two books of non-fiction, including *1915, Mr Darwin's Shooter, Shearers' Motel* and *The Tree in Changing Light*. His most recent novel, *The Ballad of Desmond Kale*, won the 2006 Miles Franklin Award. He lives near Braidwood, New South Wales.

Shane Maloney is the author of the Murray Whelan series of novels. He has almost won several awards.

David Malouf's latest work of fiction is *Every Move You Make* (Chatto & Windus, London, 2007). *The Colected Stories* was published by Pantheon, New York, in June 2007.

Amy T. Matthews was born in 1975. She has a PhD in creative writing, teaches at the University of Adelaide and has co-edited two anthologies of poetry and short stories. Her novel, *End of the Night Girl*, was long-listed for the 2006 Australian/Vogel literary award.

Michael Meehan grew up in north west Victoria. We won the NSW Premier's Prize for fiction with his first novel, *The Salt of Broken Tears*, and has published novels in Australia, the US and the UK. He teaches at Deakin University.

Jennifer Mills has published short stories, poems and essays in several journals and anthologies, and recently completed a novel. She lives near Alice Springs, and she has never been a government bureaucrat. Her website is <www.jenjen.com.au>.

Frank Moorhouse's most recent book is *The Martini Memoir*. All his books are at present being republished by Random House as the 'Moorhouse Collection.' This year he won the Alfred Deakin Prize for Best Essay Contributing to Public Discussion.

Ryan O'Neill has had two short-story collections published by Ginninderra Press, *Six Tenses* and *A Famine in Newcastle*, which was short-listed for the Steele Rudd Award in 2007's Queensland Premier's Literary Awards. He lives in Newcastle with his wife and daughter.

Paddy O'Reilly is a Melbourne writer. 'Speak to Me' is from her collection of award-winning stories, *The End of the World* (UQP). She has also published a novel, *The Factory*, and a novella, *Deep Water*. Her stories have been published in Australia, the USA and Europe.

Alice Pung is a Melbourne writer and lawyer. Her book *Unpolished Gem* won the 2007 Australian Book Industry Newcomer of the Year Award, and was nominated for the Victorian and NSW Premiers' awards. Her work has also appeared in the *Monthly*, *Good Weekend* and *Meanjin*.

Tim Richards is a Melbourne-based script editor. He is the author of two collections, *Letters to Francesca* and *Duckness*, and a novella, *The Prince*.

Beth Spencer's first book of fiction, *How to Conceive of a Girl*, was published by Vintage in 1997 and was runner-up for the Steele Rudd Award. She is currently writing a novel called *A Short (Personal) History of the Bra and its Contents*, and has a website at <www.bethspencer.com>.

Shane Strange is a writer living in Ipswich, Queensland. His work has appeared in various publication, including *Griffith Review* and *Verandah*. He is currently studying for a Master of Writing and Literature at Deakin University.

Louise Swinn, as well as being a writer, is the editorial director of Sleepers Publishing.

Michael Wilding's stories are collected in *This is For You*, *Great Climate*, *Her Most Exciting Sexual Experience*, *The Man of Slow Feeling* and *Under Saturn*. His recent novels include *Academia Nuts* (Wild & Woolley), *Wild Amazement* and *National Treasure* (CQUP).

Robert Williams studies professional writing and editing at RMIT. His second published work won the *Age* short-story competition in 2006. He is currently working on his first novel. He lives with his family in Coburg.

Sean Williams writes for adults, young adults and children, and is the author of over sixty published short stories and twenty-two novels. Multiple winner of Australia's speculative fiction awards, a *New York Times* bestseller and judge of the Writers of the Future Contest, he lives with his family in Adelaide.